Isaac Asimov was born in Russia in 1920. At the age of
three he went with his family to Brooklyn, New York,
where he grew up. In 1948 he received his Ph.D at
Columbia University and joined the faculty of Boston
University School of Medicine.
Dr. Asimov is one of today's most prolific and widely read
authors. His books range from science fiction and pure
science to history, religion, literature, geography and
humour. His recent novel, 'The Gods Themselves', was
granted both the Nebula Award and the Hugo Award.
Dr. Asimov currently lives in New York City.

D0822861

Also edited by Isaac Asimov

Edited by Isaac Asimov

Before the Golden Age
Volume One

A Science Fiction Anthology of the 1930's

Futura Publications Limited
An Orbit Book

An Orbit Book

First published in Great Britain in 1975 by
Futura Publications Limited
49 Poland Street,
London W1A 2LG

Copyright © Doubleday & Company, Inc. 1974

PUBLISHER'S NOTE
The four volumes of 'Before the Golden Age' edited by
Isaac Asimov, published by Futura Publications Limited,
appeared originally in one complete volume under the
title 'Before the Golden Age'. The Introduction to the
complete volume will be repeated in each of the four
volumes.

This book is sold subject to the condition
that it shall not, by way of trade or
otherwise, be lent, re-sold, hired out or
otherwise circulated without the publisher's
prior consent in any form of binding or
cover other than that in which it is
published and without a similar condition
including this condition being imposed on the
subsequent purchaser.

ISBN 0 8600 78035
Printed in Great Britain by
Hazell Watson & Viney Ltd
Aylesbury, Bucks

Futura Publications Limited
49 Poland Street,
London W1A 2LG

'The Man Who Evolved,' by Edmond Hamilton, copyright © 1931 by Gernsback Publications, Inc.; reprinted by permission of the author and the agents for the author, Scott Meredith Literary Agency, Inc.

'The Jameson Satellite,' by Neil R. Jones, copyright © 1931 by Radio-Science Publications, Inc.; reprinted by permission of the author.

'Submicroscopic,' by Capt. S. P. Meek, copyright © 1931 by Radio-Science Publications, Inc.

'Awlo of Ulm,' by Capt. S. P. Meek, copyright © 1931 by Teck Publishing Corporation.

'Tetrahedra of Space,' by P. Schuyler Miller, copyright © 1931 by Gernsback Publications, Inc.; reprinted by permission of the author.

'The World of the Red Sun,' by Clifford D. Simak, copyright © 1931 by Gernsback Publications, Inc.; reprinted by permission of the author.

To Sam Moskowitz, and myself, and all the other members
of First Fandom (those dinosaurs of science fiction),
for whom some of the glitter went out of the world in
1938

INTRODUCTION

TO MANY science fiction readers who are now in their middle years, there was a Golden Age of Science Fiction—in capital letters.

That Golden Age began in 1938, when John Campbell became editor of *Astounding Stories* and remolded it, and the whole field, into something closer to his heart's desire. During the Golden Age, he and the magazine he edited so dominated science fiction that to read *Astounding* was to know the field entire.

In that sense, the Golden Age endured till 1950, when other magazines, such as *Galaxy* and *The Magazine of Fantasy and Science Fiction,* entered the field. The editorial personalities of H. L. Gold and Anthony Boucher were as strong in their ways as Campbell's, so the field grew wider and more diverse. In many ways, it improved still further as it spilled out of the magazines and into the books, the paperbacks, and the electronic media.

But then the individual could no longer comprehend the field entire. It grew too large for one to do more than sample, and the Golden Age, when all of science fiction could belong to the reader, was over.

I lived through the Golden Age in the best possible way, for I was among the first of the new writers Campbell discovered, and I am sure there was no other in whom he took so personal and paternal an interest. My book *The Early Asimov* (Doubleday, 1972) is both my memorial to those years and my tribute to John.

But let us forget the capital-letter Golden Age, and let us be more personal. To anyone who has lived a life that has not been utterly disastrous, there is an iridescent aura permeating its second decade. Memories of the first decade, extending back to before the age of ten, are dim, uncertain, and incomplete. Beginning with the third decade, after twenty, life becomes filled with adult responsibility and turns to lead. But that second decade, from ten to twenty, is gold; it is in those years that we remember bliss.

It is the second decade that is the golden age for each individual; it is the memory of life as it was then, that we consider to be life as it ought to be. For any science fiction reader, the gold of the second decade of his life permeates the stories he read at that time, so I frequently hear enthusiasts of thirty speak of "the golden age of the 1950s." If I live out my normal lifetime, I fully expect to hear some rotten kid talk to me of "the golden age of the 1970s." (I will rise from my wheel chair and hit him with my cane.)

Well, then, what about me? My own golden age (small letters) lay in the 1930s. It came in the decade just before the Golden Age (capital letters), and it had a glory for me—and a glory for everyone, for it was in *my* golden age that the personalities that molded the Golden Age, including Campbell himself, were themselves molded.

The science fiction stories I read in the 1930s were in magazines I could not keep. I took each magazine, as it arrived, from my father's newsstand and then, having read it as quickly as I could, I returned it to my father's newsstand so that it might be sold. I cultivated a light hand, which left the magazine in its pristine crispness even though I had read, rabidly, every word on every page. (I *had* to, for if the magazine suffered, my father would have issued a ukase forbidding me to touch any of them, and I don't know about you, but *my* father expected, and got, instant obedience.)

So I never reread those science fiction stories of my personal golden age after that first reading. Oh, a very few of them, yes, when they were reprinted. However, very few stories published before the Golden Age have been reprinted. The Coming of Campbell wiped out all that went before.

The science fiction of the thirties seems, to anyone who has experienced the Campbell Revolution, to be clumsy, primitive, and naïve. The stories are old-fashioned and unsophisticated.

All right, grant that they are all those things. Nevertheless, there was a rough-hewn vigor about them that sophistication has, to some extent, lost us.

Besides, I remember them. Some of them, although I read them only once at a very early age, I remember over a space of forty years. Through all that has happened and all that I have read and, for that matter, written, I remember them—and love them still.

Those stories were dear to me because they roused my enthusiasm, gave me the joy of life at a time and in a place and under conditions when not terribly many joys existed. They helped shape me and even educate me, and I am filled with gratitude to those stories and to the men who wrote them.

And aside from my personal involvement, the stories form an essential part of the history of science fiction, a part that has been unfairly neglected and is in danger of being forgotten altogether, since virtually no important anthologies have dealt with pre-1938 science fiction.

You would have thought that a person of my incredible ingenuity would have conceived *years ago* the notion of repairing this omission and editing an anthology of the great stories of the 1930s. Oddly enough, that is not so. Never once, in my conscious moments, did so obvious a project occur to me.

Fortunately, I am not always conscious.

On the morning of April 3, 1973, I woke and said to my good lady, "Hey, I remember a dream I had." (I virtually never remember my dreams, so this came under the heading of a stop-the-presses bulletin.)

My good lady is professionally interested in dreams, so she said, "What was it?"

"I dreamed," I said, "I had prepared an anthology of all those good old stories I read when I was a kid and I was getting a chance to read them again. There was 'Tumithak of the Corridors' and 'Awlo of Ulm' and 'The World of the —' "

I think that's about as far as I got. I had been chuckling as I talked about the dream, because it seemed like such a ridiculous thing to do. But was it ridiculous?

Simply talking about it filled me, quite suddenly, with a burning urge to do it. I've had those burning urges before, and I know it means I will have to do it at once regardless of any commitments I may have. But who would publish such a thing?—A ridiculous question. After all, in a quarter century of association, the good people at Doubleday & Company, Inc., had never once said "No" to me.

It was at 7 A.M. that I told my dream, and I had to wait for the opening of the business day to do something about it. At 9:05 A.M. (I gave them five minutes' grace) I was on the phone, talking rapidly and earnestly to Lawrence P. Ashmead and to Michele Tempesta, two splendid editorial representatives of that estimable publishing house. They did not say "No" to me.

I then thought about it some more. As I told you, I did not have those old magazines, and it is most difficult to get copies these days. Difficult, but not impossible.

There was always my old friend Sam Moskowitz, who shared my golden age but bought and kept every magazine that was published, memorized them all, and can quote them all word by word at any time of day or night.

He has put his knowledge and expertise to good use by becoming a historian of science fiction, perhaps the only true specialist in this unusual section of human knowledge in the whole world. He has written two volumes of biographies of great science fiction writers, *Explorers of the Infinite* and *Seekers of Tomorrow*. (One of these biographies dealt with none other than your un-humble servant, Isaac Asimov. Sam, never one to skimp on hyperbole, called that one *Genius in a Candy Store*.)

He also produced *Science Fiction by Gaslight*, a history and anthology of science fiction in the popular magazines of the period from 1891 to 1911, and *Under the Moons of Mars*, a history and anthology of science fiction in the Munsey magazines from 1912 to 1929.

Doubleday published his *The Crystal Man*, dealing with nineteenth-century American science fiction. Sam even wrote an account of the tremendous and earth-shaking feuds among the handful of science fiction fans in the American Northeast, which he very dashingly entitled *The Immortal Storm*.

It was to Sam Moskowitz that I therefore turned. Swearing him to secrecy, I asked him if he had ever himself done an anthology of this sort and if he was in the process of doing so. He answered, no, he hadn't and he wasn't. He would like to if he could find a publisher.

"Well, I can," I said, "and I would make it an autobiographical anthology. Would you object if I moved in on your territory?"

He sighed a little and said that he didn't.

Then I reached the crucial point. "Would you get me the stories, Sam?" I asked.

And goodhearted Sam said, "Oh, sure!" and in three weeks he had them, every one, with word counts and copyright information and comments on each. (I was only too glad to pay him for the time and trouble he took.)

So now here I am, all set to do the anthology, and, if you don't mind, I intend to make it more than a mere anthology. I am not going to include the stories bareboned.

With your permission (or without, if necessary), I intend to do as I did in *The Early Asimov* and place the stories within the context of my life.

As I told Larry, Michele, and Sam, I intend the book to be autobiographical.

I am doing this partly because one pronounced facet of my personality is a kind of cheerful self-appreciation ("a monster of vanity and arrogance" is what my good friends call me) but also, believe it or not, as a matter of self-protection and as almost a kind of public service.

My numerous readers (bless them, one and all) never tire of writing letters in which they ask eagerly after all the most intimate statistics of my early life, and it has long since passed the point where I can possibly satisfy them, one by one, and still find time to do anything else. *The Early Asimov* has already performed miracles in that respect, since I can send back post cards saying, "Please read *The Early Asimov* for the information you request."

And now I will be able to add, "Also read *Before the Golden Age.*"

Part One

1920 TO 1930

I HAVE always wanted to start a book in the fashion of a nineteenth-century novelist. You know: "I was born in the little town of P_____ in the year 19__." Here's my chance:

I was born in the little town of Petrovichi (accent on the second syllable, I believe), in the U.S.S.R. I say the U.S.S.R. and not Russia, because I was born two years after the Russian Revolution.

More than once, I have been asked where Petrovichi is relative to some place that might be considered reasonably familiar. It is thirty-five miles due west of Roslavl and fifty-five miles due south of Smolensk (where a great battle was fought during Napoleon's invasion of 1812, and another during Hitler's invasion of 1941), but that doesn't seem to help any. I had better say, then, that Petrovichi is 240 miles southwest of Moscow and fifteen miles east of the White Russian S.S.R., so I was born on the soil of Holy Russia itself, for what that's worth.

The date of my birth is January 2, 1920. For those of you who are interested in casting horoscopes, forget it! I am not only unaware of the exact hour and minute of my birth but even, actually, of the exact day. January 2 is the official day and that's what I celebrate, but at the time of my birth the Soviet Union was on the Julian calendar, which was thirteen days behind our Gregorian, and my parents in those days didn't even pay much attention to the Julian. They dated things according to the holy days of the Jewish calendar.

Under the Tsars, Russia had never indulged in careful statistical accounting of its less important subjects, and during World War I and the hectic years immediately following, things were more slovenly than ever. So when a birth certificate finally had to be drawn up for me, my parents had to rely on memory, and that worked out to January 2.

And that's good enough. Anyway, it's official.

I remained in the Soviet Union for less than three years and remember nothing of those days except for a few vague impressions, some of which my mother claims she can date back to the time I was two years old.

About the only event of personal note worth mentioning from those years is the fact that sometime in 1921 I fell ill of double pneumonia at a time when antibiotics were non-existent and such medical care as did exist was extremely primitive. My mother tells me (though I never know how much to allow for her innate sense of the dramatic) that seventeen children came down with it in our village at that time and that sixteen died. Apparently, I was the sole survivor.

In 1922, after my sister, Marcia, was born, my father decided to emigrate to the United States. My mother had a half brother living in New York who was willing to guarantee that we would not become a charge on the country; that, plus permission from the Soviet Government, was all we needed.

I am sometimes asked to give the details of how we left the Soviet Union, and I get the distinct feeling that the questioners will be satisfied with nothing less than having my mother jumping from ice floe to ice floe across the Dnieper River with myself in her arms and the entire Red Army hot on our heels.

Sorry! Nothing like that at all! My father applied for an exit visa, or whatever it's called, got it, and off we went by commercial transportation. While we were getting the visa, the family had to go to Moscow, so in the year 1922 I was actually there. My mother says the temperature was forty below and she had to keep me inside her coat lest I freeze solid, but she may be exaggerating.

Needless to say, I am not sorry we left. I dare say that if my family had remained in the Soviet Union, I would have received an education similar to the one I actually did get, that I might well have become a chemist and might even have become a science fiction writer. On the other hand, there is a very good chance that I would then have been killed in the course of the German invasion of the Soviet Union in 1941 to 1945, and while I hope I would have done my bit first, I am glad I didn't have to. I am prejudiced in favor of life.

The four of us—my father Judah, my mother Anna, my sister Marcia, and myself—traveled by way of Danzig, Liverpool, and the good ship *Baltic*, and arrived at Ellis Island in February 1923. It was the last year in which immigration was relatively open and in which Ellis Island was working full steam. In 1924, the quota system was established and the

United States began to welcome only sharply limited amounts of the tired, the poor, and the wretched refuse of Europe's teeming shores.

One more year, then, and we wouldn't have made it. Even if we could have come in at some later time, it wouldn't have been the same. Arriving at the age of three, I was, of course, already speaking (Yiddish), but I was still young enough to learn English as a native language and not as an acquired one (which is never the same).

My parents, both of whom spoke Russian fluently, made no effort to teach me Russian, but insisted on my learning English as rapidly and as well as possible. They even set about learning English themselves, with reasonable, but limited, success.

In a way, I am sorry. It would have been good to know the language of Pushkin, Tolstoy, and Dostoevski. On the other hand, I would not have been willing to let anything get in the way of the complete mastery of English. Allow me my prejudice: surely there is no language more majestic than that of Shakespeare, Milton, and the King James Bible, and if I am to have one language that I know as only a native can know it, I consider myself unbelievably fortunate that it is English.

Now my memory starts. I remember, quite distinctly, the first place we lived in after having arrived in the United States. I even remember the address. It was 425 Van Siclen Avenue, in the East New York section of Brooklyn.* I lived in Brooklyn for nineteen years after my arrival in the United States, and my Brooklyn accent is with me to this day.

The Van Siclen Avenue abode was nothing lavish. There was no electricity; we used gas jets. There was no central heating; we had a cast-iron stove, which my mother started with paper and kindling.

Fortunately, I didn't know that this represented slum living. It was home to me, and I was happy. I was particularly fascinated by the stove, and I was always on hand to watch the fire start and my mother knead dough and make noodles. In 1925, when we moved to more advanced quarters, at 434 Miller Avenue, one block away, I cried bitterly.

In February 1925, shortly after my fifth birthday, I began school: kindergarten. If you want further statistics, the school was P.S. 182.

In the ordinary course of events, I would have entered first grade a year

---

* I feel a little silly giving statistics of this sort. I mean, who could possibly care what the exact address is? However, these are among the questions I am sometimes asked: "Exactly where did you live when you first came to the United States?" I hope that no one is thinking of making a pilgrimage to the site. It was a slum when I lived there and it has gone downhill steadily ever since.

later, shortly after my sixth birthday. My mother, however, could not wait.

You see, I had already taught myself to read by hounding the older boys to write out the alphabet for me (which I had learned from a rope-skipping game) and identify each letter and tell me what it "sounds like." I then practiced on street signs and newspaper headlines, sounding the letters till words made sense. To this day, I remember the sudden surge of triumph when I realized there must be such things as silent letters and that the word I was trying to pronounce, ISland, which meant nothing to me, was really EYEland. That made "Coney Island" luminously clear all of a sudden. On the other hand, I remember being completely defeated by "ought." I could not pronounce it, nor could any of the other boys tell me what it meant when *they* pronounced it.

My parents, of course, couldn't read English and so couldn't help me, and the fact that I learned to read without their help seemed to impress them the more. (My sister was much luckier. When she was five years old, I was seven and a past master at the art. Considerably against her will, I taught her to read quite efficiently, so that when it came time for her to enter school, they put her into the second grade directly.)

In September 1925, I remember, my mother took me to school. My mother's half brother came along, too, as interpreter. (He was my "Uncle Joe.") At the time, I did not know what they were doing, but in later years it dawned on me that they must have been altering my birth date. My mother, backed by Uncle Joe, assured the school authorities that I was born on September 7, 1919. (Considering the uncertainty of my birth date, it was less of a lie than it looked, but it was a little of a lie, because, allowing for all uncertainties, I could not possibly have been born earlier than October at the outside.)

With a September 7, 1919 birthday, that made me six years old the day before the fall term started in 1925, and I was allowed to enter the first grade.

The reason I know that this is what must have happened is that when I was in the third grade, the teacher (for some reason) had the children recite their birth dates. In all innocence, I said January 2, 1920, and she frowned and told me it was September 7, 1919.

Well! I have always been quite certain of knowing what I *know*, and I became very emphatic about having been born on January 2, 1920. So energetic did I become in the matter, in fact, that the school records were changed accordingly. If that had not been done, my official birthday would have been September 7, 1919, to this day.

Oddly enough, that turned out to have an important influence on my life. During World War II, I was working at the U. S. Navy Yard in Philadelphia as a chemist and was periodically deferred from the draft because of the war-related importance of my labors. After V-E day, May 8, 1945, the upper age for those liable to the draft was lowered to twenty-six, and those who were still under that age and had thus far escaped being drafted were scrutinized with special care.

On September 7, 1945, I received my notice of induction, and, two months later, was taken into the warm bosom of the Army of the United States as a private. It was no great tragedy, as it turned out, since by that time the war was over, and I remained in the Army only nine months. However, had I kept my little third-grade yap shut, my birthday would have stayed September 7, 1919, and that notice of induction would have arrived on my twenty-sixth birthday and I would have been ineligible for the draft.

My stay in grade school was hectic. On two different occasions, my despairing teachers got rid of me by shoving me ahead a semester. This had its elements of trauma, for on each occasion I lost the friends I had made in the old class and was forced to associate with the strangers of the new one.

Besides that, there was always that panic-laden moment when I realized the class had learned things I didn't yet know and that it would take me days of frightened activity to catch up and move ahead again. On the first occasion on which I was "skipped," I found myself in a class that was solving problems in multiplication, something I had never heard of.

I went home crying. My mother, unable to tell what it was that I did not know, called in a neighboring girl, aged twelve. (I found out in later years that she had been aged twelve; at the time, I thought she was a grownup.) The girl began drilling me in $2 \times 1 = 2$, $2 \times 2 = 4$, $2 \times 3 = 6$, and so on.

After a while it began to seem very familiar. I asked her to wait a moment and got my five-cent copybook. On the back were reference tables telling me that there were 12 inches to a foot, 16 ounces to a pound, and so on. There was also a large square array of mysterious numbers.

"What is this?" I asked.

"That," she said, "is the multiplication table."

"In that case," I said, "I know how to multiply," and I sent her home. Having nothing better to do, I had memorized the numbers long before, and from what she told me, I saw how the multiplication table worked.

The other time when I was pushed ahead, I found the class was studying geography, something of which I was utterly innocent. I remember the teacher had asked me where Yucatan was, and I drew a complete blank and the class laughed. (The less advanced a student was, the louder he laughed at someone else's ignorance.)

Quite humiliated, I asked the teacher after class if we had a book on the subject, and she pointed out the largest of the new books I had been given and said it was the geography book. That night, I went over every map in the book, and you can bet I was never caught again.

It turned out quite early, you see, that I was a child prodigy. My parents apparently knew it, but never told me so, because they didn't believe in giving children swelled heads. I wish they had, though, since then I wouldn't have thought it so unreasonable that every time I came back with less than 100 in any test I took, it would be interpreted as an unsatisfactory performance deserving of punishment. (And my mother, who knew nothing about modern child psychology, always punished by means of a physical assault.)

But then I didn't really need the information from them, since I gathered it by myself when I made the astonishing discovery that other people didn't understand something till it was explained and then didn't remember it after it was explained.

I don't know how it is with other prodigies, for I have never gone into the subject. Perhaps many of them have had a sense of unhappiness, of isolation, of drudgery, and may have wanted to be like other people.

Not so in my case, however. I enjoyed every minute of my prodigiousness, because, nasty little devil that I was, I enjoyed knowing more than the other kids and being far quicker on the uptake.

Of course, it had its difficulties. By the time I entered the fourth grade, I was a year and a half younger than anyone else in the class, and small for my age at that. And since I was still the smartest kid in the class and very self-appreciative about it, there were many of my schoolmates who lusted for my life. I found, however, that if I picked out the biggest and dumbest kid in the class and did his homework for him, he constituted himself my protector.

Another point that may have helped save my life was that I was never a teacher's pet. Never! I was a loudmouthed extrovert then, as I am now, and I could never resist the chance of upsetting the class with a funny remark. I was forever being disciplined, and when that was insufficient I was sent to the principal's office. (Believe it or not, I was evicted from class as a disruptive influence even as late as my college days.) So, of course, the other kids decided that anyone as badly behaved as I couldn't be all bad, and they resisted the impulse to eradicate me.

During our first years in the United States, my father worked in a knitting factory for a while, and then tried his hand at being a door-to-door salesman. Finally, in 1926, in a search for some sort of security, he put what money he had been able to accumulate into a candy store that existed on Sutter Avenue (good Heavens, I've forgotten the street number), right around the corner from our apartment.

A candy store is a good thing in some ways. You work for yourself and the work is steady. The profits are small but they're there, and we went through the entire period of the Great Depression without missing a meal and without ever having to spend one moment's anxiety that my father might lose his job and that we might all be on the bread lines. To those of you who know nothing of the Great Depression firsthand, let me assure you as earnestly as I can that we were very lucky.

On the other hand, a candy store is a rotten thing in some ways. Back before World War II, candy stores stayed open from 6 A.M. to 1 A.M. seven days a week, with no holidays. It meant that from the age of six I never had any but an occasional, fugitive hour of leisure with either parent. Furthermore, a candy store can be operated only by an entire family, which meant that I had to pitch in. Each year, I did a larger share of the chores.

The work wasn't hard, but it kept me behind the counter for much of my spare time, dishing out candy and cigarettes, making change, delivering papers, running a block and a half to call someone to the telephone, and so on. It kept me from the gay social life of my peers, eliminating punchball and ring-a-levio and many other things of the sort.

Not entirely, of course. In those days (and maybe in ours, too, for all I know) there were "seasons." One day, everyone was playing complicated games with marbles. The next day, all the marbles had disappeared and everyone was out with tops, or checkers (with which to play a marvelous game called "skelly"). I could play all the games with moderate ability, but I was considerably hampered by the fact that I was under strict instructions not to play "for keeps," because my father disapproved of gambling and it was difficult to get others kids to play me "for fun." ("There's no fun in playing for fun," they would say.)

Life was not all work, of course. There was a movie immediately across the street from the candy store. Every Saturday afternoon, my mother gave me a dime and supervised my crossing of the street. For that dime I saw two (silent) movies, a comedy, a cartoon, and, best of all, "an episode," which is what we called the movie serials of those days.

Then, too, I read a good deal. We had no books in the house (they were one of the very many luxuries we could not afford), but my father wangled a library card for me before I was seven. My very first taste of independence was that of going to the library *alone* by bus in order to pick out books.

I could go to the library only at certain times, however, and I could take out only two books at a time when I did go, and I generally finished them both before it was time to go to the library again, no matter how slowly I tried to make myself read. As a result, I constantly felt myself gravitating toward the magazine rack in my father's candy store. It was filled with apparently fascinating reading material.

Along a string stretched across the window, there were draped a dozen paper-backed novels featuring Frank Merriwell and Nick Carter, which I yearned for. There were other paper-backed objects with pictures on the cover, which I learned were called magazines, and some were particularly fascinating; there were pictures of people shooting other people with guns, and that looked great. There were even magazines with names like *Paris Nights*, whose purpose I didn't quite understand but with color illustrations that roused the most intense curiosity in me.

But, standing in the way of all this was my father. He simply would not let me read any of the magazines he sold, for he considered every one of them cheap and sensational trash that would only blunt and ruin my razor-sharp mind. I disagreed, of course, but my father was a remarkably stubborn man and he still had the European notion that Papa was boss.

My fate, however, all unknown to me, was approaching.

In the spring of 1926, the first magazine ever to be devoted to science fiction exclusively was placed on the newsstands for sale. It was entitled *Amazing Stories,* the first issue was dated April, and the publisher was Hugo Gernsback.

To fill the magazine, Gernsback was at first compelled to make heavy use of reprints of the works of European writers. It wasn't till the August 1928 issue that a new world really opened. In that issue there appeared the first installment of a three-part serial entitled *The Skylark of Space,* by Edward E. Smith and Lee Hawkins Garby.

As literature, it was a total flop (may the shade of good old Doc Smith forgive me!), but it had something more than good writing, much more. It had adventure of an unprecedented kind. There was the first introduction of interstellar travel. There were mind-boggling distances and encounters; a kind of never-slowing action centered about indestructible heroes.

The readers whom *Amazing Stories* had been attracting went wild. It became the first great "classic" of American magazine science fiction, and it was the forerunner of native American science fiction, which ever since has dominated world literature in that field.

But, alas, *The Skylark of Space* came and went and I knew nothing of it. I don't even recall seeing *Amazing Stories* on my father's newsstand during the years 1926 to 1928. I must have, but no trace of it is left in my memory.

Yet 1928, the year of *The Skylark of Space*, was notable for me in a number of ways.

For one thing, I briefly made the acquaintance of a remarkable youngster, who influenced me far more strongly than I could possibly have realized at the time.

He was roughly my age, rather smaller than I was, and rather darker in complexion. Somehow I discovered he had the ability to tell stories that held me enthralled, and he discovered simultaneously that I was an audience most willing to be enthralled.

For some months, we sought each other out so that we could play the roles of storyteller and audience. He would rattle on eagerly while we walked to the library and back, or when we just sat on someone's front steps.

The importance of it was just this: for the first time, I realized stories could be "made up." Until then, I had naturally assumed that stories existed only in books and had probably been there unchanged, from the beginning of time, without human creators.

Of the tales my friend told me, I have only the dimmest of recollections. I seem to remember that they involved the adventures of a group of men who were forever facing and overcoming dangerous villains. The leader of the group, an expert in the use of all conceivable weapons, was named Dodo "Weapons" Windrows, and his lieutenant was one Jack Winslow.

Whether my friend actually made up the stories or retold me material he had read, with adaptations, I don't know. At the time, I had no doubt whatever that he was inventing it as he went along. And looking back on it now, his enthusiasm seems to me to have been that of creation and not of adaptation.

Both of us were careful never to let anyone overhear us in our enjoyment of the process. My friend once explained that the other kids would "laugh at us." I suppose he felt his stories weren't first class and that while I seemed to appreciate them, others might not. Like any true artist, he did not care to expose himself needlessly to the possibility of adverse criticism.

As for myself, my chief fear was that my father would become aware of this. Instinctively, I was certain that my friend's tales would come under the heading of "cheap literature" and that I would be forcibly rescued from their baneful influence. This I most earnestly did not want to happen, and, in so far as I recognized that my friend's stories were akin in spirit to the tales to be found in sensational magazines, my hunger for those magazines sharpened.

Ah, well, it didn't last long. The storytelling spree could not have gone on for more than a few months when my friend's family moved away from the neighborhood and, of course, took my friend with them. He never returned; he never visited; he never wrote. I never knew where they had moved, and shortly my family moved, too. Contact was broken forever.

It seems to me now that my storytelling friend could not possibly have gotten the pleasure he clearly got out of telling stories that he (to all appearances) made up as he went along, without having tried to be a writer as he grew older. I know something about that particular compulsion, and I am certain he would have tried. And if he tried, it would seem to me that he must have succeeded.

And yet I remember his name and I am certain that there is no writer by that name. Can he have used a pseudonym? Is he dead? I don't know; I wish I did.

On a less personal note, and for the sake of statistics, 1928 was also the year of our citizenship. My parents had completed their five-year residency requirement, and in September received their papers. As minor children, my sister and I were mentioned on my father's citizenship papers and automatically became American citizens in consequence. (After I married and left home, I got citizenship papers of my own, dated 1943, so that I need not be forced to send my father to his safe-deposit box every time I needed proof of citizenship. To any future biographer who may find documentation of the 1943 citizenship, however, this is to inform him that I have been a citizen since 1928.)

The year ended with another change of residence. My father, having increased his savings, thanks to the candy store, felt it was time to sell it and buy another. Partly, I suppose, he felt he would welcome a change, and partly there was always the hope that another candy store would be more profitable.

In December 1928, therefore, we moved to 651 Essex Street, on the corner of New Lots Avenue. There the second candy store was located. I had to transfer from P.S. 182 to P.S. 202, something that involved another traumatic readjustment of friendships.

Then came the crucial summer of 1929, in which everything seemed to conspire to change the direction of my life. (It was the last summer of the Roaring Twenties, the last merry spark before the stock-market crash and the beginning of the Great Depression, but no one knew that, of course.)

For one thing, it was a time of crisis for *Amazing Stories*. Though it had been doing well, there were business machinations of a kind that go beyond the capacity for understanding of my essentially simple mind (Sam Moskowitz knows the story in detail), and Gernsback was forced out of ownership of the magazine.

The last issue of what we can call the "Gernsback *Amazing*" was the June 1929 issue, I believe. (I may be wrong by one or two months here.) It had gone thirty-nine issues. The magazine was taken over by Teck Publications, so with the July 1929 issue we can speak of the "Teck *Amazing*."

Gernsback, a man of considerable resource, had no intention of leaving the magazine field or, for that matter, of abandoning science fiction. Without missing a step, he founded another science fiction magazine, which was thereafter to compete with *Amazing Stories* and was to double the supply of reading matter for the science fiction public. Gernsback's new magazine was called *Science Wonder Stories*, and its first issue was dated June 1929.

Gernsback went further indeed and started a companion magazine called *Air Wonder Stories*, which began with the July 1929 issue. The supply of science fiction was thus tripled, and the existence of these new magazines was to prove of crucial importance to me.

The June in which those two new magazines were both on the stands for the first time, I was completing my stay in the fifth grade. The teacher of the course had offered to take a selected group in the class on a post-term trip to the Statue of Liberty. I did not qualify, since my marks in "Deportment" did not meet the minimum standards. I looked so stricken, however, that the teacher (presumably recalling that I was the brightest student in the class) asked the class permission to include me. The nice kids gave it and I went.

The trip was on July 2, 1929. I remember because I was nine and a half years old that day. It was exciting in itself, but the most remarkable thing about it was that for the first time in my life I had gone a considerable distance without my parents. The fact that the teacher was along didn't count. She did not have parental authority. It gave me an extraordinary feeling of having reached manhood.

The third event of the period was the fact that my mother had entered a third pregnancy (this one, I have reason to believe, unplanned) and, in July, was nearing term. It meant she couldn't help much in the store, and my poor father with only a nine-year-old assistant was terribly harried.

Now observe the concatenation of events.

Not long after my trip to the Statue of Liberty, I noted the new magazine *Science Wonder Stories* on the newsstand. It was the August 1929 issue, the third of its existence. I noticed it, first, because it had a cover by Frank R. Paul, the artist Gernsback always used, a man who painted in primary colors exclusively, I think, and who specialized in complex, futuristic machines.

But I also noticed it because it was a new magazine and my eye hadn't grown dulled to it. Finally, I noticed it because of the word "Science" in the title. That made all the difference. I knew about science; I had already read books about science. I was perfectly aware that science was considered a mentally nourishing and spiritually wholesome study. What's more, I knew that my father thought so from our occasional talks about my schoolwork.

Well, then, the loss of my storytelling friend had left a gnawing vacancy within me; my trip to the Statue of Liberty filled me with a desire to assert my independence and argue with my father; and the word "science" gave me the necessary leverage.

I picked up the magazine and, not without considerable qualms, approached my formidable parent. (It is hard for me to believe that at the time he was only thirty-two years old. I took it for granted he was infinitely old—at least as old as Moses.)

I spoke rapidly, pointed out the word "science," pointed to paintings of futuristic machines inside as an indication of how advanced it was, and (I believe) made it plain that if he said "No" I had every intention of throwing a fit. And that's where the final item in the concatenation of events came in: my father, driven to distraction by the new baby that was on its way, was in no mood to concern himself with trivia. He granted me permission.

I then scanned the newsstand for any other magazine of the same type, planning to maintain with all the strength at my disposal the legal position that permission for one such magazine implied permission' for all the others, even when the word "science" was not in the title.

Promptly I found the August 1929 issue of *Amazing Stories* and, of course, the August 1929 issue of *Air Wonder Stories*. I girded myself for the battle. It never came. My mother went to the hospital and my father conceded everything. On July 25, my brother, Stanley, was born.

I wish I could remember the stories in the very first science fiction magazines I ever read, but I can't. The nearest I can come to it is the fact that I remember the cover story in the August 1929 *Amazing Stories* to be "Barton's Island" by Harl Vincent, but I don't remember the plot.

One of the factors that surely must have helped induce my father to let me read the science fiction magazines was their respectable appearance.

At that time, there were two types of magazines on the stands. There were the smaller magazines, 7 by 10 inches in size, which were printed on cheap paper made of wood pulp, unglazed and with ragged edges. These "pulps" featured action stories in different categories, one magazine being devoted to Westerns, another to mysteries, still another to jungle stories, another to sports stories, yet another to air-war stories, and so on.

My father read some of the pulps himself (to improve his English, he said), but nothing could have induced him to let *me* read them. We quarreled over *The Shadow* and *Doc Savage* for years, and eventually, in my mid-teens, I began to read them defiantly without his permission. He would look at me sorrowfully whenever he caught me reading one of them, too; but though those looks stabbed me to the soul, I kept on reading them.

There were, however, also large-size magazines, 8½ by 11 inches or larger, published on glazed paper of good quality with smooth edges. These were the "slicks." I doubt that very many of them were any higher in literary quality than the pulps, but they looked better.

Well, *Amazing Stories, Science Wonder Stories,* and *Air Wonder Stories,* though printed on pulp paper and sometimes featuring authors who wrote regularly for the pulp magazines, were large-size and had smooth edges. They were kept with the slicks on the newsstands, not with the pulps (oh, what a kiss of death that would have been), and they therefore were to be found in respectable company.

What's more, where the pulp magazines usually charged ten cents an issue, the three science fiction magazines charged a lordly twenty-five cents, and, as always, high charge was equated with high quality.

In 1927, Gernsback had been faced with an overflow of stories and had put out a special issue of *Amazing Stories,* which he then still owned, made it thicker than an ordinary one, and called it *Amazing Stories Annual.* It was a success, and from then on he put out such issues at quarter-year intervals. This *Amazing Stories Quarterly* continued under the Teck regime, too, and Gernsback, when he started his new magazines, also began *Science Wonder Quarterly.*

The quarterlies were magnificent. Whereas the ordinary issues of the science fiction magazines contained 96 pages and about 100,000 words of fiction, the quarterlies contained 144 pages and about 150,000 words. The ordinary issues ran novels as serials (usually in three parts), but the quarterlies could run novels entire. Of course, the quarterlies cost fifty cents, an enormous price for those days, and my father didn't always receive them from the distributing companies, so I missed some copies. When I saw them, though, what an enormous feast they were!

(It occurs to me that if my father had not had a newsstand, there would not have been the slightest possibility of my ever reading science fiction magazines at that time except for such issues as I might—a very unlikely supposition—have borrowed. There was no way on Earth that I could have afforded quarters and half dollars for something as un-essential as reading matter. . . . Pardon me while I overcome my trembling fit at the thought, and then I will continue.)

Toward the end of 1929, still another science fiction magazine hit the newsstands, with its first issue dated January 1930. It was called *Astounding Stories of Super-Science.* The final phrase was soon dropped and it became *Astounding Stories.* It was published by Clayton Publications and is now referred to as the "Clayton *Astounding*" to differentiate it from later incarnations.

The Clayton *Astounding* was clearly a poor relation. For one thing, it was the size and quality of the pulp magazines and was placed with them on the newsstands. I was taken aback, and almost hesitated to try to read it, thinking that I would surely be stopped. However, my father said nothing. Having retreated, he was not prepared to renew the battle.

Astounding Stories published tales that were heavy on adventure and that seemed, to my boyish mind, to be less sophisticated than those in *Amazing Stories.* In fact, though I read every issue of the Clayton *Astounding,* all thirty-four, there was not one story in any of those issues that has remained with me to this day, and none are included in this anthology.

The very early stories that I still remember almost all appeared in *Amazing Stories,* which called itself "The Aristocrat of Science Fiction." And so it was, in my opinion. During the first four years of my science fiction reading, it was *Amazing Stories* all the way with me.

And it was the novels that were most impressive. The plots were most intricate, the adventures most detailed, and, most of all, there was the cliff-hanger with which each installment ended. You then had to wait the length of an arid month for the next installment. Some readers, I later discovered, saved their issues so that they could read the serials all at once, but I couldn't do that, of course. I had to return each issue to the newsstand.

The earliest serial I remember reading and slavering joyously over was *Cities in the Air,* by Edmond Hamilton, which ran in two parts in *Air Wonder Stories,* in the November and December 1929 issues.* I still remember the dramatic Paul cover illustration for that serial, with sky-scraper cities shown on huge circular slabs in mid-air.

The next serial I remember is *The Universe Wreckers,* a three-parter in *Amazing Stories,* in the May, June, and July 1930 issues. This one was also by Edmond Hamilton. Considering that, and the fact that Ed is the best-represented in this anthology (three stories) of any of the authors included, I can only deduce that Ed was my favorite author in those very early days.

I have met Ed and his charming wife, Leigh Brackett—also a writer —on many occasions in my grown-up days, and I've never thought to tell him this. I guess I didn't really realize it myself till I began sorting out my memories for this book.

Then, too, there was *The Drums of Tapajos,* by Capt. S. P. Meek, another three-parter in *Amazing Stories,* the November and December 1930 and January 1931 issues. Also *The Black Star Passes,* by John W. Campbell, Jr., published complete in the fall 1930 *Amazing Stories Quarterly.*

* I have a marvelous memory, but it is not so marvelous that I can remember exact issues for all the stories that I quote, or the exact date for the various items of historical interest I refer to in connection with early magazine science fiction. Actually, I am making liberal use of Donald B. Day's *Index to the Science-Fiction Magazines, 1926–1950* (Perri Press, Portland, Ore., 1952), which I bought twenty years ago and which has paid me back a hundredfold in its constant usefulness as a reference book to the early history of magazine science fiction. There have been a number of supplements put out for the period since 1950 by computers at M.I.T., but they lack the taste and flavor of the Day *Index.*

These stories, which are full-length novels, can't be included, alas, in this anthology, which is restricted to stories of fewer than forty thousand words.

In my first couple of years as a science fiction reader, I was given an unexpected bonus of time in which to read. When my brother was an infant, I was freed of some of my candy-store chores because I was put in charge of his welfare.

Watching Stanley was much better than standing behind the counter, because virtually no work was required. Aside from giving him his bottle if he cried (or shaking the carriage) and making sure that he didn't fall out or that no eagle swooped down to carry him off, I had only to sit there. I remember the warm summer days of 1930 when I was counting the hours till the Monday after Labor Day, when I could start the adventure of junior high school. I would be sitting next to the carriage, my chair tipped back against the brick wall of the house, and reading a science fiction magazine, dead to all the world beside except for my automatic response to any wail from the carriage.

Sometimes, to avoid being cramped, I would wheel the carriage sixty or seventy times around the block with the science fiction magazine propped against the handlebar.

Of course the nation as a whole was not going through my own idyllic experience that summer. The stock market had crashed in October 1929, and the economic situation had grown steadily worse ever since. The Great Depression was on. My father's customers had less money, so less money was spent in the candy store. Things grew tighter, and the second candy store, after half a year of moderate promise, showed clearly that it was to be no more a highway to riches than the first.

The science fiction magazines suffered along with everyone else. *Amazing Stories* and *Science Wonder Stories*, which never paid their authors very much, paid them more and more slowly. (The grim joke was that they paid a quarter cent a word on lawsuit.) *Astounding Stories*, for all its lower quality, paid higher rates more quickly, and it began to draw the authors its way, which made things harder than ever for the large-size magazines.

Amazing Stories withstood the strain stolidly and continued without apparent alteration. The Gernsback magazines, however, underwent ominous changes.

Air Wonder Stories was simply too specialized. Its stories dealt with futurized air travel in one way or another, and that did not allow for sufficient variety. I presume its circulation suffered, and the May 1930 issue, its eleventh, was also its last. With the next issue, that of June 1930, it was combined with *Science Wonder Stories* and the combined magazine was given the logical name of *Wonder Stories*.

After five issues, however, the combined magazine found that matters were still too tight for it and it attempted to improve its competitive stance by more closely imitating *Astounding Stories*. With the November 1930 issue, *Wonder Stories* went pulp size and left *Amazing Stories* as the only large-size science fiction magazine.

Part Two

1931

IN 1931, I finished my first year at Junior High School 149. It gave a three-year course: seventh, eighth, and ninth grades. For the better students, it offered, however, a "rapid advance" course in which both seventh and eighth grades were completed in the first year. That was the course I took.

On promotion day in June 1931, therefore, I received my final report card and was told that I would enter ninth grade in September. This was the equivalent of first year high school. I had expected this, of course, and had arranged with my mother that I would not go directly home. I ran to the library instead and came up against the librarian's desk with a bang.

"I want an adult library card, please," I panted, handing her my children's card.

I was still a week short of being eleven and a half, and very skinny, so the librarian said to me, kindly, "You can't have an adult card till you're in high school, little boy."

"I *am* in high school," I snarled, and slammed down my report card. She consulted another official, and I got my card.

This meant I could roam at will among the mysterious stacks containing adult books. The card was stamped "H.S.," however, which still restricted me to two books at a time.

Science fiction helped fill the gaps, and, as it happened, that spring, three months before my exciting promotion to an adult library card, I had read the first science fiction short story (as opposed to novel) that impressed me so much it stayed in my mind permanently.

I never read it again after that first reading, *never*, until I got a copy of old, fading, and brittle tear sheets of the story from Sam Moskowitz for the preparation of this anthology. And then, when I read it again, after forty-two years, I found I remembered it all in complete detail.

This cannot merely be a quirk of my excellent memory, for there are hundreds of science fiction stories I read both before and after this one that I have completely forgotten, including one or two that I read last month.

No, it's the story, "The Man Who Evolved," by (no surprise!) Edmond Hamilton. It appeared in the April 1931 *Wonder Stories*.

THE MAN WHO EVOLVED

by Edmond Hamilton

THERE were three of us in Pollard's house on that night that I try vainly to forget. Dr. John Pollard himself, Hugh Dutton and I, Arthur Wright—we were the three. Pollard met that night a fate whose horror none could dream; Dutton has since that night inhabited a state institution reserved for the insane, and I alone am left to tell what happened.

It was on Pollard's invitation that Dutton and I went up to his isolated cottage. We three had been friends and room-mates at the New York Technical University. Our friendship was perhaps a little unusual, for Pollard was a number of years older than Dutton and myself and was different in temperament, being rather quieter by nature. He had followed an intensive course of biological studies, too, instead of the ordinary engineering courses Dutton and I had taken.

As Dutton and I drove northward along the Hudson on that afternoon, we found ourselves reviewing what we knew of Pollard's career. We had known of his taking his master's and doctor's degrees, and had heard of his work under Braun, the Vienna biologist whose theories had stirred up such turmoil. We had heard casually, too, that afterwards he had come back to plunge himself in private research at the country-house beside the Hudson he had inherited. But since then we had had no word from him and had been somewhat surprised to receive his telegrams inviting us to spend the week-end with him.

It was drawing into early-summer twilight when Dutton and I reached a small riverside village and were directed to Pollard's place, a mile or so beyond. We found it easily enough, a splendid old pegged-frame house that for a hundred-odd years had squatted on a low hill above the river. Its outbuildings were clustered around the big house like the chicks about some protecting hen.

Copyright 1931 by Gernsback Publications, Inc.

Pollard himself came out to greet us. "Why, you boys have grown up!" was his first exclamation. "Here I've remembered you as Hughie and Art, the campus trouble-raisers, and you look as though you belong to business clubs and talk everlastingly about sales-resistance!"

"That's the sobering effect of commercial life," Dutton explained, grinning. "It hasn't touched you, you old oyster—you look the same as you did five years ago."

He did, too, his lanky figure and slow smile and curiously thoughtful eyes having changed not a jot. Yet Pollard's bearing seemed to show some rather more than usual excitement and I commented on it.

"If I seem a little excited it's because this is a great day for me," he answered.

"Well, you *are* in luck to get two fine fellows like Dutton and me to trail up to this hermitage of yours," I began, but he shook his head smilingly.

"I don't refer to that, Art, though I'm mighty glad you've come. As for my hermitage, as you call it, don't say a word against it. I've been able to do work here I could never have done amid the distractions of a city laboratory."

His eyes were alight. "If you two knew what—but there, you'll hear it soon enough. Let's get inside—I suppose you're hungry?"

"Hungry—not I," I assured him. "I might devour half a steer or some trifle like that, but I have really no appetite for anything else today."

"Same here," Dutton said. "I just pick at my food lately. Give me a few dozen sandwiches and a bucket of coffee and I consider it a full meal."

"Well, we'll see what we can do to tempt your delicate appetites," said Pollard, as we went inside.

We found his big house comfortable enough, with long, low-ceilinged rooms and broad windows looking riverward. After putting our bags in a bedroom, and while his housekeeper and cook prepared dinner, Pollard escorted us on a tour of inspection of the place. We were most interested in his laboratory.

It was a small wing he had added to the house, of frame construction outside to harmonize with the rest of the building, but inside offering a gleaming vista of white-tiled walls and polished instruments. A big cube-like structure of transparent metal surmounted by a huge metal cylinder resembling a monster vacuum tube, took up the room's center, and he showed us in an adjoining stone-floored room the dynamos and motors of his private power-plant.

Night had fallen by the time we finished dinner, the meal having been prolonged by our reminiscences. The housekeeper and cook had gone, Pollard explaining that the servants did not sleep in the place. We sat smoking for a while in his living-room, Dutton looking appreciatively around at our comfortable surroundings.

"Your hermitage doesn't seem half-bad, Pollard," he commented. "I wouldn't mind this easy life for a while myself."

"Easy life?" repeated Pollard. "That's all you know about it, Hugh. The fact is that I've never worked so hard in my life as I've done up here in the last two years."

"What in the world have you been working at?" I asked. "Something so unholy you've had to keep it hidden here?"

A Mad Scheme

Pollard chuckled. "That's what they think down in the village. They know I'm a biologist and have a laboratory here, so it's a foregone conclusion with them that I'm doing vivisection of a specially dreadful nature. That's why the servants won't stay here at night."

"As a matter of fact," he added, "if they knew down in the village what I've really been working on they'd be ten times as fearful as they are now."

"Are you trying to play the mysterious great scientist for our benefit?" Dutton demanded. "If you are you're wasting time—I know you, stranger, so take off that mask."

"That's right," I told him. "If you're trying to get our curiosity worked up you'll find we can scram you as neatly as we could five years ago."

"Which scramming generally ended in black eyes for both of you," he retorted. "But I've no intention of working up your curiosity—as a matter of fact I asked you up here to see what I've been doing and help me finish it."

"Help you?" echoed Dutton. "What can we help you do—dissect worms? Some week-end, I can see right now!"

"There's more to this than dissecting worms," Pollard said. He leaned back and smoked for a little time in silence before he spoke again.

"Do you two have any knowledge at all of evolution?" he asked.

"I know that it's a fighting word in some states," I answered, "and that when you say it you've got to smile, damn you."

He smiled, himself. "I suppose you're aware of the fact, however, that all life on this earth began as simple uni-cellular protoplasm, and by successive evolutionary mutations or changes developed into its present forms and is still slowly developing?"

"We know that much—just because we're not biologists you needn't think we're totally ignorant of biology," Dutton said.

"Shut up, Dutton," I warned. "What's evolution got to do with your work up here, Pollard?"

"It *is* my work up here," Pollard answered.

He bent forward. "I'll try to make this clear to you from the start. You know, or say you know, the main steps of evolutionary development. Life began on this earth as simple protoplasm, a jelly-like mass from which developed small protoplasmic organisms. From these developed in turn sea-creatures, land-lizards, mammals, by successive mutations. This infinitely slow evolutionary process has reached its highest point so far in the mammal man, and is still going on with the same slowness.

"This much is certain biological knowledge, but two great questions concerning this process of evolution have remained hitherto unanswered. First, what is the cause of evolutionary change, the cause of these slow, steady mutations into higher forms? Second, what is the future course of man's evolution going to be, what will the forms into which in the future man will evolve, and where will his evolution stop? Those two questions biology has so far been unable to answer."

Pollard was silent a moment and then said quietly, "I have found the answer to one of those questions, and am going to find the answer to the other tonight."

We stared at him. "Are you trying to spoof us?" I asked finally.

"I'm absolutely serious, Arthur. I have actually solved the first of those problems, have found the cause of evolution."

"What is it, then?" burst out of Dutton.

"What it has been thought by some biologists for years to be," Pollard answered. "The cosmic rays."

"The cosmic rays?" I echoed. "The vibrations from space that Millikan discovered?"

"Yes, the cosmic rays, the shortest wavelength and most highly penetrating of all vibratory forces. It has been known that they beat unceasingly upon the earth from outer space, cast forth by the huge generators of the stars, and it has also been known that they must have some great effect in one way or another upon the life of the earth."

"I have proved that they do have such an effect, and that that effect is what we call evolution! For it is the cosmic rays, beating upon every living organism on earth, that cause the profound changes in the structure of those organisms which we call mutations. Those changes are slow indeed, but it is due to them that through the ages life has been raised from the first protoplasm to man, and is still being raised higher."

"Good Lord, you can't be serious on this, Pollard!" Dutton protested.

"I am so serious that I am going to stake my life on my discovery tonight," Pollard answered, quietly.

We were startled. "What do you mean?"

"I mean that I have found in the cosmic rays the cause of evolution, the answer to the first question, and that tonight by means of them I am going to answer the second question and find out what the future evolutionary development of man will be!"

"But how could you possibly—"

Pollard interrupted. "Easily enough. I have been able in the last months to do something no physicist has been able to do, to concentrate the cosmic rays and yet remove from them their harmful properties. You saw the cylinder over the metal cube in my laboratory? That cylinder literally gathers in for an immense distance the cosmic rays that strike this part of earth, and reflects them down inside the cube.

"Now suppose those concentrated cosmic rays, millions of times stronger than the ordinary cosmic rays that strike one spot on earth, fall upon a man standing inside the cube. What will be the result? It is the cosmic rays that cause evolutionary change, and you heard me say that they are still changing all life on earth, still changing man, but so slowly as to be unnoticeable. But what about the man under those terrifically intensified rays? He will be changed millions of times faster than ordinarily, will go forward in hours or minutes through the evolutionary mutations that all mankind will go forward through in eons to come!"

"And you propose to try that experiment?" I cried.

"I propose to try it on myself," said Pollard gravely, "and to find out for myself the evolutionary changes that await humankind."

"Why, it's insane!" Dutton exclaimed.

Pollard smiled. "The old cry," he commented. "Never an attempt has been made yet to tamper with nature's laws, but that cry has been raised."

"But Dutton's right!" I cried. "Pollard, you've worked here alone too long—you've let your mind become warped—"

"You are trying to tell me that I have become a little mad," he said. "No, I am sane—perhaps wonderfully sane, in trying this."

His expression changed, his eyes brooding. "Can't you two see what this may mean to humanity? As we are to the apes, so must the men of the future be to us. If we could use this method of mine to take all mankind forward through millions of years of evolutionary development at one stride, wouldn't it be sane to do so?"

My mind was whirling. "Good heavens, the whole thing is so crazy," I protested. "To accelerate the evolution of the human race? It seems somehow a thing forbidden."

"It's a thing glorious if it can be done," he returned, "and I know that it can be done. But first one must go ahead, must travel on through stage after stage of man's future development to find out to which stage it would be most desirable for all mankind to be transferred. I know there is such an age."

"And you asked us up here to take part in that?"

"Just that. I mean to enter the cube and let the concentrated rays whirl me forward along the paths of evolution, but I must have someone to turn the rays on and off at the right moments."

"It's all incredible!" Dutton exclaimed. "Pollard, if this is a joke it's gone far enough for me."

For answer Pollard rose. "We will go to the laboratory now," he said simply. "I am eager to get started."

I cannot remember following Pollard and Dutton to the laboratory, my thoughts were spinning so at the time. It was not until we stood before the great cube from which the huge metal cylinder towered that I was aware of the reality of it all.

Pollard had gone into the dynamo-room and as Dutton and I stared wordlessly at the great cube and cylinder, at the retorts and flasks of acids and strange equipment about us, we heard the hum of motor-generators. Pollard came back to the switchboard supported in a steel frame beside the cube, and as he closed a switch there came a crackling and the cylinder glowed with white light.

Pollard pointed to it and the big quartz-like disc in the cubical chamber's ceiling, from which the white force-shafts shot downward.

"The cylinder is now gathering cosmic rays from an immense area of space," he said, "and those concentrated rays are falling through that disk into the cube's interior. To cut off the rays it is necessary only to open this switch." He reached to open the switch, the light died.

The Man Who Evolved

Quickly, while we stared, he removed his clothing, donning in place of it a loose white running suit.

"I will want to observe the changes of my own body as much as possible," he explained. "Now, I will stand inside the cube and you will turn on the rays and let them play upon me for fifteen minutes. Roughly, that should represent a period of some fifty million years of future evolutionary change. At the end of fifteen minutes you will turn the rays off and we will be able to observe what changes they have caused. We will then resume the process, going forward by fifteen-minute or rather fifty million year periods."

"But where will it stop—where will we quit the process?" Dutton asked.

Pollard shrugged. "We'll stop where evolution stops, that is, where the rays no longer affect me. You know, biologists have often wondered what the last change or final development of man will be, the last mutation. Well, we are going to see tonight what it will be."

He stepped toward the cube and then paused, went to a desk and brought from it a sealed envelope he handed to me.

"This is just in case something happens to me of a fatal nature," he said. "It contains an attestation signed by myself that you two are in no way responsible for what I am undertaking."

"Pollard, give up this unholy business!" I cried, clutching his arm. "It's not too late, and this whole thing seems ghastly to me!"

"I'm afraid it is too late," he smiled. "If I backed out now I'd be ashamed to look in a mirror hereafter. And no explorer was ever more eager than I am to start down the path of man's future evolution!"

He stepped up into the cube, standing directly beneath the disk in its ceiling. He motioned imperatively, and like an automaton I closed the door and then threw the switch.

The cylinder broke again into glowing white light, and as the shafts of glowing white force shot down from the disk in the cube's ceiling upon Pollard, we glimpsed his whole body writhing as though beneath a terrifically concentrated electrical force. The shaft of glowing emanations almost hid him from our view. I knew that the cosmic rays in themselves were invisible but guessed that the light of the cylinder and shaft was in some way a transformation of part of the rays into visible light.

Dutton and I stared with beating hearts into the cubical chamber, having but fleeting glimpses of Pollard's form. My watch was in one hand, the other hand on the switch. The fifteen minutes that followed seemed to me to pass with the slowness of fifteen eternities. Neither of us spoke and the only sounds were the hum of the generators and the crackling of the cylinder that from the far spaces was gathering and concentrating the rays of evolution.

At last the watch's hand marked the quarter-hour and I snapped off the switch, the light of the cylinder and inside the cube dying. Exclamations burst from us both.

Pollard stood inside the cube, staggering as though still dazed by the impact of the experience, but he was not the Pollard who had entered the chamber! He was transfigured, godlike! His body had literally expanded into a great figure of such physical power and beauty as we had not imagined could exist! He was many inches taller and broader, his skin a clear pink, every limb and muscle molded as though by some master sculptor.

The greatest change, though, was in his face. Pollard's homely, good-humored features were gone, replaced by a face whose perfectly-cut features held the stamp of immense intellectual power that shone almost overpoweringly from the clear dark eyes. It was not Pollard who stood before us, I told myself, but a being as far above us as the most advanced man of today is above the troglodyte!

He was stepping out of the cube and his voice reached our ears, clear and bell-like, triumphant.

"You see? It worked as I knew it would work! I'm fifty million years ahead of the rest of humanity in evolutionary development!"

"Pollard!" My lips moved with difficulty. "Pollard, this is terrible—this change—"

His radiant eyes flashed. "Terrible? It's wonderful! Do you two realize what I now am, can you realize it? This body of mine is the kind of body all men will have in fifty million years, and the brain inside it is a brain fifty million years ahead of yours in development!"

He swept his hand about. "Why, all this laboratory and former work of mine seems infinitely petty, childish, to me! The problems that I worked on for years I could solve now in minutes. I could do more for mankind now than all the men now living could do together!"

"Then you're going to stop at this stage?" Dutton cried eagerly "You're not going further with this?"

"Of course I am! If fifty million years development makes this much change in man, what will a hundred million years, two hundred million make? I'm going to find that out."

I grasped his hand. "Pollard, listen to me! Your experiment has succeeded, has fulfilled your wildest dreams. Stop it now! Think what you can accomplish, man! I know your ambition has always been to be one of humanity's great benefactors—by stopping here you can be the greatest!

You can be a living proof to mankind of what your process can make it, and with that proof before it all humanity will be eager to become the same as you!"

He freed himself from my grasp. "No, Arthur—I have gone part of the way into humanity's future and I'm going on."

He stepped back into the chamber, while Dutton and I stared helplessly. It seemed half a dream, the laboratory, the cubical chamber, the godlike figure inside that was and still was not Pollard.

"Turn on the rays, and let them play for fifteen minutes more," he was directing. "It will project me ahead another fifty million years."

His eyes and voice were imperative, and I glanced at my watch, and snicked over the switch. Again the cylinder broke into light, again the shaft of force shot down into the cube to hide Pollard's splendid figure.

Dutton and I waited with feverish intensity in the next minutes. Pollard was standing still beneath the broad shaft of force, and so was hidden in it from our eyes. What would its lifting disclose? Would he have changed still more, into some giant form, or would he be the same, having already reached humanity's highest possible development?

When I shut off the mechanism at the end of the appointed period, Dutton and I received a shock. For again Pollard had changed!

He was no longer the radiant, physically perfect figure of the first metamorphosis. His body instead seemed to have grown thin and shrivelled, the outlines of bones visible through its flesh. His body, indeed, seemed to have lost half its bulk and many inches of stature and breadth, but these were compensated for by the change in his head.

For the head supported by this weak body was an immense, bulging balloon that measured fully eighteen inches from brow to back! It was almost entirely hairless, its great mass balanced precariously upon his slender shoulders and neck. And his face too was changed greatly, the eyes larger and the mouth smaller, the ears seeming smaller also. The great bulging forehead dominated the face.

Could this be Pollard? His voice sounded thin and weak to our ears.

"You are surprised to see me this time? Well, you see a man a hundred million years ahead of you in development. And I must confess that you appear to me as two brutish, hairy cave-men would appear to you."

"But Pollard, this is awful!" Dutton cried. "This change is more terrible than the first . . . if you had only stopped at the first . . ."

The eyes of the shrivelled, huge-headed figure in the cube fired with anger. "Stop at that first stage? I'm glad now that I didn't! The man I was fifteen minutes ago . . . fifty million years ago in development . . . seems now to me to have been half-animal! What was his big animal-like body beside my immense brain?"

"You say that because in this change you're getting away from all human emotions and sentiments!" I burst. "Pollard, do you realize what you're doing? You're changing out of human semblance!"

"I realize it perfectly," he snapped, "and I see nothing to be deplored in the fact. It means that in a hundred million years man will be developing in brain-capacity and will care nothing for the development of body. To you two crude beings, of what is to me the past, this seems terrible; but to me it is desirable and natural. Turn on the rays again!"

"Don't do it, Art!" cried Dutton. "This madness had gone far enough!"

Pollard's great eyes surveyed us with cold menace. "You will turn on the rays," his thin voice ordered deliberately. "If you do not, it will be but the work of a moment for me to annihilate both of you and go on with this alone."

"You'd kill us?" I said dumfoundedly. "We two, two of your best friends?"

His narrow mouth seemed to sneer. "Friends? I am millions of years past such irrational emotions as friendship. The only emotion you awaken in me is a contempt for your crudity. Turn on the rays!"

The Brain Monster

His eyes blazed as he snapped the last order, and as though propelled by a force outside myself, I closed the switch. The shaft of glowing force again hid him from our view.

Of our thoughts during the following quarter-hour I can say nothing, for both Dutton and I were so rigid with awe and horror as to make our minds chaotic. I shall never forget, though, that first moment after the time had passed and I had again switched off the mechanism.

The change had continued, and Pollard—I could not call him that in my own mind—stood in the cube-chamber as a shape the sight of which stunned our minds.

He had become simply a great head! A huge hairless head fully a yard in diameter, supported on tiny legs, the arms having dwindled to mere hands that projected just below the head! The eyes were enormous, saucer-like, but the ears were mere pin-holes at either side of the head, the nose and mouth being similar holes below the eyes!

He was stepping out of the chamber on his ridiculously little limbs, and as Dutton and I reeled back in unreasoning horror, his voice came to us as an almost inaudible piping. And it held pride!

"You tried to keep me from going on, and you see what I have become? To such as you, no doubt, I seem terrible, yet you two and all like you seem as low to me as the worms that crawl!"

"Good God, Pollard, you've made yourself a monster!" The words burst from me without thought.

His enormous eyes turned on me. "You call me Pollard, yet I am no more the Pollard you knew, and who entered that chamber first, than you are the ape of millions of years ago from whom you sprang! And all mankind is like you two! Well, they will all learn the powers of one who is a hundred and fifty million years in advance of them!"

"What do you mean?" Dutton exclaimed.

"I mean that with the colossal brain I have I will master without a struggle this man-swarming planet, and make it a huge laboratory in which to pursue the experiments that please me."

"But Pollard—remember why you started this!" I cried. "To go ahead and chart the path of future evolution for humanity—to benefit humanity and not to rule it!"

The great head's enormous eyes did not change. "I remember that the creature Pollard that I was until tonight had such foolish ambitions, yes. It would stir mirth now, if I could feel such an emotion. To benefit humanity? Do you men dream of benefitting the animals you rule over? I would no sooner think of working for the benefit of you humans!

"Do you two yet realize that I am so far ahead of you in brain power now as you are ahead of the beasts that perish? Look at this . . ."

He had climbed onto a chair beside one of the laboratory tables, was reaching among the retorts and apparatus there. Swiftly he poured several compounds into a lead mortar, added others, poured upon the mixed contents another mixture made as swiftly.

There was a puff of intense green smoke from the mortar instantly, and then the great head—I can only call him that—turned the mortar upside down. A lump of shining mottled metal fell out and we gasped as we recognized the yellow sheen of pure gold, made in a moment, apparently, by a mixture of common compounds!

"You see?" the grotesque figure was asking. "What is the transformation of elements to a mind like mine? You two cannot even realize the scope of my intelligence!

"I can destroy all life on this earth from this room, if I desire. I can construct a telescope that will allow me to look on the planets of the farthest galaxies! I can send my mind forth to make contact with other minds without the slightest material connection. And you think it terrible that I should rule your race! I will not rule them, I will *own* them and this planet as you might own a farm and animals!"

"You couldn't!" I cried. "Pollard, if there is anything of Pollard left in you, give up that thought! We'll kill you ourselves before we'll let you start a monstrous rule of men!"

"We will—by God, we will!" Dutton cried, his face twitching.

We had started desperately forward toward the great head but stopped suddenly in our tracks as his great eyes met ours. I found myself walking backward to where I had stood, walking back and Dutton with me, like two automatons.

"So you two would try to kill me?" queried the head that had been Pollard. "Why, I could direct you without a word to kill yourselves and you'd do so in an instant! What chance has your puny will and brain against mine? And what chance will all the force of men have against me when a glance from me will make them puppets of my will?"

A desperate inspiration flashed through my brain. "Pollard, wait?" I exclaimed. "You were going on with the process, with the rays! If you stop here you'll not know what changes lie beyond your present form!"

He seemed to consider. "That is true," he admitted, "and though it seems impossible to me that by going on I can attain to greater intelligence than I now have, I want to find out for certain."

"Then you'll go under the rays for another fifteen minutes?" I asked quickly.

"I will," he answered, "but lest you harbor any foolish ideas, you may know that even inside the chamber I will be able to read your thoughts and can kill both of you before you can make a move to harm me."

He stepped up into the chamber again, and as I reached for the switch, Dutton trembling beside me, we glimpsed for a moment the huge head before the down-smiting white force hid it from our sight.

The minutes of this period seemed dragging even more slowly than before. It seemed hours before I reached at last to snap off the rays. We gazed into the chamber, shaking.

At first glance the great head inside seemed unchanged, but then we saw that it had changed, and greatly. Instead of being a skin-covered head with at least rudimentary arms and legs, it was now a great gray head-like shape of even greater size, supported by two gray muscular tentacles.

The surface of this gray head-thing was wrinkled and folded and its only features were two eyes as small as our own.

"Oh, my God!" quaked Dutton. "He's changing from a head into a brain—he's losing all human appearance!"

Into our minds came a thought from the gray head-thing before us, a thought as clear as though spoken. "You have guessed it, for even my former head-body is disappearing, all atrophying except the brain. I am become a walking, seeing brain. As I am so all of your race will be in two hundred million years, gradually losing more and more of their atrophied bodies and developing more and more their great brains."

His eyes seemed to read us. "You need not fear now the things I threatened in my last stage of development. My mind, grown infinitely greater, would no more now want to rule you men and your little planet than you would want to rule an anthill and its inhabitants! My mind, gone fifty million years further ahead in development, can soar out now to vistas of power and knowledge unimagined by me in that last stage, and unimaginable to you."

"Great God, Pollard!" I cried. "What have you become?"

"Pollard?" Dutton was laughing hysterically. "You call that thing Pollard? Why, we had dinner with Pollard three hours ago—he was a human being, and not a thing like this!"

"I have become what all men will become in time," the thing's thought answered me, "I have gone this far along the road of man's future evolution, and am going on to the end of that road, am going to attain the development that the last mutation possible will give me!"

"Turn on the rays," his thought continued. "I think that I must be approaching now the last possible mutation."

I snapped over the switch again and the white shaft of the concentrated rays veiled from us the great gray shape. I felt my own mind giving beneath the strain of horror of the last hour, and Dutton was still half-hysterical.

The humming and crackling of the great apparatus seemed thunderous to my ears as the minutes passed. With every nerve keyed to highest tension, I threw open the switch at last. The rays ceased, and the figure in the chamber was again revealed.

Dutton began to laugh shrilly, and then abruptly was sobbing. I do not know whether I was doing the same, thought I have a dim memory of mouthing incoherent things as my eyes took in the shape in the chamber.

It was a great brain! A gray limp mass four feet across, it lay in the chamber, its surface ridged and wrinkled by innumerable fine convolutions.

It had no features or limbs of any kind in its gray mass. It was simply a huge brain whose only visible sign of life was its slow, twitching movement.

From it thoughts beat strongly into our own horror-weighted brains.

"You see me now, a great brain only, just as all men will be far in the future. Yes, you might have known, I might have known, when I was like you, that this would be the course of human evolution, that the brain that alone gives man dominance would develop and the body that hampers that brain would atrophy until he would have developed into pure brain as I now am!

"I have no features, no senses that I could describe to you, yet I can realize the universe infinitely better than you can with your elementary senses. I am aware of planes of existence you cannot imagine. I can feed myself with pure energy without the need of a cumbersome body, to transform it, and I can move and act, despite my lack of limbs, by means and with a speed and power utterly beyond your comprehension.

"If you still have fear of the threats I made two stages back against your world and race, banish them! I am pure intelligence now and as such, though I can no more feel the emotions of love or friendship, neither can I feel those of ambition or pride. The only emotion, if such it is, that remains to me still is intellectual curiosity, and this desire for truth that has burned in man since his apehood will thus be the last of all desires to leave him!"

The Last Mutation

"A brain—a great brain!" Dutton was saying dazedly. "Here in Pollard's laboratory—but where's Pollard? He was here, too . . ."

"Then all men will some day be as you are now?" I cried.

"Yes," came the answering thought, "in two hundred and fifty million years man as you know him and as you are will be no more, and after passing all the stages through which I have passed through tonight, the human race will have developed into great brains inhabiting not only your solar system, no doubt, but the systems of other stars!"

"And that's the end of man's evolutionary road? That is the highest point that he will reach?"

"No, I think he will change from this great brain into still a higher form," the brain answered—the brain that three hours before had been Pollard!—"and I am going to find out now what that higher form will be. For I think this will be the last mutation of all and that with it I will reach

THE MAN WHO EVOLVED

the end of man's evolutionary path, the last and highest form into which he can develop!

"You will turn on the rays now," the brain's order continued, "and in fifteen minutes we will know what that last and highest form is."

My hand was on the switch but Dutton had staggered to me, was clutching my arm. "Don't, Arthur!" he was exclaiming thickly. "We've seen horrors enough—let's not see the last—get out of here . . ."

"I can't!" I cried. "Oh God, I want to stop but I can't now—I want to see the end myself—I've got to see . . ."

"Turn on the rays!" came the brain's thought-order again.

"The end of the road—the last mutation," I panted. "We've got to see— to see—" I drove the switch home.

The rays flashed down again to hide the great gray brain in the cube. Dutton's eyes were staring fixedly, he was clinging to me.

The minutes passed! Each tick of the watch in my hand was the mighty note of a great tolling bell in my ears.

An inability to move seemed gripping me. The hand of my watch was approaching the minute for which I waited, yet I could not raise my hand toward the switch!

Then as the hand reached the appointed minute I broke from my immobility and in a sheer frenzy of sudden strength pulled open the switch, rushed forward with Dutton to the cube's very edge!

The great gray brain that had been inside it was gone. There lay on the cube's floor instead of it a quite shapeless mass of clear, jelly-like matter. It was quite motionless save for a slight quivering. My shaking hand went forth to touch it, and then it was that I screamed, such a scream as all the tortures of hell's cruelest fiends could not have wrung from a human throat.

The mass inside the cube was a mass of simple *protoplasm!* This then was the end of man's evolution-road, the highest form to which time would bring him, the last mutation of all! The road of man's evolution was a circular one, returning to its beginning!

From the earth's bosom had risen the first crude organisms. Then sea-creature and land-creature and mammal and ape to man; and from man it would rise in the future through all the forms we had seen that night. There would be super-men, bodiless heads, pure brains; only to be changed by the last mutation of all into the protoplasm from which first it had sprung!

I do not know now exactly what followed. I know that I rushed upon that quivering, quiescent mass, calling Pollard's name madly and shouting things I am glad I cannot remember. I know that Dutton was shouting too, with insane laughter, and that as he struck with lunatic howls and fury about the laboratory the crash of breaking glass and the hiss of escaping gases was in my ears. And then from those mingling acids bright flames were leaping and spreading, sudden fires that alone, I think now, saved my own sanity.

For I can remember dragging the insanely laughing Dutton from the room, from the house, into the cool darkness of the night. I remember the chill of dew-wet grass against my hands and face as the flames from Pollard's house soared higher. And I remember that as I saw Dutton's crazy laughter by that crimson light, I knew that he would laugh thus until he died.

So ends my narrative of the end that came to Pollard and Pollard's house. It is, as I said in beginning, a narrative that I only can tell now, for Dutton has never spoken a sane word since. In the institution where he now is, they think his condition the result of shock from the fire, just as Pollard was believed to have perished in that fire. I have never until now told the truth.

But I am telling it now, hoping that it will in some way lessen the horror it has left with me. For there could be no horror greater than that we saw in Pollard's house that night. I have brooded upon it. With my mind's eye I have followed that tremendous cycle of change, that purposeless, eon-long climb of life up from simple protoplasm through myriads of forms and lives of ceaseless pain and struggle, only to end in simple protoplasm again.

Will that cycle of evolutionary change be repeated over and over again upon this and other worlds, ceaselessly, purposelessly, until there is no more universe for it to go on in? Is this colossal cycle of life's changes as inevitable and necessary as the cycle that in space makes of the nebulæ myriad suns, and of the suns dark-stars, and of the dark-stars colliding with one another nebula again?

Or is this evolutionary cycle we saw a cycle in appearance only, is there some change that we cannot understand, above and beyond it? I do not know which of these possibilities is truth, but I do know that the first of them haunts me. It would haunt the world if the world believed my story. Perhaps I should be thankful as I write to know that I will not be believed.

■ ■ ■ ■

As I reread "The Man Who Evolved," I tried to remember when I had first learned about cosmic rays and evolution. I failed. It is as though I always knew about both phenomena, even though I was clearly not born with the knowledge.

I honestly believe that I learned about both from science fiction stories to begin with. I might even have come across them first in this story.

There are some pieces of knowledge that I remember clearly having learned from science fiction stories.

For instance, in Hamilton's *The Universe Wreckers,* much of the action took place on the planet Neptune, which was treated in the story as the most distant of the planets. (Pluto had not yet been discovered, and when I heard news of the discovery, in 1931, my first thought was that it messed up Hamilton's novel.) It was in that novel that, for the first time, I learned Neptune had a satellite named Triton. I remember that piece of learning quite clearly.

It was from *The Drums of Tapajos* that I first learned there was a Mato Grosso area in the Amazon basin. It was from *The Black Star Passes* and other stories by John W. Campbell, Jr., that I first heard of relativity.

The pleasure of reading about such things in the dramatic and fascinating form of science fiction gave me a push toward science that was irresistible. It was science fiction that made me want to be a scientist strongly enough to eventually make me one.

This is not to say that science fiction stories can be completely trusted as a source of specific knowledge. In the case of "The Man Who Evolved," Hamilton was on solid ground when he maintained cosmic rays to be a motive force behind evolution. They are, but only in so far as they help create random mutations. It is natural selection that supplies the direction of evolutionary change, and this works, very painfully and slowly, upon large populations, not upon individuals.

The notion that a concentration of cosmic rays would cause an individual human being to evolve, personally, in the direction inevitably to be taken by the entire species is, of course, quite wrong. Concentrated radiation would merely kill.

However, the misguidings of science fiction can be unlearned. Sometimes the unlearning process is not easy, but it is a low price to pay for the gift of fascination over science.

It was the mark of the early and rather unsophisticated science fiction stories of the 1930s, by the way, that they often opened with one scientist lecturing others on subjects those others could not fail to know in real life (but of which the readers had to be informed).

I remember that the very first story I ever wrote for publication (but which was never published), "Cosmic Corkscrew," began that way, with the scientist-hero lecturing a friend on cosmic rays and neutrinos. No doubt, that opening helped Campbell decide on an immediate rejection (see *The Early Asimov*).

In the very month in which I completed the eighth grade, I read another story that stayed with me: "The Jameson Satellite," by Neil R. Jones, in the July 1931 *Amazing Stories*.

THE JAMESON SATELLITE

by Neil R. Jones

PROLOGUE

The Rocket Satellite

IN THE depths of space, some twenty thousand miles from the earth, the body of Professor Jameson within its rocket container cruised upon an endless journey, circling the gigantic sphere. The rocket was a satellite of the huge, revolving world around which it held to its orbit. In the year 1958, Professor Jameson had sought for a plan whereby he might preserve his body indefinitely after his death. He had worked long and hard upon the subject.

Since the time of the Pharaohs, the human race had looked for a means by which the dead might be preserved against the ravages of time. Great had been the art of the Egyptians in the embalming of their deceased, a practice which was later lost to humanity of the ensuing mechanical age, never to be rediscovered. But even the embalming of the Egyptians—so Professor Jameson had argued—would be futile in the face of millions of years, the dissolution of the corpses being just as eventual as immediate cremation following death.

The professor had looked for a means by which the body could be preserved perfectly forever. But eventually he had come to the conclusion that nothing on earth is unchangeable beyond a certain limit of time. Just as long as he sought an earthly means of preservation, he was doomed to disappointment. All earthly elements are composed of atoms which are forever breaking down and building up, but never destroying themselves. A match may be burned, but the atoms are still unchanged, having resolved themselves into smoke, carbon dioxide, ashes, and certain basic elements. It was clear to the professor that he could never accomplish his

Copyright 1931 by Radio-Science Publications, Inc.

purpose if he were to employ one system of atomic structure, such as embalming fluid or other concoction, to preserve another system of atomic structure, such as the human body, when all atomic structure is subject to universal change, no matter how slow.

He had then soliloquized upon the possibility of preserving the human body in its state of death until the end of all earthly time—to that day when the earth would return to the sun from which it had sprung. Quite suddenly one day he had conceived the answer to the puzzling problem which obsessed his mind, leaving him awed with its wild, uncanny potentialities.

He would have his body shot into space enclosed in a rocket to become a satellite of the earth as long as the earth continued to exist. He reasoned logically. Any material substance, whether of organic or inorganic origin, cast into the depths of space would exist indefinitely. He had visualized his dead body enclosed in a rocket flying off into the illimitable maw of space. He would remain in perfect preservation, while on earth millions of generations of mankind would live and die, their bodies to molder into the dust of the forgotten past. He would exist in this unchanged manner until that day when mankind, beneath a cooling sun, should fade out forever in the chill, thin atmosphere of a dying world. And still his body would remain intact and as perfect in its rocket container as on that day of the far-gone past when it had left the earth to be hurled out on its career. What a magnificent idea!

At first he had been assailed with doubts. Suppose his funeral rocket landed upon some other planet or, drawn by the pull of the great sun, were thrown into the flaming folds of the incandescent sphere? Then the rocket might continue on out of the solar system, plunging through the endless seas of space for millions of years, to finally enter the solar system of some far-off star, as meteors often enter ours. Suppose his rocket crashed upon a planet, or the star itself, or became a captive satellite of some celestial body?

It had been at this juncture that the idea of his rocket becoming the satellite of the earth had presented itself, and he had immediately incorporated it into his scheme. The professor had figured out the amount of radium necessary to carry the rocket far enough away from the earth so that it would not turn around and crash, and still be not so far away but what the earth's gravitational attraction would keep it from leaving the vicinity of the earth and the solar system. Like the moon, it would forever revolve around the earth.

He had chosen an orbit sixty-five thousand miles from the earth for his rocket to follow. The only fears he had entertained concerned the huge meteors which careened through space at tremendous rates of speed. He had overcome this obstacle, however, and had eliminated the possibilities of a collision with these stellar juggernauts. In the rocket were installed radium repulsion rays which swerved all approaching meteors from the path of the rocket as they entered the vicinity of the space wanderer.

The aged professor had prepared for every contingency, and had set down to rest from his labors, reveling in the stupendous, unparalleled results he would obtain. Never would his body undergo decay; and never would his bones bleach to return to the dust of the earth from which all men originally came and to which they must return. His body would remain millions of years in a perfectly preserved state, untouched by the hoary palm of such time as only geologists and astronomers can conceive.

His efforts would surpass even the wildest dreams of H. Rider Haggard, who depicted the wondrous, embalming practices of the ancient nation of Kor in his immortal novel, "She," wherein Holly, under the escort of the incomparable Ayesha, looked upon the magnificent, lifelike masterpieces of embalming by the long-gone peoples of Kor.

With the able assistance of a nephew, who carried out his instructions and wishes following his death, Professor Jameson was sent upon his pilgrimage into space within the rocket he himself had built. The nephew and heir kept the secret forever locked in his heart.

Generation after generation had passed upon its way. Gradually humanity had come to die out, finally disappearing from the earth altogether. Mankind was later replaced by various other forms of life which dominated the globe for their allotted spaces of time before they too became extinct. The years piled up on one another, running into millions, and still the Jameson Satellite kept its lonely vigil around the earth, gradually closing the distance between satellite and planet, yielding reluctantly to the latter's powerful attraction.

Forty million years later, its orbit ranged some twenty thousand miles from the earth while the dead world edged ever nearer the cooling sun whose dull, red ball covered a large expanse of the sky. Surrounding the flaming sphere, many of the stars could be perceived through the earth's thin, rarefied atmosphere. As the earth cut in slowly and gradually toward the solar luminary, so was the moon revolving ever nearer the earth, appearing like a great gem glowing in the twilight sky.

The rocket containing the remains of Professor Jameson continued its endless travel around the great ball of the earth whose rotation had now ceased entirely—one side forever facing the dying sun. There it pursued its lonely way, a cosmic coffin, accompanied by its funeral cortege of scintillating stars amid the deep silence of the eternal space which enshrouded it. Solitary it remained, except for the occasional passing of a meteor flitting by at a remarkable speed on its aimless journey through the vacuum between the far-flung worlds.

Would the satellite follow its orbit to the world's end, or would its supply of radium soon exhaust itself after so many eons of time, converting the rocket into the prey of the first large meteor which chanced that way? Would it some day return to the earth as its nearer approach portended, and increase its acceleration in a long arc to crash upon the surface of the dead planet? And when the rocket terminated its career, would the body of Professor Jameson be found perfectly preserved or merely a crumbled mound of dust?

CHAPTER I

40,000,000 Years After

Entering within the boundaries of the solar system, a long, dark, pointed craft sped across the realms of space towards the tiny point of light which marked the dull red ball of the dying sun which would some day lie cold and dark forever. Like a huge meteor it flashed into the solar system from another chain of planets far out in the illimitable Universe of stars and worlds, heading towards the great red sun at an inconceivable speed.

Within the interior of the space traveler, queer creatures of metal labored at the controls of the space flyer which juggernauted on its way towards the far-off solar luminary. Rapidly it crossed the orbits of Neptune and Uranus and headed sunward. The bodies of these queer creatures were square blocks of a metal closely resembling steel, while for appendages, the metal cube was upheld by four jointed legs capable of movement. A set of six tentacles, all metal, like the rest of the body, curved outward from the upper half of the cubic body. Surmounting it was a queer-shaped head rising to a peak in the center and equipped with a circle of eyes all the way around the head. The creatures, with their mechanical eyes equipped with metal shutters, could see in all directions. A single eye pointed directly upward, being situated in the space of the peaked head, resting in a slight depression of the cranium.

These were the Zoromes of the planet Zor which rotated on its way around a star millions of light years distant from our solar system. The Zoromes, several hundred thousand years before, had reached a stage in science, where they searched for immortality and eternal relief from bodily ills and various deficiencies of flesh and blood anatomy. They had sought freedom from death, and had found it, but at the same time they had destroyed the propensities for birth. And for several hundred thousand years there had been no births and few deaths in the history of the Zoromes.

This strange race of people had built their own mechanical bodies, and by operation upon one another had removed their brains to the metal heads from which they directed the functions and movements of their inorganic anatomies. There had been no deaths due to worn-out bodies. When one part of the mechanical men wore out, it was replaced by a new part, and so the Zoromes continued living their immortal lives which saw few casualties. It was true that, since the innovation of the machines, there had been a few accidents which had seen the destruction of the metal heads with their brains. These were irreparable. Such cases had been few, however, and the population of Zor had decreased but little. The machine men of Zor had no use for atmosphere, and had it not been for the terrible coldness of space, could have just as well existed in the ether void as upon some planet. Their metal bodies, especially their metal-encased brains, did require a certain amount of heat even though they were able to exist comfortably in temperatures which would instantly have frozen to death a flesh-and-blood creature.

The most popular pastime among the machine men of Zor was the exploration of the Universe. This afforded them a never ending source of interest in the discovery of the variegated inhabitants and conditions of the various planets on which they came to rest. Hundreds of space ships were sent out in all directions, many of them being upon their expeditions for hundreds of years before they returned once more to the home planet of far-off Zor.

This particular space craft of the Zoromes had entered the solar system whose planets were gradually circling in closer to the dull red ball of the declining sun. Several of the machine men of the space craft's crew, which numbered some fifty individuals, were examining the various planets of this particular planetary system carefully through telescopes possessing immense power.

These machine men had no names and were indexed according to letters and numbers. They conversed by means of thought impulses, and were neither capable of making a sound vocally nor of hearing one uttered.

"Where shall we go?" queried one of the men at the controls questioning another who stood by his side examining a chart on the wall.

"They all appear to be dead worlds, 4R-3579," replied the one addressed, "but the second planet from the sun appears to have an atmosphere which might sustain a few living creatures, and the third planet may also prove interesting for it has a satellite. We shall examine the inner planets first of all, and explore the outer ones later if we decide it is worth the time."

"Too much trouble for nothing," ventured 9G-721. "This system of planets offers us little but what we have seen many times before in our travels. The sun is so cooled that it cannot sustain the more common life on its planets, the type of life forms we usually find in our travels. We should have visited a planetary system with a brighter sun."

"You speak of common life," remarked 25X-987. "What of the uncommon life? Have we not found life existent on cold, dead planets with no sunlight and atmosphere at all?"

"Yes, we have," admitted 9G-721, "but such occasions are exceedingly rare."

"The possibility exists, however, even in this case," reminded 4R-3579, "and what if we do spend a bit of unprofitable time in this one planetary system—haven't we all an endless lifetime before us? Eternity is ours."

"We shall visit the second planet first of all," directed 25X-987, who was in charge of this particular expedition of the Zoromes, "and on the way there we shall cruise along near the third planet to see what we can of the surface. We may be able to tell whether or not it holds anything of interest to us. If it does, after visiting the second planet, we shall then return to the third. The first world is not worth bothering with."

The space ship from Zor raced on in a direction which would take it several thousand miles above the earth and then on to the planet which we know as Venus. As the space ship rapidly neared the earth, it slackened its speed, so that the Zoromes might examine it closely with their glasses as the ship passed the third planet.

Suddenly, one of the machine men ran excitedly into the room where 25X-987 stood watching the topography of the world beneath him.

"We have found something!" he exclaimed.

"What?"

"Another space ship!"

"Where?"

"But a short distance ahead of us on our course. Come into the foreport of the ship and you can pick it up with the glass."

"Which is the way it's going?" asked 25X-987.

"It is behaving queerly," replied the machine man of Zor. "It appears to be in the act of encircling the planet."

"Do you suppose that there really is life on that dead world—intelligent beings like ourselves, and that this is one of their space craft?"

"Perhaps it is another exploration craft like our own from some other world," was the suggestion.

"But not of ours," said 25X-987.

Together, the two Zoromes now hastened into the observation room of the space ship where more of the machine men were excitedly examining the mysterious space craft, their thought impulses flying thick and fast like bodiless bullets.

"It is very small!"

"Its speed is slow!"

"The craft can hold but few men," observed one.

"We do not yet know of what size the creatures are," reminded another. "Perhaps there are thousands of them in that space craft out there. They may be of such a small size that it will be necessary to look twice before finding one of them. Such beings are not unknown."

"We shall soon overtake it and see."

"I wonder if they have seen us?"

"Where do you suppose it came from?"

"From the world beneath us," was the suggestion.

"Perhaps."

CHAPTER II

The Mysterious Space Craft

The machine men made way for their leader, 25X-987, who regarded the space craft ahead of them critically.

"Have you tried communicating with it yet?" he asked.

"There is no reply to any of our signals," came the answer.

"Come alongside of it then," ordered their commander. "It is small enough to be brought inside our carrying compartment, and we can see with our penetration rays just what manner of creatures it holds. They are intelligent, that is certain, for their space ship does imply as much."

The space flyer of the Zoromes slowed up as it approached the mysterious wanderer of the cosmic void which hovered in the vicinity of the dying
world.

"What a queer shape it has," remarked 25X-987. "It is even smaller
than I had previously calculated."

A rare occurrence had taken place among the machine men of Zor.
They were overcome by a great curiosity which they could not allow to
remain unsatiated. Accustomed as they were to witnessing strange sights
and still stranger creatures, meeting up with weird adventures in various
corners of the Universe, they had now become hardened to the usual run of
experiences which they were in the habit of encountering. It took a great
deal to arouse their unperturbed attitudes. Something new, however, about
this queer space craft had gripped their imaginations, and perhaps a
subconscious influence asserted to their minds that here they have come
across an adventure radically unusual.

"Come alongside it," repeated 25X-987 to the operator as he returned to the control room and gazed through the side of the space ship
in the direction of the smaller cosmic wanderer.

"I'm trying to," replied the machine man, "but it seems to jump away a
bit every time I get within a certain distance of it. Our ship seems to
jump backward a bit too."

"Are they trying to elude us?"

"I don't know. They should pick up more speed if that is their object."

"Perhaps they are now progressing at their maximum speed and cannot increase their acceleration any more."

"Look!" exclaimed the operator. "Did you just see that? The thing has
jumped away from us again!"

"Our ship moved also," said 25X-987. "I saw a flash of light shoot
from the side of the other craft as it jumped."

Another machine man now entered and spoke to the commander of
the Zorome expedition.

"They are using radium repellent rays to keep us from approaching,"
he informed.

"Counteract it," instructed 25X-987.

The man left, and now the machine man at the controls of the craft
tried again to close with the mysterious wanderer of the space between
planets. The effort was successful, and this time there was no glow of
repulsion rays from the side of the long metal cylinder.

They now entered the compartment where various objects were transferred from out of the depths of space to the interplanetary craft. Then

patiently they waited for the rest of the machine men to open the side of their space ship and bring in the queer, elongated cylinder.

"Put it under the penetration ray!" ordered 25X-987. "Then we shall see what it contains!"

The entire group of Zoromes were assembled about the long cylinder, whose low nickel-plated sides shone brilliantly. With interest they regarded the fifteen-foot object which tapered a bit towards its base. The nose was pointed like a bullet. Eight cylindrical protuberances were affixed to the base while the four sides were equipped with fins such as are seen on aerial bombs to guide them in a direct, unswerving line through the atmosphere. At the base of the strange craft there projected a lever, while in one side was a door which apparently opened outward. One of the machine men reached forward to open it but was halted by the admonition of the commander.

"Do not open it up yet!" he warned. "We are not aware of what it contains!"

Guided by the hand of one of the machine men, a series of lights shone down upon the cylinder. It became enveloped in a haze of light which rendered the metal sides of the mysterious space craft dim and indistinct while the interior of the cylinder was as clearly revealed as if there had been no covering. The machine men, expecting to see at least several, perhaps many, strange creatures moving about within the metal cylinder, stared aghast at the sight they beheld. There was but one creature, and he was lying perfectly still, either in a state of suspended animation or else of death. He was about twice the height of the mechanical men of Zor. For a long time they gazed at him in a silence of thought, and then their leader instructed them.

"Take him out of the container."

The penetration rays were turned off, and two of the machine men stepped eagerly forward and opened the door. One of them peered within at the recumbent body of the weird-looking individual with the four appendages. The creature lay up against a luxuriously upholstered interior, a strap affixed to his chin while four more straps held both the upper and lower appendages securely to the insides of the cylinder. The machine man released these, and with the help of his comrade removed the body of the creature from the cosmic coffin in which they had found it.

"He is dead!" pronounced one of the machine men after a long and careful examination of the corpse. "He has been like this for a long time."

"There are strange thought impressions left upon his mind," remarked another.

One of the machine men, whose metal body was a different shade than that of his companions, stepped forward, his cubic body bent over that of the strange, cold creature who was garbed in fantastic accoutrements. He examined the dead organism a moment, and then he turned to his companions.

"Would you like to hear his story?" he asked.

"Yes!" came the concerted reply.

"You shall, then," was the ultimatum. "Bring him into my laboratory. I shall remove his brain and stimulate the cells into activity once more. We shall give him life again, transplanting his brain into the head of one of our machines."

With these words he directed two of the Zoromes to carry the corpse into the laboratory.

As the space ship cruised about in the vicinity of this third planet which 25X-987 had decided to visit on finding the metal cylinder with its queer inhabitant, 8B-52, the experimenter, worked unceasingly in his laboratory to revive the long-dead brain cells to action once more. Finally, after consummating his desires and having his efforts crowned with success, he placed the brain within the head of a machine. The brain was brought to consciousness. The creature's body was discarded after the all-important brain had been removed.

CHAPTER III

Recalled to Life

As Professor Jameson came to, he became aware of a strange feeling. He was sick. The doctors had not expected him to live; they had frankly told him so—but he had cared little in view of the long, happy years stretched out behind him. Perhaps he was not to die yet. He wondered how long he had slept. How strange he felt—as if he had no body. Why couldn't he open his eyes? He tried very hard. A mist swam before him. His eyes had been open all the time but he had not seen before. That was queer, he ruminated. All was silent about his bedside. Had all the doctors and nurses left him to sleep—or to die?

Devil take that mist which now swam before him, obscuring everything in line of vision. He would call his nephew. Vainly he attempted to shout the word "Douglas," but to no avail. Where was his mouth? It seemed as if he had none. Was it all delirium? The strange silence—perhaps he had lost his sense of hearing along with his ability to speak—and he could see nothing distinctly. The mist had transferred itself into a confused jumble of indistinct objects, some of which moved about before him.

He was now conscious of some impulse in his mind which kept questioning him as to how he felt. He was conscious of other strange ideas which seemed to be impressed upon his brain, but this one thought concerning his indisposition clamored insistently over the lesser ideas. It even seemed just as if someone was addressing him, and impulsively he attempted to utter a sound and tell them how queer he felt. It seemed as if speech had been taken from him. He could not talk, no matter how hard he tried. It was no use. Strange to say, however, the impulse within his mind appeared to be satisfied with the effort, and it now put another question to him. Where was he from? What a strange question—when he was at home. He told them as much. Had he always lived there? Why, yes, of course.

The aged professor was now becoming more astute as to his condition. At first it was only a mild, passive wonderment at his helplessness and the strange thoughts which raced through his mind. Now he attempted to arouse himself from the lethargy.

Quite suddenly his sight cleared, and what a surprise! He could see all the way around him without moving his head! And he could look at the ceiling of his room! His room? Was it his room! No— It just couldn't be. Where was he? What were those queer machines before him? They moved on four legs. Six tentacles curled outward from their cubical bodies. One of the machines stood close before him. A tentacle shot out from the object and rubbed his head. How strange it felt upon his brow. Instinctively he obeyed the impulse to shove the contraption of metal from him with his hands.

His arms did not rise, instead six tentacles projected upward to force back the machine. Professor Jameson gasped mentally in surprise as he gazed at the result of his urge to push the strange, unearthly looking machine-caricature from him. With trepidation he looked down at his own body to see where the tentacles had come from, and his surprise turned to sheer fright and amazement. His body was like the moving machine which stood before him! Where was he? What ever had happened to him so suddenly? Only a few moments ago he had been in his bed, with the doctors and his nephew bending over him, expecting him to die. The last words he had remembered hearing was the cryptic announcement of one of the doctors.

"He is going now."

But he hadn't died after all, apparently. A horrible thought struck him! Was this the life after death? Or was it an illusion of the mind? He became aware that the machine in front of him was attempting to communicate something to him. How could it, thought the professor, when he had no mouth. The desire to communicate an idea to him became more insistent. The suggestion of the machine man's question was in his mind. Telepathy, thought he.

The creature was asking about the place whence he had come. He didn't know; his mind was in such a turmoil of thoughts and conflicting ideas. He allowed himself to be led to a window where the machine with waving tentacle pointed towards an object outside. It was a queer sensation to be walking on the four metal legs. He looked from the window and he saw that which caused him to nearly drop over, so astounded was he.

The professor found himself gazing out from the boundless depths of space across the cosmic void to where a huge planet lay quiet. Now he was sure it was an illusion which made his mind and sight behave so queerly. He was troubled by a very strange dream. Carefully he examined the topography of the gigantic globe which rested off in the distance. At the same time he could see back of him the concourse of mechanical creatures crowding up behind him, and he was aware of a telepathic conversation which was being carried on behind him—or just before him. Which was it now? Eyes extended all the way around his head, while there existed no difference on any of the four sides of his cubed body. His mechanical legs were capable of moving in any of four given directions with perfect ease, he discovered.

The planet was not the earth—of that he was sure. None of the familiar continents lay before his eyes. And then he saw the great dull red ball of the dying sun. That was not the sun of his earth. It had been a great deal more brilliant.

"Did you come from that planet?" came the thought impulse from the mechanism by his side.

"No," he returned.

He then allowed the machine men—for he assumed that they were machine men, and he reasoned that, somehow or other they had by some marvelous transformation made him over just as they were—to lead him through the craft of which he now took notice for the first time. It was an interplanetary flyer, or space ship, he firmly believed.

25X-987 now took him to the compartment which they had removed him to from the strange container they had found wandering in the vicinity of the nearby world. There they showed him the long cylinder.

"It's my rocket satellite!" exclaimed Professor Jameson to himself, though in reality every one of the machine men received his thoughts plainly. "What is it doing here?"

"We found your dead body within it," answered 25X-987. "Your brain was removed to the machine after having been stimulated into activity once more. Your carcass was thrown away."

Professor Jameson just stood dumfounded by the words of the machine man.

"So I did die!" exclaimed the professor. "And my body was placed within the rocket to remain in everlasting preservation until the end of all earthly time! Success! I have now attained unrivaled success!"

He then turned to the machine man.

"How long have I been that way?" he asked excitedly.

"How should we know?" replied the Zorome. "We picked up your rocket only a short time ago, which, according to your computation, would be less than a day. This is our first visit to your planetary system and we chanced upon your rocket. So it is a satellite? We didn't watch it long enough to discover whether or not it was a satellite. At first we thought it to be another traveling space craft, but when it refused to answer our signals we investigated."

"And so that was the earth at which I looked," mused the professor. "No wonder I didn't recognize it. The topography has changed so much. How different the sun appears—it must have been over a million years ago when I died!"

"Many millions," corrected 25X-987. "Suns of such size as this one do not cool in so short a time as you suggest."

Professor Jameson, in spite of all his amazing computations before his death, was staggered by the reality.

"Who are you?" he suddenly asked.

"We are the Zoromes from Zor, a planet of a sun far across the Universe."

25X-987 then went on to tell Professor Jameson something about how the Zoromes had attained their high stage of development and had instantly put a stop to all birth, evolution and death of their people, by becoming machine men.

CHAPTER IV

The Dying World

"And now tell us of yourself," said 25X-987, "and about your world."

Professor Jameson, noted in college as a lecturer of no mean ability and perfectly capable of relating intelligently to them the story of the earth's history, evolution and march of events following the birth of civilization up until the time when he died, began his story. The mental speech hampered him for a time, but he soon became accustomed to it so as to use it easily, and he found it preferable to vocal speech after a while. The Zoromes listened interestedly to the long account until Professor Jameson had finished.

"My nephew," concluded the professor, "evidently obeyed my instructions and placed my body in the rocket I had built, shooting it out into space where I became the satellite of the earth for these many millions of years."

"Do you really want to know how long you were dead before we found you?" asked 25X-987. "It would be interesting to find out."

"Yes, I should like very much to know," replied the professor.

"Our greatest mathematician, 459C-79, will tell it to you." The mathematician stepped forward. Upon one side of his cube were many buttons arranged in long columns and squares.

"What is your unit of measuring?" he asked.

"A mile."

"How many times more is a mile than is the length of your rocket satellite?"

"My rocket is fifteen feet long. A mile is five thousand two hundred and eighty feet."

The mathematician depressed a few buttons.

"How far, or how many miles from the sun was your planet at that time?"

"Ninety-three million miles," was the reply.

"And your world's satellite—which you call moon from your planet—earth?"

"Two hundred and forty thousand miles."

"And your rocket?"

"I figured it to go about sixty-five thousand miles from the earth."

"It was only twenty thousand miles from the earth when we picked it up," said the mathematician, depressing a few more buttons. "The moon and sun are also much nearer your planet now."

Professor Jameson gave way to a mental ejaculation of amazement.

"Do you know how long you have cruised around the planet in your own satellite?" said the mathematician. "Since you began that journey, the planet which you call the earth has revolved around the sun over forty million times."

"Forty—million—years!" exclaimed Professor Jameson haltingly. "Humanity must then have all perished from the earth long ago! I'm the last man on earth!"

"It is a dead world now," interjected 25X-987.

"Of course," elucidated the mathematician, "those last few million years are much shorter than the ones in which you lived. The earth's orbit is of less diameter and its speed of revolution is greatly increased, due to its proximity to the cooling sun. I should say that your year was some four times as long as the time in which it now takes your old planet to circumnavigate the sun.

"How many days were there in your year?"

"Three hundred and sixty-five."

"The planet has now ceased rotating entirely."

"Seems queer that your rocket satellite should avoid the meteors so long," observed 459C-79, the mathematician.

"Automatic radium repulsion rays," explained the professor.

"The very rays which kept us from approaching your rocket," stated 25X-987, "until we neutralized them."

"You died and were shot out into space long before any life occurred on Zor," soliloquized one of the machine men. "Our people had not yet even been born when yours had probably disappeared entirely from the face of the earth."

"Hearken to 72N-4783," said 25X-987, "he is our philosopher, and he just loves to dwell on the past life of Zor when we were flesh and blood creatures with the threat of death hanging always over our heads. At that time, like the life you knew, we were born, we lived and died, all within a very short time, comparatively."

"Of course, time has come to mean nothing to us, especially when we are out in space," observed 72N-4783. "We never keep track of it on our expeditions, though back in Zor such accounts are accurately kept. By the way, do you know how long we stood here while you recounted to us the history of your planet? Our machine bodies never get tired, you know."

"Well," ruminated Professor Jameson, giving a generous allowance of time. "I should say about a half a day, although it seemed scarcely as long as that."

"We listened to you for four days," replied 72N-4783.

Professor Jameson was really aghast.

"Really, I hadn't meant to be such a bore," he apologized.

"That is nothing," replied the other. "Your story was interesting, and if it had been twice as long, it would not have mattered, nor would it have seemed any longer. Time is merely relative, and in space actual time does not exist at all, any more than your forty million years' cessation of life seemed more than a few moments to you. We saw that it was so when your first thought impressions reached us following your revival."

"Let us continue on to your planet earth," then said 25X-987. "Perhaps we shall find more startling disclosures there."

As the space ship of the Zoromes approached the sphere from which Professor Jameson had been hurled in his rocket forty million years before, the professor was wondering how the earth would appear, and what radical changes he would find. Already he knew that the geographical conditions of the various continents were changed. He had seen as much from the space ship.

A short time later the earth was reached. The space travelers from Zor, as well as Professor Jameson, emerged from the cosmic flyer to walk upon the surface of the planet. The earth had ceased rotating, leaving one-half its surface always toward the sun. This side of the earth was heated to a considerable degree, while its antipodes, turned always away from the solar luminary, was a cold, frigid, desolate waste. The space travelers from Zor did not dare to advance very far into either hemisphere, but landed on the narrow, thousand-mile strip of territory separating the earth's frozen half from its sun-baked antipodes.

As Professor Jameson emerged from the space ship with 25X-987, he stared in awe at the great transformation four hundred thousand centuries had wrought. The earth's surface, its sky and the sun were all so changed and unearthly appearing. Off to the east the blood red ball of the slowly cooling sun rested upon the horizon, lighting up the eternal day. The earth's rotation had ceased entirely, and it hung motionless in the sky as it revolved around its solar parent, its orbit slowly but surely cutting in toward the great body of the sun. The two inner planets, Mercury and Venus, were now very close to the blood red orb whose scintillating, dazzling brilliance had been lost in its cooling process. Soon, the two nearer planets would succumb to the great pull of the solar luminary and return to the flaming folds, from which they had been hurled out as gaseous bodies in the dim, age-old past, when their careers had just begun.

The atmosphere was nearly gone, so rarefied had it become, and through it Professor Jameson could view with amazing clarity without discomfort to his eyes the bloated body of the dying sun. It appeared, many times the size he had seen it at the time of his death, on account of its relative nearness. The earth had advanced a great deal closer to the great star around which it swung.

The sky towards the west was pitch black except for the iridescent twinkle of the fiery stars which studded that section of the heavens. As he watched, a faint glow suffused the western sky, gradually growing brighter, the full moon majestically lifted itself above the horizon, casting its pale, ethereal radiance upon the dying world beneath. It was increased to many times the size Professor Jameson had ever seen it during his natural lifetime. The earth's greater attraction was drawing upon the moon just as the sun was pulling the earth ever nearer itself.

This cheerless landscape confronting the professor represented the state of existence to which the earth had come. It was a magnificent spread of loneliness which bore no witness to the fact that it had seen the teeming of life in better ages long ago. The weird, yet beautiful scene, spread in a melancholy panorama before his eyes, drove his thoughts into gloomy abstraction with its dismal, depressing influence. Its funereal, oppressive aspect smote him suddenly with the chill of a terrible loneliness.

25X-987 aroused Professor Jameson from his lethargic reverie. "Let us walk around and see what we can find. I can understand how you feel in regard to the past. It is quite a shock—but it must happen to all worlds sooner or later—even to Zor. When that times comes, the Zoromes will find a new planet on which to live. If you travel with us, you will become accustomed to the sight of seeing dead, lifeless worlds as well as new and beautiful ones pulsating with life and energy. Of course, this world being your own, holds a peculiar sentimental value to you, but it is really one planet among billions."

Professor Jameson was silent.

"I wonder whether or not there are any ruins here to be found?" queried 25X-987.

"I don't believe so," replied the professor. "I remember hearing an eminent scientist of my day state that, given fifty thousand years, every structure and other creation of man would be obliterated entirely from off the earth's surface."

"And he was right," endorsed the machine man of Zor. "Time is a great effacer."

For a long time the machine men wandered over the dreary surface of the earth, and then 25X-987 suggested a change of territory to explore. In the space ship, they moved around the earth to the other side, still keeping to the belt of shadowland which completely encircled the globe like some gigantic ring. Where they now landed arose a series of cones with hollow peaks.

"Volcanoes!" exclaimed the professor.

"Extinct ones," added the machine man.

Leaving the space ship, the fifty or more machine men, including also Professor Jameson, were soon exploring the curiously shaped peaks. The professor, in his wanderings had strayed away from the rest, and now advanced into one of the cup-like depressions of the peak, out of sight of his companions, the Zoromes.

CHAPTER V

Eternity or Death

He was well in the center of the cavity when the soft ground beneath him gave way suddenly and he catapulted below into the darkness. Through the Stygian gloom he fell in what seemed to be an endless drop. He finally crashed upon something hard. The thin crust of the volcano's mouth had broken through, precipitating him into the deep, hollow interior.

It must have been a long ways to fall—or so it had seemed. Why was he not knocked senseless or killed? Then he felt himself over with three tentacles. His metal legs were four broken, twisted masses of metal, while the lower half of his cubic body was jammed out of shape and split. He could not move, and half of his six tentacles were paralyzed.

How would he ever get out of there? he wondered. The machine men of Zor might never find him. What would happen to him, then? He would remain in this deathless, monotonous state forever in the black hole of the volcano's interior unable to move. What a horrible thought! He could not starve to death; eating was unknown among the Zoromes, the machines requiring no food. He could not even commit suicide. The only way for him to die would be to smash the strong metal head, and in his present immovable condition, this was impossible.

It suddenly occurred to him to radiate thoughts for help. Would the Zoromes receive his messages? He wondered how far the telepathic messages would carry. He concentrated the powers of his mind upon the call for help, and repeatedly stated his position and plight. He then left his mind clear to receive the thought answers of the Zoromes. He received none.

Again he tried. Still he received no welcoming answer. Professor Jameson became dejected.

It was hopeless. The telepathic messages had not reached the machine men of Zor. They were too far away, just as one person may be out of earshot of another's voice. He was doomed to a terrible fate of existence! It were better that his rocket had never been found. He wished that the Zoromes had destroyed him instead of bringing him back to life—back to this!

His thoughts were suddenly broken in upon.

"We're coming!"

"Don't give up hope!"

If the professor's machine body had been equipped with a heart, it would have sung for joy at these welcome thought impressions. A short time later there appeared in the ragged break of the volcano's mouth, where he had fallen through, the metal head of one of the machine men.

"We shall have you out of there soon," he said.

The professor never knew how they managed it for he lost consciousness under some strange ray of light they projected down upon him in his prison. When he came to consciousness once more, it was to find himself inside the space ship.

"If you had fallen and had smashed your head, it would have been all over with you," were the first thought impulses which greeted him. "As it is, however, we can fix you up first rate."

"Why didn't you answer the first time I called to you?" asked the professor. "Didn't you hear me?"

"We heard you, and we answered, but you didn't hear us. You see, your brain is different than ours, and though you can send thought waves as far as we can you cannot receive them from such a great distance."

"I'm wrecked," said the professor, gazing at his twisted limbs, paralyzed tentacles and jammed body.

"We shall repair you," came the reply. "It is your good fortune that your head was not crushed."

"What are you going to do with me?" queried the professor. "Will you remove my brains to another machine?"

"No, it isn't necessary. We shall merely remove your head and place it upon another machine body."

The Zoromes immediately set to work upon the task, and soon had

Professor Jameson's metal head removed from the machine which he had wrecked in his fall down the crater. All during the painless operation, the professor kept up a series of thought exchanges in conversation with the Zoromes, and it seemed but a short time before his head surmounted a new machine and he was ready for further exploration. In the course of his operation, the space ship had moved to a new position, and now as they emerged 25X-987 kept company with Professor Jameson.

"I must keep an eye on you," he said. "You will be getting into more trouble before you get accustomed to the metal bodies."

But Professor Jameson was doing a great deal of thinking. Doubtlessly, these strange machine men who had picked up his rocket in the depths of space and had brought him back to life, were expecting him to travel with them and become adopted into the ranks of the Zoromes. Did he want to go with them? He couldn't decide. He had forgotten that the machine men could read his innermost thoughts.

"You wish to remain here alone upon the earth?" asked 25X-987. "It is your privilege if you really want it so."

"I don't know," replied Professor Jameson truthfully.

He gazed at the dust around his feet. It had probably been the composition of men, and had changed from time to time into various other atomic structures—of other queer forms of life which had succeeded mankind. It was the law of the atom which never died. And now he had within his power perpetual existence. He could be immortal if he wished! It would be an immortality of never-ending adventures in the vast, endless Universe among the galaxy of stars and planets.

A great loneliness seized him. Would he be happy among these machine men of another far-off world—among these Zoromes? They were kindly and solicitous of his welfare. What better fate could he expect? Still, a longing for his own kind arose in him—the call of humanity. It was irresistible. What could he do? Was it not in vain? Humanity had long since disappeared from the earth—millions of years ago. He wondered what lay beyond the pales of death—the real death, where the body decomposed and wasted away to return to the dust of the earth and assume new atomic structures.

He had begun to wonder whether or not he had been dead all these forty millions of years—suppose he had been merely in a state of suspended animation. He had remembered a scientist of his day, who had claimed that the body does not die at the point of official death. According to the claims of this man, the cells of the body did not die at the moment at which respiration, heart beats and the blood circulation ceased, but it existed in the semblance of life for several days afterward, especially in the cells of the bones, which died last of all.

Perhaps when he had been sent out into space in his rocket right after his death, the action of the cosmic void was to halt his slow death of the cells in his body, and hold him in suspended animation during the ensuing millions of years. Suppose he should really die—destroying his own brain? What lay beyond real death? Would it be a better plane of existence than the Zoromes could offer him? Would he rediscover humanity, or had they long since arisen to higher planes of existence or reincarnation? Did time exist beyond the mysterious portals of death? If not, then it was possible for him to join the souls of the human race. Had he really been dead all this time? If so, he knew what to expect in case he really destroyed his own brain. Oblivion!

Again the intense feeling of loneliness surged over him and held him within its melancholy grasp. Desperately, he decided to find the nearest cliff and jump from it—head-first! Humanity called; no man lived to companion him. His four metal limbs carried him swiftly to the summit of a nearby precipice. Why not gamble on the hereafter? 25X-987, understanding his trend of thought, did not attempt to restrain him. Instead, the machine man of Zor waited patiently.

As Professor Jameson stood there meditating upon the jump which would hurl him now into a new plane of existence—or into oblivion, the thought transference of 25X-987 reached him. It was laden with the wisdom born of many planets and thousands of centuries' experience.

"Why jump?" asked the machine man. "The dying world holds your imagination within a morbid clutch. It is all a matter of mental condition. Free your mind of this fascinating influence and come with us to visit other worlds, many of them are both beautiful and new. You will then feel a great difference.

"Will you come?"

The professor considered for a moment as he resisted the impulse to dive off the declivity to the enticing rocks far below. An inspiration seized him. Backing away from the edge of the cliff, he joined 25X-987 once more.

"I shall come," he stated.

He would become an immortal after all and join the Zoromes in their never-ending adventures from world to world. They hastened to the space ship to escape the depressing, dreary influence of the dying world, which had nearly driven Professor Jameson to take the fatal leap to oblivion.

■ ■ ■ ■ ■

"The Jameson Satellite" is a notable example of the faults of pre-Campbell science fiction. The scientific background is not blended with the story but is presented in indigestible blocks that halt the action. The science, moreover, is inaccurate even by the standards of its own time.

In 1931, for instance, radium still had glamour as the richest practical source of radioactivity, so it is natural to have it used vaguely as propulsive power for a satellite (launched in 1958, by the way, almost on the nose). There was no indication, however, in 1931 (or since) that radium possesses "repulsion rays."

Then, too, Jones, at this early stage in his career (he had been publishing for only a year and a half, and this was his fourth science fiction story) was clearly in imperfect command of the English language. He used the words "soliloquized upon" when he should rather have used "considered," "inspiration" rather than the more accurate "impulse," and so on. On the whole, "The Jameson Satellite" is probably the least skillfully written story in this anthology.

None of the flaws in language and construction were obvious to my eleven-and-a-half-year self, however. What I responded to was the tantalizing glimpse of possible immortality and the vision of the world's sad death, to say nothing of the contracting spirals of the planetary orbits forty million years hence (not long enough, by the way; forty billion would have been better if that were the way the Solar System were to end, which it isn't).

More important still were Jones's Zoromes, who were robots really. Their organic brains were just a detail. Jones treated them as mechanical men, making them objective without being unfeeling, benevolent without being busybodies. They made no effort to use force to keep Professor Jameson from committing suicide if he really wanted to, but they did use dignified persuasion.

One of the marks of reader enthusiasm for a story is the demand for more, and an author often wrote a sequel to a popular story. The readers (not just myself) were so taken by "The Jameson Satellite" that Jones wrote about a dozen "Professor Jameson stories" over the next seven years, carrying his Zoromes to a new and startling world in each. Although the Zoromes remained without individual personality, I could easily recite the number-letter combinations of those who appeared most often.

It is from the Zoromes, beginning with their first appearance in "The Jameson Satellite," that I got my own feeling for benevolent robots who could serve man with decency, as these had served Professor Jameson. It was the Zoromes, then, who were the spiritual ancestors of my own "positronic robots," all of them, from Robbie to R. Daneel.

Something else that was very prevalent in the science fiction of the 1930s was the adventure story fitted out with just enough scientific trappings to enable it to pass muster. And in the science fiction magazines of the early part of the decade, no one was better at it than Captain S. P. Meek.

He published some thirty stories in the magazines between 1930 and 1932—his heyday—and of them all, the best was *The Drums of Tapajos*, a lost-civilization-in-the-Amazon story I have already mentioned twice.

Equally typical, and short enough to include here, are his "Submicroscopic" and its sequel, "Awlo of Ulm," which ran in successive issues of *Amazing Stories* (August and September 1931), and which won my heart with their boy-and-girl romance. It was at a level that just suited my time in life.

SUBMICROSCOPIC

by Capt. S. P. Meek

AFTER many weary months of toil my task has been completed. As the sun sank to rest today, I soldered up the last connection on my Electronic Vibration Adjuster and in the fading twilight I tested it. It functions perfectly and as soon as the sun rises tomorrow I will leave this plane, I hope forever. I had originally intended to disappear without trace, as I did once before, but as I sit here waiting for the dawn, such a course seems hardly fair. This plane has treated me pretty well on the whole and I really ought to leave behind me some record of my discoveries and of my adventures, possibly the strangest adventures through which a man of this plane has ever passed. Besides, it will help to pass the time which must elapse before I can start on my journey.

My name is Courtney Edwards. I was born thirty-four years ago in the city of Honolulu, the only child of the richest sugar planter in the Islands. When I arrived at high school age I was sent to the mainland to be educated and here I have stayed. The death of my parents left me wealthy and rather disinclined to return to the home of my youth.

I did my bit in the Air Corps during the war and when it was over I shed my olive drab and went back to the University of Minneconsin to finish my education. My interest in science started when I attended a lecture on the composition of matter. It was a popular lecture intended for non-science students, and so it wasn't over my head. Dr. Harvey, one of our most popular professors, was the speaker and to this day I can visualize him standing there and can even recall some of his words.

"To give you some idea of the size of an atom," he said, "I will take for an, example a cubic millimeter of hydrogen gas at a temperature of 0 degrees Centigrade and at sea-level pressure. It contains roughly ninety

Copyright 1931 by Radio-Science Publications, Inc.

quadrillions of atoms, an almost inconceivable number. Consider this enormous number of particles packed into a cube with an edge less than one-twentieth of an inch long; yet so small are the individual atoms compared with the space between them that the solar system is crowded in comparison.

"In order to get at the ultimate composition of matter, however, we are forced to consider even smaller units. An atom is not a solid particle of matter, but instead consists of smaller particles called protons and electrons. The protons are particles of positive electricity which exist at the center or the nucleus of the atoms and the electrons are particles of negative electricity some of which revolve about the central portion and in most elements some are in the nucleus. Each of these particles is as small compared to the space between them as is the case with the atoms in the molecule."

I left the lecture hall with my head in a whirl. My imagination had been captured by the idea of counting and measuring such infinitesimal particles and I went to Dr. Harvey's office the next day and sought an interview.

"I wish to ask some questions relative to your talk last night, Doctor," I said when I faced him.

His kindly grey eyes twinkled and he invited me to be seated.

"As I understood you, Doctor," I began, "the space between the atoms and between the electrons and protons in each atom is so vast compared to their bulk that if you were to jam the protons and electrons of a cubic mile of gas together until they touched, you couldn't see the result with a microscope."

"Your idea is crudely expressed, but in the main accurate," he answered.

"Then what in the name of common sense holds them apart?" I demanded.

"Each of the atoms," he replied, "is in a state of violent motion, rushing through space with a high velocity and continually colliding with other atoms and rebounding until it strikes another atom and rebounds again. The electrons are also in a state of violent motion, revolving around the protons and this combination of centrifugal force and electrical attraction holds the atom in a state of dynamic equilibrium."

"One more question, Doctor, and I'll quit. Are these things you have told me cold sober fact susceptible of proof, or are they merely the results of an overactive imagination?"

He smiled and then leaned over his desk and answered gravely.

"Some of them are solid facts which I can prove to you in the laboratory," he said. "For instance, you, yourself, with proper training could count the number of atoms in a given volume. Other things I have said are merely theories or shrewd guesses which best explain the facts which we know. There is in physical chemistry a tremendous field of work open for men who have the ability and the patience to investigate. No one knows what the future may bring forth."

The Doctor's evident enthusiasm communicated itself to me.

"I'll be one of the ones to do this work if you'll have me as a student!" I exclaimed.

"I'll be very glad to have you, Edwards," he replied. "I believe you have the ability and the will. Time alone will tell whether you have the patience."

I resigned·from my course the next day and enrolled as a special student under Dr. Harvey. After a period of intensive study of methods, I was ready to plunge into the unknown. The work of Bohr and Langmuir especially attracted me, and I bent my energies to investigating the supposed motion of the electrons about the nuclear protons. This line of investigation led me to the suspicion that the motion was not circular and steady, but was periodic and simple harmonic except as the harmonic periods were interfered with by the frequent collisions.

I devised an experiment which proved this to my satisfaction and took my results to Dr. Harvey for checking. He took my data home with him that night intending to read it in bed as was his usual custom, but from that bed he never rose. Death robbed me of my preceptor and Dr. Julius became the head of the Chemistry Department. I took my results to him only to meet with scorn and laughter. Dr. Julius was an able analyst, but he lacked vision and could never see the woods for the trees. The result of my interview with him was that I promptly left Minneconsin, and resolved to carry on my work at another school.

The problem on which I wished to work was the reduction of the period of vibration of the atoms and of their constituent parts. If my theory of their motion were correct, it should be possible to damp their vibrations and thus collapse matter together and make it occupy a smaller volume in space. I soon found that men like Dr. Harvey were scarce. Not a man at the head of a university department could I find who had the vision to see the possibilities of my work and in a rage I determined to conduct my experiments alone and hidden from the world until I had proved the truth of my theories.

I was still flying for amusement and one day while flying from Salt Lake City to San Francisco, I passed over a verdant fertile valley hidden in the almost inaccessible crags of the Timpahute range in southern Nevada. I abandoned my trip temporarily and landed at Beatty to make inquiries. Not a person could I find who had ever heard of my hidden valley. Even the old desert rats professed ignorance of its location and laughed at me when I told them that I had seen flowing water and deciduous trees in the barren stretches of the Timpahutes.

I had taken the bearings of my valley and I flew on to San Francisco and made my arrangements. I flew back to Beatty and picked up a pack outfit and landed at the foot of the crags sheltering the valley and started on foot to seek an entrance. It took me a month of careful searching to find it, but find it I did. With a little blasting, the way could be made practicable for pack burros. The stuff I had ordered at San Francisco had been delivered to Beatty and I hired packers to take it out to the Timpahutes for me. I established a dump about a mile from my valley entrance and had the stuff unloaded there. When the packers had left I took my own burros and packed it in to the valley. I didn't care to have anyone find out where I was locating and so far as I know no one ever did.

When I had everything packed in, I started to work.

A few days enabled me to rig an undershot waterwheel in the stream and get enough power to turn an electric generator and thereafter I had the strength of twenty men at my call. I built a small wooden building for a laboratory with a room in it for my cooking and sleeping.

I was fortunate enough not to meet with a single major setback in my work, and in about fourteen months I had my first piece of apparatus completed. I don't intend to tell how I did it, for I do not believe that the world is ready for it yet, but I will give some idea of how it looked and how it was operated. The adjuster has a circular base of silvery metal (it is a palladium alloy) from which rise six supports which hold up the top. The top, which is made of the same alloy as the base, is parabolic in shape and concave downward. In the parabola is set an induction coil with a sparkgap surmounting it, so set that the gap is at the focus of the reflector, which is what the top really is. The coil and gap are connected with other coils and condensers which are actuated by large storage batteries set around the edge of the base. To each of the six uprights is fastened a small parabolic reflector with a small coil and gap at the focus. These small reflectors are so arranged that they bathe the top with the generated ray while the large gap in the top bathes the rest of the apparatus.

When the gaps and coils are actuated by the current, they throw out a ray of such a wavelength that it has the same period as the electronic and atomic vibrations but is half a wavelength out of phase. The ray is effective only when it can flow freely, and the base and top serve not only as conductors, but also as insulators, for they absorb and transform the vibrations falling on them so that nothing outside of the apparatus itself and anything lying between the base and the top is affected.

When I had it completed, I naturally tested it. The whole thing was controlled by a master switch and I reached in with a small steel rod and closed the switch. Immediately the whole apparatus began to shrink. I gave a loud cheer and patted myself on the back. I got down on my knees and watched it as it rapidly diminished in size until I suddenly realized that it would soon get too small to see unless I opened my switch. I tried to reach the switch with my rod but I had waited too long. The rod would not go through the interval between the side columns. I had the mortification of seeing a year's work grow smaller and smaller until it finally vanished.

The loss of my adjuster was a blow, but at least I had proved my theory and as soon as I had rested for a few days I started in to build a duplicate. The way had already been blazed and it took me less than a year to complete my second piece of apparatus. When I tested this one I stopped the shrinking process when the adjuster was about half its original size and reversed the polarity of my coils. To my delight the adjuster began to expand until it had resumed its original proportions. Then I shut it off and began to experiment to find out its limitations.

When I had determined to my satisfaction that inanimate objects placed on the base would be expanded or contracted, I tried it on living organisms. A jack rabbit was my first subject and I found that I could increase this rabbit to the size of a Shetland pony or reduce it to the size of a mouse without visible ill effects. When I had completed this experiment, I tried the adjuster on myself.

My first experiment was to increase my size. I stepped on the base plate and turned on the current, but I could feel no effects. I looked at the landscape and found to my amazement that something had gone wrong. I was remaining the same size but the house and the surrounding country had come under the influence of my device and was shrinking rapidly. In alarm I shut off my current and got out. The house had shrunk to one-half its normal size and I could not get in the door, even on hands and knees. An idea struck me and I reached in and hauled out a pair of scales and weighed myself. *I weighed a trifle over twelve hundred pounds.* I suddenly realized that I had succeeded beyond my wildest dreams and I reentered the adjuster and shrunk myself down to four inches tall, again with no ill effects and merely the impression that the house and landscape were growing. I returned myself to my normal size and while I was weak from excitement, otherwise I felt perfectly normal.

My first thought was to return and confound the men who had scoffed at me but the more I considered the matter, the more I realized the importance of my invention and the need of caution in introducing it. I felt that I needed a rest anyway, so I remained in my valley to perfect my plans before announcing my discovery.

Time soon lagged on my hands. I have always been fond of big game hunting and I had an excellent rifle and plenty of ammunition, but game does not abound in the Timpahutes. There were quite a few ants in the valley and it struck me that, were I to reduce myself and my rifle to the proper dimensions, I would have some good sport. The novelty of the idea fascinated me as much as the thought of the hunting and I promptly belted on a pistol and a full belt of ammunition and entered the adjuster.

I closed the switch and the house and landscape began to grow to Brobdingnagian proportions, but I kept my power on until the grains of sand began to look like huge boulders and then I tried to open the switch. *It was stuck.* Thoroughly alarmed, I tried to wrench it open and as a result broke the handle—the device kept on functioning and I grew smaller and smaller. The grains of sand grew to be huge mountains and presently I felt myself falling. I realized that my adjuster had been balanced on a grain of sand and that it had slipped and was falling into the chasm between two grains. Soon it became wedged in a gloomy chasm, but it was still functioning and presently I was falling again.

A glance at the dial of my relative size indicator showed me that the needle had almost reached the point which I had indicated as infinity. Desperately I battered at the switch with my rifle butt, but it was solidly made. At last I broke it loose and the whine of my coil became audible and ran down the scale until it was silent. I had stopped shrinking but I was already far smaller than any microscope could detect and an examination of the switch soon convinced me that it was completely wrecked and that it would take me hours to repair it.

When I had finished my examination, I looked around for the first time. I could hardly believe my eyes. My adjuster was standing in a beautiful sunlit glade, which was carpeted with grass and dotted with varicolored flowers. Now I will have to explain one thing. As I said, I felt no change when my size was increased and reduced; it only seemed that the familiar landscape was undergoing a change. As a result, I could never realize while I was in Ulm, that everything was really submicroscopic, but persisted in referring everything to my normal six feet of height. In actual fact, the glade in which the adjuster stood was only a minute fraction of an inch across, but to me it looked like about half a mile and it took me ten minutes to walk it. Even now I have no idea of how small I actually was, so I will not try to describe the *absolute* size of everything, but will speak of things as they appeared to me; in other words, their *relative* size to me.

I looked over that landscape and rubbed my eyes, trying to convince myself that I was dreaming, but the scene didn't change and I realized that I had stumbled on something heretofore unsuspected—namely that our world is a very complex affair and supports many kinds of life unknown to us. Everything within the range of my vision looked normal, grass, trees and even mosquitos were buzzing around and one lit on my wrist and bit me. Imagine, if you can, what the actual measurements of that mosquito must have been!

Convinced that I was not dreaming, I stepped out of the adjuster to the grass. Before I repaired that switch I meant to have a look around and see what this miniature world was like. I had gone only a few steps from the adjuster when a lordly buck rose from the grass and bounded away. Instinctively I threw up my rifle and fired and the buck went down kicking. Assured that my weapons were functioning properly, I set off at a brisk pace across the glade. I took careful bearings with my pocket compass and expected to have no trouble in finding my way back. During the ten minutes it took me to cross the glade, I had several more chances to shoot at deer, but I passed them up. I didn't wish to waste ammunition or to call attention to myself until I knew what was ahead of me.

It was hot and sultry in the glade and I glanced up at the sun, expecting it to appear enormous, but it appeared no larger than usual, a matter which I could not explain at the time and cannot even yet. Before I reached the woods which fringed the glade I noticed that the horizon was walled in on all sides with enormous mountains, higher than any I had ever seen and it gave me a shock to realize that these mighty and imposing masses of rock were in reality only grains of sand, or perhaps even smaller; they might be particles of the impalpable dust which lies between the sand grains.

It took me perhaps ten minutes to reach the edge of the jungle, for such it proved to be. Most of the trees were of species unknown to me, although I recognized several trees of peculiarly tropical habit, among them the baobab or one of its relatives and the *lignum vitae.* The scene reminded

me more of the Brazilian jungles than anything else. The ground underfoot was deep with rotting vegetation and the creepers made the going
hard. I plunged into the tangle and in ten minutes I was as thoroughly
lost as I have even been in my life. The gloom under the trees prevented
me from using the sun as a guide and I had not read my compass when I
entered the tangle.

I set a compass course and floundered forward as best I could but half
an hour of steady going convinced me that I had taken the wrong direction.
The jungle was too dense to back trail, so I laid a new course by compass
and plunged ahead. I kept on for perhaps ten minutes on my new course
when I heard a sound that brought me up standing, hardly able to believe
my ears. From ahead of me came a shout, a shout given in a human voice.
I strained my ears and soon I heard it again from the same direction and
somewhat closer. Some one was coming toward me and I looked for a
hiding place. A tangle of baobab roots concealed me pretty well and I
crouched, my rifle ready, waiting for what might appear.

In a few moments I heard a sound of running footsteps and I peered
out from my cover. Imagine my surprise when a girl, a white girl, came
into view, running at top speed. Not fifty yards behind her came a group
of men, or beasts, for I couldn't tell at first glance which they were. They
were as black as pitch, with thick heavy lips, flat noses and almost no
foreheads. They were or rather seemed to be about seven feet tall on the
average, with enormously powerful chests and arms that hung below their
knees. At times they dropped forward so that their knuckles rested on the
ground and came ahead on all fours at a more rapid rate than their
relatively short bandy legs could carry them when they were in an upright position. They were covered on the head, chest and arms with
coarse black hair, although their legs, abdomens and backs were almost
free from it. Their mouths were wide with the lower jaw protruding
somewhat with yellow fangs showing between their lips, giving them a
horribly bestial expression. They had two eyes, but they were not placed
as is usual with animals of the monkey or human species. One eye was
set in the middle of the forehead and the other in the back of the head.
They were naked except for a G string and a belt from which hung a
short heavy sword, and in their hands they carried spears about ten feet
long. The average weight of a full grown male in our world would have
been about four hundred pounds. Of course I didn't see all of this at first
glance, but later I saw enough of the Mena, as they were called, to get
pretty familiar with their appearance.

A glance was enough to show me that the girl was tired and that these brutes were gaining on her. She was human and the sight of these savages made my next action purely instinctive. With a shout I stepped from my hiding place and threw my rifle to my shoulder. The girl saw me and altered her direction to come toward me. The blacks saw me, too, and they turned in my direction, brandishing their spears.

I am a pretty good shot and they were close and an easy target. I had four shells in my rifle and four of the blacks went down as fast as I could work my bolt. The rest paused for a moment and gave me time to ram a fresh clip of cartridges into my rifle. As I reloaded, I picked out one of them who seemed to be a leader and I dropped him on the next shot. This made them pause again but another black devil sprang forward to take the lead and I presented him with a bit of lead in the face. He went down like a thunderbolt and as none of the rest seemed to aspire to leadership, I distributed the other three bullets where I thought they would do the most good. As I lowered my rifle to reload, another one of the blacks jumped forward and charged me, and the rest followed. I had no time to load, so I jerked out my Colt .45 and when he was about twenty-five yards away I let him have a pill in the chest and then started a little miscellaneous slaughter. By the time the Colt was empty, there were fourteen of the blacks down and the rest were retreating at full speed. I first reloaded my rifle and slipped a clip into my pistol and then looked for the girl.

I didn't see her for a moment and then I spied a lock of golden hair in the tangle at my feet. She had burrowed into the vegetation and had got pretty well covered in the few moments I was shooting. I reached down and touched her, but as soon as she found that her hiding place was discovered, she bounded up and took to her heels like a scared rabbit. I called to her and she threw a glance back over her shoulder and when she saw that I was alone she checked her speed and stood her ground. She hesitated for a moment and then came back and dropped to her knees at my feet. I lifted her up and patted her on the shoulder.

"'There, little girl, don't cry,'" I quoted inanely, partly because I didn't know what else to say and partly because I was completely bowled over by her appearance. She was absolutely the most beautiful girl I have ever seen in my life—tall and lithe, all curves and grace, with eyes as blue as the sea around Oahu and hair where sunbeams had been imprisoned and where they struggled continuously for liberty, throwing their glints out through the meshes of their prison. Bound around her head was a golden filet with a huge square cut stone of beautiful sparkle and radiance set in it. Around her waist and confining her garments of flowing green gauze was another golden band with a gold-encrusted, gem-set pouch depending from it. On the buckle of her girdle was another of the square cut gems such as adorned her head band.

I have always been pretty much at ease in the presence of girls, principally because I never cared much for them, but to this dirty little savage, as beautiful as dawn, I didn't know what to say. I could just gulp and stammer.

"Er, do you think these rapscallions will come back for more?" I blurted out at last.

She cast a sideways glance at me that made my head whirl, and my heart do all sorts of funny flip-flops, and then she spoke. Her speech was beautifully liquid and hauntingly familiar. I couldn't understand her, but I was sure that I had heard that language before. Presently I caught a word and like a flash I knew. She was speaking some dialect of Hawaiian. Desperately I strove to recall the speech of Leilani, my old nurse, but the only phrase I could remember was *"E nac iki ne puu wai."* It didn't seem quite appropriate to say "Be true to me, fair one" to a girl I had just met, but it was for the moment the only phrase I could remember so I blurted it out.

She understood it all right and she flew into a royal rage. She shot out a stream of fluent speech so fast that I couldn't understand a word of it. I thought rapidly and then brought fourth another gem of speech, *"Hawaiian pau."* I had to repeat it twice before she understood and then she didn't get the word Hawaiian, but she understood *pau,* finished, all right and she presently realized that my first speech was the only bit of her language which I knew. When she understood my predicament, she forgot her anger and laughed. I was glad to see her cheerful again, but I was still worried about whether those blacks would return.

For lack of language I was forced to fall back on pantomime in order to make myself understood. She readily understood me and looked worried for a moment until her eye fell on my rifle. She touched it questioningly and then spurned the body of the nearest black with her foot and laughed.

Evidently she thought that my weapon made me invincible, but I knew better. I had only two more clips of pistol cartridges and eighty-five rounds for my rifle, not enough to repel a real attack. I tapped my rifle, shook my head sadly and said *"pau."*

The worried look again came into her face and she started talking very slowly and distinctly, repeating the word *"Ulm"* several times. Gradually my Hawaiian was coming back and while her speech was not the language I had learned in my youth, for she made use of the consonants "s" and "t," both of which are unknown in Hawaiian, presently I made out her meaning. She was asking me to go with her to Ulm. I had no idea of where Ulm was but I had given up hopes of finding my adjuster and besides, since I had met this girl, I wasn't so very anxious to find it at once. It seemed to me that it might be a good idea to go to Ulm for a while, and then make a fresh start for the glade with a competent guide. I therefore gave her to understand that her program suited me. She nodded brightly and stepped in front of me and set off toward the northeast.

For perhaps three hours we made our way through the jungle, keeping a pretty straight line as I could tell by my compass. I found later that the people of Ulm have an uncanny sense of direction and can find their way from place to place in their miniature world without the aid of any other guide. The girl kept up a steady talk in her language and as I recalled more of my early Hawaiian, I found that I could understand the sense of most of what she said if she talked very slowly and I was even able to answer her after a fashion.

"What is your name?" I asked her.

"Awlo Sibi Tam," she replied, raising her head proudly as she did so.

"My name is Courtney," I told her.

She tried to repeat it, but she had a little trouble with the "r" sound which was evidently strange to her. She repeated it several times as we went along and at last managed to get a very fair rendition. Anyhow, I thought that I had never heard it pronounced so beautifully before.

Suddenly Awlo paused in her talk and listened intently. She turned a terror-stricken face toward me and said, "They are coming."

"Who?" I asked.

"The Mena," she replied.

I listened but I could hear nothing.

"Are there many of them?" I asked.

"Many," she replied, "hundred, I believe. They are following our trail. Can't you hear them?"

I laid my ear close to the ground and could detect a faint murmur but I would never have recognized what it was.

"What shall we do?" I asked. "This," I held up my rifle, "will kill about a hundred but no more."

"Run," she said, "run as fast as we can. It will be of little use, because the Mena can catch us. You are slow and I am tired, but if we are lucky, we may win to the plains of Ulm and there we are safe."

Her advice sounded good and I started after her as swiftly as I could.

I am a fair average runner, but I could not keep up with Awlo, who fled over the ground like an antelope. I was handicapped by the weight of my rifle but I hung to it like grim death. It was not long before I could plainly hear the shouts of the pursuing Mena.

"Have we far to go?" I gasped.

"No," she replied over her shoulder. "Hurry!"

I panted along in her wake. The jungle thinned before us and we debouched onto a huge open plain. Awlo stopped and uttered a cry of dismay.

."What is it?" I demanded.

She did not answer but pointed ahead. Our way was barred by a wide, gently flowing river. Over it had been thrown a bridge but a glance showed me that the center span had been removed and a gap twenty feet wide yawned in the middle of the structure.

"Can you swim?" I asked.

She looked at me interrogatively. Evidently the word was a new one.

"Swim, run through the water," I explained.

An expression of absolute terror passed over her face.

"It is *tabu*," she replied. "It is death to enter."

"It is death to stay on this side," I told her.

"It is better to die at the hands of the Mena than at the hands of the Gods," she answered.

She meant it too. She would rather face certain death at the hands of those hideous savages than to enter the stream. There was only one thing to do and that was to look for a place where I could sell my life dearly. With this in mind, I started along the river bank looking for a depression which would shelter us from the spears of the Mena. We made our way through a clump of trees in front of us and it was my turn to cry out, only the cry was one of joy and not of apprehension. There, between the trees and the river bank, stood a familiar looking object—an Electronic Vibration Adjuster.

"We are saved, Awlo," I cried joyously as I raced for the machine. A glance showed me that it was my first model which I had sent, as I thought, to infinite smallness nearly a year before. I was puzzled for a moment at the fact that it had not shrunk to nothing, but I had no time for philosophical reasoning. The shouts of the Mena were already perilously close.

"Run off a few yards, Awlo," I commanded, "and don't be frightened. I can save you easily."

She obeyed me and I entered the adjuster. A momentary fear came over me that the batteries might be exhausted but I seized the switch and threw it on in the direction of increasing size. The landscape began to diminish its size, although as before, I could feel nothing. I kept my eye on the river until it had shrunk to a point where I knew that I could easily leap it and then I opened my switch and stepped out.

For a moment I could not see Awlo, but I detected her lying face downward on the ground. I bent over her and then I saw something else. The Mena, hundreds of them, had emerged from the jungle and were coming along our trail. I hesitated no longer. As gently as I could, I picked up Awlo and leaped over the river with her. I waited to see whether the Mena were going to make any attempt to follow, but they had evidently caught a glimpse of my gargantuan proportions and they were in full retreat. I found out later that the river was as much taboo to them as it was to Awlo and they would under no circumstances have crossed the stream except by means of a bridge or in boats.

I raised Awlo to the level of my eyes to talk to her but she had fainted. I leaped back to the other side of the river, reentered my adjuster and closed the reducing switch. Since I had the machine under control, I determined not to stop it until I found what had made it cease functioning when it did. My size rapidly grew smaller until I was correctly scaled to my surroundings and then the machine abruptly ceased working. I could not make it reduce either itself or me any further. The only explanation which has ever occurred to me is that the land of Ulm must be at the limit of smallness, that is, the period of vibration of the atoms and their component parts must be at the lower limit of motion and any further reduction would result in contact and consequent nothingness.

My intention had been to swim the river while Awlo was unconscious but it occurred to me that the adjuster might be useful on the other side of the river so I again increased my size until I could step over it. Knowing that the machine would only get so small, I reached in with a piece of wood and closed the reducing switch and watched it grow to toy size. With it in my hand, I again leaped the river and used my pocket knife blade to close the increasing switch. When it had grown to the right size, I stopped it, reentered it and soon had both the adjuster and myself down to the minimum to which it would go.

Awlo was still unconscious and I bent over her and chafed her hands. She soon recovered and sat up. Her gaze wandered and it fell on the adjuster, she shuddered and turned to me with fear in her eyes.

"What happened, Courtney Siba?" she asked with a quaver in her voice.

"I thought that you had changed into a *kahuma*, a wizard of the old days. Was I dreaming?"

I thought rapidly. Evidently a *kahuma* was something to be revered but also something not quite human. The advantage and disadvantages of being one flashed before me but a glance at Awlo's scared face decided me.

"I am no *kahuma*, Awlo," I replied. "What I did, I did with the aid of that. It made me appear to the Mena to be larger than I am and they ran. While they were gone, I carried you and the machine over the river. We are perfectly safe now and unless the Mena find some way of crossing, they won't bother us again."

Awlo seemed satisfied with my explanation. I suggested that she rest for a while to recover from her scare but she laughed at the idea.

"Ulm is near at hand," she told me, "and we must hurry on. I would not that my father be unduly worried by my absence."

"That reminds me of something I have been meaning to ask you, Awlo," I said as we resumed our onward way. "How did you happen to be in the jungle with the Mena after you when I found you."

"I was visiting my uncle, Hama, at his city of Ame," she replied. "My visit was at an end and I started homeward yesterday. It has been three years since the Mena have ventured to attack us and the guard was small, only about three hundred soldiers. We were about half way between the two cities and were going peaceably through the jungle when, without warning, the Mena attacked. The soldiers fought desperately but the Mena were too many and too powerful for them and they were all killed. I and two of my maidens were captured. The Mena took us to one of their cities in the jungle and prepared for a feast."

"For a feast?" I inquired.

"We are food for the Mena," she replied simply.

I shuddered at the thought and gritted my teeth as I thought of those flying monsters who were at my mercy a few minutes before. Had I known what brutes they were, I could have taken glorious vengeance on them.

"Last night," went on Awlo, "they took first one and then the other of my maidens out from the cave where we were confined, and killed them and dragged them away to the pot. My turn was next and two of them seized me and dragged me out. They released me and one of them raised a spear to end my life. I dropped to the ground and the spear passed over my head and then I fled. I tried to run toward Ulm, but they suspected the course I would pursue and a party went to head me off while others

followed my trail. As long as it was dark I was able to baffle them and
go faster than they could trail me, but with the coming of light they found
my trail and soon I heard them after me. I ran as fast as I could, but they
gained rapidly and I thought that I was lost when I heard your shout.
Awlo Sibu Tam will never forget how you saved her and neither will
Ulm. My father, Kalu, will honor you highly, Courtney Siba."

"If these Mena are such brutes, why don't your soldiers wage war on
them until there are none left?" I asked.

"They have waged war for ages," she replied, "but the Mena are too
many and we cannot hunt them all down. In ages past, there were no
Mena and then Ulm and Ame fought together. Sometimes one would be
victorious and sometimes the other, but always they ceased warring before either was destroyed. Then came the Mena through the passes from
the wilderness to the north. They came in thousands and they attacked
Ame. The men of Ulm forgot their hatred of their old rival and our armies
marched to the assistance of the threatened city. For a time our armies
drove the invaders back but more and more came from the north and
carried the battle to the gates of Ame itself. There our armies stopped
them for they could not climb the walls nor could they break in.

"When they saw that they could not win the city, they attacked Ulm.
Our army hurried back to defend the city and the men of Ame came
with them, leaving only enough to man the walls. Again the Mena fought
their way to the city walls and again they were stopped. When they found
they could not take either city, they drew back into the jungle and established cities of huts. Such is the condition today. The Mena fight among
themselves and when they are weakened in numbers, the armies of Ulm
and Ame march out to attack them. They have always defeated them and
tried to hunt them down and sometimes for a generation the Mena are
not seen, but eventually they return stronger than ever and attack one of
the cities. It has been many years now since war was waged on them and
it may be that they are planning to attack again."

"Do Ulm and Ame ever fight now?" I asked.

"No, there is peace between them. Brothers of one blood sit on the
two thrones and the old enmity is forgotten. But see, there lies Ulm!"

We had topped a little rise and had come to the cultivated fields. Before
us lay row after row of cultivated plots, most of them planted with *keill*
bushes, the nut of which is the staple food of the poorer classes of Ulm.
Two miles or so across the plain rose a massive walled city. Dotted about
on the plain were small stone structures, which reminded me of the old

blockhouses which used to be erected on our own plains to guard against Indian raids. That, in fact, was the exact function of these structures.

As we approached the nearest of them a figure appeared on the wall and scrutinized us closely. He called out a musical greeting and Awlo raised her face.

"Awlo Sibi Tam commands your presence," she cried imperiously.

The sentry rubbed his eyes and looked and then came down from that wall in a hurry. The massive gates swung open and an officer appeared and prostrated himself and kissed the ground before Awlo.

"Rise!" she commanded.

He rose and half drew his sword from its sheath and presented the hilt to Awlo. She touched it and he returned it to its scabbard with a sharp motion and stood upright.

"I would go to Ulm," she said. "Send couriers to warn my father of my approach and bid my guard come hither to escort me."

He bowed deeply and Awlo took me by the hand and led me into the building. It was a typical guardroom such as are found in all nations and at all times. We seated ourselves and I heard the sound of hoof-beats rapidly dying away in the direction of the city.

"Who are you, Awlo?" I asked. "Are you a Chief's daughter or what?"

"I am Sibi Tam," she replied.

"I don't know that rank," I answered. "How important is it?"

She looked at me in surprise and then laughed.

"You will find out in time, Courtney Siba," she said with a laugh.

I tried to press the question but she refused to answer and turned the talk to other matters. Half an hour passed and then I was aware of a confused murmur approaching from the city. Awlo rose.

"It is doubtless our escort," she said. "Let us greet them."

I followed her out into the courtyard and up on the thick wall which surrounded the building. Coming down the road was the most gorgeous cavalcade I had ever seen. First came a band of cavalry mounted on superb horses and carrying long lances. They wore golden helmets with nodding crimson horsehair plumes rising from them, a cuirass of gold and golden shin guards. Their thighs were bare. Besides the armor they wore a short crimson garment like a skirt, which fell half way to the knee, and a flowing crimson cape trimmed with brown fur. Heavy swords on the left side of their belts and a dagger on the right, together with their twelve-foot lances made up their offensive weapons.

Following the cavalry came a number of gorgeously decorated chariots, occupied by men gorgeously dressed in every imaginable hue. Another troop of cavalry, similar to the first except that their plumes and clothing were blue, brought up the rear.

As the leading troop came opposite the gate, Awlo stepped to the edge of the wall. Her appearance was greeted by a roar of applause and salutation and the red cavalry reined in their horses and pointed their lances toward her, butt foremost. She answered the salute with a wave of her hand and the troop charged forward at a word of command past the tower and then whirled to form a line facing her. The chariots came up and an elderly man dismounted from the first one and passed in through the gate. He came up the steps to the wall and dropped on one knee before Awlo, half drawing his sword and thrusting the hilt toward her as he did so.

She touched the sword and he returned it and rose to his feet.

"Greeting, Moka," she said. "Come with me for I desire a word with you."

Submissively he followed her a short distance along the wall and I could see that she was speaking rapidly. I could tell from the direction of Moka's glances that I was the topic of conversation, and his actions when Awlo had finished amply proved it. Moka came forward and drew his sword and cast it at my feet. I drew my pistol and placed it beside his weapon. Moka laid his left hand against my breast and I did the same.

"My brother and my lord," he said as he rose.

Awlo interrupted before I could say anything.

"I would go to Ulm," she said.

Moka bowed deeply and we each picked up our weapons. I followed Awlo toward the chariots. The largest and most ornate was empty and into it she sprang lightly, motioning to me to go with Moka in his chariot. I entered it and the whole cortège turned about and proceeded toward the city.

We drove in through a huge gate which was opened before us and down a wide thoroughfare which led directly into the center of the city. This avenue ended in a park in the center of which stood the largest and most beautiful building in the city. We left our chariots and made our way on foot across the park and entered the palace between rows of guards who, as Awlo passed, presented their spears, butt foremost.

At the end of the hall, Awlo paused.

"Courtney Siba," she said, "you are doubtless weary as I am. Go then with Moka, who will supply you with clothing fitting to your rank and with proper refreshment. My father will meet you when you have rested and reward you as you merit."

I had learned a little about the customs of Ulm and I dropped on one knee and presented her my pistol, butt first. She smilingly touched it and I rose and followed Moka. He led me up a flight of steps and into an apartment fit for a Prince of the Blood. Here he summoned servants and surrendered me to their tender mercies.

I did not realize how tired I was until a hot bath revealed the true extent of my fatigue. One of my servants approached and by motions indicated that I was to lie down on a couch. I did so and he massaged me thoroughly with a sweet-smelling oil, which banished my fatigue marvelously. When he had finished, other servants approached with garments which they evidently desired me to put on. I strove to talk to them but they merely shook their heads. Small wonder, for I later found that they were dumb.

The clothing which they brought me consisted of such a skirt, as I had seen on the soldiers, except that it was pure white. In addition they brought me a white cloak which hung well below the waist and which was fastened at the throat with a diamond the size of a walnut. On my feet they placed leather sandals which were thickly encrusted with gold and diamonds and around my calves they wound leather straps also heavily gemmed. About my head they bound a golden filet with a square cut diamond set in the center and around my waist they fastened a belt with a diamond buckle with a long straight sword hanging from the left and a heavily jeweled dagger from the right. As a final touch they set on my head a golden helmet somewhat like those I have seen on ancient Grecian coins, with a white horsehair plume. When they had finished they stood me in front of a mirror to see if I was suited.

I was, in every respect except one. I dug into my old clothes and got my Colt and hung the holster on my belt instead of the silly dagger. It may not have been as handsome, but if I was going to need weapons where I was going, I knew which would be of the most value to me. When I signified that I was suited, my servants withdrew with many bows and left me alone.

I hardly knew what to expect next but I threw myself on the couch to rest a little. For close to an hour I waited before the door swung open to admit Moka.

"My lord," he said with a bow, "Kalu Sabama awaits your presence."

"I am ready," I replied as I rose.

As we passed through the doorway, a detachment of guard met us. As we appeared, they grounded their spears with a ringing clash and closed around us. We passed down a corridor and down a flight of stairs to the main entrance hall and across it to a great closed double door, where we were halted by another detachment of guards and challenged. Moka answered the challenge and the great doors swung open and there was a peal of trumpets. When they had ceased a sonorous voice called out some words which I did not understand, although I was pretty sure that I caught the words "Awlo" and "Courtney." It was evidently an introduction, for, when the voice ceased, Moka motioned me to go forward. I stepped out with my head held high. The guards went with me for a few paces and then opened out and formed a line, leaving me to advance alone down the hall.

It was an immense and spacious hall and while the center was open, the sides were crowded with gaily dressed people. Guards were on all sides and at the far end was a dais or platform raised seven steps above the floor. On the topmost level were four thrones. Before the throne, on the various levels, were a number of men and women, dressed in every color imaginable except the green which was worn by the occupants of the thrones. On the step next to the top level stood a lone figure, who also wore green.

Down the hall I marched until I stood at the foot of the dais. I heard a murmur run down the hall as I passed, but whether of approval or disapproval I could not tell, so I went straight ahead until I came to the foot of the dais and then I bowed deeply. I looked up and looked the occupants of the thrones straight in the eye.

The two center seats were occupied by an elderly couple of great grace and dignity of manner, the throne on the right was vacant and in the one on the left sat Awlo. I had known by the respect accorded her that she must be a rather important personage, but it startled me to realize that she was one of the biggest of them all. She threw me a momentary smile and then looked at me gravely and impersonally as the other two were doing.

The man who occupied one of the center thrones rose and spoke to me.

"Courtney Siba," he said gravely in a sonorous and ringing voice, "my daughter has told before me, where all could hear, the mighty deeds which you have wrought against the Mena. And you who have saved her, in whom the hopes of the dynasty of Kalu are bound up, merit and will receive the gratitude of a nation. The gratitude of a father for the life of his only child I freely give you.

"There is no reward within my power to grant that is great enough for your merits, but if you will name your wishes, they shall be yours if Ulm can supply them. Your rank of Siba I hereby confirm in Ulm and

Ame and give orders that your rank is above all others in the empire save only the royal blood. Is there any reward you desire?"

"I thank you, oh King," I replied, "and I will bear your gracious words in mind. Already you have honored me above my poor deserts but the time may come when I will remind you of your words."

"My words are engraven on my memory, Courtney Siba," said the King with a gracious smile, "and time will not erase them. Your rank entitles you to a place on the second level of my throne, below only my beloved nephew, Lamu Siba."

He motioned toward the man who stood on the next to the topmost level and who I noticed was attired in green as was Kalu. I glanced at him and found that he was watching me with a face like a thundercloud. I returned the scowl with interest and took stock of him. He was about two inches shorter than I was and ruggedly built and showed evidence of a great deal of strength. His black hair, which like the hair of all the men of Ulm, was worn long enough to reach his shoulders, matched the swarthy complexion. The thing that set me against him was a crafty expression in his close-set eyes, which were grey instead of the honest black or brown which should have gone with his complexion.

At a gesture from the King (or Sabama as his title really was), I mounted the dais and took my stand on the step below Lamu and directly in front of Awlo. When I had taken my place, the Sabama turned to the court and began again in his sonorous voice what was evidently a regularly recited formula.

"The house of Kalu," he said, "is as a withered tree with but one green branch. Should this branch be cut, the tree would die without trace of life remaining. Already the branch has been almost cut. It is the hope of all Ulm that this branch will make that new life may be given to the tree, yet the immemorable laws of Ulm decree that the Sibi Tam shall be free to choose her own husband when and how she will, nor may even the Sabama force her choice. Awlo, my daughter, the green branch of the tree of the house of Kalu, are you yet ready to declare your choice?"

Awlo rose and stepped forward.

"I am," she declared in ringing tone.

The reply made a sensation. The audience had been listening politely to the words of the Sabama but they evidently expected Awlo to say that she had not yet made up her mind and her reply electrified them. A hastily suppressed murmur ran through the hall and the Sabama started. I noticed that Lamu bit his lip and closed his hand on his dagger hilt.

"Whom, my daughter, have you chosen to be your prince?" asked Kalu.

Awlo stepped down two steps and stood beside me.

"When the branch was about to be cut, one arose who stayed the hand of the Mena and who saved the tree from being a desolate dying trunk today. Who but that one should be chosen to the highest honor in Ulm and as her future ruler. My father, for my husband, I choose Courtney Siba."

As she ended, she took my right hand and raised it high above my head. There was a moment of silence and then cheer after cheer rent the hall. Evidently Awlo's choice was popular. The Sabama stepped forward and held up his hand for silence. The uproar instantly hushed and he started to speak. He was interrupted in a dramatic manner.

Sword in hand, Lamu faced him.

"Grant you permission to the Sibi Tam to make such a choice?" he demanded.

"The Sibi Tam chooses whom she pleases," said Kalu sharply. "Sheath your weapon. You are in the presence of the Sabama."

"My weapon remains drawn until the honor of Ame is revenged," cried Lamu hoarsely. "Have you lost your senses, my uncle, that you give your only child, the pride and hope of Ulm, to a nameless adventurer who comes from no one knows where? Who knows that he is not a *kahuma* who will destroy the land? Awlo says that he slew the Mena by witchcraft."

"Awlo has chosen," said Kalu quietly but with an ominous ring in his voice. "By what right do you assume to question her choice?"

"For years I have sought her, seeking to consolidate the rule of Ulm and Ame," replied Lamu, "and until this stranger came into Ulm, I had reason to think that my suit was favored. Are you seeking, my uncle, to raise a barrier of blood between Ulm and Ame that the Mena may destroy both?"

"What mean you?" thundered Kalu.

"I demand that the stranger be tested before the Court of Lords to prove that he is not a *kahuma*."

"And Lamu presides over the Court of Lords," broke in Awlo with biting sarcasm. "Do you expect me to let my chosen go before your creatures for judgment?"

The shot struck home and Lamu bit his lips.

"Do you approve Awlo's choice?" he demanded of the Sabama.

"I do," was the reply.

"Then I call upon the ancient laws of Ulm for redress. It is the right of every Siba of royal blood to challenge and fight to the death with the choice of the Sibi Tam. You, Courtney, who claim the rank of Siba, I challenge you to fight to the death."

"Courtney Siba," said Kalu gravely, "do you accept this challenge? Either you must give up your rank or fight for it."

I hesitated but Awlo touched me on the arm. I looked at her and she glanced meaningly at my pistol. An idea came to me.

"I will gladly fight him," I cried, "but not to his death. If he overcomes me, he may do as he wishes, but I fight with my own weapons and if I overcome him, I spare his life."

"Then draw your weapon, Courtney Siba and defend yourself," cried Lamu as he rushed forward.

He aimed a vicious thrust at me before I had time to draw my own weapon and I avoided it only by leaping nimbly back. He came on again and I side-stepped and whipped out my Colt. As he rushed me the third time, I raised my weapon and fired. As I have said, I am a good shot and the range was close, so I didn't shoot to kill. Instead I fired at his sword hand and was lucky enough to hit the hilt of his weapon. The heavy forty-five bullet tore his sword from his grasp and sent it flying through the air. I instantly sheathed my pistol and waited for his next move. It came quickly enough.

He rubbed his right hand for a moment; it must have stung damnably, and then he whipped out his dagger and came at me with it in his left hand. I was a little taller than he was and had the reach on him so I met him half way. He made a sweep at me with his knife which I avoided and then I took his measure and landed my right full on the point of his chin and he went down like a poled ox. A tremendous murmur went around the room and then came a volley of cheers. I judged that Lamu was not popular. When the noise subsided, the Sabama spoke.

"Does any one else wish to challenge the choice of the Sibi Tam?" he asked sardonically.

There was no reply and he nodded to Awlo. She stepped forward and took my right hand in hers and turning it over, she kissed me on the palm and then set my hand on top of her head. When she had finished the ceremony, she looked expectantly at me. I wasn't exactly sure what to do so I took her hand and kissed it and then placed it on top of my head as she had done. In a moment her arms were around me and the assembly room rang with cheers.

Presently Awlo drew back and the Sabama stepped down from his throne. Some officers came forward and removed my white cloak and replaced it with a green one and the Sabama himself bound about my brow a golden filet with a square cut stone in it, similar to the ones which he and Awlo wore, and took me by the hand and led me up the dais and seated me on the vacant throne. There came another blare of trumpets and then the Sabama formally addressed me as "Courtney Siba Tam." Thus it was that I, Courtney Edwards, a citizen of the United States of America, in the year of our Lord one thousand, nine hundred and twenty-two became a Prince of the House of Kalu, the Crown Prince of the Empire of Ulm and the husband of the reigning monarch's only child.

I quickly became settled in my position of Siba Tam. My first official task was to pronounce judgment on Lamu. When I learned the circumstances, I hardly blamed him for his outburst. He was the only son of the ruler of Ame and he had been Awlo's suitor for years. By virtue of his rank he was Commander-in-Chief of the combined armies of Ulm and Ame and when he saw me, a stranger, come in and oust him from his proud position and take his sweetheart as my wife into the bargain, he lost his head. The Sabama wished to reduce him to the grade of commoner and confine him, but Awlo and I interceded and he was eventually pardoned and I appointed him as my second in command of the army. Whatever his faults, he was a good soldier and quite popular with the military. He acted rather formally to me for a couple of years, but he got over it and became one of my closest friends.

One of my first acts was to send a detail of troops out to bring my adjuster into Ulm. There I drained the batteries and went over it thoroughly and stored it in the palace vault. I was perfectly happy and had no idea at all of ever leaving Ulm, but I was guarding against accidents. At any time some prospector might find my valley and wash out a pan of dirt and dump the rubbish on Ulm. If that happened, I meant to take Awlo and increase our size and break up through it.

For five years everything was quiet and peaceful in Ulm and Awlo and I were the happiest pair in the whole empire. She was the idol of the city and my rescue of her had given me a good start. I soon grew quite popular and when Lamu grew to be my friend, the army joined the populace in their affection for me.

In the fall of 1927 we first began to get rumors of a great gathering of the Mena. At first both Lamu and I were disposed to scout the idea, but the rumors came with more definiteness and at last we had to face the fact that the Mena were gathering for an attack in real force. We made what preparations we could for the siege and waited for them to attack. One of the peculiar things which had struck me about Ulm was that the art of projecting weapons was unknown to them. Even the crudest bow and arrow had not been developed. I thought that I saw my way clear to thrash the Mena handsomely and I made up a bow and arrow and showed it to Kalu, proposing that our army be so equipped. He smiled enigmatically and advised me to lay it before the council.

I did so and to my surprise Lamu and the council would not listen to the suggestion. When they explained their reasons, I saw that they were sound ones. The Mena, while they have no inventive ability, are adept at copying the ideas of others and the council were afraid that, while we might smash the first attack by fire superiority, on the next attack we would find the Mena armed with bows, and in such a case we would suffer heavily, even if we finally beat off the attack. The principle of the bow and arrow were well known to them, but they had never used it for this reason.

About a year ago the Mena attacked. There were millions of them, it seemed to me, and they were utterly reckless and willing to put up with huge losses to gain a small point. Man for man they were our superiors, so we did not meet them outside the walls, but contented ourselves with defending the city. They brought ladders and tried to climb the walls and they brought rams and tried to batter down the gates and we stood on the walls and dropped rocks on them and poured hot oil on them and when they got a ladder hoisted we hurled it back and killed with sword and spear those who had gained a footing on the walls. I had read of such defenses in history, and I was able to introduce a few new wrinkles which gave the Mena some rather unpleasant surprises. After three months of fighting, the situation hadn't changed a bit. I learned that a siege of ten or even twenty years was nothing unusual. We had enough *keili* nuts stored in the city to last for fifty years and we had an abundant supply of water. We weren't strong enough to take the offensive, so all we could do was to defend ourselves and wait until the Mena got tired and quit or got to fighting among themselves; the latter always happened when the siege drew out to too great a length.

The continual fighting kept me away from Awlo a great deal and I was naturally anxious to end it as soon as possible. As I passed the arsenal one day, I saw my adjuster standing there and a great idea struck me. I was confident that if I could use propelled projectiles, I could break the back of the Mena attack in no time. The council wouldn't let me use bows and arrows for fear our enemies would copy them and use them against us, but I defied any artisan of the Mena, or any artisan of Ulm for that matter, to copy a modern rifle and its ammunition. Why couldn't I use the adjuster to increase my size to the plane where such things were to be had, load it with guns and ammunition and shrink the whole business to usable size. I hastened to lay my idea before Kalu and the council.

I doubt whether any of the council had ever believed the story I told of my origin, although they had never said so. It is never safe to dispute the word of those in high authority. When I soberly offered to increase my size and get them guns and ammunition, they shook their heads and began to wonder. I took them up on the wall and showed them what a rifle would do to the Mena and any opposition to my going vanished. Highly elated, I refilled my batteries with the electrolyte I had drawn years before and got ready for the trip. I soon found that I had reckoned without Awlo. My Princess flatly refused to be separated from me.

For a while I was baffled but Awlo herself suggested a solution of the problem she had raised.

"Why can't I go with you, Courtney?" she asked. "If we come back safely, the trip will be an interesting one and if we do not return, at least we will be together."

The idea had merit and I presented it to Kalu. He didn't like Awlo to leave him, but he gave consent at last on my solemn promise to come back with her. I knew that some of the work up here would be rather heavy and I asked for a volunteer to accompany me. To my surprise, Lamu asked to go. I was glad of his company but I didn't want both the head of the army and the second in command to leave at once. He insisted and pointed out that the danger of the trip should be shared by the two highest ranking men in the army and I gave way and consented.

The adjuster was carried to the palace roof and I made a few adjustments to increase the speed of its action so that it wouldn't crush the whole city beneath its weight before the base expanded enough to get a wider support. At last everything was ready and the three of us crowded in and with final farewells to all I closed the switch.

I had set the machine to work faster than I realized and before I could open the switch we were twelve feet tall. I threw it back into slow speed and reduced our size until the indicator showed that I was my normal six feet and we stepped out into a new world to Awlo and Lamu and almost a new one to me.

We went into my shack and looked it over. Nothing had been disturbed and no one had been there, so there was no reason why Awlo couldn't stay there safely while Lamu and I trekked into Beatty and I got in touch with my bankers and arranged to buy the munitions that I wanted. We talked it over and Awlo wanted to come. There was no real reason why she couldn't come and indeed make a trip to New York with me if she wished, so I agreed to her coming. Lamu suggested that it might be a good idea for me to teach him how to operate the adjuster so that, in case we found it advisable to send the stuff down in several loads, he could take it down and return and thus avoid separating Awlo and me. The thought was a good one so I set the machine on slow speed and soon taught him the simple manipulation. He caught on readily and manipulated it several times to quite a small size and then professed himself satisfied with his ability. I wish that I could have seen what was in the black villain's heart!

The next morning I was in the cabin making up packs for us to carry on our hike to Beatty when I was alarmed by Awlo outside. I dropped everything and rushed out at top speed. For a moment I didn't see either her or Lamu and then I heard a low faint wail in her voice. I looked in the direction from which it came and saw the adjuster. It was less than one-tenth the size it should have been and I realized that it was shrinking. I sprinted toward it hoping to reach the switch and reverse the action, but I was too late. On my hands and knees I dropped and stared into it. Lamu had my Princess captive and his hand was on the switch. He stopped the action for a minute but the thing was already so small that I could not get my finger between the side bars had I tried and I was afraid of wrecking it. Stooping closer, I heard their tiny voices.

"Courtney Siba Tam," cried Lamu with triumph in his voice, "he laughs best who laughs last as I have heard you say. You robbed me of my kingdom once but when we return and tell them how you planned to desert Ulm in her hour of need and to steal away her Princess, I shall win back all I have lost. For years I have planned to thwart you in your ambition and for that reason I throttled my impulses and seemed your friend. Say farewell to Awlo for this is your last glimpse of her."

"Awlo," I cried in a whisper, "can't you free yourself?"

"No, Courtney," came back her tiny voice, "he is too strong for me and I dare not struggle. Come after me, Courtney! Rescue me from this dog who is worse than the Mena from whom you saved me once. I will watch for you, Courtney!" Thus I heard her voice for the last time and responded.

"I'll be after you as soon as I can, my darling," I cried. "As for you, Lamu Siba, the game is not played out yet. When I return, your heart's blood will pay for this!"

"Ah, yes, Courtney Siba Tam," came his mocking voice, *when* you return."

He turned again to the switch and the adjuster carrying with it all that is dear in life to me disappeared.

I don't remember much about the next few days. Somehow, I made my way to Beatty and established my identity. I made the wires hum to San Francisco, ordering the materials I needed to construct a duplicate of my adjuster. Nor did I forget my people. I ordered the guns and ammunition which I wanted shipped in with the rest of my stuff. It seemed to take forever to get to my valley, but at last it came and I have worked almost day and night since. This afternoon I finished my apparatus and moved it over to the spot where the other had stood and in the morning I will leave this plane and try to take my guns and ammunition to Ulm.

I hope to land in Ulm but I am not at all sure that I will do so. I marked the place where my former machine stood but I may have easily missed placing my new model over the old one. If I have missed setting the center point where it should be by even a fraction of an inch I may come down in Ulm miles from the city. I may even come down into a strange world far from my empire and with no knowledge of which way to go. I have done my best and time alone will tell how well I have done. One thing I know. No matter what Lamu may have done or said, Awlo is still waiting for me and she is still true to me. I have my rifle and plenty of ammunition and even though the whole Mena race block my path, some way I will fight my way through them and once more hold my Princess in my arms.

AWLO OF ULM

by Capt. S. P. Meek

WHEN I allowed my manuscript, "Submicroscopic," to be published, I had no intention of telling to the world the balance of my adventures. Frankly, I did not expect to be believed. The events of which I told were so fantastic, so contrary to the ordinary experiences and preconceived notions of men of this plane of existence, that I expected the story to be passed off as an idle tale, told only to amuse. The editor of AMAZING STORIES was kind enough to forward to me a number of comments received. When I read them over I found, to my astonishment, that there were a small number of discerning thinkers who realized that my story was one of actual facts. Most of them expressed regret that the end of the story was, so they thought, a sealed book to them. It is to this select group, who I feel are my friends, that this story is addressed. The interest they have shown in my welfare and in that of my beloved princess is so heartfelt that I feel that I can do no less than publish for their benefit the extraordinary events which followed that seemingly endless night in my hidden Nevada valley before I started in pursuit of Awlo and her abductor.

Impatiently I watched the sun rise over the Timpahutes. The sunrise is a little later in Ulm than in this plane because of the height of the mountain (grains of sand!) which surround the empire. I judged it best to wait for broad daylight before I plunged into what might easily be the unknown. I had set my electronic vibration adjuster as nearly as possible over the spot where Lamu and my princess had disappeared but I know that a distance which could not be detected under the microscope in this plane might be miles in Ulm and I had little hope of landing in the beleaguered city.

At last I felt that the time had come. I entered my newly completed adjuster, closed the switch and was on my way. Rapidly the scenery

Copyright 1931 by Teck Publishing Corporation

grew to Brobdingnagian proportions and then disappeared as it grew too
large for my eyes to see or my mind to comprehend. I watched the indicator
dial as the needle crept toward infinity. Presently its motion ceased and
the high whine of my generators became audible. The note ran down the
scale of audibility and subsided into silence. I looked out from my adjuster and my heart sank. The landscape resembled not in the least the
scenery around Ulm. There was no doubt that I had missed my goal by
many miles.

My first inclination was to increase my size and move the adjuster but
a sober second thought made me realize the futility of such an action. I
had set the machine as nearly as I could over the spot where Ulm lay and
any change I made would be just as likely to be away from the city as
toward it. The only thing to do was to set out on my travels in the
hope that I would meet some one, even were it one of the hostile Mena,
who could give me some idea of the direction in which to travel. I slung
a couple of extra bandoliers of ammunition over my shoulders, picked up
my rifle and stepped out of the adjuster. A second thought made me pause.
I retraced my steps and opened an arm locker. From it I took two small-
caliber .32, automatic pistols, which I placed in shoulder holsters under my
shirt. The little guns held six rounds each and while they were small, they
carried hollow point bullets which would have a deadly effect at short
range. With my armament thus reenforced, I was ready to start my travels.

The country in which I found myself was wild beyond description. In
place of the dense semi-tropical vegetation which I had been accustomed
to associate with my submicroscopic empire, there was nothing but rock,
bare rugged rock. Huge masses of stone, hundreds and even thousands of
feet high, lay piled one on another as though a race of giants had tossed
them about in sport, recking little of where they fell. There was none
of the solidity and symmetry which marks the mountains of the larger
plane. Many of the stones seemed to be precariously balanced and even
where they were wedged together, the effect was one of insecurity. I
shuddered and caught myself afraid to stir lest even my tiny weight
would start one of the masses of rock into motion and engulf me and all
my possessions in cataclysmic ruin. I walked in a gingerly fashion over
to one of the unstable appearing masses of rock and rested my hand
against it. It was solid to the touch and I pressed, gently at first, and
then with all my strength, trying in vain to budge the mass which must
have weighed thousands of tons, if my own negligible weight be taken
as being its normal one hundred and eighty pounds. Satisfied that it was
beyond my strength to move it, I felt safer, and began to consider in
which direction I should start my travels.

I racked my brain for a clue. Somewhere in memory's vaults there was an elusive something that this jumbled phantasmagoria of rock reminded me of. Suddenly I remembered it.

In the days when I had been hailed as the Crown Prince of Ulm, the husband of its ruler's only child, I had been much interested in the ancient legends which told the history of the empire. Ulm had no written language and no records to which I could refer other than the traditions and legends which had been handed down from father to son. These legends were preserved in metrical form. The learning and reciting of them on occasion was the principal duty of the class of persons known as *tamaaini,* * generally elderly men who were not of the noble class, but who, because of their profession, had an *entrée* to the court and many of the privileges of nobility. Some of them had marvelous memories and could repeat without faltering thousands after thousands of lines of the old legends. It was from them that I learned that the Mena had originally come down from the north through the barren passes in the mighty mountains which border Ulm on all sides. I had never been able to gather much information as to derivation of the people of Ulm themselves. It seemed that so far as the *tamaaini* knew, they had always lived in their present location. There were, however, here and there in the legends dim and little understood references to other places and it was one of these passages that I strove to recall. Suddenly, like a flash, the long forgotten tale came to my mind.

It told of the flight of the natural son of a ruler of Ulm who had tried to wrest the throne from his legitimate half-brother, after his father's death, and it described his own defeat and death. The victor pursued him with a handful of guards and caught him in a place where "giants played as children, tossing mountains hand to hand." There they encountered a race of *kahumas* or wizards who flew through the air like birds and who shot fire from their many hands. They could "kill from afar with fire" and they allowed no one who entered their land to return. Evidently, at least one of the party returned to Ulm with the record of the attempted usurper's death, which the legend goes on to detail at great length. The passage had always interested me, for it seemed to hint at a higher civilization than was possessed by the brave and chivalrous warriors of Ulm.

I looked about me and I did not blame the fancy of the ancient bard who had laid the condition of the landscape to the gambols of giants or to the evil machinations of wizards. Certainly his description was an apt

* Compare the Hawaiian word, "*kamaaini,*" an old inhabitant.

one. The forbidden land lay, according to the legend, "toward the setting sun." If the tale were true and if I were looking on the scene of that ancient tragedy, Ulm should lie to the east and not more than a few days' journey away. It was a pretty slender clue but it was the only one I had. Without it I had no idea of which direction to take, so I decided to trust to the accuracy and authenticity of a legend of unknown antiquity and make my way eastward.

My first step was to fix the landscape in my mind and to take bearings with my marching compass on the most prominent points of the scenery. If I found my way back to Ulm my entire labor and travail would be lost unless I were able to return to the adjuster and its precious load of weapons. Three huge peaks dominated the scene to the north and they stood so that the farther one lay exactly in the middle of the interval between the two nearer ones. The bearing of the farther peak was a quarter point west of magnetic north. Exactly south east was another peak with a peculiar cleft near its summit. A short study enabled me to fix the location of the adjuster so firmly in my mind that I was certain that I could find the place again. With a final look around, I shouldered my rifle, set my face to the east and set out.

Despite the ruggedness of the country I was able, by the aid of my marching compass, to keep going in the general direction of east pretty well although I had to make several lengthy detours around masses of rock. For several hours I pushed on and found the country gradually getting a little less rugged. There were no signs of animal life but once in a while I came across a tuft of vegetation resembling the bunch grass so common in some parts of the West.

As the sun got higher it grew intolerably hot and I began to regret that I had loaded myself so heavily with food and especially ammunition and had brought only two quarts of water. It was too late to retrace my steps, so I husbanded my water as carefully as possible and kept going. Before noon the heat got so bad that I began to look for a place where I could find a little shelter.

Ahead of me I spied what looked like a cave in the rock and I pressed forward to investigate it. It was not a true cave but it was a fair imitation of one made by two huge masses of rock leaning against one another. I had no idea how far into the rock the cavity extended but it was cool in the shade and I discarded my pack with a sigh of relief. I also unslung the heavy bandoliers of ammunition which I carried and leaned my rifle against the wall of the cavern. According to my pedometer, I had covered about ten miles. I secured a pencil and notebook from my pack and stepped to the mouth of the cavern to sight the directions of the peaks by which I had marked my landing.

I located them without any trouble and was engaged in trying to locate myself by a process of triangulation on a crude map which I had made of my morning's journey when an unfamiliar sound brought me up with a start. I listened intently and the sound faded for a moment only to increase in volume. I puzzled my brains as to what was causing it. It was a dull humming sound and the only thing it reminded me of was the whirling of an airplane propeller, a patent impossibility in Ulm.

The sound came nearer and I started back to the cave and took up my rifle when the cause of the noise came in sight. My flyer's ears had not misled me. Flying along at a moderate speed about a thousand feet above my level was an airplane. It was not of the conventional pattern with which I was familiar although it bore certain resemblance to the planes I had flown. The main difference was in the size and shape of the wings. Instead of the usual rectangular wing spread on each side of the fuselage, this machine had a single heart-shaped wing mounted above the fuselage with the point of the heart to the rear. Above the wing was a crisscross network of wires which reminded me of an aerial.

The passenger car was long and cigar-shaped although it did not extend backward much beyond the point of the heart. The sides were pierced with windows which were glazed with glass or some other transparent material through which I fancied I could see figures moving, although the distance was too great for me to be sure.

The machine had three propellers, one mounted directly in front of the car and about on a level with the wing while the other two, which were smaller, were set lower and about midway from the center line of the craft to the extremities of the wing. Not only the small wing spread and other unconventional features of the design attracted my attention but also the complete absence of all motor noise although the three propellers were whirling rapidly.

Stupidly I watched the craft until it was almost overhead and then I had sense enough to start something. Even though the occupants of the ship were not handicapped by the roar of motors, I had no hope of making them hear at that elevation so I hastily took off my hat and waved it frantically. The airship moved serenely on without anyone seeing, or at any rate, heeding my signals of distress. Desperately I ransacked my brains for a means of attracting their attention and inspiration visited me. An old friend of mine had been experimenting with some illuminating bullets and he had given me a handful of cartridges loaded with them.

I suddenly remembered that my pistol was loaded with them for I had intended to try them out but had forgotten to do so. Here was an excellent chance to test their value. I pulled my pistol from its holster and fired up into the air.

From the muzzle of the gun a bell of fire rose into the air. Up past the airship it went and still up. It must have traveled fully eight hundred yards before the flame died. I fired again and then turned my attention to the airplane. My signal had evidently been seen, for the ship was swinging around on a wide arc. Again I waved my coat. There was no question that my signal was seen for the ship glided on a long slant toward the ground. I looked at the small open space before me and knew that it would be impossible to land an ordinary plane in it without a crash, but I had not yet learned the possibilities of that stubby ship with its diminutive wing spread. The plane curved down and came to a stop not over a hundred feet from where it first touched ground. The center propeller ceased turning but the two side propellers kept up a steady hum until after the ship had come to a complete stop.

A door opened in the side of the ship and four figures climbed out and came toward me. I hastened to meet them but I stopped short in my stride before I had gone far. They had the general conformation of men but they suddenly gave me an uncanny feeling as though I were looking at huge spiders. I could not understand the feeling for a moment until I concentrated my attention on the one who was leading the advance. From his shoulders projected not one pair of arms but three. The rest of him appeared to be normal as well as I could tell through the bulky shapeless garment which he wore and the helmet which concealed his features.

The four figures spread out as they advanced and I did not interpret the action as a friendly one. I thought momentarily of retreating to the cave where I had left my rifle but I had no idea of how fast these newcomers could travel and they were as close to the cavern mouth as I was. I backed against a nearby boulder and drew my pistol. They might mean no harm but I preferred to be ready for all eventualities.

The four drew near until they were within twenty feet of me. I raised my pistol but hesitated about commencing hostilities until I was sure that they were not friendly. At my action they all stopped and stared and one of them raised an arm and pointed it at me. At this close distance I could see their features through the glass windows which formed the front of their helmets and I realized that they were like no men I had seen before. Their faces were a bright saffron yellow and their eyes were set obliquely in their heads. I raised my left hand in the universal gesture of peace and spoke.

"*Pehea oc, malahini?*" I said.

The leader looked doubtfully at me for a moment before he replied. He spoke in a strange guttural voice and while his language was not that of Ulm, I was able to understand it.

"Whence came you and what seek you here?" he demanded.

"I come from Ulm," I replied. "I came from the capital which is beleaguered by the race of the Mena and I am seeking to bring assistance to Kalu Sibama, my sovereign lord. I am lost and am trying to find my way thither. Can you direct me?"

"Ulm?" he said slowly and then burst into a harsh laugh. "You lie," he went on. "Ulm is more than a memory. Kalu Sibama has rested, well I hope, in the stomachs of the Mena for many moons."

"Is Ulm fallen?" I gasped, hardly able to believe my ears.

"Ulm is fallen," he said, evidently amused at my horror. "As fleas desert a dying dog, so her leaders deserted her. The Mena stormed the walls and but a remnant fought their way out. That remnant are slaves of my lord, Kapioma Sibama of the Empire of Kau. He will be pleased when I bring him two slaves in place of the one I was sent to seek."

His words answered my question as to his intentions. I thought grimly that he had not captured his slave yet as I carefully covered his chest with my pistol. The illuminating bullet struck him fair in the center of his chest and exploded in a flash of red light. He staggered back under the shock of impact but did not fall. I raised my pistol for a second shot but I never fired it. A flash of blinding green light came from one of his arms and my pistol clattered to the ground. My right arm hung numb and paralyzed from the shoulder. A second flash came and my left arm was in the same condition. I turned to run but I was too late. A dozen hands gripped me and held me helpless.

At a word from their leader, the three subordinates jerked me rudely along the ground toward the strange craft and pulled me inside. I gave a rapid glance around as I entered the craft for I desired to see what type of motors they had which operated so silently. There were none in sight. In the front of the long cabin were a set of dual flying controls of the type with which I was familiar. In the forward end were three tiny motors of an unfamiliar type but there were no batteries, no generators and above all no prime movers, unless such a term could be applied to a large panel board set with switches and dials which was between the two sets of controls. One man stood at this board. There were no other occupants of the ship evident at first glance.

My captors dragged me to the rear end of the cabin and forced me to a sitting position. Two more green flashes filled the interior of the cabin momentarily and my legs from the knee down were as useless as my arms were. The three retreated to the upper end of the cabin and divested themselves of their flying suits. They were men of middle height with rather slight physique but with high foreheads and an air of great intelligence. The leader turned his slanting eyes toward me. There was power in them and intelligence but there was also the very quintessence of cruelty in them. So obsessed was I with his face, that for a moment I failed to notice that four of his six arms had disappeared.

An explanation flashed through my mind and I looked at the rest of the crew. Each of them had only the normal two arms which I had expected. On the wall was a rack and hung there were five flying suits, from the shoulders of each of which projected three sets of arms. As I examined them more closely, I saw that only two arms on each suit ended in gloves. The other arms ended in hollow tubes from which the paralyzing rays had evidently come. The sight of these garments did as much as the coldly merciless faces to impress on my mind the fact that I was dealing, not with the brave chivalrous savages of Ulm, but with a race who had developed their mental powers highly and who were well acquainted with scientific laws.

The leader gave an order and two of the crew stepped to the flying controls. The man at the switchboard manipulated some dials. The ship started upward with a rocketing motion, climbing at what was, to my judgment an entirely unsafe angle. However, the ship made it without any difficulty and leveled off at an elevation of about a thousand feet and continued on her way east. I took a rapid glance at the compass set on the roof and mentally resolved to keep track of our course.

Two of the crew stepped forward and tossed to one side a piece of cloth which had covered some long object lying on the floor. They picked it up and I suppressed an exclamation with difficulty. The object was a man and it needed only a glance to tell me that he was of a different race from the crew of the ship. Long curling yellow locks fell from his head in place of the short black hair of the Kauans and his skin was as white as mine instead of the disgusting saffron yellow which marked our captors.

His arms and legs hung limp and useless as they picked him up and bore him aft. They dumped him unceremoniously on the floor beside me and returned to the forward part of the cabin. I looked at my fellow captive with interest, an interest which he quite evidently felt as well.

"Where from?" he asked me in an undertone. His voice had none of the guttural quality which marked the speech of the crew. It was as soft and liquid as the speech of any man of Ulm.

"Ulm," I replied, also in an undertone.

"But Ulm fell months ago," he said wonderingly. "Surely you did not survive the sack of the city. If you did, how have you survived since then?"

"I was not at the fall of the city," I replied. "I was away seeking aid for Ulm when it fell. I have just returned."

He looked at me curiously.

"What was your rank?" he demanded.

"I was Siba Tam," I replied proudly.

An expression of joy crossed his face.

"My hilt to your hand, Siba Tam," he said, "had I a sword to offer. I have long hoped for a sight of the son of my ruler."

"I was not the son of Kalu," I answered, "I was the husband of his only child."

"Still my hilt to your hand," he replied. "I have not seen my native land since I was a child but no more loyal subject of her Sibama lives. Do you wish to continue on to Kau?"

"I hardly wish to go anywhere as a slave," I said briefly.

"Then we can escape," he replied. "I had planned to try to win my freedom before we reached the city, although I had little hope of success. Two of us should be more than a match for five men of Kau."

"But my legs and arms are paralyzed," I objected.

"That is of no moment. Can you keep them quiet and simulate paralysis if I remove the effects of the ray?"

"I think so."

"Then be careful and do not move them while I work."

He rolled over and fell against me. The Kauans glanced around at him for a moment but paid no further attention. In a moment I felt a sharp pain in my back and then another in my shoulder.

"Now remain perfectly quiet," said my new friend. A dull whir sounded behind me for a moment and an excruciating pain racked my limbs. I bit my lip to keep from crying out. The pain passed and to my joy I found that both feeling and motion had been restored.

"What are your orders?" asked my fellow captive softly.

"I have no plans made. You know what to do much better than I do. Issue your orders and I will obey."

"Then when I give the word, leap to your feet and rush them," he said. "Get between them and their fighting suits and keep them away from them. If they get to their weapons, we are dead or worse. Without them they have nothing but their strength to rely on."

"Wait a moment," I said cautiously, "I think I have a weapon here. I have one that will kill ordinary men but it failed against these men. However, they had their fighting suits on when I tried it. Tell me, are they vulnerable to a sword thrust?"

"Without their fighting suits, yes; with them, no."

"Fine. Lie still and let me try my hand on them. Can you fly the ship after we capture it?"

"Certainly."

"All right, I'll see what I can do. If my weapon fails, we can still rush them with bare hands."

I braced myself for an effort. The distance was short and I felt sure that the little thirty-two automatic pistols which I had providentially armed myself with would be accurate enough for my purpose. Both rested in holsters—one under each arm.

With a sudden swift movement, I sprang to my feet, a pistol in each hand. I raised the right one and fired at the leader. I watched breathlessly for a moment. He swayed back and forth and then fell headlong. The gun was effective.

The other members of the crew stared stupidly at their fallen leader. Again the little gun spoke and the odds were reduced to three to two. The remaining members of the crew made a rush for their fighting suits but they never reached them. Three times the little automatic spat forth a message of death and each time my aim was good. My companion had risen to his feet and he now raced for the controls. He got them just in time, for the pilotless ship was careening badly. In a moment he had it flying once more on a level keel.

I made the rounds of the prostrate crew. At short range the mushroom bullets with which my gun was loaded had done their work. Only one of our enemies lived and it was evident that his wound was fatal. Assured of their helplessness to harm us, I moved up to the control board.

"Which way, Siba Tam?"

I reflected before answering. There was no use in returning to fallen Ulm. The ship would be an excellent aid to me in pursuing my search for my lost princess and I had gained a loyal follower. The first step was to arm him.

"Go back to the place where I was captured and then straight west for a few miles. In the meantime, teach me how to fly this ship. What is your motive power? I see no signs of any source of energy."

"Our power is drawn from the central power house in Kaulani."

"Radio transmission of power!" I gasped.

"I do not understand your words," he said (I had unconsciously spoken in English) "The power to turn our propellers and to actuate the fighting suits is generated in Kaulani and is sent out in the form of waves which are received by wires on the top of the ship."

"I noticed them," I replied, "but did not suspect their use. I thought they were used to receive and probably transmit messages."

"Could messages be sent or received through them?"

"Certainly. Isn't that done?"

"No, Siba Tam."

"In that case we have one bit of knowledge that the Kauans don't have," I said cheerfully. "I will show you how it is done later. Now show me how to control the ship."

He motioned me to take the dual set of controls and started his explanations. It was ridiculously simple for one already well versed in flying and in five minutes I was maneuvering the ship like a veteran. The secret of the small wing spread and the short take-off and landing distance lay in the setting and position of the side propellers. They were so inclined that their blast struck the wings and gave a lifting effect to aid the take-off. Reversing them made them act as a brake and brought the craft to a standstill in a few feet. The central propeller did practically all the work of moving the ship forward.

In a short time we were over the place where I had been captured and we landed and secured my rifle and pack. We took off again and in ten minutes landed safely by the side of my adjuster.

"Now I will repay you for teaching me to fly our ship," I said with a smile, "by teaching you to manipulate a machine which I doubt if even the leader of that crew of brigands who captured us could understand. However, before I do so, tell me about yourself. Who are you and how did you get here? I have lived for years in Ulm and do not know your face and my face was not familiar to you."

"I was taken from Ulm as a child and reared in Kau."

"How did that happen?"

"My name is Olua; Olua Alii by right, for I was born the son of Muana Alii, one of the Council of Lords. When I was a child, I accompanied my father on a trip to Ame. On the way home, the Mena attacked us. My father was killed but I was saved alive and taken as a present to their chief. I was destined for his larder but he never saw me. On the way to his resting place, an airship like this one swooped down on us. The Mena fled in all directions. Men of Kau in fighting suits came from the ship and one of them, a great Alii, picked me up. His only son had died a few days before and for that reason he spared me, although the men of Kau are entirely without mercy in their dealings with those of other races. He took me to Kau and raised and educated me as his own child. There are few of the scientific secrets of Kau that I do not know."

"How did you come to be a prisoner?"

"Through loyalty to the land of my birth. Although raised in Kau, I never forgot that I was by birth an Alii of Ulm, one of the Council of Lords. I read all I could of Ulm and the more I learned of their bravery and chivalry, the more glad I became that I was one of them and not a treacherous Kauan. My loyalty was always to Kalu Sibama of Ulm and not Kapioma Sibama of Kau, although I did not speak openly of it.

"When Ulm fell to the Mena, a handful of the warriors of Ulm won their way through to the mountains between Kau and Ulm, where they were captured and brought as slaves to Kaulani. My heart leapt when I saw them come in. They were such men as I had always dreamed of, men who fought their enemies with steel and not with weapons of stealth and treachery. The dream of my life was to rescue them and flee with them to Ame, which had not fallen to the Mena. I laid my plans carefully. I was going to capture one of the largest warships, and fly with them.

"The day before I was to act, I was betrayed. A faithful slave warned me that the Sibama's guards were on their way to arrest me. I did not delay, but raced for the roof of the power house, where I know that the Sibama's private flyers, the fastest craft in Kau, were kept. I selected a fast one-man flyer and fled in the night to the west. My flight was fore-doomed to be a failure.

"The power sent out by the power house in Kaulani is sent in five wavelengths. One of them is used for all machines of peace, for lighting the house, preparing the food and similar uses. A second actuates the fighting suits and other weapons of war. The other three are assigned to the ships; one to commercial ships, one to war vessels and one to the Sibama's private flyers. All they had to do was to shut down the wavelength on which I was flying and my ship crashed to the ground, a wreck.

"By their meters at Kaulani they can tell where every ship is and warships were dispatched after me. They could not locate me. Before leaving, I had rigged the flyer with a device I had perfected, which made the meters give false readings and I was many miles from the place where they sought me, I hid the wreckage of my ship under rocks and eked out a precarious living in the hope that some day I would be able to capture a small flyer and make my way to Ame alone. I knew that they would use the paralyzing ray on me when I was found and I labored to make a pocket device which would remove the effects of the ray. After seven months of toil, I perfected it. The search for me had never ended, for the Kauans knew that I could not be beyond the limits of their empire. Many times I had seen the patrol vessels pass over me and each time I had hidden myself. This morning one passed and I deliberately showed myself. Everything went as I had planned. They paralyzed my arms and legs but my pocket neutralizer destroyed the effects. I simulated paralysis and was carried on the ship a prisoner. I bided my time and was about to attack, when they saw your signal and stopped to capture you. You know the rest."

"One question, Olua Alii; you said that the survivors of Ulm were taken to Kaulani. Were there any women among them?"

"There were not, Siba Tam. They were all warriors."

Evidently Awlo and Lamu had not made their way to Ulm. Well, that was about what I had expected.

"Perhaps you had better teach me to use one of these fighting suits," I suggested.

"Certainly, Siba Tam, whatever you desire. As you can see, each suit has six arms. Two of these are control arms, the other four are weapons. Each of the weapons is different. The green ray is a paralyzing ray with whose effects you are familiar. It can be used as a crippling weapon or as a killing weapon. If the heart is paralyzed, death ensues instantly.

"In the second arm is an orange ray which neutralizes the effect of the green ray. It is used as a defensive weapon against an enemy equipped with the green paralyzing ray. It will also restore the functioning of any part of the body which has been paralyzed. The third arm contains a red or heat ray. I will show you the effect of it."

He donned a suit and directed the middle arm on the left side toward a boulder. A ray of intolerable brightness shot from the arm. The granite boulder glowed bright for a moment and a stream of molten rock ran down its face. Olua shut off the ray.

"The fourth ray is a blue one which has the effect of neutralizing the red ray of an opponent," he went on. "You see, each suit is equipped with two offensive and two defensive weapons. These are all that the common soldiers carry. The Alii have suits with more arms and more deadly weapons, both offensive and defensive. It is said that Kapioma Sibama has made a suit with forty arms but it is so heavy that he cannot walk with it on. It operates, not on the usual wavelength, but on the private wavelength on which his flyers operate.

"That, however, is not the most effective suit in Kaulani. The most deadly suit is one which I manufactured in secret and which is hidden there. I had no opportunity to bring it with me or all the forces of Kau could not have harmed me. I will tell you, Siba Tam, where it is concealed. The knowledge may never benefit you but it will do you no harm. In the power house is a laboratory where fighting suits are made and tested. One entire end of the laboratory is taken up by a screen against which all rays are helpless. Unknown to everyone, I have tampered with that screen. If you ever wish to get the suit, go to the laboratory and turn the ordinary red ray, the heat ray of the common suits, against the upper corner of the screen, fourteen inches from the top and eleven inches from the left end. Leave the ray on full force for eight seconds and then apply the orange ray for twelve seconds. A portion of the screen will open and the suit is behind it. It operates on the same wave as Kapioma's."

"Thank you, Olua," I said, after I had practised with one of the suits until I could manipulate it rapidly, "you have told me what I wished to know very frankly and fully. I will reward your confidence by being equally frank with you. Although I am Siba Tam of Ulm, I was not born in that empire. I was born in a much larger world. Do you understand the composition of matter?"

I soon found that the education of an Alii of Kau left little to be desired from a scientific standpoint. Olua was perfectly familiar with the division of matter into molecules and atoms and of the atoms into protons and electrons. One of his statements surprised me a great deal until I had time to reflect on it. He said that the atoms were static instead of in motion and that the same was true of the electrons. I started to correct him, when a sudden thought made me pause. A moment of reflection told me that he was right. In his plane, both atoms and electrons were static.

When I had first started my electronic vibration adjuster, which reduced the amplitude of vibration of the electrons, my switch had jammed and I had broken it in trying to open it. Despite this fact, the adjuster had reduced me to the size of the men of Ulm and had then ceased operation. On each subsequent trip, the same phenomenon had occurred. The reason, on reflection, was obvious. I had reduced the amplitude of vibration to zero and in this minute plane, the electrons did not vibrate.

Once I had that idea in my head, it was a simple matter to explain to Olua the theory of the vibrating atoms of the larger planes. He did not question my theory of simple harmonic vibration of the electrons, which theory had brought so much ridicule on me at one time. He realized at once how the size of a body could be increased under such circumstances but when I told him of the world from which I had first come to Ulm, his eyes opened. He had no more idea of the existence of such a world than we of the larger plane had of the existence of Ulm before my first trip there. His first thought was to flee to the larger plane from the pursuing Kauans.

"There we will be safe," he said. "They will be after us in a few hours with ships of greater speed equipped with fighting suits against which we have no defence."

"You may go if you wish Olua," I said, "but I have returned to Ulm for a purpose and that purpose has not been accomplished. I will stay and continue my search."

"Where the Siba Tam of Ulm stays, there stays Olua Alii of Ulm," he said quietly. "What are your plans?"

"The only place where I can obtain the information I seek is at Kaulani, where the survivors of Ulm are," I replied. "Let me tell you why I am here and what I seek."

In a few words I told him of Lamu's treachery and of my search for my lost princess.

"You will not find her in Kaulani," he said thoughtfully, "for there were no women brought there. However, some of the prisoners can tell you whether they returned to Ulm before it fell. Since that is your desire, we will wait here until the Kauans come and capture us."

"No, we won't," I replied. "If they come here, they will capture not only us but also my adjuster and the weapons I brought from the larger plane. How long will it be before they are after us?"

"At least four hours."

"Good. In that length of time, I can teach you how to manipulate a rifle and a pistol as well as the adjuster. There is one other thing you want to learn to use. Here is a wireless transmission set. It will enable you to send messages through the air, which a similar instrument will receive, and also to receive messages sent to you. If I can, I will construct one in Kaulani so that we can get into communication. You are not going back to Kaulani with me."

"I will stay with my lord."

"You will obey my orders. If you go there, it will not aid me at all and will result in your death. If you hide out here, it is possible that you may aid me. In the event that I am killed, it is my order that you take up the search for Awlo of Ulm and never abandon it while you live until you have rescued her from Lamu or have looked on her dead body. Do you understand?"

"I do, sire. It will be as you order."

"Good. Now I want to teach you all I can before we have to pull out of here."

Olua was an apt pupil and in two hours he was able to manipulate a rifle and a pistol as well as I could and even to shoot fairly well at short ranges. The weapons would be useless against men equipped with fighting suits, the simplest of which threw about the wearer a repulsive screen which no bullet could penetrate, but I felt that no knowledge was useless, since my ability with a pistol had saved us once. The radio set was elementary to him, his only wonder being that no Kauan had ever thought of so simple a device.

When he was fully instructed we entered the adjuster and increased our size slowly until we were perhaps a hundred yards tall, compared to Ulm standards. We stepped out and I used a rifle to start the adjuster and let it reduce its size to Ulmite standards. When this was done, I could pick it and its entire load up and carry it without difficulty. Olua picked up the Kauan ship and together we set out across the hills for the point where I was captured. I resolved to make that cavern our base of operations.

We found it with no trouble and reduced ourselves to our former dimensions. It was quite a task for us to move the adjuster and its load into the cavern but we did so. When the task was completed, I bade a temporary farewell to Olua and entered the Kauan ship. I drove it about thirty miles due east and then landed. I set the controls of the ship for a maximum climb and pulled the power lever to full speed forward. The ship sprang up into the air and I leaped out just in time. Upward it went for several miles before it fell out of control. When it did, it gave a sickening lurch or two and then dove at full speed toward the ground. I sat down and waited for the next Kauan ship to appear.

I did not have long to wait. In less than an hour a speck appeared in the blue to the east. The new ship was a larger one than the first and it seemed to me to be traveling at a higher speed. I was fearful lest the occupants would see the remains of the ship which had crashed but the Gods of Fate were kind to me and it escaped their notice. It probably dove into some deep dark ravine, for none of the scouts which went out from Kau in search of it ever located it. Hunting for so small an object as a five-man cruiser in the wastes of the Kau mountains was a great deal like the proverbial search for a needle in a haystack.

When the ship came in sight, I walked slowly out into the open and stood quietly awaiting its approach. I thought, and as it turned out I thought rightly, that the figure of a man would hardly escape the attention of an airship sent out to seek for one. The ship swung down on a long slant and came to a standstill less than fifty feet from where I stood. A door opened in the side of the cabin and a half a dozen figures wearing eight-armed fighting suits emerged. I advanced toward them confidently.

"Greetings, men of Kau," I said when I had approached to within twenty feet of them. They paused and their leader stepped a pace in front.

"Greetings, man of Ulm," he replied in his guttural voice. "What seek you in the mountains of Kau?"

"I seek audience with Kapioma Sibama of Kau," I said. "The way to Kaulani is long and weary and I ask your aid in traveling there."

"What manner of man are you?" he demanded. "Your color and speech mark you as a man of Ulm, yet what man of Ulm knows of Kau and Kaulani?"

"I know many things," I said haughtily, "things which I have come to Kau to impart to your Sibama."

"What is your name and rank?"

"I am Courtney Siba Tam, Crown Prince of Ulm."

A peculiar expression flickered for a moment over his face and he bowed low to me.

"Neimeha of Kau is honored to be of service to such a one," he said smoothly. "My poor ship is at your Highness' disposal to carry him to the court of Kapioma Sibama. There you may meet some of your compatriots."

"I believe that a few of my subjects did escape into the Kau mountains when Ulm fell," I said carelessly, "and I would like to see them again. I will mention your courtesy to Kapioma Sibama."

He bowed again at my words and motioned to me to precede him into the flyer. I did so, expecting every moment to feel a paralyzing ray strike me, but evidently my bluff had worked. Neimeha followed me in and he and his followers divested themselves of their fighting suits.

"It is fortunate for me that you took this path," I said cheerfully. "I had little hope of meeting a ship so soon."

"We seek one who has fled from Kau," he replied. "As long as the light holds we will continue our search. Such were my orders."

"It is unfortunate that you men of Kau do not understand some of the laws of nature with which I am familiar," I said. "If you were, it would be a simple matter to communicate with your sovereign and ask for a modification of your orders. The waves which come from your power house could easily carry a message to you."

"How would such a thing be possible?" demanded Neimeha in amazement.

I smiled enigmatically.

"It is but one of the things which I can teach you," I replied. "I could instruct one of your learning in a short time, but I do not choose to do so. Perhaps your Sibama will desire to confine this new knowledge to his Alii. How long will it take us to fly to Kaulani?"

He turned to a map hanging on the wall and I walked over and studied it. It was the first map of the submicroscopic country I had ever seen, for Ulm had not progressed to the stage of map making and probably never would have. The Ulmites were possessed of an uncanny sense of direction which enabled them to find their way readily about their domain without other aid.

I had been captured in what was apparently a "no man's land" between the empires of Ulm and Kau. Ulm lay, as nearly as I could scale distances by the eye, about ninety miles *due west* of where we were. The old legend had lied after all. Kaulani was roughly two hundred miles to the east, a hundred and fifty of which were over barren mountains.

"We can fly to Kaulani in an hour and a half," said Neimeha. "In view of your presence, I am going to alter my instructions on my own initiative and take you directly to the city."

"I thank you," I said. "I am fairly familiar with this type of ship. With your permission, I will take the dual set of controls and guide the ship a part of the way."

He nodded and for the rest of the trip I devoted my attention to improving my technique. There was really nothing to it and long before we reached Kaulani, I was as confident of my ability to fly any ship in the country as I was of my ability to fly a Bach or a Douglas.

It was nearly dark when we landed in Kaulani. The plan of the city resembled the plan of Ulm, but the architecture was of a much lighter and more graceful type. Not that Ulm had not been a beautiful city but its beauty was the beauty of grandeur and massiveness with utter simplicity marking its architectural lines. Kaulani, as well as I could tell in the gathering dusk, was made up of buildings of a much more graceful style.

I could not place the type of architecture, although in the daylight it had a strong note of the best Grecian style in it.

We landed in the huge grounds surrounding the royal palace. Neimeha and two of his guards escorted me into the palace to a floor below the level of the ground.

"I am placing you in the slave's quarters," he explained, "not that your status as a guest has changed, but that it is necessary that you be kept under surveillance, until it is learned whether Kapioma Sibama will receive you. The slave's quarters are the only place where this can be done. Besides, I thought that you might like to see some of your old subjects," he added with a touch of malice in his voice.

The room into which I stepped was the central recreation room of a large suite of rooms. It was well lighted and ventilated and was fitted with a number of comfortable looking chairs and divans. At the far end of the room a half dozen men clothed in coarse white garments were grouped together talking. They turned as I entered and surveyed me from head to foot. As I approached them, one stepped in front of the rest and looked at me keenly. I suddenly became aware that I was dressed in corduroy breeches and a flannel shirt and not in the gorgeous robes of the Crown Prince of Ulm with the diadem indicative of my royal rank blazing on my brow. These garments were not suitable for rough work and I had left them at my adjuster in the care of Olua. With as much of an air of dignity as I could command, I stepped forward to face the group. Suddenly I recognized the man who had stepped forward.

"Moka!" I shouted with joy. It was indeed Moka Alii, Lord Chamberlain of Kalu's court.

The old nobleman stared at me in unbelief for a moment and then a red flush stole over his haughty face. Pointedly he turned his back on me.

"Moka!" I cried again, "Don't you remember me? I am Courtney Siba Tam, your prince; Courtney Sibama, if Olua spoke the truth when he said that Kalu Sibama was no more."

Moka turned and faced me coldly, entirely ignoring my outstretched hand.

"I recognize you, Courtney," he said in a biting tone, carefully avoiding giving me any title, "to my regret, but my lips will never touch the hand of a traitor, though I be boiled in oil for my refusal!"

"Moka!" I cried in real anguish, for the coldness of the first friend I had made in Ulm cut me to the heart. "It is not true. I am no traitor to Ulm. I was delayed in my task and was on my way to Ulm with aid when I learned that it had fallen. I surrendered to the Kauans and hastened here to bring what aid and comfort I could to those of my subjects who still lived. Never have I deserted Ulm and never has the thought of her welfare been absent from my thoughts."

"Traitor! Doubly dyed traitor!" said Moka slowly and bitingly, "and now, it seems, liar to boot! Well, I know the plan with which you left Ulm. You planned to aid her enemies and to depose Kalu Sibama, your lord, and reign in his stead. Thankful I am that Kalu, who foolishly loved you, died before he knew of your treachery."

"I am no traitor, Moka," I cried, "and who says I am, lies in his throat! Hold up, old friend," I exclaimed as he sprang at me, "I am not hitting at you but at the one who told you this pack of lies. Where did you learn what you thought were my plans?"

"Your smooth tongue, which deluded Kalu Sibama, will not avail you, Courtney," he said coldly. "Cover your face in confusion and learn that your treachery was told by Lamu Siba, whom you tried to corrupt and failed."

"Lamu!" I gasped—"Did Lamu return to Ulm?"

"He is here and he has told of the plans which you broached to him to destroy Kalu and of how he fled from you when he learned of your baseness. Your treachery is proven indeed, Courtney."

"So he got back to Ulm safely," I said. Somehow I had always had an idea that he must have missed the city as I did and thought that he and Awlo were wandering somewhere in the submicroscopic world. The news that he had reached Ulm and had managed to turn my friends against me was a bitter blow for it could mean only one thing, that Awlo was dead. Had she been alive, he could never have told that tale and been believed. With a sinking heart I put my next question.

"What of Awlo?" I asked.

I reeled back as Moka struck me a blow on the mouth.

"Dog!" he cried. "The name of a Sibama of Ulm must not be uttered by the lips of a perjured traitor! To complete your confusion, I will tell you that the Sibama of Ulm is in Kaulani."

"Said she that I was a traitor?" I demanded bitterly. Moka paused.

"No," he admitted slowly, "she did not, but it is unnecessary. Lamu Siba has told enough. We men of Ulm need no word from her to damn you further."

My heart leaped with joy at the thought that Awlo was alive and in the same city with me, and while her silence was inexplicable, I knew that she must have some good reason for it. Awlo knew that I was no traitor to Ulm and I would have staked my life on her love and loyalty.

"Listen, old friend," I said to Moka, "it was never your way to condemn a man unheard in his own defense on the testimony of his enemies. You have known me as your lord and as your friend for years; have you ever known me to speak an untruth?"

"No," he admitted.

"Then listen, old friend, while I tell you the truth. Lamu Siba is the traitor, not I."

Rapidly, but in great detail, I told him all that had happened since the fatal day when I left Ulm in my adjuster with Awlo and Lamu to bring back the guns and ammunition with which I hoped to rout, if not destroy the besieging Mena. I told how Lamu had learned to operate the adjuster, how he had stolen my princess and had fled with her, leaving me desolate. I told of my struggle to get material and of the months of feverish work while I had constructed a duplicate of my machine and gone in pursuit. Last, I told of how I had landed with my guns and ammunition and had met Olua and how I had surrendered to the Kauans in order to be brought to Kaulani.

Moka's face grew graver as my story progressed. My sincerity almost convinced him, but for months he had thought me a traitor. The struggle was evident in his face. He wanted to believe and yet could not. When I had ended my tale and again held out my hand to him, he hesitated, but another of the auditors, a young officer named Hiko, who had at one time been my personal aide, had no doubts.

"My sword to your hand, Courtney Sibama!" he cried, as he dropped on one knee and pressed my hand against his forehead and then to his lips. "My life is yours to command!"

His enthusiasm carried the day and in a moment, not only Moka, but the rest of the group were on their knees professing their loyalty to me.

"Forgive me for doubting you, Courtney Sibama," cried Moka with tears in his voice, "but the words of a Siba carry weight."

"Where is my Sibimi?" I demanded.

"Alas, my lord," said Moka, "she is a prisoner in the palace of Kapioma Sibama, Lord of Kau. I have seen her twice but none of us has ever spoken to her."

"Did you not speak to her in Ulm?" I asked.

"No, my lord. She or Lamu never returned to Ulm. Four months after you left us, Ulm fell to a night assault of the Mena. Had you been there, it would never have happened, but discipline was relaxed after you left and they kept watch poorly. Besides, the Mena had never before attacked at night.

"The city was given over to slaughter, but a remnant of the royal guard gathered about the palace of the Sibama and we held them at bay for eight days. At the end of that time they fired the palace and we fought our way out hardly. Both Kalu and the Sibimi were killed and most of the guards, but a few of us held together and fought our way toward the waste places where we hoped the kahumas, who were said to rule, would either defend us or kill us with honor.

"The Mena ringed us about and mile by mile our numbers lessened. There were but a hundred and twenty left and many of them sore wounded when the pressure of the Mena suddenly ceased and we saw them flying like leaves before a gale. We heard a strange noise overhead and looked up and saw a multitude of strange birds flying over us. Some of these birds lit near us and disgorged men with many arms who took us prisoners and dragged us into the interior of the birds. We thought they were kahumas. When they were in the birds they divested themselves of all their arms but two and we prepared for death. They did not kill us but saved us alive and brought us here to Kaulani.

"We had been here about a month when we learned that an Alii of Kau had planned to rescue us. We rejoiced but his plot failed and he had to flee for his life. Two months later Lamu Siba was brought to us as a slave. He told us a tale of treachery on your part and of how he and Awlo Sibimi had fled from you but had been captured in the waste places of Kau. Him we foolishly believed, the more because Awlo Sibimi was a prisoner in the palace of Kapioma and none of us could speak with her.

"Aside from the fact that we are slaves and not free men, we have no complaint. The kahumas have treated us well and mercifully, although we are forced to labor, and dire is the punishment of one who shirks. We hope that our condition will be improved, for Kapioma means to make Awlo his Sibimi as soon as the present one is killed."

"Is killed?" I echoed.

"Yes. The kahumas have a barbarous custom in Kau. A Sibimi is chosen and in one year, unless she is with child, she is slain and a new one is chosen. The present Sibimi dies in a month. Thinking you dead, Kapioma meant to make Awlo Sibimi of Kau. Hark! Here come the others from work. Hide behind us for a moment, Courtney Sibama, until I tell them of your presence."

I knew the love of the men of Ulm for dramatic scenes and I stepped behind the ranks of my followers. The door opened and in trooped a hundred men, all attired alike, in the coarse white garb which is the Kauan mark of a slave. Moka stepped forward and held up his hand for silence.

"We harbor in our midst a traitor!" he cried dramatically. "One who is a traitor to his Sibama, a worse traitor to his Sibimi and a traitor to Ulm. What is the punishment for such a one?"

"Death!" came a cry from the men of Ulm. Lamu stepped forward and confronted Moka.

"Death is his punishment and it shall be meted out when he is known," he said. "Name this traitor."

This was the answer that Moka had hoped for. He drew himself up to his full height and pointed his finger dramatically at the prince.

"Thou art the man!" he thundered. "On your knees and beg for mercy from Courtney, Sibama of Ulm!"

Taking my cue from his words I stepped forward into full view. Lamu started and turned pale as he saw me, but an ominous growl rose from the rest.

"What means this, Moka?" demanded one of them. I recognized the man as Hama Alii, a noble of Ulm and one of the Council of Lords. He was, if my memory did not play me false, a distant cousin of Lamu's. "Courtney is a traitor, as we all well know. To him shall the sentence of death be meted out."

A murmur of assent came from the ranks of the Ulmites behind him and my handful of followers closed up behind me.

"Slay him!" cried Lamu pointing at me. The crowd surged forward.

"Hold!" I cried and they paused for a moment. "Every man is entitled to a hearing. Let me tell my tale and then let the Council of Lords judge my tale. One of royal blood may be tried only by that tribunal."

My point was well taken and it appealed to the justice of the men and a cry of assent went up. Briefly, and as eloquently as I could, I retold my story. It made an impression but there was no loyal aide to turn the tables in my favor this time and at the end of my speech there was silence for a moment.

"It is a lie!" cried Lamu suddenly. "Kill the traitor and make an end of it."

There was a murmur, half of assent and half of dissent and I played the same card again.

"How many of the Council of Lords of Ulm are here?" I asked.

"Hama Alii and I," replied Moka.

"A matter touching the royal family of Ulm can be decided only by the Council of Lords," I insisted. "Neither Lamu Siba nor I can be tried by any lesser tribunal. Let Hama and Moka decide."

There was a roar of assent to my proposition and the two nobles retired into a corner to talk the matter over. For half an hour they argued the matter back and forth. Knowing Hama's relation to Lamu, I had rather expected a deadlock, and that was what eventually happened. The two came forward and Moka, as the elder, announced their decision.

"When the Council of Lords is evenly divided, the decision rests with the Sibama," he said, "but here the Sibama is an interested party and it would not be fair to let him decide the matter, for traitor or not, Courtney is Sibama of Ulm until the Council of Lords declare the throne vacant. Both Courtney Sibama and Lamu Siba have spoken and the voice of each sounds as that of a true man in our ears. It is our decision that Courtney Sibama and Lamu Siba be each given the honors of their rank and both held blameless, until the matter can be laid before the Sibimi for decision. In the meantime, the disputants shall swear friendship to one another for the time being, and we will all live in harmony as becomes brothers in misfortune."

Lamu and I looked speculatively at one another. After all, there was nothing that we could do except agree with the decision, which was manifestly a just one. I knew that once Awlo spoke, the question would be settled and he doubtless hoped that she would get no chance to speak or else he had another idea in the back of his head. At any rate, he spoke first.

"The Prince of Ame defers to the Council," he said. "As Moka Ali has spoken, so shall it be."

"So shall it be," I echoed.

As Lamu and I approached one another for the ceremony of swearing temporary friendship, there came an interruption. The door opened and there stood Neimeha with a detachment of guards.

"Courtney Sibama," he said, "Kapioma Sibama requires your presence in his throne room."

With a shrug of my shoulders I followed him out of the slaves' quarters and to the ground floor of the palace. The building was a beautiful one, much more ornate than Kalu's palace in Ulm, but what it gained in beauty, to my mind at least, it lost in grandeur. At the door of the throne room we were challenged, but a word from Neimeha opened a way for us.

The scene was very similar to one of the dozens of Kalu's audiences I had taken part in. On all sides blazed the colors of the nobles and ladies, their flashing gems set off by the sombre black worn by the guards. The throne room was long and impressive, with a dais at the head bearing four thrones, the central two of which were occupied. Kapioma Sibama of Kau was a tall, slender man of about my age. He had a splendid breadth of forehead but his slanting eyes, like those of all the Kauans, were mercilessly cold and cruel. The first thing, however, that attracted my attention was the sadness of the face of the Sibimi who sat beside him. She was a slim young girl and despite her yellow skin, was beautiful, but the sadness of the ages was in her tragic eyes. Suddenly I remembered what Moka had told me of the customs of Kau and I realized that she saw death before her in a few short weeks. I squared my shoulders and advanced to the foot of the dais. Slave or prisoner, condemned to death, I might come from that interview, but as Sibama of Ulm I would go to it. I looked Kapioma squarely in the eye and he returned my gaze with an expressionless face.

"Courtney of Ulm," he said in a guttural voice, "Neimeha tells me that the wonders we have heard of you are true and that your subjects in Ulm looked on you as a powerful kahuma because you knew more of nature and her laws than they dreamed of. You are no barbarian of Ulm, fit only to be a slave, but a man of intelligence and learning. He tells me that you are able to navigate a flyer."

I bowed without speaking.

"I am duly sensible of the misfortunes which have thrown you from your high position, where you might with propriety have sat by my side, and it is not my desire to add to the burdens or sorrows of a man of royal rank. Since you are able to take your part in this community as an equal with my nobles, it is in my mind to create you an Alii of Kau and attach you to my court."

Again I bowed deeply in silence.

"Neimeha tells me further that you know ways of sending messages through the air from the power house to a ship many miles away."

"I do, sire, it is a relatively simple matter."

"I am glad to hear it, for I believe that the art will be of much use. To the rank of Alii of Kau I will raise you, but in return I will ask of you one small favor."

"I will be glad to put my knowledge at your service," I replied.

He frowned slightly at my answer.

"It is not that; that I took for granted. The favor I ask of you is of a different nature. You were married in Ulm to Awlo, daughter of Kalu Sibama. Since his death she is now Sibimi of Ulm. In a month or so," here he paused and shot a glance at the Sibimi, who quailed under it as though under a lash, "there will be no Sibimi in Kau and it is my intention to elevate the daughter of Kalu to that exalted rank in lieu of the throne she has lost. The favor I ask of you is that you divorce her."

"Divorce Awlo? Never!" I cried.

"You had better consider well before you decide so," he said with a frown. "As the wife of an Alii, I could not marry her without first getting rid of you. Were I to order your execution, I would be no better off, for the widow of an executed criminal could not be elevated to the rank of Sibimi. However, under the laws of Kau, a slave may not legally have a wife. Unless you consent, I will degrade you to the position of a slave, which will effectually dissolve the tie which binds her and leave her free to mount the throne by my side. It is immaterial to me, but it means much to you. You may have a day in which to decide. Either you become an Alii of Kau and divorce her, or you become a slave of Kau and I will marry her in either event."

"It doesn't take a day or a minute to decide that, Kapioma Sibama," I replied, "I will never divorce her."

He shrugged his shoulders.

"At any rate, I tried to be kind to you," he replied. "Neimeha, this man is a slave of Kau. Clothe him as such and take him to the slaves' quarters. He will work in the laboratory of the power house and show us a method of sending messages to our ships, which he boasts is so simple. If he refuses, or fails, flay him alive."

The guards seized me and half dragged and half led me from the throne room. Once outside the room, my clothing was stripped from me and the white garb of a slave thrown over my shoulders. Thus dressed, I was led back to the slaves' quarters which I had left a short time before. Moka and my other friends hastened to greet me and to express their indignation at the tale I had to tell. They applauded my action vociferously, although Lamu suggested that it might have been a good plan for me to have fallen in with Kapioma's plan and won the rank of Alii, which might have enabled me to aid all of them to escape. A withering glance from Moka stopped his mouth. After a short talk we dispersed to our beds in the dormitories attached to the central room.

I lay awake for some time making my plans. So far everything had fallen out better than I had dared to hope. Awlo was alive and well and in no immediate peril. I had a hundred loyal friends at my back and best of all, I was assigned to work in the laboratory to construct a wireless set, the very thing I needed to communicate with Olua with. I dropped to sleep with a feeling that fortune was favoring me.

When the slaves were turned out for work the next morning, a guard was waiting for me. He took me to the power plant, which was located in the grounds of the royal palace. I was taken to the laboratory and told shortly to show how I proposed to send messages over power waves. I protested that I was unfamiliar with their methods of power transmission and that I would have to familiarize myself with their methods and equipment before I could be expected to show them anything new. After a consultation, my stand was decided to be a reasonable one and I was handed over to one of the laboratory men with orders that I be taught all that could be taught about power transmission.

My guide and instructor was a young man, about my own age. Despite his slant eyes and yellow skin, he proved to me quite a likeable fellow as well as an erudite scientist. He was a son of one of the higher Alii of Kau. During the period I worked with him, we became in a measure friends and he confided to me one day that one of his great-grandmothers had been a slave brought from Ame, the second city of the empire of Ulm. This probably accounted for the fact that he showed less interest in science and more in human beings than most of his compatriots. Altogether, I found him the most human and likeable person I met among the Kauans. Only the fact that he was passionately loyal to Kapioma prevented me from approaching Waimua, which was his name, on the subject of joining forces with us. His tragic death later was a source of lasting sorrow to me.

I had little trouble following Waimua's explanations. The power for the entire empire of Kau was generated in the one building in Kaulani and was sent out broadcast for general use. There were five distinct and separate installations, each sending out one of the five wave-lengths earlier described to me by Olua. I was appalled at first by the enormous waste of energy involved in general broadcasting until I found out that only a low-power pilot wave was so sent out. The generators were so built that when a demand was received by the pilot wave, a directional wave of the proper power was automatically sent out to fill the demand. Meters registered the direction and distance from the power house of the consumption and, as a result, the location of any ship flying over the empire could be plotted to within a dozen miles on a map hung near the flying broadcasters. The smallest installation of the five was naturally the one on which the Sibama's private flyers and his fighting suits were operated.

The day passed before we were half through with the power installation but I took the time to give Waimua a rough outline of the methods of radio telegraphy. He understood the principle at once and promised to assemble everything we needed for our experiments and start the best instrument

makers in the empire making tubes according to my specifications. As soon
as the needed equipment could be got together, we would be in a position
to start our experiments. I readily located the screen in the laboratory, behind which Olua had hid his fighting suit, but naturally I made no attempt
to get possession of it and did not mention its existence to Waimua.

While I was going over the power plant, a germ of an idea came to me,
which seemed to make our escape not altogether impossible. While I had
no intention to strike before I had established communication with Olua
and given him orders as to the part he was to play in it, nevertheless, I
broached the idea to Moka in strict confidence. He promptly promised to
see that our men gathered as promptly as possible certain information
which I needed. He proposed to speak at first only to the most discreet
and trustworthy of our men and avoid giving out information until the time
came for action. As we were not interrupted that night, the remnant of the
Council of Lords decided that the moment was propitious and Lamu and I
swore a temporary oath of friendship.

The next day I finished my course of instruction and on the third day the
instrument makers presented for my approval a dozen radio tubes which
they had manufactured. Considering the fact that they had never seen a
small tube for the sending of messages, they had done a very creditable job
and I had little doubt of the success of my efforts. Waimua and I at once
started assembling a transmitter and two receivers. One of the receivers
was constructed to work only on one definite wavelength, but the other was
made adjustable, so that I could not only receive from my own transmitter
but also from Olua, if I finally established communication with him. A
week passed before I was ready to make a test.

The receivers worked all right while they were in the room with the
transmitter and on the pretext of testing them at a longer distance, I sent
Waimua fifty miles away in a military flyer. As soon as he was out of the
way, I set my transmitter to the wave-length of the receiver on the adjuster and called frantically. It seemed hours before an answer came. Olua
had diligently studied the international code since I had left him and he
had no difficulty in receiving my messages and answering them. I quickly
acquainted him with the state of affairs in Kau and told him of our plans.
He was able to make some excellent suggestions, based on his knowledge
of Kaulani, suggestions which I gladly fitted into my plans. On the off-
chance that they might be useful, I directed him to make a trip to the
larger plane in the adjuster and bring back certain supplies. I had left
quite a sum in gold in my hidden Nevada valley and I told him where to

find it. He promised faithful performance of his duties and I turned to the
wave-length on which the receiver, which Waimua was carrying, was set.

I sent out a garbled message, varying my power from time to time so
that the signals would come in strong and then fade out. I was fairly sure
that Waimua would be able to get only a few words of the message, yet he
would feel much encouraged. By means of a proposed modification, I intended to prolong the work for a few more days until we were ready to
strike for freedom. My plan worked perfectly and Waimua came back
wildly enthusiastic about the partial success we had achieved on our first
attempt. We tore down both the receivers and the transmitters and proposed rebuilding them with slight modifications, which I assured him would
make them entirely successful.

That night Moka reported that Hiko had brought in the last bit of information we had needed and there was no need to delay longer. Everyone, even Lamu, had by this time been informed of the plan and of the
part assigned to him in carrying it out.

Briefly, our plan was this. At a given time, we were to divide into two
bands. One band, under my personal leadership, was to attack the power
house and shut off all power. As soon as this was done, the remainder,
under the command of Moka, was to enter the palace and secure Awlo.
The rest of us would sally out and meet them and we would all take refuge
in the power house. We expected to capture several of the Kauan scientists
in the power plant and we would force them to modify a hundred-man
military flyer, which was always kept in a hangar on the roof of the power
house, to fly on the Sibama's private wave-length. We would disable all
generating units except the small one which sent out this power. All but a
picked detail were then to leave on this modified ship and the devoted
band who remained would try to hold the power plant until we were well
away from Kau.

The plan was a risky one but it was the best we could think of and I
resolutely refused to allow any discussion of what would happen after
those staying behind had been overpowered and our ship brought to the
ground. I had another plan, which I did not divulge, even to Moka. I
meant to head for my adjuster and arm my band. Kau had no firearms so
far as any of us had seen and before a hundred well-armed and resolute
men, the entire army of Kau would be helpless, once their fighting suits
were put out of business by the shutting off of the power which actuated
them. What we would do after our escape would depend on Awlo's wishes.
We might wipe out the Mena and refound the empire of Ulm (Ame had

not yet fallen to the Mena so far as we knew), or we might found a new empire in some remote part of our tiny world some place where neither the Mena nor the Kauans would find us.

The weakest part of our plan was the fact that we were forced to strike in broad daylight, for we were locked in at night. This could not be helped, however, and we set high noon for our attempt. We trusted to the surprise and to the fact that many of the palace attendants would be at lunch. When we left our quarters in the morning, I could not help wondering how many of my brave subjects would be alive that night.

About ten o'clock, as Waimua and I were working away at the radio transmitter, two guards appeared in the laboratory and ordered me to follow them. They refused to answer any questions, merely stating that I was wanted at once in the throne room. With a few words of instruction to Waimua, I took my place between them and walked out. As we emerged from the power house, I saw that something had gone wrong with our plans. Between rows of guards wearing fighting suits, the Ulmites were being herded to the slave's quarters. I was taken to the door of the throne room, where I found Lamu, Moka, and Hama all waiting under guard. The door opened and I was ordered to enter the presence of the Sibama. Shaking off the hands of my guards, I walked with my head up, to the foot of the dais and stared defiantly at Kapioma. He stared back at me with an expressionless face.

"I have been informed, Courtney," he said in his guttural voice, "that there is a plot on foot among the slaves from Ulm to capture the power plant and then to escape in a military flyer, with you at the controls. What have you to say?"

"Nothing, sire," I replied briefly.

"All of the details of the plot are in my hands," he went on, "and any denial would be useless. As the ringleader, your fate is naturally death. What form it will take, I have not yet decided, nor has my Council of Lords yet debated the fate of your followers."

"Of course, I realized long ago that you had decided on my death, Kapioma Sibama," I said coldly, "since only thus can you free Awlo from her bonds to me. The laws of Kau may say what they please about a slave but we were wed by the laws of Ulm when I was free and a Prince. My enslaving does not dissolve the tie which may be set aside only by the Sibama of Ulm with the consent of his Council of Lords. I would like to know how you learned of our plan."

"One of your members, whom you basely planned to leave behind through jealousy, overheard the plan and found out the details and told them," he replied.

"None were to be left," I exclaimed in surprise.

"Did you not plan to leave Lamu here?"

"We did not. He was the leader of the band who were to seize and protect the power installation by means of which we hoped to escape."

"Then Lamu lied," said Kapioma slowly. "This is not the first lie in which he has been detected. Courtney, it seems that even a Prince of Ulm may be a traitor. Bring in the slave, Lamu!"

The trembling Lamu was dragged by guards to the foot of the dais. He prostrated himself at the foot of the throne and looked abjectly upward. His subserviency disgusted me and I kicked him sharply.

"Get up and take your medicine like a man!" I said.

Kapioma smiled coldly as Lamu struggled to his feet with a black look at me.

"Lamu," he said, "you have lied once too often. The penalty for lying to the Sibama of Kau is death and that fate you have merited. The reward for treachery to your ruler in all countries is death and you have betrayed him who is your lawful Sibama, slave though he may be in Kau. Twice do you merit death and so slowly shall you die that it will seem to you that twice have you passed through the agonies of dissolution. You were planning to escape despite what you told me."

"I was not," cried Lamu. "I first learned of the plot last night through overhearing Moka and Courtney talk. I told my guards at the first opportunity."

"Bring in Moka and Hama," directed Kapioma.

The two Alii were brought in and it pleased me to see that each of them bowed with just the right amount of deference due to a throned monarch and not a speck more.

"Was the slave, Lamu, included in the plot to escape and did he know of it before last night?" demanded the Sibama.

The two nobles glanced at me for orders.

"Speak the truth!" I said.

"He was included in the plot to escape and he was told of it four nights ago, Kapioma Sibama," said Hama. Moka nodded assent.

"By the voices of your countrymen are you condemned, Lamu," said Kapioma. "His death shall be a thing to bring the sweat of terror to the brows of condemned criminals for a generation. Courtney, the laws of Kau are not inexorable. You have been the victim of one you trusted and your suffering to learn that one of your Princes is a traitor is already a heavy punishment. It may be that you may not have to die. If you will divorce Awlo as I have requested, I will submit the question to my Council of Lords with a recommendation for clemency. No, do not answer me now; I know what your answer will be before you have had time to think the matter over. Reflect on this matter. If you die, with you will die every one of your followers who were concerned in the plot. As criminals shall they die by torture. For you, I decree a soldier's death."

"Not through any regard for me, Kapioma Sibama, but because you cannot elevate the widow of one who has died as a criminal to the rank of Sibimi," I replied hotly.

"Exactly, Courtney. Your refusal to accede to my terms will accomplish nothing. You may have two days in which to make your decision. In the meanwhile, it is my pleasure that any reasonable wish of yours be granted. Have you a desire?"

"Yes," I replied with my blood boiling, "let me be the one to execute your decree of death on that rat who has been the source of all my trouble."

Kapioma smiled slightly, while Lamu shuddered.

"Gladly," said the Sibama. "It will be an amusing spectacle. I will even let you choose the manner of his death."

"I wish to kill him in fair fight."

Kapioma studied the two of us for a moment.

"So be it," he said. "Should he kill you, the question of Awlo would be settled pleasantly. If he is the victor, his life will be spared and he shall serve as a slave in Kau for the rest of his days. If you kill him, both you and your subjects will be free. You will be taken to the Kau mountains and liberated with two weeks' supply of food and water and with arms. If any of you return to Kau, you will be put to death with torture. If you win through the mountains, the Mena will kill you? What say you?"

"And Awlo?" I asked.

"In any event, Awlo remains here and becomes my Sibimi," he said sharply.

"Then I will——" I paused in thought. I had been about to declare my preference for death in Kau rather than for a separation from Awlo, but a plan occurred to me. My death in Kau would rob Awlo of her only protector and the Kau mountains were where my precious firearms were stored.

"I accept your terms, Kapioma Sibama," I said.

"Bring fighting suits!" commanded the Sibama.

A guard hastened up with two fighting suits, each equipped with eight arms.

"A scientist such as you are, Courtney, needs no instruction to use such a simple appliance," said Kapioma in a cold voice. "Since Lamu has not your knowledge, I will personally instruct him so that the fight may be more even."

I saw at once that it was his plan that Lamu should kill me and I thought regretfully of the thirty-armed suit which Olua had told me was concealed in the laboratory. However, there was no use in crying for the moon and I devoted my attention to studying the six controls with which my suit was equipped. I soon had them located.

Kapioma put in some time instructing Lamu. When he was satisfied that my adversary understood his weapons, he gave orders for us to don the suits. We did so and the guards brought in a huge dome of some transparent crystalline material which they sat down over us. I have no idea what it was made of. It looked like glass, but since it was thirty feet in diameter and ten feet high and four men carried it with ease, it must have been made of some exceedingly light material. I could hear Kapioma's voice as plainly as though the dome were not over us.

"Let no one interfere," said the Sibama. "I will count to five. When I have given the final number you may fight, but not before. Are you ready? One! Two!"

A blinding green flash came from one of the arms of Lamu's suit. My left arm fell useless, paralyzed by the deadly ray. Lamu threw back his head and raised an arm to shield his eyes from the brilliance. The ray passed from me with no further damage. I waited for the further counting of Kapioma. I was sure that he had instructed Lamu to start the battle before the final count, but I was equally sure that I would be punished if I did the same.

"Three!" came his voice after a pause. "Four!"

Lamu had recovered from the shock and with a crafty expression he was slowly bringing his green ray, which had been blazing harmlessly against the crystalline dome covering us, to bear on me. Nearer and nearer it came and still Kapioma did not give the final word. The ray touched my paralyzed arm and traveled down toward my leg.

"Five!" came Kapioma's voice at last.

My orange ray blazed forth and Lamu's green ray disappeared. I wasted a moment by turning my orange ray against my paralyzed arm and restoring it to usefulness. With it again normal, I could use two of my weapons at once.

I turned the orange ray again on Lamu and then turned on in rapid succession my red and my green. This was a fighting trick which Olua had taught me. There was a blinding flash from Lamu's suit and his green ray disappeared. One of his most powerful weapons was out of commission.

A scared look came on his face and his red ray blazed out. I was resolved to act only on the defensive until his weapons were destroyed and I turned off my orange, green and red rays and let my blue one blaze forth. Vainly Lamu strove to pierce the shield of blue light with which I covered myself. He reached toward his suit again and a white ray began to play beside the red. Olua had told me of this terrible ray, which extracted the water from any substance on which it struck and I hurriedly turned on my yellow ray to combat it. Round and round one another we circled, his rays trying vainly to find a hole in my armor of light. I strove to remember other tricks which Olua had told me of and one came to my mind. I suddenly turned off both my rays. Lamu swung the two blazing arms of his fighting suit toward my heart. I waited until the two rays overlapped one another and then turned on my green and yellow. With only one ray to guard against, it was a simple matter to keep him at bay.

I could remember no method of putting his white ray out of operation and to avoid prolonging the battle indefinitely, I turned on my green ray suddenly and directed it against his legs. Before he could switch on his orange ray to combat it, the paralyzing ray had got in its deadly effect and he fell in a heap. I hastened forward and stood over him. Olua had told me that almost any ray was deadly against the force which generated it. I seized the arm from which the white ray was blazing and slowly twisted it around. Lamu strove to fight, but a touch of my paralyzing ray made his arms as useless as were his legs. Slowly I twisted his arm until the white ray bore back against the arm from which it came. In another moment the ray ceased to glow and Lamu was shorn of his weapons.

A touch of either of my three offensive rays would have finished him, but I was not minded to kill him in that way. I bent over him and stripped his wrecked fighting suit from him. I tossed it to one side and stepped back. My orange ray glowed for an instant and Lamu rose as well and strong as he had been at the start of the battle.

"This fight is between you and me, Lamu Siba," I said slowly and menacingly. "Prepare to die at my hands."

Quickly I ripped my fighting suit from me. Lamu watched me like a cat.

Once my arms were engaged in getting out of the suit he straightened up and rushed. I stepped back and to one side and gave him an opening. His right foot flew out and caught me a violent blow in the groin. With a cry of anguish I doubled up in pain and Lamu threw himself on me, a dagger gleaming in his hand.

I had sense enough left to twist to one side and Lamu's dagger merely scored my back. The pain of his foul blow was terrible and I was un-armed, but as he closed again I wriggled out of my suit and launched my-self at his throat. His dagger flashed before my eyes but I disregarded it and closed with him. I grasped him by the throat and hurled myself to the ground, dragging him with me. I felt a burning pain in my shoulder and another in my side before my knee found his chest and I could wrench the dagger from his grasp and hurl it away. My hands closed again on his throat and I began to squeeze. His face grew purple and he looked at me appealingly. I released the pressure for a moment and put my head down.

"Mercy, Courtney Sibama," came in a coarse whisper from his lips.

"When did you show mercy?" I demanded. "Where is Awlo? Where is Kalu Sibama? Where is ravaged Ulm? Your life is trebly forfeit for your treachery and there is no mercy in my heart."

Slowly I tightened my grip on his throat. His breath came in gasps and then in a rattling wheeze. His head sank back, his eyes starting from their sockets and staring horribly. I can see those eyes yet. Still kneeling on his chest, I released my grip on his throat and seized his head and twisted it slowly around. Further and further it went until the vertebrae gave with a snap and his head fell limp. So died Lamu Siba, Prince of Ame of the Empire of Ulm at the hands of his ruler, whom he had betrayed.

I staggered to my feet and faced Kapioma.

"Your decree has been executed, oh Sibama," I cried between gasps. "When may I and my subjects depart?"

"As soon as you are recovered from your wounds and can travel, Court-ney," he said gravely. "I am disappointed at the showing that dog made, but the word of the Sibama once pledged, may not be recalled. You are only changing the quick and honorable death of a soldier for a lingering death of thirst and starvation in the mountains. You have made your choice. Remember, however, that my offer of your life is still open. Di-vorce Awlo and I give it to you freely."

I straightened up to hurl a defiance into his teeth, but I could do no more. I had lost more blood than I realized and I swayed a moment and then everything went black. I seemed to be falling through an endless distance and then I could remember nothing more.

It was four days before I recovered consciousness, but when I did, I was ready to travel. The physicians of Kau had treated me with healing rays which had healed my wounds and restored my strength. I really felt little the worse for the terrible battle I had been through. Moka wished me to rest for a few more days, but I did not dare. The date of the death of the Sibimi of Kau was only fourteen days away and unless we could return to Kau before that time, I shuddered to think of the fate of Awlo. Accordingly, I sent word to Kapioma that I held him to his promise and desired to depart at once.

Somewhere in his heart there must have been a speck of chivalry which had not been bred out, for he came to the power house in person to see our departure.

"Farewell, Courtney Sibama," he said, "for once I have released you from slavery, your royal rank returns. I am sorry that you would not accede to the very lenient terms I offered you, for I believe you would be a useful member of my court. However, I have pledged my word and you may depart. I am merely changing the form of your death. You cannot return to Kau. If you stay in the mountains, you starve, and if you go to Ulm the Mena will kill you. In any event, you will be removed from my path in a few weeks."

I humbled myself to ask one favor before I left.

"Since I am going to death, Kapioma Sibama," I said, "I ask of your mercy one thing. I wish to see Awlo before I go."

His brow darkened.

"That is impossible," he coldly. "Awlo does not know of your presence here and thinks you are dead. You soon will be and I have no wish to refresh her memory and reawaken her sorrows. It would turn her against me."

I did not trust myself to speak further but entered the waiting transport. My men followed me and in a few moments we rose rapidly into the air and headed away to the west.

"Where shall we land you, Courtney Sibama?" asked Neimeha, who was in command.

"Land us at the spot where you found me," I replied.

He shrugged his shoulders and spoke to the pilot. Two hours after leaving Kaulani, the transport dropped to a landing and we debarked. The ship hovered over us for a few minutes and then turned back toward the capital of Kau. Moka approached me as the Kauan ship disappeared.

"What are your plans, Courtney Sibama?" he asked.

"We will return to Kau and rescue our Sibimi. Thereafter we will do as circumstances direct."

"We are but a hundred and two," said Moka doubtfully, "and the army of Kau numbers thousands. Can we hope to win through to victory?"

"A hundred men properly armed can do wonders, Moka," I replied. "Have you forgotten the weapons which I went from Ulm to bring? They are hidden in these mountains. We will go to where they are and then make our plans. With them we will find an Alii of Ulm who has lived in Kau for years and knows their weapons. Do you think that the Kauan ship will return to watch our movements?"

"Since we are forbidden to return, I think it will."

"I hope so. If they do, I have an idea that may enable us to reach Kaulani without a fight. The first thing to do is to get proper arms."

My marching compass was one of the things which the Kauans had returned to me before they left us. My automatic pistols they had kept, although they were not familiar with their use. I laid off a course with the compass and, laden down with food and water, we started our journey toward the adjuster.

Moka had been right when he said that the Kauans would keep track of us. Late that afternoon, while our cavalcade was struggling wearily over the bare rocks, the transport which had brought us to the mountains sailed over us at a low elevation. The sight of our progress evidently satisfied them, for, after a careful survey of our column, they returned toward Kaulani. Night fell before we had covered more than half the distance which I calculated separated us from the adjuster, but I was confident that we were going in the right direction.

The night was bitterly cold and as we had nothing resembling blankets, all we could do was to huddle together and pass the night as best we could. The men of Ulm were unaccustomed to cold weather and they suffered horribly but none of them complained. The next morning we took up our march.

By noon I was confident that we had come far enough, yet none of the landscape was familiar. I halted the column and sent parties of scouts off in various directions. They were all ordered to reassemble at the central point before sundown.

It was a hard task to find one's way about the rugged country, even with a compass. I nearly got lost and the sun was setting when my party

returned to camp. Two of the parties were still unaccounted for. We had
no material with which to make fires and all we could do was to send up
occasional shouts to guide the stragglers. One party came in about eight
o'clock but morning dawned without trace of the other one. I was surprised
at this, for I knew of the wonderful sense of direction and location which
is the gift of all Ulmites. I made some tests and soon found that this sense
was not operative in the mountains. Why, I can't explain. It just wasn't.

I held a consultation with Hama and Moka the next morning. I was
sure that we were close to the adjuster and the ammunition and yet we had
combed the country the day before and found nothing. I had a feeling that
we were too far south and favored moving the camp, but the problem of
the lost party remained to be solved. We finally decided to leave ten men
under Hama at our first camp and move the rest some five miles north,
keeping in touch by means of messengers. At the new camp I would send
out fresh search parties. This programme we carried out, but another
two days of combing the hills failed to locate the adjuster and I began to
fear that the Kauans had found it and moved it. The fourth and fifth days
passed in similar fashion and even my staunchest supporter, Moka, began
to look dubious.

The morning of the sixth day we were about to start fresh parties out
on their interminable search when a faint shout was heard from the
south and we saw one of Hama's party approaching at top speed. As he
came nearer, it was evident that he was laboring under great excitement.

"We have found the place, Sibama!" he gasped as he came within
hearing. "Hiko's party found it the first day but the messenger they sent
fell and broke a leg. It was not until today that he crawled into our camp,
nearly dead from pain and thirst. He says that Hiko and two men stayed
there, but he does not know where it is."

The fact that the adjuster had been found near our camp was a heart-
ening thing and we swiftly broke camp and retraced our steps to join
Hama's party. We found that Hama had sent off all his men in the direction in which Hiko had left the camp and all we could do was to wait until
they found the place. We had not waited more than three hours when a
man arrived and told us that he had located it. He said that they had
found the cave and the boxes in it, but that there were no signs of Olua
or the adjuster. I started at once with a party with food and water for
Hiko's men, leaving most of the men in camp until all of Hama's men returned. They were to move camp and join me the next morning.

The report of the scout was correct. In the cave were the arm chests and the boxes of ammunition, but there was no trace of either Olua or the adjuster. I racked my brains as to what could have happened. The only explanation which seemed logical was that when he had returned to the larger plane at my orders, his adjuster got moved. In such a case he might easily have come down miles away and was earnestly seeking us. The loss of the adjuster was a blow, but we still had our arms and ammunition and everything was not lost.

It was a short task to break open the rifle chests and the ammunition boxes and I felt better when I saw my tiny force armed with modern rifles and pistols, even though none of them had the slightest idea of their use and I had grave doubts of their value against the fighting suits of the Kauans. The fact that they did not know how to use the weapons did not worry me especially, for I knew that I had eight days before the Sibimi of Kau was doomed to die and I had a plan which, if successful, would enable us to travel over the two hundred miles which separated us from Kaulani in a short time. The Kauan transport had flown over us each afternoon, evidently checking our movements and my plan was a no less daring one than attempting its capture. I blessed the fact that I had not completed my radiotelegraphic apparatus before I left the city.

My first task was to teach my men the use of the pistols and rifles. I had loaded a hundred rifles and thirty thousand rounds of ammunition on the adjuster together with a hundred pistols and ten thousand rounds of pistol ammunition. I felt that I could safely expend one hundred rounds of rifle ammunition per man and half that amount of pistol ammunition on target practise. We improvised a range and posted guards to warn us of the approach of Kauan ships. The Ulmites took to the guns as ducks take to water. In five days I felt my fire discipline was adequate and I anxiously awaited the arrival of the ship I had planned to capture.

To my horror, the ship did not appear on that day, nor the next day, nor yet on the next. Our food and water were about exhausted, for we had been allowed only a fourteen-day supply. Apparently the Kauans knew that we could not return to their country and had decided that we were afraid to face the Mena and thought it useless to keep further track of us. As the sun went down on the fourteenth day after we had left Kaulani, I was in black despair. That was the day set for the execution of the Sibimi of Kau and the thought of my princess at the mercy of Kapioma nearly drove me insane.

We could not possibly cover the two hundred miles separating us from Kaulani in less than five days of forced marching, even were we adequately supplied with food and water and unopposed. I had based all my plans on the capture of a Kauan ship. The morning of the fifteenth day found us with no water and almost no food and despair settled over the camp. We felt the urge to be moving but there was no place where we could go and nothing that we could do. We went through some rifle drill in the morning in a perfunctory manner and with the feeling that it was merely a waste of time.

In an endeavor to keep my men from brooding, I took them out on the improvised range again in the afternoon, but there was no enthusiasm. We were all suffering badly from thirst. I was about to order them back to camp when a shout from one of the lookouts whom we had posted as a routine matter, brought us to our feet. The lookout was shouting and pointing to the east. In the sudden silence which fell, I could feel rather than hear, the distant hum of propellers. Our plans had been made long ago and my men rapidly took the ambush formation I had laid out, while others, as the Kauans appeared, started a dropping fire at the distant targets.

I had counted on the curiosity of the Kauans to bring them to the ground to see what we were doing, nor was I disappointed. The ship hovered over our range for fifteen agonizing minutes before it swooped to a landing, a hundred yards from our firing point. A detachment of Kauans, wearing six-armed fighting suits, debarked and approached the firing line. I was hidden behind a rock perhaps fifty yards from the ship. The angle at which the ship landed was such that I could not see the control board through the open door, a vital necessity, if we were to capture the ship. I waited until the Kauans had passed me and blew my whistle.

A burst of fire came from the line and the Kauans staggered back under the impact of the heavy bullets at short range. The fighting suits held and none of them were injured. Green and red rays shot out from the arms of the fighting suits. Half a dozen of my men dropped helpless and the Kauans advanced slowly in a line. This was the moment for which I had been waiting. Holding my fire at ready, I raced across the ground behind the fighters. The angle at which I ran brought the control panel into view through the open door. I dropped prone and cuddled my rifle to my cheek. I had been nervous, but when the moment came to fire, I was as steady as a rock. I picked out the switch which controlled the current which fed the fighting suits. The switch sat for a moment on top of my front sight as I slowly squeezed my trigger. With a crash the rifle went off. In an instant the rays died out in midair, and with a cheer my men leaped to their feet. A volley rang out and the ground was sprinkled with dead and dying Kauans. I had effectually disabled every fighting suit in the ship.

The pilot of the ship was not napping. My men raced toward the ship, but when the nearest was still fifty yards away, the central propeller began to whir and the ship moved forward. Hiko was the nearest and he almost reached it when a blinding white flash came from its side and he dropped in his tracks. The ship moved forward with rapidly gathering momentum.

My men raced after it, but I knew the use of a rifle better than they did. I rammed a fresh shell into my piece and took careful aim. As my shot rang out, the central propeller slowed down for a moment and I hastily reloaded my gun. My second shot went wild, but the third scored a bull's-eye and the propeller slowed visibly and ran out of true. A fourth shot, the last in my magazine, stopped it entirely and the ship, with only the two wing propellers turning, sank toward the ground.

"After it!" I shouted, and my men toiled valiantly toward the dropping ship. I did not dare to risk a shot at a wing propeller lest the ship crash so badly that we would be unable to repair it. The ship touched the ground and came to a standstill. My men rushed forward with a shout of triumph. They had almost reached it when another blinding crash came from the side and two of the Ulmites crumpled in their tracks.

It was apparent that the Kauans possessed other means of offense than their fighting suits, but they seemed to be effective only at short range. I called my men back and a volley from our rifles riddled the transport. A second and third volley were poured into the cabin for safety's sake before we cautiously approached. No flash greeted us and we opened the doors to find the interior of the cabin a shambles.

The soldiers removed the dead bodies while I inspected the ship. Aside from my first shot, not a one had struck the control panel, but the central propeller was wrecked. A cursory inspection showed me that the switch which controlled the fighting suits was hopelessly wrecked, but as my men did not know how to use those terrible weapons, it was a matter of small moment. I knew that every Kauan ship carried a set of spare propellers and I soon located them and set some of my men at work removing the damaged one. The Ulmites were about as clumsy with tools as it is possible to imagine and in the end I had to do most of the work myself. The result was that the sun had nearly set before I tested the new propeller with the control panel and found that it had been properly installed. Our party embarked and I took my place at the controls. A hundred-man transport was not built for one man to fly and I had my troubles. How I cursed the luck which had made Olua miss the place when he returned to Kau in the adjuster. I would have given a great deal to have had him at my side. However, what must be done can be done and I got the ship into the air and headed for Kaulani.

For half an hour we made our way east without incident. A shout from the forward lookout apprised us of danger and Moka hastened to his side. He glanced through the telescope and informed me that three Kauan warships were approaching at high speed. I dared not leave the controls for an instant, so I hastily gave him directions for the fight which I felt was approaching and I drove forward.

The leading Kauan ship approached to within fifty yards and a string of illuminated signals broke out above her wings. I had no idea what they meant. The ship passed by, swung around in a circle and flew parallel to us about a hundred yards away with the strange signals flying. I gave the word to Moka.

A burst of rifle fire came from our ports and I had the satisfaction of seeing the Kauan ship reel wildly for a moment and then plunge headlong toward the ground. The other ships had not been fired on and they approached rapidly, one on either side. As the first one swept past us there was a blinding flash of purple light from her side. I was conscious of a feeling as though I had been struck a heavy blow, but they had miscalculated the range. While our ship reeled in the air, she righted herself and went on. The fire of our riflemen was deadly and the second ship plunged to the ground after the first.

The third ship had learned caution. It swung past us at a much greater range. When it was opposite us, a tiny spot of intense light shone for an instant and every switch on our power panel flew open. Our ship reeled and started to fall, but I dropped the flying controls and rushed to the panel. With both hands I closed the switches and then grasped the controls again and tried to right the ship. I had barely succeeded when the spot of light shone again and I had to repeat the task.

"Fire at them, Moka!" I cried. "Never mind the range!"

At my words, the burst of fire came from our ship but again the light glowed, this time before I had the ship under control. We turned nose down and fell rapidly. Apparently satisfied that they had put us out of commission, the Kauan ship turned her tail to us and sped away in the gathering darkness. I closed the switches and with all three propellers whirling at top speed, I strove desperately to right the ship. Nearer and nearer we came to the ground, but I wrenched at the controls with all my strength. Just before we struck I felt the craft respond to my efforts and slowly start to gain altitude. A dropping fire had been kept up at the flying Kauan and just as we started to climb, a shout of joy from Moka, who was at the telescope, told us that it was in trouble. At our best speed we drove it and soon it was again visible, flying slowly and in evident distress. A few well-directed shots ended the fight. We left it in ruins and resumed our course for Kaulani. Again I thanked my lucky stars that Kau did not have wireless communication.

Darkness came on rapidly, but I held my course by compass and in less than an hour the lights of Kaulani loomed before us. With all my lights blazing I headed boldly for the power house and landed on the roof. A detachment of the guard came to meet us and we opened the door and emerged. Ten of my men had donned the useless fighting suits of the dead Kauans and they led the way with me in their midst and the rest of the Ulmites trooped along after as though they were prisoners.

"What means this, Homena?" demanded the officer who had approached us.

These were the last words he spoke, for Moka had him by the throat before he could utter another. Before the menace of the lifted arms of the fighting suits, the unarmed Kauan guards surrendered and were taken into the flyer and bound and gagged. The ten men equipped with fighting suits, with me again an apparent prisoner in their midst, trooped down the stairs to the laboratory. We paused outside and I heard the buzz of a wireless transmitter. Waimua was apparently at work.

I motioned my men aside and softly opened the door. Waimua was alone in the laboratory and he looked up with a smile when I entered.

"Ah, Courtney," he said, "you are just in time. I have been hearing some signals on my receiver—"

He broke off as I covered him with my pistol.

"I want to save your life, Waimua," I said, "for you were kind to me, but to do so you must surrender to me. I am in control of the power house and my men are outside. If you make a sound, I will kill you where you stand."

"What do you mean?" he asked in amazement.

"Exactly what I say. We have returned from the Kau mountains to rescue our Sibimi and we will brook no interference. Raise your hands in token of surrender or I'll shoot."

Slowly he raised his hands as I had ordered. I turned to call my men, and he sprang. Not at me, but toward a button which was on his laboratory table. I liked Waimua, but it was his life or mine and with mine, Awlo's.

My pistol spat out a message of death and the luckless scientist fell in a heap. At the sound of my weapon, my men burst in. We barred the door and waited breathlessly. Not a sound came from outside. Apparently the Kauans were enough accustomed to strange sounds from the laboratory to remain unalarmed at my shot.

Satisfied that we would not be interrupted, I took an ordinary six-armed fighting suit from the wall and donned it. I measured a distance of fourteen inches from the top of the huge testing screen, which covered one entire end of the laboratory and eleven inches from the left edge. I marked the place and stepped back. I pointed my red ray at the intersection of the two lines I had drawn and left it on full force for eight seconds. I shut it off and supplied the orange ray for twelve seconds. As I shut the orange ray off, a section of the screen opened slowly forward and there, in a recess cut behind the screen, lay the fighting suit of which Olua had told me. I drew it out and examined it.

The suit weighed less than twenty pounds, despite its thirty arms. I took off the six-armed suit which I was wearing and donned the new garment. It fit me like a glove and was not much more uncomfortable than an ordinary suit of clothes.

Olua had explained the suit to me and I found detailed instructions with it. I stepped back and spent several minutes in practising the use of the various controls against the protective screen. I did not have time to try all of them and no time to learn which control actuated which weapons, but I did locate the master control, which threw on all of the protective rays at once. Satisfied that I had learned enough, I led the way out of the laboratory.

For some unknown reason, we passed through the building and into the grounds without a challenge, although the sight of a detachment of eleven men in fighting suits in the Sibama's palace ground was enough to attract attention. We stole quietly toward the royal palace until we were under the south wing, where we knew Awlo to be confined. Moka pointed out her window to me and I gave my rifle to him and grasped a creeper which clothed the wall. It was a hard climb and I was tempted several times to return to the ground and take off the cumbersome fighting suit which I wore, but better judgment prevailed and I struggled on. At last I climbed to a point where I could look into her room. It was apparently empty and I inserted the point of my dagger and pried the window open and stepped into the room.

I found myself in a luxuriously furnished apartment, but a hasty search through the rooms proved them to be as empty as the grave. My heart fell, for I feared that Awlo had already been dragged to Kapioma's chambers. I tried the doors leading from the rooms and one of them opened at my touch. I found myself in a deserted corridor and I stole softly along it. I had almost reached an intersecting way when a slight noise behind me made me swing around. A hidden panel in the wall I had just passed was slowly opening and I stepped beside it. A Kauan Alii made his appearance and turned toward me. As he saw me, he opened his mouth to shout, but my green ray blazed forth for an instant and he stopped petrified. He had done me no harm and with my orange ray I removed the paralysis from his brain. His tongue I left helpless and before I left him I treated both his legs with a dose from my paralyzing ray. I left him helpless and went on.

I found myself in a secret passage, dimly lighted, and I stole along it for a few yards and found it ended in a stairway. I debated for a moment as to what course to pursue and then stole back to the panel. It was closed and I could not find the spring or lever which operated it. It would have been an easy matter to have burnt my way through with my heat ray, but I did not care to start a possible fire in the palace. I thought of restoring to speech the Alii who lay helpless before me, but knowing the Kauans as I did, I felt certain that his first action would be to give the alarm. Despite their cruelty and treachery, they were intensely loyal to their Sibama.

There was only one alternative. With a prayer in my heart, I returned to the stairway and proceeded down it. I went down a long flight and paused on a landing place where I could hear a murmur of voices. I touched the wall before me and found that it was no wall but a hanging. Cautiously I cut a slit with my dagger and peered through.

I was looking into the throne room from a point behind and slightly to one side of the two central thrones. The room was empty save for a small group which stood before the throne. I didn't stop to count them, for my eyes were focused on one of them and my heart gave a bound which threatened to burst my ribs. The central figure was my adored princess, Awlo of Ulm. I could hear a voice speaking from the throne which was concealed from my gaze and I recognized it as Kapioma's.

"The Sibimi's throne of Kau is empty," he said in a voice which sounded as though he were repeating an argument for the hundredth time, "and I offer you the honor of filling it. I could take you without this formality, but such is not my wish. Your blood is royal and your children would be worthy of the throne of Kau, which they would occupy some day. Will you bid me lay aside the panoply of war and don the robes of peace that I may wed you honorably?"

Awlo threw back her proud head.

"Never!" she cried. "My lord, Courtney Sibama, lives and will rescue me. I could not be your Sibimi if I wished and would not if I could."

"I tell you that Courtney is dead," protested Kapioma.

"Not until I see his corpse will I believe that and when I do, my life will end as well," she said haughtily. "Beware what you do, Kapioma Sibama, the arm of my lord is long and he knows how to avenge any indignity to which I am subjected."

"Enough of this!" cried Kapioma angrily. "I am offering you no indignity but honorable marriage and the rank of Sibimi of the greatest empire in the world. If you will not wed me willingly, you will by force. Wedlock is essential that your children may be lawfully called to the throne of Kau. Where is the Mayor of the Palace?"

A gorgeously dressed functionary stepped forward.

"You shall wed us, Wiki," said Kapioma, "and as I have won her by conquest, I will be wed in the panoply of war."

He stepped down from the dais into the range of my vision. Had it not been for his voice, I would not have known him, for he wore a fighting suit from which fully forty arms protruded. The weight must have been great for he moved slowly and as if with an effort. As he approached, the Mayor of the Palace stepped forward toward Awlo, but recoiled as though she had been a deadly snake. In her hand gleamed a jeweled dagger.

"One step nearer and I will sheath this weapon in my heart!" she cried.

The Mayor stopped but Awlo could not fight alone the weapons of Kau. A green flash came momentarily from Kapioma's suit and the dagger dropped from her paralyzed arm. She turned to run but another flash, this time of a paler green, filled the room for an instant and she stopped in her tracks. Kapioma's guttural laugh rang out as he advanced to where she stood motionless. He took her hand in his and kissed it and then placed it for a moment on top of his head. He held out his hand and the Mayor of the Palace took it respectfully and raised it toward Awlo's lips. A sharp report rang out and the Mayor staggered and fell headlong. Unfamiliar as I was with Olua's fighting suit, I preferred to use the weapon I knew. I have mentioned before that I am a good shot, especially at short range.

A sweep of my dagger opened a way for me through the tapestry and I stepped out into view. The time for ordinary weapons had passed and

I dropped both pistol and dagger and placed my hands on the control buttons of my fighting suit. I swung the deadly offensive arms toward Kapioma and prepared to launch my deadly assortment of rays at him. The guards, armed with spears, were approaching from all sides.

"One step nearer and your Sibama dies!" I shouted.

The Sibama stared at me for a moment and a look of wonder came into his eyes.

"Courtney Sibama!" he cried.

I bowed my head in acknowledgement but I did not take my eyes off him. It was well that I did not. Slowly his hands sought the control buttons of his massive fighting suit.

"Stop that!" I warned sharply. "If you try to use a weapon you are a dead man."

He dropped his hand and stared fixedly at me. The situation was a stalemate. Kapioma did not dare to move and I could not pick the helpless Awlo up and leave with her. I thought of trying a blast of one of my rays at Kapioma but I was not sure just which ones his fighting suit would stop instantly. Besides, if I opened hostilities, Awlo might be killed in the blasts of rays which would fill the throne room. For a full minute we stared at one another and then Kapioma spoke.

"Courtney Sibama," he said slowly, "one of us will never leave this room alive. You are wearing a fighting suit of a type I do not recognize. I wear the most powerful suit in Kau. Which of the two will win in a conflict, neither of us knows. If we fight in the open, no one can prophesy what the result to all in this room will be."

He paused and I nodded assent to his word but did not relax my vigilance.

"We both desire the same thing—the life and person of Awlo of Ulm," he went on, "and one of us will win it. Let her be won in fair fight and to the victor she shall belong."

"What do you mean?" I asked.

"Let a fighting dome be brought and placed over us. When the signal is given, we will prove which of our fighting suits is the most powerful. To the survivor shall belong the princess."

"If I win, have I the promise that Awlo and I can leave Kau with our subjects without hindrance?" I demanded.

"You may, without hindrance from me. Further than that I cannot promise. The word of a dead Sibama does not bind his successor. However, if you win, you should be able to fight your way out of the kingdom with fighting suits."

I hesitated for a minute. If I fought him and lost, my princess was doomed. If I won, all I could hope for was the chance to battle my way out with her in my arms. If, on the other hand, I refused his terms, she might easily be sacrificed during the battle in the open, which would ensue. I quickly made up my mind.

"Bring your fighting dome," I cried.

Guards hastened out to get it. Still keeping my hands on the control buttons of my suit, I walked down the steps of the dais and took my place facing Kapioma. The dome was brought in and placed over us.

"Take your hands from your controls, Courtney Sibama," said Kapioma, "in order that we may start equally." ·

I dropped my hands to my side. The Sibama turned to the ring of spectators.

"Noma," he said to an Alii who stood there, "take a spear from a guard and drop it. When that spear strikes the ground, the battle will commence."

The Alii took a spear and poised it. He stood in such a position that each of us could see him equally well. He poised the spear above his head for an instant and then let it fall.

The fractions of a second that passed before that spear reached the floor seemed like days and weeks. It seemed to move with infinitesimal slowness. I stole a glance around and the scene burned itself on my brain. Kapioma stood a few feet from me with a confident smile on his yellow face, his slant black eyes gleaming fiercely. All about us stood the Alii and guards of Kau, their yellow faces alight with excitement. Like a white flower stood out the form of my beloved princess, rigid in the grasp of the rays which Kapioma had poured out on her. I looked back and saw that the spear had almost reached the floor. Another glance at Kapioma showed that he had not moved but stood with muscles tense, waiting for the signal. At least, he was a fair fighter.

The spear struck the floor and my hands flew to the control buttons of my suit. I tugged the master button of the defensive weapons in the nick of time for the red and green rays flashed out from half a dozen of the arms of Kapioma's suits. They were absorbed harmlessly in the refulgence with which I was bathed. He stepped back a moment and shifted his hands. His first attack with his simpler weapons had failed and he was prepared to use weapons which were individual to his suit.

I remembered what Olua had told me and shut off my general protective ray. I hastily tugged at my fifth, sixteenth and seventeenth buttons. A dazzling kaleidoscope of colors surrounded me and I heard a report from Kapioma's suit. His simple paralyzing and heat rays had been rendered useless.

His hand found the buttons he wished and a fresh menace threatened me. From him came a cloud of purple gas which rolled rapidly toward me. I knew the weapon to use against that and I tugged at my eleventh button. The cloud of gas was drawn rapidly into one of the arms of my suit. I pressed my twelfth button and a cloud of yellow vapor rolled toward him. As his hands sought his defensive weapons, I tugged my ninth button and the gas dissolved into a blinding flash which rushed toward him. It struck him full on the chest and drove him back with the violence of the shock. I followed up my advantage with my violet ray, but he had recovered from the momentary effects of the surprise he had received and shot out a furry spiral of red flame, which twisted in and out before him and rendered the purple ray helpless.

From another arm came alternate flashes of red and white. I pulled on a defensive weapon but it had no effect. Through my protective screens the deadly ray was eating its way. I felt as though my veins were filled with liquid fire. Frantically I tugged at button after button. Cloud of deadly gases and vivid rays of various sorts leaped from the arms of my suit but Kapioma met each attack with a weapon of his own and rendered my efforts futile. And still that deadly red and white ate into my screen. It was a matter of seconds only before the end would come.

In desperation I used my final weapon. Olua had cautioned me not to use it, except as a last resort. With a sob I tugged at my thirtieth button. As I did so, a blinding flash came from one of the arms of my suit. It struck Kapioma and coiled itself around him. Fighting against the strange power at every step, he was dragged relentlessly toward me. The red and white still glowed and my body seemed parched and dried up but I could not think of that. In another moment he would be within reach.

Despite his struggles, he was drawn closer until I could reach him with my hands. I understood why Olua had warned me against this weapon for my strength was rapidly oozing away. It took a tremendous toll of the user. Kapioma reached for other buttons but he was unable to use them. This thirtieth weapon of Olua's was nothing less than an electrical harnessing of the will of the user and while Kapioma was in its grasp, his will was a slave to mine. As I realized the nature of the strange force I was wielding, I concentrated on what I wished him to do. Slowly and reluctantly his hand sought his controls. He tugged at one and the deadly red and white which was eating into my very brain died out. I was temporarily safe.

I threw all the force of my will into the struggle and the force I exerted was magnified a thousand times by the instrument which Olua's genius had evolved. Kapioma tugged button after button, until not a ray gleamed from his suit and not a single deadly gas even oozed from it. With almost my last effort I pulled my second button and bathed him for an instant in the common green paralyzing ray carried by even the simplest fighting suits. He wavered a moment and then dropped in a heap. I shut off the terrible weapon with which I had conquered and swayed in weakness for a moment.

I thought I was going to fall, but I didn't. My eyes caught a glimpse of Awlo and it acted like a dash of cold water in my face. I braced myself up and faced the spectators.

"Remove the fighting dome!" I cried, "and make way for Courtney, Sibama of Ulm!"

The dome was hastily lifted from me. As I approached Awlo, there was a disturbance at the door. I looked up and a more welcome sight never met my eyes. In the doorway stood Moka with a half dozen Ulmites with rifles in their hands ranged behind him. Four figures in six-armed fighting suits stood beside him.

"Way!" I cried imperiously, "Way for the men of Ulm! Way ere I blast a path through your living bodies!"

There was a general scurry at my words and the space between Moka and me opened. Down the path came my loyal Ulmites. At my orders two of them handed their rifles to comrades and tenderly picked up the form of my beloved princess. Down through the ranks of the scowling Kauans we passed until the door of the palace opened before us. Guards stepped forward to bar our way, long black tubes in their hands. I hesitated only a moment. The poor fellows wore no fighting suits and it was almost murder but I did not dare to hesitate. I tugged my fourteenth button and a flash of violet flame leaped in front of me. The guards went down like tenpins, their black tubes exploding with brilliant flashes of light. As we emerged from the doorway, a distant crackle of rifle fire told us that Hama's party had left the roof and were fighting their way down through the power house. In a compact group we raced across the lawn toward the building.

We had covered about half the distance before we were opposed. I heard a shout behind us and turned and looked. Emerging from the trees at one side were a group of figures in fighting suits. We were a little closer

to the power house than they were, but we were handicapped by our
rifles and we had to carry Awlo. It looked as though we would arrive at
the door at about the same moment. My decision was made in an instant.
Warning Moka to hold straight for the door, I turned at an angle and
raced to meet them.

As I approached the newcomers stopped and rays began to flash from
the arms of their fighting suits. None of the suits carried more than ten
arms, so I pulled on my general protective rays and charged them. They
strove to run but they were too late. Again my fourteenth button came
into play and they toppled in heaps. I glanced over my shoulder and saw
that Moka's party had gained the doorway.

I bounded through the door and Hama slammed it shut behind me. I
was positive that there were protective rays of some sort that could be
brought into action but I did not dare to look for them. Hama told me
that the power house was clear of Kauans except for one room in which
a few were barricaded. I knew that they would soon emerge wearing
fighting suits and that more men from the palace would be using more
potent weapons against us in a few minutes. With Hama and Moka at
my back, I ran for the central control room. I reached it just in time.

My hand was on the switch controlling the fighting suit power when a
door opened and a dozen figures wearing many-armed suits entered. I let
them approach a few feet and pulled the switch just as their hands were
seeking the control buttons. When I pulled that switch every fighting suit
and every weapon of war in the empire of Kau became useless. It took
me only a few seconds to pull the other four controlling switches and
everything which depended on power in the empire was useless. The science
of our enemies was at an end and the battle, if battle there was, would be
fought out hand to hand in the same manner as the old battles with the
Mena. The only power left in the land was a tiny auxiliary generator
which fed the lights in the power house itself. As we saw in the morning,
my action in pulling the switches came none too soon. Two huge Kauan
warships had crashed in ruins not a hundred yards from the building. Had
I been a little slower, they would have landed on the roof and we would
have been caught between two fires.

I left Awlo in the laboratory and hastened out to look after our defense.
Although crippled by the loss of power, the Kauans were not altogether
helpless. They were present in tremendous numbers and they still had a
quantity of the black tubes which I had noticed in the hands of the
guards at the palace gates. These tubes were not dependent on power
for their discharge, although once fired, they could not be reloaded while

the generators were shut down. They carried a large charge of static electricity and at short range they were very deadly.

Armed with the tubes and with spears, the Kauans made a determined assault on our fortress. The attack was doomed to failure from the first. The flash tubes were not dangerous at ranges of over fifty yards and we mowed down the attackers with our deadly rifle fire. The attack waned after a few minutes and I returned to the laboratory.

Awlo lay on a table, cold and rigid. There was a complete absence of respiration and I could not detect the slightest flicker of a pulse. I would have unhesitatingly pronounced her dead, had I not seen what had happened to her. I knew that Kapioma would never have fought for the possession of a dead body and I was confident that there was some method of reviving her, could I only find it. I ordered Moka to turn on the switch which controlled the fighting suit I had worn. He did so and I bathed her in a refulgence of the orange anti-paralysis ray. It had not the slightest effect. For an hour I experimented with various rays and combinations of them without result. I did not dare to use most of the weapons in Olua's fighting suit for I was not aware of all of their properties and I might easily do more harm than good.

As I studied her prostrate figure, I was alarmed by a crash at the main door of the house. I started down to investigate, but a messenger from Hama met me before I got there.

"A Kauan!" the man gasped, "a Kauan in a fighting suit has broken in the door and has killed a dozen of our men!"

The explanation rushed to my mind. When I had connected up the generator which had actuated my fighting suit, I had also supplied power to Kapioma's, which worked on the same wave-length. I hurried to the control room and pulled off the switch. A crackle of rifle fire from below told me that my men were engaged. I rushed down the steps to take charge, but I was no longer needed. When the fighting suit was rendered helpless, our rifles came into their own and they made short work of the Kauans, who had followed their leader in through the wrecked door.

In an hour the door was repaired and we were again in a position to bid defiance to the armies of Kau, but I learned with regret that the fleeing Kauans had carried off the body of their leader and so, of course, his fighting suit. If we had it, two of us could have walked unopposed throughout Kaulani. As it was, I did not dare to again turn on any of the generators which would arm our enemies. Since I had no idea of what to do for Awlo, even had I had plenty of power, it did not seem to matter much.

In point of fact, our situation had many elements devoid of cheer in it.

To be sure we were comparatively safe in the power house, but we had no way of getting out. We had a hundred-man flyer at our service, but if we turned on power to run it, we mobilized every warship in Kau. We had plenty of powerful fighting suits, but there were more powerful ones in the hands of some of the Alii of Kau and arming our suits meant arming theirs. As far as I could figure out, in capturing the power house, I had put myself in the classic position of the man who had caught the bear by the tail; I needed a lot of help to hang on and a darned sight more help to let go.

I went back to the laboratory and studied the rigid figure of Awlo, but no new suggestion came to me and I lay down for a few minutes of rest, hoping that time would solve the problem. In any event, I felt sure that we could hold the power house indefinitely. In thinking this, however, I had underestimated the power and resourcefulness of the Alii of Kau, as the morning showed.

All night we heard the sounds of men working and saw faint lights flickering back and forth across the lawn. We tried them with a shot occasionally but we had no ammunition to waste and I ordered the men to hold their fire. When day broke, we saw on the lawn between the palace and the powerhouse, an enormous machine made of metal. As we watched, it moved slowly forward toward the power house. I had forgotten that the Alii and even the soldiers and commoners of Kau were familiar with electricity in all of its forms. The obvious thing had occurred to them. Since their regular source of power had been shut off, they had collected or constructed batteries and were driving this tank, for that is what it looked like, toward us with direct current. From the moving mass of metal, heavy cables trailed back toward the palace.

I took a rifle and fired at that cable, directing my best shots to do the same. Despite the fire we poured in, the machine continued to advance until it was only a few yards from the building. From its side a bolt of what looked like lightning came and the power house door was again splintered and driven from its hinges. The machine moved forward for a few feet and stopped. No fresh bolts came from it and it was apparently helpless. At last a lucky shot had severed their connection with the source of power. We were temporarily saved.

As no fresh attack seemed imminent, I left Moka in charge of the defense and returned to the laboratory. It had occurred to me that direct current might have some effect on Awlo.

As I entered the laboratory, a familiar sound struck my ear. I paused and looked around but I could not locate the source. It was an intermittent buzzing and crackling and as I listened, it began to form itself into letters and words in my mind. "——·—, —— —— ···—— ·—·, —— ——·. ·—·—·—," I heard and then "——·—, —— —— ···—— ·—·, ·—··—· —— ··· ·—·—

——·—" "COURTNEY, COURTNEY SIBAMA." There was only one person in the world who would be calling me by wireless and calling me by that title. I jumped for the radio set which had stood unheeded on the laboratory table since Waimua's death. As I clamped the headphones on my ear, the message came through plainly and distinctly. It was a matter of seconds only until I had the transmitter hooked up and ready to send. Luckily both sender and receiver drew their power from the auxiliary generator which normally supplied only the lights in the power house. I pounded my key rapidly.

"Olua," I called. "Olua, can you hear me?"

"Yes, Courtney Sibama," came the reply.

"Where are you?" I tapped out.

"At the cave, where we parted. The arms are gone. Did you return for them or did the Kauans get them?"

"I have the arms here."

"Where is here?"

"At the power house in Kaulani. I'll tell you the situation."

"All right, but send a little slower."

As briefly as possible I told him the events which had happened and the situation in which we were. I told him of the deadlock and that we were afraid to turn on any power. Last I told him of the attack launched by battery driven appliances that morning.

"How long can you hold out?" he asked.

As the message came in, a crash from below, followed by a burst of rifle fire, told me that a fresh attack had been launched. I told Olua of this fact.

"Battery apparatus won't do much harm," he answered. "If you can hold out for a few hours, I'll be with you and help you."

"How can you get here?" I asked, "there is no power being broadcast."

"I'll get there," he replied. "Look for me in three hours or less."

"Wait," I demanded. "I want one bit of information."

In a few words I described the condition of Awlo.

"Was it a light green ray with yellow flecks?" he asked.

"Yes."

"Use button twenty-eight on my suit for two seconds. Goodbye. I'll be with you soon."

Without regard to the risk I was running, I dashed to the control room and threw on the switch which actuated Olua's fighting suit. Back in the laboratory, I donned the garment and with trembling hands pulled button twenty-eight. Nothing happened for two seconds and then Awlo sat up. With a shout of joy I released the button and started for her. She gave a cry of terror and strove to run. I stopped aghast at her reception of me, until I remembered the fighting suit which I wore. She took me for a Kauan.

"Awlo!" I cried as I threw back my helmet. "It is Courtney, your Courtney! Don't you know me?"

She looked at me in wonder and then with a sob of utter thankfulness threw herself into my arms. As I clasped her, there came an interruption. Moka dashed into the room.

"Sibama!" he cried. "Come quickly or we are lost. The Kauans are winning their way in."

So excited was he that he failed to notice Awlo. As I released her, his jaw dropped and he fell on one knee.

"Sibimi!" he cried and the worship in his voice made me realize anew the depth of affection which these tiny men had for their rulers. I gave him no further time.

"Come, Moka," I cried, as I pulled my helmet back into place, "we must go to the rescue."

I led the way down the stairs to the doorway. A number of Kauans equipped with fighting suits from which long leads trailed back to the palace, had crossed the lawn and forced their way through the shattered door. Bullets had no effect on them and my men went down like tenpins before the deadly rays which poured from them. Their feeble fighting suits, however, were no match for the one I wore and in three minutes after I arrived, not a live Kauan remained in the powerhouse. My violet ray disposed of them. As the last one fell, a figure wearing Kapioma's forty-armed suit came from the palace and lumbered slowly across the lawn. Before he was close enough to do any damage I had the power shut off and he fell before a well aimed bullet from Hama's rifle. The danger was again temporarily averted and I turned my attention to my men. The improvised suits did not have enough power to kill, or else it was not a killing ray that was used, for they were merely stunned and a few minutes of care brought them to, as well as ever.

Leaving Moka in command, I hurried back to the laboratory. Awlo threw herself into my arms again as I entered. I embraced her fervently and then turned to the key of my wireless. Not an answering signal could I get. I gave up at last and devoted my attention to Awlo. Her story was soon told.

The adjuster must have been moved slightly without our knowledge when Lamu had stolen it and fled with her, for they landed in Kau, not far from Kaulani. Lamu had attempted to force his attentions on her and had threatened her with death if she did not substantiate his story of my treachery. When I heard this, I gritted my teeth and wished that I had killed Lamu more slowly and painfully.

They attempted to make their way to Ulm but they were seen and taken prisoners. They were taken to Halekala, one of the cities of Kau, several hundred miles from the capital. There they were held as prisoners for several months. Word of their presence was finally brought to Kaulani and Kapioma had ordered them sent to him. He had at once made Lamu a prisoner and confined him with the survivors of Ulm who had been meanwhile captured and brought to the city. Awlo he treated at first as an honored guest, but during the last few months he had tried unavailingly to win her consent to their union. The final scene of his attempt was the one which I had interrupted in the throne room.

She had consistently refused to give him any cause for hope, for she assured me that she never would believe that I was dead but always expected me to rescue her. Until I entered the throne room she had no idea that I had been in Kaulani.

An hour later the Kauans attacked in earnest. Wearing their improvised direct current fighting suits they came in force and repaired the broken cable which led to their machine. I went down in my fighting suit to rout them, but I did not dare to turn the power on. One of them was wearing Kapioma's suit and any attempt to render mine active would have activated his. He kept behind a screen of men and was effectually protected from our rifles.

Slowly the huge tank-like machine moved forward. We poured a storm of rifle and pistol bullets into it but they had no effect. Like the heroes they were, the loyal Ulmites threw themselves before it and strove to stop it with their bodies, only to fall before the deadly rays which it poured out. Half of my men were down and the tank was slowly but inexorably approaching the open doorway. At intervals blinding flashes of white light came from it and whatever stood in their path, be it man, wood or stone, was shattered to fragments. On it came despite all our efforts. I was about to order the power turned on and make a last desperate attempt to stop it with Olua's fighting suit, despite the one I would have opposing me, when an unfamiliar sound stopped the fighting for a moment. There was a silence and I heard a sound I had never expected to hear again, the drone of an airplane motor. The Kauans looked up and gave vent to cries of surprise. Half of them raced back toward the hangars where their war machines were kept.

Louder and louder became the sound and over the palace grounds swooped the familiar form of a tri-motored Fokker. I gave a shout of joy when I saw it and another one of exultation when I realized who the pilot must be. I suspected what Olua was up to and I called my men under shelter.

The Fokker swooped down low over the palace grounds and then up. A second time it swooped, and as it passed, a few hundred feet above our heads, something was thrown from the cockpit. It was a long black object and it fell slowly toward the ground. Square on the Kauan machine it landed. There was a deafening crash and a burst of smoke. Fragments of the machine flew in all directions. The Kauans who remained on their feet fled with cries of alarm.

Again the Fokker swept up and back over the palace. Another black cylinder fell and a huge hole was torn in one corner of Kapioma's stately residence. Apparently satisfied with the damage he had done, the pilot swung down with idling motor. I raced to the roof to meet him. The Fokker came down and made a perfect landing, although it would have rolled off the roof had not several of my men been there to check it. Removing his flying goggles, Olua climbed out and knelt at my feet.

"You came just in time, Olua Alii," I said as I raised him to his feet. "I feared that your adjuster had been moved and that you could not find your way back."

"I had no trouble, Courtney Sibama," he replied. "I exceeded your orders somewhat but I felt certain that you would approve what I did. I got to the larger plane all right and learned to fly your ship with no trouble but it took me a long time to get the explosives you wanted. I could make myself understood only with difficulty and when they understood, they would not give me what I wanted, although I offered them the metal you told me to use. At last I found one who knew you in the place they call Beatty and he got them for me. Then I returned as quickly as I could."

"And just in time," I repeated, "and you are more than welcome. I was about at the end of my resources, but with your knowledge of Kauan fighting methods, the battle will be on a more even footing now."

Olua inquired as to the details of the fight and expressed himself as surprised at the stubborn resistance we had made. As a member of the Council of Lords, he requested a private interview with Moka and Hama, a favor which I promptly granted. In an hour the three of them entered the laboratory where I was talking to Awlo and requested permission to speak.

"Speak on," I said puzzled at their grave faces.

"It is the law of Ulm," said Moka gravely, "that when dire peril threatens the persons of the Sibama or the Sibimi, the word of the Council of Lords shall rule, if it will promise safety. Is that not so, my lord?"

"It is," I replied.

"Grave danger now threatens you and Awlo Sibimi, my lord. It is the word of the Council of Lords that you take the flying ship in which Olua Alii arrived and take the Sibimi to a place of safety."

"I'll do nothing of the sort," I said shortly.

"You must, Courtney Sibama," said Moka earnestly. "All of us have risked our lives and Olua Alii has returned from a place of safety to one of peril to assure the safety of our rulers. Unless you avail yourself of this chance, the sacrifice of those who have already died for you will be in vain. For countless generations my fathers have served the royal family of Ulm and it is just and fitting that the last member of my family should die that the royal family of Ulm should live on. Besides, the ammunition is running short."

This last was serious news. I inquired and found that we had less than sixty rounds of rifle cartridges per man left and another serious attack would settle matters. Olua gave another argument.

"You do not know the power of Kau," he said. "They have tried to conquer you quickly so far but now I think they will settle down to do it slowly. It is only a matter of time until they will construct a new power house or at least a power unit sufficient to power their fighting suits and when they do, the battle is over. I can make suits for our men but they would be outnumbered by a thousand to one. No, Courtney Sibama, what Moka says is true. You and our Sibimi must fly to safety. For this reason, I brought you your ship."

Thus reenforced, Moka returned to the attack.

"Ame has not yet fallen to the Mena," he said, "and there you and the Sibimi will find refuge and can build up again the empire of Ulm. We here are few and worthless, but the hopes of a mighty people are bound up in you. It may even be that when the Mena are defeated that you can lead a rescue party here for us."

"Wait a minute," I cried. His voice gave me an idea. I had forgotten the possibilities of my electronic vibration adjuster. Could I win my way to that, I could make my Fokker large enough to carry the entire population of Ulm, Ame and Kaulani. As the possibilities of the plan became clear, I gave a shout of joy.

"We will go," I exclaimed. "We will go, but we will return and carry you all to Ame."

In a few words I outlined my plan and Moka, Hama and Olua enthusiastically agreed to it. I don't think that any of the three expected me to succeed but the fact that Awlo and I would be safe was the thing that was uppermost in their loyal minds. In a few minutes we were on the roof and I was examining the Fokker prior to taking off. Satisfied with my inspection, Awlo and I went the rounds of our subjects to say farewell. Our plan had been told to them and man after man, the brave fellows thrust forward their gun butts for me to touch and knelt at Awlo's feet. To each of them we gave a hearty hand clasp and then, with only the three Alii in attendance, we ascended to the roof to take our departure. At the last moment I suggested that Olua accompany me to help me with the adjuster but he objected on the grounds that his knowledge would be needed to ward off the next attack. Moka dropped on one knee with the tears suspiciously near overflowing in his blue eyes.

"Farewell, my lord; farewell, my lady," he said. "It is the best end to die bravely for those we love."

"Die, nothing!" I exclaimed. "I'll be back here in five hours at the outside to take you all to Ame and safety."

"If it be so written," he replied, "but if not, remember ever, my friends, that Ulm was loyal to the last."

Awlo was sobbing openly and the tears were coming into my own eyes, so I brusquely put my princess into the plane and took the controls. Olua spun the propeller and the little craft soared into the air and at her best speed flew to the west toward the Kau mountains.

In two hours we were over the mountains and I was searching for my adjuster. At last I saw it and on a long slope we glided down toward it. We were within a hundred yards of the ground when the sun suddenly darkened and a terrific gust of wind turned the ship completely over. I strove to right it, but we were too close to the ground and in the semi-darkness, we crashed. I staggered to my feet and found that neither of us had been more than badly shaken by the fall.

As we climbed free from the wreck, the wind nearly carried us from the ground while crashes which shook the earth came from all around us. The sun was still partially obscured and I looked up and saw a marvel.

Through the air were flying rocks the size of mountains, some of them apparently miles in diameter. The were flying toward the east and I realized that some of them must be falling on or near Kaulani.

"The kahumas! The giants!" cried Awlo.

"Kahumas, nothing!" I replied. "I don't know what it is, but it is no witchcraft."

As I spoke, another blast of wind came and again the sun was darkened. When it cleared, more of the huge masses of rock were flying through the air. One boulder, which must have weighed a million tons, fell not over two miles from us.

"Quick, Awlo!" I gasped. "Come with me!"

I grasped her hand and we raced for the adjuster. The only defence against such masses of rock was to increase our size until they were small in comparison to our bulk. We entered the machine and I turned the speed control to maximum, at the same time setting an automatic stop I had put on my new model, which would halt our increase when I arrived at my normal six feet. My hand reached for the increasing switch when a fresh cloud of rock masses came hurtling through the air, this time falling to the west of us. One of them struck the mountain above us and started a slide. I looked up and saw thousands of tons of rock rushing madly toward us. Awlo gave a cry of despair and fear but before they reached us, my hand closed on the switch and I pulled downward with all my strength.

I stepped from the adjuster and faced with clenched fists a grizzled old prospector, who lay on the ground where he had been thrown by the adjuster, as it had grown almost instantaneously to its original size.

"What do you mean by digging here and killing my friends?" I demanded hotly. "This is private property."

"Taint so on the map," he retorted as he rose. "It's a public domain and I reckon a man can prospect where he pleases. Where in hell did you come from?"

Without bothering to answer him, I hastily pulled the adjuster to one side. Under where it stood was piled dirt that that wretched fool had thrown and the weight of the adjuster had packed it smooth. Ulm, Ame, Kau; all were gone; buried under what was to them miles on miles of rock.

"Where did you come from?" demanded the prospector again as he dusted off his knees. "You weren't here a minute ago!"

"I came from a better land than you'll ever see," I replied grimly. "Hand me your shovel for a moment."

I took his tool and reached in and changed the speed of the adjuster to slow and closed the reducing switch. Sadly I watched it as it shrunk down to nothing and vanished from our sight. When it disappeared, I turned to Awlo, ignoring for the moment the ancient prospector who had watched the proceedings with dropping jaw and eyes as big as saucers.

"Farewell, Awlo, Sibimi of Ulm," I said solemnly. "My dear, you have lost forever your royal title but you have gained another fully as honorable, if it is slightly less exclusive."

"What do you mean, Courtney?" she asked.

"I mean that through the action of God and this ignorant agent of his, the Empire of Ulm had ceased to exist. You have ceased to be Awlo, Sibimi of Ulm, and will henceforth have to content yourself with being Mrs. Courtney Edwards, citizen of the United States of America."

■ ■ ■ ■ ■

When I reread "Submicroscopic" and "Awlo of Ulm," I was made very uneasy by the touches of racism it contained. The thought crossed my mind that I ought to try to edit them out, but, you know, I can't do that. Once I started tampering with stories, where would I stop?

The trouble is that racial stereotypes, unfavorable to everyone but white men of northwest European extraction, were completely accepted and, indeed, scarcely noted in those days of only forty years ago (except perhaps by members of the groups victimized thereby).

I'm sure the readers of that day were not particularly disturbed by the fact that the brave and chivalrous people of Ulm were blond, white people; and that so was the Earthman hero. (That hero is rich, athletic, and the kind of square-shooter who longs to kill ants for sport, and who does kill an inoffensive deer the instant he sees it, even though he is not hungry at the time and has no intention of eating it.) The one member of the Ulm group who is villainous is, of course, swarthy in complexion.

The chief villains in "Submicroscopic," however, are the Mena, who are black, brutal, disgusting, and cannibalistic. In "Awlo of Ulm" the villains are the men of Kau, who are intelligent and scientifically advanced, but who are yellow in color and very, very cruel. This picture of the savage Black (given in almost every adventure story dealing with the far corners of the world, from *Robinson Crusoe* on) and the cruel Oriental (remember Fu Manchu and Ming the Merciless) was drummed into young heads until it became second nature.

Indeed, when my storytelling friend of 1928 told his tales of derring-do, the band of heroes he invented included both a Black and an Oriental, each with a full and insulting list of stereotypical characteristics. Neither he nor I knew there was anything wrong in that.

That we have come as far as we have in forty years is hopeful, though I believe it is more through the fact that Hitler's excesses made racism poisonous to any humane individual than through our own virtue. That we have much farther to go even now is incontestable.

The stories also include naïvetés of drama characteristic of the adventure stories of the day. There is the love at first sight, the princess who accepts a strange adventurer as her husband, and who threatens, "One step nearer and I will sheath this weapon in my heart!" (I had to read that line twice to make sure it was there.)

There are also the naïvetés of science that assume that slowing atomic and subatomic movement reduces size (it actually cools an object) or that mass automatically increases and decreases with size, or that the living creatures of the submicroscopic world would be of the same species as ourselves and would speak a kind of Hawaiian (which the hero fortunately understands).

But never mind. The action is rapid and violent; the hero is utterly heroic, the heroine utterly beautiful, the various villains utterly despicable. Everything breathed a kind of knightly chivalry, and at the time I asked no more.

"Submicroscopic" and "Awlo of Ulm" did not directly affect my own writing. I have never been able to throw myself into the kind of tale in which virtue just happens to have stronger muscles, readier fists, and better weapons.

Two things lingered, though. One was the seductive vision of a world in a grain of dust (something handled with much superior force in "He Who Shrank," which will appear later in the book). The notion is an old one, but it seemed to gain scientific backing in 1910, when the atom was briefly pictured as an ultramicroscopic Solar System.

Science quickly abandoned the picture as impossibly simplistic, but it caught on with science fiction writers. I never used it, because by the time I became a writer I had too good a grounding in the physical sciences to make me comfortable with the notion.

However, in 1965, when I was asked to do a novelization of a motion picture that had already been made, I found myself brought face to face with a similar notion. The picture was *Fantastic Voyage,* and it dealt with the miniaturization of human beings to the size of bacteria and with their adventures in a human blood stream. It was not the type of situation I would have chosen to use of my own accord, but since it was handed me, the dim memory of "Submicroscopic" helped persuade me to accept the task.

The other aspect of the stories that particularly impressed me was the duel with the rays in "Awlo of Ulm." The ray gun was a staple of science fiction (and came true, after a fashion, with the laser). That and the disintegrator gun were the two great hand weapons of the future. No one, however, had gone as all out as had Meek in "Awlo of Ulm."

I don't think I ever actually used ray guns myself in my stories, but the "neuronic whip" in my book *Pebble in the Sky* is a definite reminiscence of the weapons of "Awlo of Ulm."

It was not long after "Awlo of Ulm" that I read "Tetrahedra of Space," in the November 1931 issue of *Wonder Stories*, and was nearly as impressed. That was an important issue to me anyway, for after twelve months of experiment with pulp size, *Wonder Stories* went back to the large size with that issue, to my great relief.

TETRAHEDRA OF SPACE

by P. Schuyler Miller

A MOON of mottled silver swam in the star-flecked sky, pouring its flood of pale light over the sea of blue-green vegetation that swelled up and up in a mighty, slow wave to break in the foaming crest of the Andes. The shadow of the plane raced far below, dipping into the troughs, breasting the summits of that vast, unbroken sea of emerald stretching on and on beyond reach of vision.

And the stars—blinking Mira nearly overhead, a great Fomalhaut blazing over the far off mountains, and to the south a host of exotic strangers, burning with a fire that we of the north seldom know—clustered like great, glowing fireflies around the invisible Pole. But I paid little heed to moon and stars and silvered jungle, for night had caught me unawares, and it is no simple matter to lay down supplies in a little clearing, marked only by a flickering camp-fire, lost somewhere among the jungles of Brazil.

Or was it Brazil? Here three great states mingled in an upland of forest and mountain and grassy valley—Peru, Bolivia, Brazil. Here ancient races had made their home, raised their massive temples in the little valleys, wrested a fortune from the mountains, given their lives to the jungles—a people more ancient by far than those others beyond the ranges whom the Incas conquered. Here none had come before to study, yet now, somewhere in the gloom beneath me, was a little oval valley hung midway between crag and forest, and there would be the tents and fires of scientists, men of my own world.

I must swoop and circle and loose my load, then soar off into the silver night like some great moth spurning the flame, out into the world of the moon and the jungles, back to the government that had sent me, to plunge once more into the hum-drum routine of government flight, the moon and the silvered jungle forgotten and forever gone.

Copyright 1931 by Gernsback Publications, Inc.

But there came no glimmer of flame in the darkness, no flicker of white tents in the moonlight. Alone the outflung cross of the plane swam the unbroken sea of green, dark and boding against its wan beauty. It takes little error of judgment to miss a tiny clearing in the dark. So, as the western ranges crept out of their alignment, I swooped and soared, and was roaring back, higher now, over the silent moon-lit forests.

But one gap had I seen in the jungle—a harsh, black scar seared by some great fire from the bowels of the planet, ugly and grim in the soft beauty of the night. Again it slipped beneath, and as the shadow of the plane vanished against its harsh blackness it seemed to me that there came a scurry of furtive motion, an instant's flicker of shadow against its deeper gloom. I half checked the course of the plane, to wheel and search it closer, then of a sudden the air about me blazed with a dull crimson fire that burned into my body with a numbing fury of unleashed energy, the drone of the engines gasped and died, and we were spinning headlong toward the silver sea beneath!

As it had come, the tingling paralysis passed, and I flattened out the mad dive of the crippled plane, cut the ignition, and dived over the side. As in a dream I felt the jerk of the parachute, saw the deserted plane, like a huge, wounded bat of the jungles, swoop and check and swoop again in a long flat dive that broke and pancaked into the upper reaches of the forest. Then the heavy pendulum of my body alone beat out the dull seconds as I swung and twisted beneath the silken hemisphere of the 'chute. And then the leafy boughs, no longer silver but like hungry, clutching talons of black horror, swept up and seized me. I crashed through a tangle of vine and brittle bough into a hot, sweet-scented darkness where little hidden things scurried away into the night and the silence.

The rain-forest is like a mighty roof stretched over the valleys of tropical America. Interlacing branches blot out the sun from a world of damp and rotting dark, where great mottled serpents writhe among tangled branches and greater vines strangle the life out of giants of the forest in the endless battle for light. And there are little, venomous things of the dark ways—savage two-inch ants with fire in their bite, tiny snakelets whose particolored beauty masks grim death—creatures of the upper reaches and of the glorious world above the tree-tops. With the sunrise, a blaze of life and flaming color breaks over the roof of the jungle—flame of orchid and of macaw, and of the great, gaudy butterflies of this upper world. Beneath, there comes but a brightening of the green gloom to a wan half-light in which dim horrors seem to lurk and creep and watch, and giant lianas twist and climb up and ever up to the living light.

And lowest of all is death and damp decay—the dull, sodden carpet of mold and rotting vegetation where fat white grubs burrow in blind fear and huge centipedes scurry underfoot.

The sun was an hour gone when I fell, but it was not until its second coming when I managed to writhe and slip through the tangle as if I too were of the jungle, moving toward the spot where my memory placed that blasted clearing, and the light. And with the deepening of the gloom in the upper branches, I came upon it, quite by accident, from above.

It was a little valley, perhaps a mile long and two thirds as wide, lying in an oval of glittering jet against the side of the mountain. Here the Andes were beginning their swift climb up from the jungles to the snows, and beneath me fifty-foot cliffs of sheer, black rock dropped to the valley floor.

I have spoken of it as blasted, seared into the living heart of the jungle. It was all of that, and more! There was a gentleness in its rocky slopes that spoke of centuries of hungry plant-life, prying and tearing at jagged ledges, crumbling giant boulders, dying, and laying down a soft, rich blanket of humus over the harsh, under-rock, forming a little garden-spot of life and light in the dark heart of the forest.

Then came fire—an awful, scourging blast of fierce heat that even Man's Hell cannot equal! It blasted that little valley, seared its verdant beauty horribly, crumbling blossoms and long grasses into dead white ash, stripping the rich soil of past ages from its sleeping rocks, fusing those rocks into a harsh, glittering slag of seared, burnt black, cold and dead and damned! The sheer cliffs of its sides, once draped with a delicate tracery of flowered tendrils, had cloven away under the terrible heat, split off in huge slabs of the living rock that had toppled into the holocaust beneath and died with the valley.

The few thin shrubs that screened me at their summit showed blackened, blistered leaves and twigs, though here the heat had been least. As no other spot on Earth that little upland valley was awfully, terribly dead, *yet at its center something moved!*

Eagerly, fearfully, I peered through the gathering dusk. Full and golden, the moon was rising over the forest, throwing new shadows across the valley floor, brightening new corners, revealing new motion. And as its smoky orange cleared to white gold and waned to limpid silver, that glorious light seemed to soften the harsh jet of the valley. It wakened a lustrous opalescence in the two great spheres that nestled like mighty twin pearls against the dark rock, to create beings of the rock and of the shadow, gliding wraithlike among the shattered boulders!

Painfully I crept through the dense growth of the brink, nearer to those great spheres and their dreadful cargo. Within me my brain whirled and throbbed, my throat froze against the cry of shocked incredulity that rushed to my lips, cold, clammy sweat oozed from gaping pores! It was beyond all reason—all possibility! And yet—it *was!* Now I could see them clearly, rank on rank of them in orderly file, some hundred of them, stewn in great concentric rings about the softly glowing spheres—harsh as the black rock itself, hard, and glittering, and angular—a man's height and more from summit to base—great, glittering tetrahedra—*tetrahedra of terror!*

They were tetrahedra, and they were alive—living even as you and I! They stirred restlessly in their great circles, uneasy in the dim light. Here and there little groups formed, and sometimes they clicked together in still other monstrous geometric shapes, yet always they moved with an uncanny stillness, darting with utter sureness among the scattered rocks. And now from the nearer of the twin spheres came another of their kind, yet twice their size, the pearly walls opening and closing as by thought-magic for his passing! He swept forward a little, into the full light of the moon, and the rings followed him, centered about him, until the spheres lay beyond the outermost and the giant tetrahedron faced alone the hosts of his lesser fellows!

Then came their speech—of all things the most mind-wracking! I felt it deep within my brain; before I sensed it externally, a dull, heavy rhythm of insistent throbbing, beating at my temples and throwing up a dull red haze before my staring eyes!

And then I knew it was no fancy—that the great things of the blasted valley were indeed speaking, chanting, in low, vibrant monotone that beat physically upon me in long, slow waves of the air! You have heard those deepest notes of a great organ, when the windows tremble, even the walls, the building itself vibrate in resonance, beat and beat and beat to its rhythm until you feel it throbbing against your skull, pulsing in your mind in a vast, relentless sea of thundrous sound!

Such was the speech of the tetrahedra, only deeper still beneath the threshold of sound—so deep that each tiny nerve of the skin sensed its monotonous pressure and shouted it to a reeling brain—so deep that it seemed like a great surf of more-than-sound thundering dismally against desolate, rocky shores!

For it was without inflection—only the dull, dead beat and beat and beat, mounting throb on throb in my pulsing brain, and bringing madness in its wake! I think now that it was a sort of chant, the concerted cry of all the scores of tetrahedra, dinning savagely, angrily at their giant leader in a dismal plaint of discontent and unease! I think they were restless, aware of unfulfilled promises and purposes, anxious to make sure their mission, or to be gone. I think that the seed of tetrahedral mutiny was sown among them, and that as angry convicts will drum at their prison bars and scream in monotone, even so these things of another world, another life-stuff, drummed their grievances at their mighty leader!

For soon I sensed a deeper, stronger voice beating against the din, drowning it out, thundering command and reproof, shouting down the mob until its lesser drumming sank to a mutter and ceased. But the voice of the giant tetrahedron rang on, inflected now as our own voices, rising and falling in angry speech and command, pouring out burning sarcasm, perhaps, cowing them with its great insistence!

Like all great leaders, his followers were as children to him, and the hard, harsh beat of sound swept off into a soothing, cajoling murmur of whispering ripples, tapping ever so lightly against the packed sand of some distant tropic beach, almost sibilant, if such a sound can be so, yet none the less dominant and definite in its message. And it sank to a far, hinting rumble and vanished.

For a long instant they lay quiet, like graven things of the stone itself, then through the circles, like a spreading wave, rose a thrill of slow motion, quickening, livening, until all were astir! The ranks parted, the giant tetrahedron swept swiftly over the valley floor to the two great spheres, his angular hordes flowing in swift, soft motion in his wake! Again, with that speed and silent mystery of thought, the spheres gaped open and the ranks of the tetrahedra were swallowed up within! Alone, the twin pearls of fire-flecked opalescence nestled among the black rocks —great orbs of soft light, glowing with the magic of the full moon.

For a long moment I lay there under the bushes at the cliff's edge, staring out over the valley, stunned by the weird unreality of the thing I had seen. Then, out of the dark behind me, came a hand, gripping my shoulder in a vise of iron! Mad with sudden terror I twisted free, struck blindly at the thing that had seized me, a thing that fastened with the grip of a Hercules upon my flailing arms, pinioned them to my sides—a thing that spoke, its words a hoarse mutter that barely penetrated the gloom!

"For God's sake, man, be still! Do you want *them* to hear?"

It was a man—a human like myself. My frozen tongue stammered reply.

"Who are you? What are those things out there? What Hell of Earth did they spring from?"

"None of Earth, you may rest sure!" came the grim answer. "But we will tell you all that later. We must get clear of this place! I am Marston of the Museum expedition—the biologist. I suppose you are the aviator—Valdez saw them burn you down last night. Follow me."

"Yes, I'm Hawkins. The plane is somewhere over there, if it didn't burn, with all your supplies in it. I was held up crossing the mountains. But tell me, first—those things, there—are they *alive?*"

"You've wondered that? I suppose anyone would. The Indians make them gods of a kind—realize they're beyond all experience and tradition. But I'm a biologist. I have had some experience in strange forms of life. They are as much alive as we—perhaps even more than we. After all, if life is energy, why should it not rest where it will? Need we—soft, puny things of carbon and water and a few unstable elements—be the only things to harbor life? But this is no place to moralize—come on!"

He vanished into the dark, and I followed, plunging blindly after the sound of his crashing progress, away from the seared valley and the tetrahedra, to safety of a sort in the sombre depths of the rain-forest.

They crouched beside a tiny fire of bark and twigs, like men of old Cro-Magnon, fifty thousand years ago—two gaunt skeletons hung and swathed with soiled rags, brooding over their pitiful little flame. With the crackle of our approach they sprang at bay—two hunted things of the jungle—then relaxed as we came into the firelight.

I will always remember them as I saw them then—Hornby, the Museum archaeologist, tall, grey-haired, his haggard face seamed with deep wrinkles of sleeplessness and fear and puzzled wonderment. Valdez, his colleague of the government that had sent me, short, dark, his Portuguese blood blended with that of the squat tribes of the interior, teeth gleaming in a snarl like that of some great jungle cat, cornered, crazed, and dangerous! He seemed plumper than the others, and I felt that he could and would care for himself very well if need be.

Now, too, I saw my guide for the first time as something more than a black hulk in blackness. Marston, the biologist, looked like an old-time blacksmith, a massive man of bone and muscle, with keen grey eyes under heavy brows and the beginnings of a mighty beard. A Hercules, I have said—more like an Atlas, upholding the burden of this little wilderness world from the shoulders of one who could not and one who would not share it! Muscles that had had scant padding of reserve flesh now lacked it utterly, jutting like knotted tree-roots from his rugged frame, making him seem a being rudely hewn from some twisted cypress stump by the master hand of a forest god, and given life.

"We're all there are, Hawkins," he rumbled, his unhushed voice bearing much of the quality of the speech of the tetrahedra. "We've got to find that plane soon, if it's still whole. Did you see flames, Valdez?"

"Flames, Senor Marston? No—as I have so often said, I saw merely the falling of the plane, like a great wounded bird seeking the shelter of the jungle, and Senor—Hawkins, is it—with his parachute. I am not certain that I can find it, now that a day and a night have passed, but I will try. With the guides gone, it is not easy to feed even three mouths—eh, Senor Marston?"

"Four is no worse than three, Valdez. I'm glad Hawkins is here. He's new blood, a new brain, and with his help we may lick the damn' things yet!"

Then Hornby's voice—dry and withered as his shrunken body—weary as his tired old eyes.

"You have seen the tetrahedra, Lieutenant Hawkins? You realize that they are living, intelligent beings? You can comprehend the menace of their presence here on our Earth?"

"Yes, Professor," I answered slowly, "I have seen them and heard them. I can see that they're not like anything I know of, on Earth or off, and that there is some sort of purpose behind them. But I saw them only in the half-light, for a few moments at best. They had a great leader, twice the size of any of them, and the rest seemed to be dissatisfied with the way he was running things."

"You hear that, Marston?" cried the Professor, almost savagely. "You hear—they are impatient—they will act, soon, as soon as they have fed again! We dare not wait longer! We must do something, Marston—we must act—now!"

"Yes, I saw them too," said Marston slowly. "They're on the brink, all right. But I don't know what we can do—four men with three rifles and a couple of machetes against a hundred of them and what they can do. I don't know that we can even puncture one—they look almighty hard to me!"

"Marston," I put in eagerly, "if it's guns you want, there are two machine-guns and plenty of ammunition in the plane—it was a government ship, fresh from the uprising in the North. If we can find that, there'll be guns as well as food. I think I could find it, from the valley, in daylight."

"Valdez—you hear that? Can you help him search? You are the one who saw him fall, and you have been out with the Indians more than once. How about it?"

"Very well, Senor Marston, I will do what I can. But do not hope for too much—remember, there has been a day and a night, and I had only a glimpse. And the guns—what can they do against those devils from the spheres? We are fools to stay here, I tell you—we would do better to flee, now that there is food, and warn the world of what has come upon it!"

"I've heard that stuff preached before, Valdez. Stow it! If it comes to announcing them to the world, those things will do it for themselves faster than we could! It would be our own hides we'd be saving, and that not for long! Besides, you know the reputation these Indians have, once they're roused! Looks like you're the fool of the lot, Valdez. You'll hunt with Hawkins in the morning!"

Professor Hornby had said little—he merely crouched against a tree, staring blankly at the flames. Now, at Marston's words, he roused again.

"Marston," his voice came petulantly, "have you seen the Indians in the forest, as I have? Have you seen them, felt them staring at your back, fingering their little darts in the dark? Marston, they take those tetrahedra for gods, or devils—things to worship and propitiate with sacrifice! The forest is full of them—I feel it—I can tell! Marston, *what are they doing?*"

CHAPTER II

The Coming of the Tetrahedra

Marston's bluff rumble drowned out that final wail. "Sure, Prof, they're here, all right—all about us, out there in the jungle with the beasts. I can feel them too—watching us from the dark. But they're harmless—just inquisitive, that's all. It's the things yonder that draw them—gods, maybe, or devils, like you said, but something out of old times and old tales, when the Old People had their forts and palaces here under the shadow of the hills. It's a legend come true, for them, and until they find out different, I reckon they link us with the things that have appeared in the place where we used to be—we, with our white magic and our questions of the Old People. They're not apt to hurt us for a while yet, but it won't hurt to slip a mite closer to the valley, where we can watch the things and keep the association fresh for the Indians."

Then Valdez slipped in his acid wedge of dissent, smoothly and blandly as ever, yet deadly sharp beneath the flashing smile.

"You remember, of couurse, Senor Marston, that these poor Indios retain the superstitions of their ancient masters, and that in time of peril it was the way of the Old People to make blood sacrifice to their gods— the blood of their most holy priests! Old customs linger long among savages, Senor! You have a proverb, I think—'Out of sight, out of mind', is it not? There is truth in such old maxims, Senor Marston."

"Meaning we can skip out and let them forget us? We're not playing that game, as I think I've said before, Valdez. None of us—get that! We're staying, and we're fighting, just as soon as you and Hawkins locate those guns, which is tomorrow. Your memory will improve with a little sleep, I think. And, Prof—I reckon Hawkins here would like to hear about those things yonder. Tell him what there is to tell—you have it clearest of any of us, I guess."

And so, huddled there by the tiny, flickering fire, I listened as the thin, dry voice of the old Professor marched through the awful story of the coming of the tetrahedra. It was graven deep in his mind, and with every telling the tale grew more vivid to him. Even now the sweat oozed from his face as he spoke, staring in fascination at the dying flames. The eyes of Marston and Valdez watched us across the embers and those other, unseen eyes in the darkness that hung its velvet shroud beyond the waning flicker of the fire-light, peered furtively out of the night.

They had come to the little valley in the hills, three white men and a half-dozen Indian guides from the more civilized tribes to the north. Here in its oval bowl they had made their camp among flowers and waving grasses, with the dark rampart of the jungle standing about them like the walls of a prison. And from those walls, in the end, came the Indians of the forests—poor, savage creatures hag-ridden by superstition and ignorance, wracked by famine and disease—a feeble remnant of those who had been servants to the Old People in days long gone.

For they treasured weird legends and aborted ceremonies where understanding of other things had passed. Perhaps they had never known the reality of the great deeds with which they had served the Masters—cunningly fitting huge boulders into smooth-cut walls and terraces, hacking long roads into jungle and mountain, eking out a livelihood for the decadent ruling race.

But true it was that they bore memories of things that even the savage mind can ponder, memories of magic and ritual, and the adoration of fierce and powerful gods. As the newer magic of this younger, paler race gripped their childish minds, they told of the things that their fathers before them had learned of grandfathers through the centuries, tales not only of custom and life in those long-gone days, but of cities swallowed up in the rain-forest, cities of massive stone and untarnishing metal—"the metal of the Sun," that sleeps in long, fat serpents in the white rock of the mountains. In Hornby's old eyes gleamed a new, young frenzy of hope and joy, and in the little eyes of Valdez another, older lust-light wakened at the tale of the golden serpents. Marston saw it, but Marston had known that it would come, and he went about his study of the plants of valley and forest as if it had not been there—worked, and watched.

Then, one day—and Professor Hornby's hoarse voice sank almost to a whisper as he told of it—there came the little group of savages who were to lead the way to the buried ruins of a great city of the Old Ones, four little brown men with blow-guns and deadly darts, waiting patiently for the great White Ones to take up their magic and follow. Hornby had stepped to the door of his tent to call their chieftain to conference, and as he went he gazed up at the towering Andes, whence the Old Ones had sprung. There, drifting like wind-tossed bubbles just above the tree-tops, floated the spheres of the tetrahedral

Gently they sank to rest at the other end of the little valley—lay there in the thick grass like the eggs of some huge moth out of fable. The Indians had fled in terror, but as Hardy and Marston raced down the slope toward the twin globes they sensed that furtive eyes would be peering from the undergrowth, half-fearful, half-wondering, waiting with timeless patience for new magic—new masters.

The three came to the spheres as they lay there in the lush grass——Hornby, Marston, Valdez—and in each heart must have been something of the wonder that I in my turn had felt. For the spheres were unbroken by any opening, were as twin orbs hewn from mother-of-pearl, iridescent, with delicate hues of blue and rose tinting their snowy white, and yet there came a force from them, a tingling of excess energy that thrilled in every nerve and set their minds on edge with unwonted keenness!

It grew in strength, slowly, and it was Marston who first sensed its lurking hostility, who turned his gaze from the enigmatic spheres to see the long grasses about their bases wither and shrivel to soft grey ash under the blasting radiation! It was he who cried the alarm, and in sudden panic they fled a little way up the valley, to stand like startled sheep, then flee anew as the surge of energy poured forth in ever-quickening pulses from the opal spheres.

It swept all life before it into sudden, luxuriant growth that as suddenly dropped into blighted destruction! Beside their tents, nearly in the shadow of the brooding forest, they stood at last and watched the slow torrent sweep the life of their little valley home into the sullen ash of death. And then its invisible van drifted up the slope to their feet, and again its subtle venom thrilled evilly in their veins, and they ran crazily, headlong, into the jungle!

But they could not long shun the brain-troubling enigma that had engulfed their little home. Marston, Hornby, Valdez—they struggled back and stared from the damp dark of the forest at the thing that was happening there in the sunlit oval on the mountainside. Then it was that Marston broke the spell of fear that had been laid upon him—seized rifles, blankets, food from the deserted tents in the ebbing of the invisible waves, and fled again as the second billow of devastation poured from the silent spheres! The grasses and delicate blossoms of the valley had passed under the first blight, but here and there grew hardier blooms and bushes, akin to the life of the forest, and higher forms of life—insects, rodents, birds. Again the wave of death surged, and again, and now they could see a faint flush of crimson burning angrily where it passed, a glow more of the atmosphere than of the blighted, seared life of the valley! Then, for a time, there came a lull—a peace almost of the days and hours when this little spot of light in the green dark was the home of happy, busy men—almost, yet not quite!

For there was a boding in it, an ominous sense of oppression, a tension of the very ether, a stress that spread to mind and brain and sucked hungrily at the dazed consciousness! Now they saw that the spheres were alight with a cold green radiance that glowed vividly even above the glare of the sun upon the bleaching ash! Almost an incandescence they might have called it, yet there was no feeling of heat, only a great, overpowering energy that was being hurled from those unearthly spheres upon the little valley and its walling forests. And they were not wrong, for of a sudden, with an awful violence that shook even the stolid Marston, the storm burst in its full fury over the valley!

It did not touch the forests—indeed, it seemed to shun their cool, damp dark—and so the three could watch its awful progress and live. In an instant's time the tension burst into a seething, chaotic turmoil of blue-green flame, electric fire akin to lightning, yet far surpassing any lightning of Earth in its fury!

In a great beating sea of horrid flame it lashed the oval valley, driving into the soil, into the very rock, waking them into an angry answer of leaping, burning crimson fires. The fires swept the thin black soil from the underlying rock and scored the naked face of the rock itself with an awful furnace of consuming fury. Filling all the bowl of the valley and beating high against its bounding walls, licking away their flowery curtain of lacing vines, rending from them huge flakes of rock that burst like monster bombs as they toppled into the fiery sea below, it rushed in a mighty pillar of roaring fires hundreds of feet into the shuddering air!

And through the curtain where fire of heavens and fire of Earth met in that terrible holocaust, those three saw the curving flames of the twin spheres gape wide, saw huge angular shapes file from the darkness within —shapes never yet associated in the Mind of Man with the meaning of life! Careless of the flame that seethed about them, they glided out over the fusing rock of the valley floor, score on score of them, showing in the fierce glare as mighty, eight-foot tetrahedra of dark, glistening crystal. They were of a purple that seemed to be of the essence of the things themselves, rather than a pigmentation of their surface; and near one apex each had two green-yellow unstaring, unseeing eyes!

Within them one glimpsed a spherical body—purple too—from which ran hundreds of curious filaments to the smooth surfaces. Tetrahedra they were—living tetrahedra of chilling terror that feared neither flame nor lightning and spread destruction on every side!

Sick at heart the three men watched, while the flames died and the winds came and stripped the blanket of dust and ash from the blasted rock. The tetrahedra meanwhile glided about their endless affairs, forming and reforming in geometric pattern. Or they clicked swiftly into many-faceted forms that in turn mounted into monolithic, crystalline monstrosities, then melted with startling suddenness into their original components. These were idle, pointless maneuverings from the human viewpoint, yet fraught with some hidden meaning and purpose as alien to Earth as the things themselves. They suggested the terrible energies that were under their control—energies such as our little science has never hinted at.

"I cannot tell you of the feeling that came to me," the weary, dried-out voice of the Professor droned despairingly on. "Here was a power absolutely at odds to all the great, painfully evolved civilization of mankind, a power that could and would crush us as a fly, if we came into conflict with the motives of the tetrahedral race! Here were beings endowed by nature with powers beyond our science—alien to our ideas of evolution, well-nigh to our imagination and reason. I felt the latent doom of mankind and of the very life-forms of all Earth, squatting here in our little, blasted valley with an ominous, cruel indifference that struck chill fear into my heart! And I knew that if Man must die, I would die too—die fighting for *my* race and *my* civilization! I think we all felt it, knew it in our hearts, and swore our oath of undying feud upon the violated rock of our valley home!"

His voice trailed off into silence as his deadened eyes saw once more the vision of that awful day. I thought he had done, but again his voice broke the quiet.

"Perhaps we can flee, even now—hide away in some corner where they can have no motive for searching—exist for a few dreadful months or years while our planet sinks under their unearthly tyranny. Perhaps, for a little, we can save our lives, and yet—I wonder if it is not better to die foolishly, futilely, but to die with the knowledge that we have been closer than any man to the unfathomable, to the reality that underlies all life."

From the dark beyond the glowing embers came Marston's quiet rumble:

"We can't do less, Prof, and we won't. We will fight, as men fight, and if our way is greater and better than their way, you know, down in your heart, that we will win as Man has always won—and that science will have another doubtful bone to quarrel over. In the morning we must lay our plans. They are getting restless—they may strike any minute, and we must be ready and waiting. We're going to die, I guess, but we'll die as men should!" That was all.

The events of the past few hours had crowded in upon me with such staggering force and complexity that I found my mind in a whirl. I could get no clear-cut impression—no broad meaning—only a blurred, fantastic cyclorama of unearthly event and taut emotion, piling thought on thought in an orgy of color and sound and feeling that completely swamped me. Even now, with it all past and much of it clarified by time, I feel that same vagueness, that groping for concepts, that I felt then. With the morning all this changed—changed swiftly and utterly as event after event rushed upon us, broke like a tidal wave upon our outraged consciousness, and vanished before the tumultuous onslaught of another, greater clash of mind and matter.

We were up with the dawn, and after a scant breakfast of dried fruits, salvaged from the tents before the destruction of the valley, Valdez and I set out to find the plane. I wanted to return to the valley to get my bearings, but Valdez protested—claimed it was uselessly dangerous, that he could make better time from where we were. We struck into the tangle of dank underwood, Valdez leading, and within seconds of our leaving camp I was utterly lost. My companion seemed sure of his way, slipping through the maze of fine growth like a beast of the jungle, almost as if he were following an invisible trail.

For nearly an hour we plunged ahead, then of a sudden came a gap in the forest roof as the level of the ground fell in a narrow ravine, and I woke to angry realization of what was happening! The sun, on our right when we started, lay behind us! *We were traveling dead away from the valley, the camp, and the plane!*

Angrily I sprang forward, seized Valdez by the shoulder! He spun like a striking snake, fury in his half-closed eyes, fury and crazed fear! In his hand was a gun!

"So—you have awakened at last, Senor Hawkins," he sneered. "You feel that things are not quite as they seemed—is it not so? You fool— did you for one moment think I would cast my lot with those idiots back there? Do I seem mad, that I should offer my life for fools like them? You—you were not invited to our little party, but you came—you are here, and on my hands—and you will do as I say or wish you had! Am I clear?"

"You're too damn' clear!" I shouted. "You're not fit to live, Valdez, and it's high time someone told you so to your sneaking face! So you're going to sneak off and leave your comrades to the tender mercies of those tetrahedra—you want to make sure of your precious hide! Why, damn you, it's *you* that's a bigger fool than any of us! How can you expect to get clear of this filthy jungle, with the guides gone? Where are you going to find food when your shells run out? What do you think these damn' stinking savages will do to you when they catch you out here alone, running away from their new gods? You haven't the least chance in the world—you're crazy, that's it! You're stark, staring mad—a damned, yellow, mad dog!"

"You say unfortunate things, Senor Hawkins," he replied coldly, the ugly sneer still on his thin, red lips. "I think that I can dispense with your company. It might interest you to know that Valdez is the name of my father by adoption, Senor. My people are those whom you have so kindly classified as 'damned stinking savages'—my home is these very forests that you seem to find so unpleasant! And, Senor Hawkins, have I not said that I can always find your plane?"

"What do you mean by that?"

"I mean, Senor, that it has always been I who could find the plane, and I who *did* find it, not very many minutes after it crashed. You would be disappointed, Senor Hawkins, were you to see it now. The food, the guns and ammunition of which you boasted—they can never have existed save in a mind disordered by jungle fevers. Or can it be that the Indios—the 'stinking savages' that even now are all about us, there behind you in the shadows, have stolen them? It would be most interesting to know the truth of the matter, would it not?"

I stared up through the matted branches at the blandly shining sun, red hate clouding my vision! I raised both hands, fists clenched, as if to crash them down upon the evilly smiling face! But the little snub-nosed gun that bored into my belly spoke eloquent warning, and of a sudden came clear thought and cool, calculated words:

"So even in this you must lie, Valdez! It is bred in the blood, I think! I do not question that you stole the food and weapons that meant life to your comrades—it is much too characteristic an act to doubt—but, Senor Valdez, no Indian would so steal another's food. *Was it, perhaps, your mother who was white?*"

Blind fury glazed his little, bloodshot eyes and drew back his thin lips in an ugly snarl of rage! I saw murder staring at me from those eyes, and in the instant when he stood frozen with his hate I leaped—swung with all my weight on the great liana that was looped over the branch above me! Even as the gun spat flame, the tautening vine caught him full at the base of the skull and toppled him forward into the black mold of the forest floor, out, and out for good!

CHAPTER III

The Tetrahedra's Power

It was his life or mine, but I had not contemplated killing him. The vine was heavy and swung loose on the limb, and it whipped taut with the force of a snapping hawser, catching him squarely at the base of his maddened brain! It was an awful blow, every bit as heavy as the swing of a sledge hammer, and it broke his spine free from his skull as I would snap an apple from its stem! I turned him over, his features purple and contorted, and as I lifted him his head flopped forward like that of a rag dummy! With a shudder I dropped him and turned away.

Yet part of him was white, and all of him was human, and so I scooped a shallow trench in the soft mold and buried him, first searching his body for weapons and food. In his breast pocket was a rough sketch-map, showing the valley, the camp, and a small cross where the plane had fallen. Across its penciled contours ran a fine dotted line, due north from the camp nearly to the place where the plane lay, then bearing off to the west, toward the mountains, and toward a little upland river that ran down from the snows.

There was the gulley where I stood, a dried-out stream-bed leading up into the lower end of the valley, and just beyond a second little cross, to the south of the trail. I knew what it meant—the food and guns from the looted plane! I could see now that the way was cunningly marked by untangled vines and diverted branches—a path of least resistance, more than a trail—and within five minutes I had uncovered Valdez' cache, under the cover of an outcropping ledge of quartz, and loaded one of the packs we had brought along.

How to return to camp with my news was another question entirely. I knew it was hopelessly futile for me to try to follow the back trail, or to run by the rude map for either plane or camp. There remained the valley —straight south along the ravine—and I felt certain that once there I could regain my lost sense of direction or wait until one of the others found me. The valley—and the tetrahedra! Driven by instinct or intuition, I shouldered one of the very light machine-guns and wrapped three belts of ammunition about my waist, under my shirt.

The going was easier along the rim of the little ravine than at its bottom, where extra moisture made the tangle thicker. Indeed, it seemed almost like the trail Valdez had followed—a path of least resistance, carved invisibly into the underbrush by unknown hands. To right and left the thicket held like a tightly woven fabric, but ahead, parallel to the gulley, the branches slipped silently apart under a slight pressure of the hand and closed us quietly behind. It was obvious that either Valdez or the Indians had made this way to the valley, and it was not on Valdez' map.

The trail finally swung away from the stream-bed, toward the east, and suddenly emerged on a sort of peninsula jutting into the valley just above the point where the twin spheres lay. I saw the glare of sunlight through the trees, for there was a sort of clearing overlooking the parade-ground of the tetrahedra. Here were gathered the forest Indians, clustered behind the thin screen of vegetation, gazing in dumb adoration at the things below. So rapt were they that my approach went unnoticed, and I was able to retreat and bear to the west, creeping up to the edge of the valley midway between clearing and ravine.

It was nearly noon, and the fury of the blazing sun made the valley a black cauldron of flickering air-currents. They boiled up from the naked rock in vast, shimmering waves of heat that made the distant jungle and the rocky valley floor seem to engage in a weird witches' caper with the unearthly things that basked at the valley's heart. '

Now, in the full light of day, I could see that it was as Professor Hornby had said. The tetrahedra were formed from some hard, crystalline mineral, black almost to invisibility, with a faint wash of rich purple running through it. As they moved, the sun sent up glittering flashes of brilliance from their polished flanks, dancing like little searchlight rays along the shadowed face of the forest. For the tetrahedra were restless, were weaving aimlessly in and out among the boulders in weird arabesques as of some unearthly dance of the crystal folk, were condensing in little groups of half a dozen or less that formed and broke again even as do restless humans, waiting impatiently for some anticipated event.

Apart from the rest, motionless in a sort of circular clearing among the rocks, squatted the giant leader of the tetrahedra. In him the deep violet of the crystal became a rich, plum-like hue, purple flushed with warm red, and the underlying black seemed less harsh. It was warmer and more like the calm velvet of the tropic night. But these are impressions, qualitative terms with which to distinguish him in some way other than by mere size from his fellows. To an observer, the distinction was apparent, but it is not easy to express in everyday terms. It must suffice that he was indefinably different from the others, that he seemed to have character and personality, where the rest were but pyramidal crystals, albeit terribly alive.

And now the giant leader was dinning out his mighty call in long, slow billows of beating sound that seemed to thrust me back, press me into the dark of the forest, away from the alien monsters of the valley! In response came thirty of the lesser tetrahedra, chosen seemingly at random from the scattered ranks, to range themselves at equal intervals about their master, forming a single great circle a dozen yards in diameter.

Again the throbbing call shattered against the cliffs about me, and now all the hordes of the tetrahedra broke into flowing motion, converging in a torrent of glittering purple crystal upon the natural amphitheater, clustering in threes at the spots that their fellows had marked—all but ten, who glided into place before every third group, forming a giant toothed wheel with hub and rim and spokes of living, sentient crystal—*crystal with a purpose!*

There under that blazing sun they lay, gleaming like giant purple gems against the jetty rock. I thought of the great stone wheel of Stonehenge, and of the other monolithic circles that men have found in England and on the Continent. Strange resemblance, between the pattern of living

monsters of another world and the ancient temples of a prehistoric race!
And yet, is it too far-fetched to suggest that the superstitious savages
should pattern their greatest temples after the unearthly gods of their
worship—gods of purple crystal that came and smote and vanished again
into the skies, leaving the memory of their inevitable circling, and the
thunder of their language in the great drums of worship? May it not be
that they have come before, and found Earth unfitted for their usage, and
passed on to other worlds? And if they have so come, and found us want-
ing, what lies beyond that has prevented them from bearing back the
tale of their findings, marking Earth as useless for their tetrahedral purposes? Why have they had to come again and again?

I could see that the groups of three that formed the toothed rim of the
giant crystal wheel were tipping inward, bringing their peaks together in a
narrow focus, and more, that the ten that were the spokes, the binding
members of the wheel, were of the same rich hue as their master. The
shadows of the myriad tetrahedra squatted short and black about their
shining bases, against the shining rock.

As the sun soared higher, pouring its blazing rays straight down upon
the sweltering world, I sensed the beginning of a vague roseate glow at the
foci of the circling trios, a glow as of energy, light, focussed by the
tetrahedra themselves, yet not of themselves, but sucked from the flood of
light that poured upon them from above. For the light that was reflected
from their sides gleamed ever bluer, ever colder, as they drank in the
warm red rays and spewed them forth again into the seething globes of
leashed energy that were forming just beyond their pointing tips!

The rose-glow had deepened to angry vermillion, seemingly caged
within the spheres defined by the tips of the tilted tetrahedra. Thirty
glowing coals against the black, ninety great angular forms gleaming
ghastly blue in the pillaged sunlight, forms that were slowly closing in
upon the center, upon their mighty master, bearing him food, energy
of the sun for his feasting!

Now the scarlet flame of the prisoned light was mounting swiftly in
an awful pinnacle of outrageous color—pure fire torn from the warm
rays of the sun—raw energy for the glutting of these tetrahedral demons
of another world! It seemed to me that it must needs burst its bounding
spheres and fuse all that crystal horde with its unleashed fury of living
flame, must win free of the unimaginable forces that held it there between
the eager, glittering facets, must burst its unnatural bonds and sweep
the valley with a tempest of awful fire that would consign the furnace of

the tetrahedra to pitiful insignificance! It did none of these, for the power that had reft it from the golden sunbeams could mould it to the use and will of the tetrahedra, as clay before the potter!

Slowly the great ring contracted, slowly the tetrahedra tipped toward their common center, bearing at their foci the globes of angry flame. Now they stopped, hung for a long moment in preparation. Then in an instant they loosed the cradled energy of the spheres in one mighty blaze of blinding crimson that swept out in a single huge sheet of flame, blanketing all the giant wheel with its glory, then rushing into the blazing vortex of its center. Here, all the freed energy of the flame was flowing into the body of the mighty ruler of the tetrahedra, bathing him in a fury of crimson light that sank into his glowing facets as water into parched sand of the desert, bringing a fresh, new glow of renewed life to his giant frame!

And now, as in recoil, there spouted from his towering peak a fine, thin fountain of pale blue fire, soundless, like the blaze of man-made lightning between two mightily energized electrodes—the blue of electric fire—the seepage of the giant's feast! Like slaves snatching at the crumbs from their master's board, the ten lesser tetrahedra crowded close. As their fierce hunger voiced itself in awful, yearning force, the fountain of blue flame split into ten thin tongues, barely visible against the black rock, that bent down into the pinnacles of the ten and poured through them into the crowding rim of the giant wheel, a rim where again the spheres of crimson fire were mounting to their climactic burst!

Again the crimson orbs shattered and swept over the horde in a titanic canopy of flame, and again the giant master drank in its fiery glory! Now the fountain of seepage had become a mighty geyser of sparkling sapphire light that hurtled a hundred feet into the shimmering atmosphere, and, bent by the fierce hungering of the lesser creatures, curved in a glorious parabola above the crystal wheel, down over them and into them, renewing their substance and their life!

For as I watched, each tetrahedron began to swell, visibly, creeping in horrid slow growth to a magnitude very little less than that of their giant leader. And as they mounted in size, the torrent of blue fire paled and died, leaving them glutted and expectant of the final stage!

It came, with startling suddenness! In an instant each of the hundred clustering monsters budded, burst, shattered into four of half its size that cleaved from each corner of the parent tetrahedron. They left an octohedral shape of transparent crystal, colorless and fragile, whence every evidence of life had been withdrawn into the new-born things—a shell that crumpled and fell in fine, sparkling crystal dust to the valley floor. Only the giant ruler lay unchanged beneath the downward slanting rays of the sun. The hundred had become four hundred! The tetrahedra had spawned!

Four hundred of the monstrous things where a hundred had lain the moment before! Drinking in the light of the noonday sun, sucking up its energy to give them substance, these tetrahedral beings from an alien world held it in their power to smother out the slightest opposition by sheer force of ever-mounting numbers! Against a hundred, or four hundred, the armies and the science of mankind might have waged war with some possibility of success, but when each creature of these invulnerable hosts might become four, with the passing of each noon's sun, surely hope lay dead! Man was doomed!

On the jutting point to my left I sensed new activity. The Indians were chanting, in weird low tones, to the rhythm of a great, deep-throated drum. It was some monotonous hymn or supplication to their ancient gods—gods now personified in the things below. Through the screen of shrubbery between us, I glimpsed their chieftain, taller by a head than the rest, his arms up-raised, leading the exhortation. Their voices rose, broke in an angry clamor as a dozen of their kind burst from the forest dragging the bound form of a white man—*of Marston!*

I must be closer. Here, separated from them by a hundred feet of space and a double screen of matted vines, I dared not fire for fear of slaying friend with foe! Headlong I dived into the tangle, shoving the machine-gun ahead of me! Had they not been utterly engrossed in their savage ritual, the Indians must surely have heard my blundering approach, ripping blindly through the undergrowth with caution flung to the winds! By chance or fortune the tangle was less matted than elsewhere, and I burst into the cleared space barely in the nick of time.

For all of his traitorous hypocrisy, Valdez had spoken truly of old customs and old sacrifices! Marston's huge, straining frame was bent back over a rounded slab of polished rock in the center of the clearing, the dwarfed forest-men fairly swarming over him to hold him in place! Arms raised in supplication, their chieftain stood over him, his features distorted by something more than fear of his gods, and frenzy of sacrifice! Hate and terrible rage had seized upon his bronzed visage, making of it a veritable devil-mask! And in his clenched fist he grasped a glittering knife of steel, a knife that half an hour ago I had seen buried in the black soil of the forest floor—*Valdez' knife!*

Again he was raising his chant of dedication and sacrifice, screeched to the thunderous rhythm of the drum in the manner of those Old Ones before the Incas! Again it mounted to its climactic crescendo of frenzied adoration and black hate—rose to a maddened scream, and broke as his arm swept down against that bearded throat! With a merry cackle of savage laughter, my gun woke the echoes, sweeping leaden death across the clearing, mowing its swath of lives in sacrifice more terrible than any savage mind could plan!

Through a bloody haze I saw the brown, broken bodies twisted and flung bodily from their feet by thudding missiles that tore their unresisting flesh from their broken bones and bathed the altar and the gaunt form stretched over it with spouting, smoking blood! Blood lust was in me as I raked their bewildered ranks with the laughing death, then the belt of cartridges was gone, and as I fumbled for a second the few cowering survivors fled screaming into the sheltering jungle!

Sanity came, and horror at the slaughter I had done, and with them an awful fear that in my unreasoning rage I had murdered friend as well as foe! Stumbling over the torn and bleeding windrows of slain humanity, I raced across the bloody clearing to where he lay, the gun forgotten! And as I reached the rude altar where he lay, Marston heaved his blood-soaked frame free of the bodies that covered it, sat up, and growled whimsically:

"Are you quite sure you've killed enough for the day? Or didn't you know it was loaded?"

"Marston, man!" I shouted frantically, "Are you all right? Did I hit you?"

"Oh, not at all. I'm quite all right. You're a rotten shot if I do say it—bring in a blasted flail, and then you can't hit me! Though I'll not say you didn't try hard enough. You did well by the innocent bystanders, and of course the public must come first in the mind of every good citizen."

As a matter of fact, I had nicked a chunk out of his arm—a nice, clean hit—and the blood on him was not all Indian. Still, his sarcastic joshing served its purpose and brought me out of my near-hysteria, where I was doing nobody the slightest good, into a sort of sanity in which I could at least talk without dithering like a crazy fool. Not until we were well clear of the shambles around the altar did he speak of Valdez.

"What happened?" he asked. "Did Valdez bolt?"

"He tried to," I replied glumly. "He had the stuff from the plane cached on the trail out, and—well, I wouldn't listen to reason, he pulled a gun, and we had it out. I broke his neck—killed him."

"I'm not blaming you for it. I saw it coming, and I reckon it was you or he. But it's stirred up merry hell among the Indians. Did you know he was a breed? He claimed to be pure Indian, son of a jungle chieftain and a princess of some remnants of the Old People, but he was a breed, and crossed the wrong way! The least hint that anyone had guessed the truth made a beast of him. I've seen him deliberately bash a man's head to jelly because the fellow, a Portuguese muleteer, claimed relationship—on his mother's side! He was one of their priests, a heritage from his father, and I guess they found his body. Hornby doesn't know, though, and if I were you I'd lay the blame to the Indians—the dead ones. Right?"

"I suppose so. It happened as you guessed. I slugged him in the neck with a heavy liana, too hard. But how did they get you?"

"I told you I was suspicious of Valdez. I tried to follow you, and they jumped me, south of here, near the ravine. It must have been shortly after they found Valdez, for they were all crazy mad. I think the Doc is safe, though. Do you realize that this spawning means that they're ready to go ahead and burn their way right through everything—make this whole planet a safer and better place for tetrahedra? Doc has figured they're from Mercury—overcrowded, probably, by this wholesale system of reproduction in job-lots, and hunting for new stamping-grounds. I don't know what our chances are of bucking them—about a quarter of what they were an hour ago—but they're mighty slim, armed as we are. You've got the other machine-gun?"

"It's at the cache, with most of the food, if the Indians didn't find it when they found Valdez. I have a map here, that he was using."

"Good. Let's have it. You keep an eye on the Professor tomorrow, now that the Indians are out for blood, and I'll get the stuff back to camp. Now I know they're hostile, I'll keep my weather eye open for trouble and I'll guarantee I won't be caught napping again. Come on—let's hunt him up now, while they're still scared."

"Wait, Marston," I replied. "You get the stuff now. I have a hunch we'll need it, and that soon. I can find Professor Hornby well enough, and I don't think the Indians will want any more for some time to come."

"Right you are!" he exclaimed. "So long then." And he swung off along my back-track.

CHAPTER IV

At Bay!

I had no trouble in finding the Professor. In truth, he found me. He was all but boiling over with excitement, for he had seen something we had not.

"Hawkins," he exclaimed, grabbing my shoulder fiercely, "did you see them spawn? It is remarkable—absolutely unequalled! The speed of it all —and, Hawkins, they do not have to grow before cleaving. I saw two that divided and redivided into three-inch tetrahedra—over a thousand of them! Think of it—Hawkins, they can overrun our little planet in a few days, once they start! We're done for!"

"I guess you're right, Professor," I replied. "But tell me—have you seen anything of the Indians?"

"The Indians? Yes—there seems to be something wrong with them now, Hawkins. They seem to have lost their reverence for the tetrahedra. These tribes do not paint much, but those I have seen were decorated for battle, and one old man was cursing the things from the edge of the forest, working himself up into a regular frenzy of invective. They may resist, now, if the tetrahedra try to start anything."

"Marston will be glad to hear that! Right now, I think we had better strike for the high ground across the ravine, where their flame is less likely to reach us. I'll leave you there and then look for Marston and the guns. We're going to need them before long."

"Very well, Hawkins. Your plan sounds good, and I'm glad you found the plane. But where is Valdez? Isn't he with Marston?"

"No. He's dead."

"Dead! You mean—the Indians?"

"Um. They nearly got Marston too, but I had one of the guns. Come on, we'll pick it up, and my pack of food, and find a place where we can see what happens and still be fairly safe. Follow me."

We found an ideal fortress, high on the west side of the ravine, where a little spur ran down from the highlands to the valley of the tetrahedra. Indeed, it had been used as a lookout by the ancient inhabitants of the region, ages ago, when great cities of cut stone lay in the valleys now choked by vegetation. Enough of the ancient walls remained to provide a decent bulwark against attack, and I left Professor Hornby with the gun to hold the fort until I could find Marston.

I had little difficulty in locating him, and between us we transferred the supplies from cache to lookout, while the Professor kept a perfunctory guard over them. As a matter of fact, he was more interested in digging around in the ancient floor of potsherds and tools of the former inhabitants. He explained that the ancient Pleistocene wave of immigration from Asia, via Alaska and North America, had split at Panama to pass down both sides of the Andes. On the west, along the coast, arose the ancient American civilizations, culminating in the Incas. On the east were the forest Indians, poor savage creatures of the thick jungles, such as we had seen. And here, on the boundary between these two regions, he sought a link between the two. Perhaps he had found it. We were never to know.

It was two days before the hostilities began. Meanwhile we had found the wreck of the plane, very nearly intact but quite useless in this dense jungle. We drained the tanks of what gasoline they contained, storing it in great glazed jars of painted earthenware that Professor Hornby had found intact in a niche below our present floor-level. His idea was to fight fire with fire, incidentally clearing a space about the spur on which our little fort was perched, so that we could see what we were about in case of trouble.

Marston and I cleared out the brush as best we could, and cut deep slots in the larger trees on the down-hill side. A back-fire is ticklish work in the forest, but we worked it, piling the quickly drying underbrush at the far side of our little swath, saturating it with gasoline, then digging in to one of the Professor's excavations while the fireworks went off. In a drier climate we would not have lived to tell the tale. As it was, we more or less leveled the thick forest for about two hundred feet on all sides, before the fire petered out, leaving a tangled mess of blackened wreckage that effectively kept us in and others out, as well as clearing the field of view.

Our fire may have served to set off the onslaught of the tetrahedra. Certainly, with the next morning, there was renewed activity in their rocky pocket. They cleared out a sizeable ring of forest before sun-set. The next noon they had another sunfeast, and now the blackened valley was fairly teeming with their angular forms, large and small, for many seemed to have split without growing, as the Professor had seen one do before.

Now, their army of destruction assembled, the tetrahedra began their conquest of Earth! In vast waves of horrid destruction with rays of angry yellow flame darting from apexes their flaming floods of energy swept over the jungle, and now not even its damp dark could resist. Mighty forest-

giants toppled headlong, by the cleaving yellow flame, to melt into
powdery ash before they touched the ground. Giant lianas writhed like
tortured serpents as their juices were vaporized by the awful heat, then
dropped away in death to lie in long grey coils along the stripped rock
of the forest floor—rock that was fast taking on the glassy glare of the
little valley, rock fused by heat such as Earth had never known.

By evening, our spur of rock was a lone peninsula, an oasis in a desert
of harsh black, a height which the tetrahedra, for some unknown reason,
had not attempted.

Now we could watch their plan of campaign, and our hearts sank in
fear for our race, for while half of the tetrahedral army engaged in its
holocaust of destruction, the remaining half fed and spawned in the
full blaze of the sun. With every day dozens of square miles were added
to their hellish domain and thousands of tetrahedra to their unnatural
army. For now we could see that more and more of them were taking
the second course, were splitting into hosts of tiny, three-inch creatures
which, within a few days' time, had swelled to full size and on the
following day could spawn anew! It was dreadful, but now we were hopelessly isolated—an island in a sea of black rock, untouched as yet by the
blasting fires, but utterly unable to save ourselves or our world.

Aside from the vegetation which they were so methodically blasting,
the Mercutian tetrahedra—for such Professor Hornby swore they were
and such we later found them to be—had not yet come into real contact
with the life of our planet, much less its master, Man. The worship of
the Indians had been carried on from afar, and we ourselves were careful
not to tempt our visitors from space. Now all that was changed in something of a double-barreled fashion. It began with the Indians. It ended
with us.

Now that we were shut off from the jungle, we no longer sensed the
unease and stealthy activity of the forest people. Their gods had betrayed
them—perhaps they thought them devils now—their sacrifice had been
interrupted and their chief men slaughtered unmercifully by the slayers
of their half-white brother. Their whole life and legend had gone wrong.
The tetrahedra were to blame, and the tetrahedra must pay!

The invaders did not start their daily program of devastation until the
sun was high. Of late, the people of the forest had become creatures of the
night, and so it was that Marston roused us about midnight to watch the
fun, as he put it. As a matter of fact, we all realized that what the Indians
did would probably be of vital importance to our own situation.

The spheres were too small to hold all the tetrahedral hosts, now, and they lay crowded in great confocal ovals about them, sleeping, if such things can be said to sleep. The first indication of the attack was a tiny fire of leaves and twigs on the rocks above the ravine, now choked with slabs of rock scaled from its walls by the terrific heat. It was barely visible—merely a smudge in size, kindled for some magical purpose. Then there came a low, wailing chant, rising swiftly in vehemence and bitter hatred—a curse designed to blast the unearthly invaders where they lay. Professor Hornby was fairly gasping at the enormously ancient background of legend and superstition which it revealed, when it suddenly broke in a shrill, senile yammer of sheer madness! The strain was more than the old priest could stand.

As in answer, other, greater fires sprang up all along the walls of the valley, and by their light we could see the Indians closing in from the edge of the forest—thousands of them, drawn to worship over untold leagues of jungle paths, and now racing into battle with all the mad fanaticism of an outraged religion! It was like a tidal wave of screeching humanity, pouring down over the black rock to break over the sleeping tetrahedra! Yet, as the last Indian burst from shelter of the jungle, the attacking force was revealed as pitifully small, compared to the ranks of those whom they attacked. Like a great city of black, tetrahedral tents the Mercutians lay, dim-lit by the failing moon, as if unaware of the savage swarm, led by its gibbering priest, that raced upon them. But they were far from unaware!

It was I who first noticed the faint, rosy glow that hung over the silent ranks—a glow like that which had brought down my plane. I whispered to Marston, and he told me that it had not been there before—that the tetrahedra must be awake, and waiting!

He was right. The red glow was spreading swiftly, out over the valley floor, and there must have been another, invisible emanation that preceded it, for I saw the old priest falter, beat with clawed fists at an unseen wall, then topple with a choking scream and lie still. Now, all round the valley, the first ranks of the savages were meeting this slowly advancing wall of unseen death—meeting it, and falling before it! In long windrows they lay, body after body piling up before the momentum of the unleashed rush of the red-skinned hordes! Stones, arrows, spears flew through the thickening red mist to clatter harmlessly upon the quiescent tetrahedra! But not as harmlessly as it seemed, for here and there among them showed a little spurt of pale blue flame as one of the smaller things was crushed by a hurtling stone! They were hard, but their skins of crystal were thin, and a well-flung stone might break them! *They were not invulnerable!*

The Indians sensed this, too, for they had deserted spears and darts in favor of a hail of stones, large and small, that clattered among the tetrahedra in a veritable downpour, dealing really telling destruction among those who had not attained a fair size.

The savages were yelling in triumph, now, thrilled with success, and their blind onslaught was checked, but still the invisible barrier crept on, dealing death all along their evilly grimacing front, and still the rose-red haze followed after, dissolving the crumpled bodies in fine white ash that in turn vanished in the deepening red. The yelling circle was thinning fast, yet they had not realized the futility of their attack when suddenly the tetrahedra deserted quiet defense for active combat!

The cause was evident. Five Indians on the upslope had shoved over the cliff a huge rounded boulder that bounded like a live thing among the rocks and crashed full into the side of a great eight-foot tetrahedron, splintering its flinty flank and freeing the pent-up energy in a blinding torrent of blue flame that cascaded over the nearby ledges, fusing them into a white-hot, smoking pool of molten lava that glowed evilly in the ill-lit gloom! It was the last straw! The mad attack had become a thing of real menace to the tetrahedra, and they sprang into swift retribution. From their apexes they flashed out the flaming yellow streaks of destruction.

Now at last the Indians broke and fled before the advancing hordes, but flight came too late, for the tetrahedra were aroused and they gave no quarter! Long tongues of yellow reached out, beating down like awful flails on the fleeing savages and searing them with swift agony, dropping them in their tracks, driving them down in shapeless horror against the smoking rock, where the scarlet sea swept over them and dissolved them in drifting, fusing ash! The doomed Indians seemed to float in a yellow sea and what the sea touched was gone in an instant! Before that awful barrage nothing living could stand!

Of a sudden the tragedy was borne forcibly to our own quarter, as a handful of Indians sought the refuge of our rocky spur! Like brown apes they scrambled up its precipitous side toward our fortress and burrowed through the tangled debris of our back-fire. They were men like ourselves, men in awful danger of their lives, and Marston and Hornby sprang to the parapet, shouting at them in their native tongue. But the frightened savage knows no friend, and their reply was a volley of long arrows that toppled the Professor into my arms and sent Marston cursing for the guns! Lips set grimly, he sprayed the rocky slope with whining leaden death, mowing down the frenzied savages as I had done in the place of sacrifice! At sight of us, their madness burst forth anew and they broke their flight to rush our pinnacle, voices raised in wild vituperation!

Laying Professor Hornby under the shelter of the wall, I dragged out the other gun and kicked open a case of ammunition, joining Marston in the defense of the fort. That other time I had had surprise and superstition to aid me in my single-handed victory, but now we two were leagued against outraged fanaticism, and the odds were great. Like locusts they came on, from every side, eyes red with blood-lust, teeth bared in hate— beasts of the jungle, ravening for the kill! It was the debris of our back-fire, piled in a matted belt around the spur, that saved us, for here the mad charge must halt and here our guns took their toll. Nor were we two alone, for now I heard the crack of a rifle and knew that Professor Hornby was covering the ledge of rock that ran back at our rear to join us to the hills.

Even so, I think our defense must have failed but for the tetrahedra. They had not been slow to recognize the changed nature of the Indians' fight, and they turned that realization to their own advantage, curving around the spur to cut off a second retreat, then laying down their fiery yellow barrage upon the rear of the clamoring savage host, licking them up as a bear licks ants. It was a matter of minutes before the last Indian lay in grey ash on the rocky slope of the crag.

For a moment matters were at a deadlock. We paused and took stock— three men with their guns against thousands of tetrahedra, armed with lightnings. Hornby had slumped back against the low wall, his eyes closed, his spare frame racked with coughs that brought back blood to his twisted lips. An arrow had pierced his lungs. Marston dropped the machine-gun, now smoking-hot, and grabbed up a rifle. I followed suit. So for perhaps two minutes the rival forces held silent, waiting.

The Mercutians took the initiative. Their yellow tongues of flame crept slowly up the hillside, scouring it clean—up, up toward our little refuge on the peak. Now they began to glide forward, on every side, beginning the ascent. In answer our rifles rang out, and now there was no doubt as to their vulnerability, for wherever the steel-jacketed lead hit, there the thin crystal splintered and the night was lit by the glare of freed energy, the life-blood of the tetrahedra! We could not save ourselves, but we would do no puny damage!

Now came a dull thunder from the rear, and by the dim light of the red mist I could see the giant leader of the Mercutians, standing at the summit of the cliff above the valley, commanding the attack. In reply, the yellow barrage began to beat upward along the rock, toward us, and with the same signal a faint, blurred scheme leapt into my fuddled brain! I raised my rifle, fired—not at the advancing front but farther back, into the body of the horde, slowly driving my fire back toward the giant commander, picking off monster after angular monster, nearer and nearer to where he squatted!

Then he was flinching, gliding back before the sea of flame that burst around him as his crystal warriors fell, and in reply I brought down one after another of those toward whom he was retreating, hemming him in with death, threatening—but not striking! I cannot tell why we did not destroy him, for Marston had followed suit, neglecting the threat of the flame, which waned and died as the tetrahedra woke to the meaning of our fire. Somehow we felt that it was wiser to spare him, and our intuition was good. For a moment he hesitated, then thundered his drumming command, and the ranks of the tetrahedra drew slowly back, leaving us in peace and safety.

So we remained, virtually prisoners, for eight days. On the third, Professor Hornby died—a blessing, for he suffered greatly. He was the only one who really understood these tetrahedra, and we shall never know how he deduced that they were from Mercury, a fact which Marston later proved. The archaeological data collected by the expedition are lost, too, since both he and Valdez are dead and we could bring out no specimens. The tetrahedra left us alone, barring us from flight with their haze of red energy, which extended up the slope to a level above that of the saddle connecting us with the forested mountain-slopes. Meanwhile they continued their barrage of the jungle, laying it waste on every side, mile after mile, day after day.

Through the binoculars we had watched them slowly advance, and noted their very human surprise as they burned the covering jungle from the great ruined city which the expedition had sought. It was their first real experience with the works of Man, and it caused a great commotion among them. Led by the purple giant, they swarmed over and through its ruined labyrinth, studying its every niche and angle, learning it. Here was their proof that Earth harbored a civilization—that they might expect real opposition. I do not think they ever realized that our puny defense was a fair example of what that civilization could do.

Later in the same day they found the wreck of the plane, and this time consternation indeed reigned. Here was a machine of some sort, evidently the product of that civilization that they feared. Moreover, it was recent where the city was ancient. Could it mean that they were watched—that the unseen creatures of this unknown ruling race were lurking in the dark of the jungle, with their engines of war and destruction —*waiting*? Now, as never before in their descent on Earth, the tetrahedra were faced by the stark blankness of the utterly unknown, and I think that they began to be afraid.

The little valley was still the center of their activity, and every day we watched their spawning as the sun rode high, saw the piling up of the hordes that would overwhelm our race and planet, and make of it a dead, black thing like that little pocket on the east slope of the Andes. There was always a double ring of the tetrahedra about us now, and their crimson sea of energy beat high about our prison. The giant who led them came often to observe us, to sit and stare with invisible eyes at our fortress and ourselves. Their drumming speech had grown familiar, too, and I felt that it would not be hard to understand, given the key to its meaning.

Marston seemed fascinated with the things and their ways. There was a spring, just above the limit of the red haze, where we got our water, and he would sit there by the hour, as close to the things as he could get, watching and listening. I could see him sway to the rhythm of their thunderous speech, see his lips move in low response, and I wondered if he were going mad.

Ever since Marston had first mentioned Professor Hornby's theory that the things were Mercutians, I had been trying to find some way of verifying it. Now that we were in semi-intimate terms with the tetrahedra, I wondered if I might not get them, somehow, to supply this evidence. I thought of stories I had read of interplanetary communication—of telepathy, of word-association, of sign-language. They had all seemed far-fetched to me, impossible of attainment, but I resolved to try my hand at the last.

There was some rather soft rock in the structure of the watch-tower, and as Valdez had rescued my tool kit from the plane, I had a hammer and chisel. With these, and a faulty memory, I set out to make a rough scale diagram of the inner planets, leaning a bit on the Professor's theory. I cut circular grooves for the orbits of the four minor planets—Mercury, Venus, Earth, Mars—and dug a deep central pit. In this I set a large nugget of gold, found in the ruins of the fortress, for the Sun, and in the grooves a tiny black pebble for Mercury, a large white one for Venus, and a jade bead from the ruins for Earth. Earth had a very small white moon, in its own deep-cut spiral orbit. Mars was a small chunk of rusty iron with two grains of sand for moons. I had a fair-sized scale, and there was no room for more.

Now I was prepared to attempt communication with the tetrahedra, but I wanted more than one diagram to work with. Consequently I attempted a map of Earth, with hollowed oceans and low mountain-ridges. All this took plenty of time and trouble, but Marston was not at all in evidence, and I was not sorry, for my scheme seemed rather pointless, and I did not relish his ridicule.

CHAPTER V

Face to Face

So things stood when the tropical storm broke over us. Its cause is not hard to explain. Remember, when those scathing fires blasted the jungle, all the superabundant moisture of the region was vaporized. Even our little spring, as it ran down into the crimson haze, vanished in plumes of steam as it passed the scarce visible boundary between life and death. To add to this, during all the long summer, the sun had been literally boiling the moisture out of the rain-forests all over the Amazon Basin. The air was nearly saturated with water-vapor, though the rainy season was normally a month off. The electrical disturbances set up by the continual barrage of fire added to the general effect. Things were ripe for a storm, and it came!

A cloud-burst, it would be called in the United States. The heavens opened in the night, and water fell in torrents, streaming from every angle of the rock, standing in pools wherever a hollow offered itself, drenching us and the world through and through. Day came, but there was no sun for the tetrahedra to feed on. Nor were they thinking of feeding, for very definite peril threatened them. *To the tetrahedra, water was death!*

As I have said, their fires had flaked huge slabs of rock from the walls of the ravine leading from the high-walled valley where they slept, choking its narrow throat with shattered stone. And now that the mountain slopes, shorn of soil and vegetation, were pouring water into its bed, the stream that had carved that ravine found its course dammed—rose against it, poured over it, but not until the valley had become a lake, a lake where only the two pearly spheres floated against the rocky wall, the thousands of tetrahedra gone forever—*dissolved!*

Water was death to them—dissolution! Only in the shelter of the spheres was there safety, and they were long since crowded. The hordes of the tetrahedral monsters perished miserably in the night, before they could summon the forces that might have spun them a fiery canopy of arching lightnings that would drive the water back in vapor and keep them safely dry beneath. A hundred had come in the twin spheres. A hundred thousand had been born. A bare hundred remained. Our way of escape was clear!

But escape had been possible before, and we stayed then as now. Flight was delay—nothing more. A miracle might save us, and I think we believed in miracles. So we vainly sought shelter from the deluge in the ruins of the tower, and stared through the falling rain at the two spheres, now clear of the water and perched on the ravine's edge, above the dam.

Our "local shower" lasted for three days. Then came the sun, and the mountains began to drain. Only the new-born lake remained to remind us of the rains, a lake stained deep violet with the slowly dissolving bodies of the crystal tetrahedra. Those in the two spheres waited for a day, then came forth to survey the ruins of their campaign—the giant leader and a scant hundred of his richly purple subordinates. And now, too, came proof of the method in Marston's madness.

The tetrahedra had resumed their guard about the base of our crag, although the crimson barrage did not beat so high nor so vividly. Their master squatted outside the ring, brooding, watching us—perhaps pondering our connection with the tempest that had wrecked his hopes. And now Marston took under his arm the great Indian drum that I had brought away from the place of sacrifice, a drum of ancient ritual, headed with well-tanned human skin, and stalked down the slope to confront the tetrahedra. I stuck by the guns and waited.

I can see them yet, giant leaders of two utterly different races, born on two planets sixty millions of miles apart at their nearest, inherently opposite and inherently enemies, squatting there on the black rock, watching each other! A rumble of speech from the great leader and the rose-hue of the barrage deepened, climbed higher about the crag. A bluff, it was. Marston did not move.

And then he took up the great drum. He had cared for it as for a child during the long rain, sheltering it as best he could, testing the tautness of its grisly membrane, drying it carefully with sun and fire during all the previous day. Now I learned the reason.

Slowly, softly, using the heel of his palm and his fingers in quick succession, he began to drum. This was not the rhythmic throb of native dances, not the choppy voice of signal drums. Faster, ever faster the great drum of sacrifice boomed forth its message, until the beats melted into a low, continuous thunder of bottomless sound, mounting in volume to a steady, rolling roar, rising and swelling in delicate inflection. His wrist must have been wonderfully strong and flexible to so control the sound! On and on in great throbbing billows rolled the drumming, and but for its thunder all the world lay still—Marston and I on the slope of the spur, the tetrahedra about its base, the purple giant beyond, on the shore of the lake. On and on, thundering through my brain in dull, insistent beatings of dead surf on the beaches of a dead world, possessing me, filling me, speaking to me in the voice of the storm—speaking—that was it! *Marston was speaking to the tetrahedra with the voice of his giant drum!*

During those long, empty days on the crag-side he had been listening, learning, drilling into his scientist's brain the meaning of every voiced command that the great master of the Mercutian tetrahedra thundered to his crystal hosts, learning their inflections, storing them in his mind! He had memorized a simple vocabulary—sounds that signified the great commander, the horde, the tetrahedra as a class; simple verbs for coming and going, for altering the barrage; words for human beings, for their planet and our own—a host of nouns and verbs that even yet seem beyond the power of any man to glean from the muttering of an alien race, coupled with the actions that fitted the words. But Marston *had* learned, and with the sullen voice of the giant drum he was replying, in rough, broken, ill-chosen words, falteringly expressed, words that the tetrahedron understood!

For the crimson mist faded, vanished. The crystal ranks split, and through the lane between them glided the giant ruler, coming to where Marston sat with his drum. He stopped, spoke in words very like those that Marston had used—simple words, such as our own babies learn, roughly connected.

"What—you?"

And the drum: "We—tetrahedra—Earth." I translate rudely, as they spoke. His words were not so literal as I must make them, to suit our limited tongue—were ideas, rather than words. And yet, they got their message across!

The giant was startled. How could we, misshapen, flabby monstrosities, be rulers of a planet, equal to themselves? He was incredulous:

"You—tetrahedra?"

The drum muttered approval, as for a fulfilled command. The idea had been transferred, but the purple giant did not seem to think much of it.

"You—weak! (Easily vulnerable, like vegetation, was the sense of the term used.) You—dead—easy. (Here he used a term with which he had designated the tetrahedra shattered in the battle with the Indians.) *We*—tetrahedra—our planet—and Earth!"

There wasn't much answer to that one. They could rule both planets with ease. And yet—Marston called to me.

"Hawkins, bring down those stones you've been chipping, and a flask of water. Wait—bring two flasks, and a gun."

So he had seen me at work and guessed my plan. Well, his own beat it hollow, but if he had an idea, I wasn't going to hinder him. I lugged the slabs down and went back for the stoppered canteens of water and the gun. At his directions I set one flask against the rock of the hillside, above him. He took the other. And all the while his drum was murmuring reassurance to the giant and his horde.

"You work the slabs, Hawkins," he said, "while I talk. I'll translate, and you act accordingly." The drum spoke:

"Sun—Sun—Sun." He pointed. "Your Sun—our Sun."

The tetrahedron approved. He came from our own Solar System.

Now he was pointing to my diagram, to the Sun, the Earth and its orbit. "Sun. Sun. Earth. Earth." I rolled the jade bead slowly along its groove, the white moon-pebble following in its spiral course. I rolled the other planets, showed him their colors and relative sizes. Marston was drumming again, as I touched planet after planet, questioning.

"You planet—your planet? Your planet—what? This?"

The giant disapproved. It was not Mars.

"This?" It was anything but Venus! Venus must have been pretty wet for the completest comfort.

Eagerly—"This?" Assent! The Professor was right! They came from Mercury! But Marston wanted to be sure. He found a white speck of quartz in the black stone that was Mercury, and now he turned it to the golden Sun—held it there as Mercury revolved slowly in its orbit. There was emphatic approval. Mercury it was—the planet with one side always to the Sun. So far, so good. Marston took my other plaque—the relief map of Earth.

"Earth—Earth."

Yes, the Mercutian recognized it. He had seen it thus from space.

With a crystal of quartz, Marston gouged our particular section of South America, pointed to the ground, to the lake, the forests. "This—this," he said.

More approval. They knew where they were, all right.

Now he reopened a closed subject. He started up the monotone of reassurance, then superimposed on it a few deft words.

"You—tetrahedra—Mercury." They sure were!

"*We*—tetrahedra—*Earth!*" Not so good! He repeated: "*You*—Mercury. *We*—Earth. *We*—tetrahedra!" There were evident signs of dissent! Marston swelled the reassurance-tone, then added a sharp call to attention, raised his gun, fired twice, threw the weapon down, and redoubled his assurance of well-meaning and safety.

His aim had been good. The flask was pierced at top and bottom, and a thin stream of water was jetting forth, trickling over the glassy rock toward us. It made a little pool at his feet, lipped over, and the double rank of tetrahedra drew back to let it pass. It formed another little pool, close to the base of their giant leader. He wasn't taking bluffs! A flash of blinding energy and the pool was steam and the rock white-hot! Marston learned another word.

"*Water—dead!* We—tetrahedra—Mercury and Earth!"

Not so good! Marston tried another.

"You—tetrahedra—Mercury. *Water*—tetrahedron—Earth!"

An alarming idea that! Water the lord of Earth!

"Water—*no*—dead!" Decided negation in the drum. He pointed. True enough, the steam was condensing and running down the smooth rock in little droplets. Water could not be killed! It always came back!

"*We*—tetrahedra—*water!*"

Phew! That *was* a statement! He proved it. He dabbled his fingers in the pool at his feet, took some up in his hand and slicked back his hair. I gave a thunderous grunt by way of attracting attention, uncapped the other canteen, and poured a long and very visible stream of water down my throat. Marston took the canteen and did the same, then sent me for more water, a pailful.

"Water—tetrahedron—Earth!" he reiterated. He illustrated his point, dipped water from the pail with much splashing and poured it over my relief of the Earth, filling the hollows of the seas. He emphasized it, with a gloomy note in his drumming. "*Water*—tetrahedron—Earth. Water. *Water!*"

He had another hunch, rolled Venus around its orbit. "What?" asked the drum. He answered, glumly. He dipped Venus in the water. Venus was pumice and floated.

"Water—tetrahedron—Venus?" Oh, decidedly. The purple giant was sure of that. Marston tried Mercury. Mercury sank. Time after time it sank. Water didn't like Mercury.

"You—tetrahedra—Mercury. Water—*no*—tetrahedron—Mercury." A pause. Then slowly, ominously—*"Water—tetrahedron—you!"*

And he was right. Water had them licked. I had a bright idea, and Marston moved camp to the brink of the lake, striding like a conqueror between the double file of tetrahedra. Arrived beside the water, with the giant fairly close and the army very much in the background, I stripped and dove in—"brought up bottom"—brought up a chunk of half-dissolved purple crystal! Marston rubbed it in, gleefully.

"Water—tetrahedron—*you!*" They had to admit it. Now he tried to coin a word—pointed to the sky and shuffled syllables on the drum. "Up—up. Water—up." The giant caught on and supplied the correct term. Marston coined a real one—a genial, murmurous "Thank-you"—on his drum. I tried my hand again, dipped up a bucket of water and doused Marston, then stepped toward the great tetrahedron with another. He retreated. I wallowed in it myself instead—childish, but convincing. By now the idea was definitely set that water was rank poison to the tetrahedra and a second home to us. Now for the real information!

Marston drummed attention and reassurance, and the great leader glided back, carefully avoiding puddles. I could see that he floated about three inches clear of the ground. Perhaps, with the lesser gravitation of Mercury, he flew.

I started demonstrating my little Solar System again, while Marston announced again that Earth was largely water—no fit place for tetrahedra—water that could be killed, but that came down again in rain. He drilled in the idea of rain, until he was sure he had made his point, securing various Mercutian expressions of disgust and dislike. He found a word for "rain" —really coined one, for it did not seem to exist in Mercutian. It was a combination of "water" and "up," so as to be quite clear, with a double-ruffle of emphasis to characterize it. The etymology of the word was quite clear to all concerned. They knew what rain was, now.

I had poked a hole through the soft, thin rock of Mercury's orbit and put clay plugs in Earth's orbit at diametrically opposite points. Now Marston demonstrated. He poured water on Mercury. It vanished.

"Mercury—no—rain. No!" The entire host had crowded in, and there was a general murmur of assent.

Venus, on the other hand, being a deep groove, held plenty of water. "Venus—rain. Water—tetrahedron—Venus."

They got that, too. Weather of Venus is ideal for ducks and frogs—*not* for tetrahedra.

He moved out one planet, and I could feel a tensing. They knew what he was driving at! He was going to describe weather-conditions of Earth. Half Earth's orbit held water to the brim. The other half was rather damp. He slowly moved Earth around her circles, showing that six months were wet and six not so wet. He took to the drum for emphasis.

"*Water*—tetrahedron—Earth. *We*—tetrahedron—water. Water—tetrahedron—*you.*" A delicate inference. Then, slowly, emphatically, "Water —Venus. Water—Earth." And now his final card.

He set Mercury in its orbit, placed Venus almost opposite, paused. The giant assented. That was where the planets were at present. He skipped Earth and went to Mars, rolled it along its orbit, stopped it. Assent. All true, so far. And now I saw his point, for when he dropped Earth in place, very nearly in line between Mars and Mercury, *it fell in the middle of the dry half of the orbit!*

A hundred tetrahedra slid back a yard or so in recoil. This rain which had drowned out practically all of their army of thousands, was an example of our *dry* season! By inference, our real wet weather must have been sheer Mercutian hell to every tetrahedron of them!

But Marston was too good a diplomat to give them a hands off without suggesting an alternative. He slowly poured water on Mars. Mars apparently, and actually, had a hole in its bottom, for it drained bone dry. Mars, now, was very nice. But Earth was nasty and wet, as bad as Venus or worse. And it was inhabited by a race of super-intelligent fish, to judge from the impression he gave the tetrahedra. He picked up the drum for a last word.

"Earth—*rain*. Mars—*no*—rain. *We*—Earth. You—*no*—Earth. You— Mars?" He dwelt on the question. "Mars? Mars???" He rolled out an endless question-mark, then suddenly quit, took a long, flashing drink of water from the flask, and dove into the lake, clothes and all. I followed him, and together we splashed to the other shore, making our mastery of the water very evident, then climbed out, waiting. If things worked out, all well and good. If they didn't—well, we had the lake between us.

And it did work! For a moment they stood motionless, the mighty sixteen-foot tetrahedron of royal purple and his eight-foot purple retinue, silent, considering. Then came a sudden command, and the hundred flowed in orderly motion to the spheres, entered. Their mighty master was alone. For an instant he hesitated, then swept forward to the very edge of the lake. From this towering peak beat the white lightnings, lashing the purple waters into great billowing clouds of steam that threw up a dense wall of mist between us! Through the hiss of the steam came his thunderous voice, in last comment upon the invasion of his tetrahedral race! Marston translated, softly:

"Water—tetrahedron—Earth. *You*—tetrahedron—water. *We—kill—water!* You—Earth. We—Mars. Mars!" And a long, rolling assent, an infinitely underlined *"YES!"*

Water and Earth seemed to be synonymous, and we were perfectly at ease in that dangerous element. For all that, they, the tetrahedra of Mercury, could "kill" it, which, by inference, we could not. They weren't going to admit defeat, by Man or water, but this was a big Solar System. We could have our soggy Earth! They were going to Mars!

Up from behind the wall of "killed" water rose two great, glorious pearls, marvelously opalescent in the rays of the setting sun—up and up, smaller and smaller, until they vanished into the deepening blue above the Andes. Ironically, it began to rain.

■ ■ ■ ■ ■

As you see, "Tetrahedra of Space" belongs in the same tradition as the stories of Meek. The setting is South America, and it is the Indians this time who are superstitious savages and clearly subhuman. When the half-breed, Valdez, is killed, the hero buries him saying, ". . . all of him was human," but also says, ". . . part of him was white."

P. Schuyler Miller has been the book reviewer for *Astounding* now for almost as many years as I have been writing, and I know him to be a liberal and humane person, one of the gentlest and most generous souls I have ever met. It is a measure of how far the unthinking stereotypes can penetrate and of how taken-for-granted they were in this type of adventure fiction, that even Miller could fall victim to them.

What fascinated me in this story and what caused it to live on in my memory was the picture of extraterrestrials who were utterly non-human. This wasn't often done in those days, or, for that matter, in the more primitive forms of science fiction even today. In so many cases, intelligent creatures are assumed to be quite human if they are virtuous, and distortedly human if they are villainous, as in "Submicroscopic."

There was, further, the picture of the tetrahedra spawning and of the final communication of the two intelligences, which was handled rather subtly, I thought then—and thought again recently, when I reread it.

One other thing that occurs to me in connection with the story is the mere word "tetrahedra." Miller doesn't define the word anywhere in the story, but the illustrations by Frank R. Paul (one of them on the cover of the magazine) made it clear to me that they were solids with four, triangular faces.

It was the first time I had ever heard the word, and, of course, I never forgot it. Any form of reading will improve one's vocabulary, but science fiction automatically improves one's scientific vocabulary.

"Tetrahedra of Space," incidentally, contains another common characteristic of early magazine science fiction: elephantiasis of the adjectives. Especially in the first portion of the story, every sentence carries a load of them that breaks it in two. Combine that with inverted word order and unnecessary italics, and you find yourself breathing heavily and losing track of the sense.

To me in my younger days, and to others in theirs, and to some, I fear, in all their days, this thick layer of fatty adjectival froth seems to be a mark of good writing. And, indeed, adjectivitis was most common in the fantasy of the time and in such admired writers as A. Merritt, H. P. Lovecraft, and Clark Ashton Smith (whom, however, I am afraid I never admired, even when I was young and might have been excused the error).

Clark Ashton Smith, in particular, had a second interesting literary aberration. He used long and unfamiliar words as another way of impressing the naïve with the quality of his writing. In the same issue with "Tetrahedra of Space," for instance, there is Smith's "Beyond the Singing Flame," and since Sam Moskowitz had sent me the complete issue in this particular case, I looked at the Smith story for old time's sake.

In the very second paragraph, I found him using "veridical" when he meant "true," and I read no further. Yes, "veridical" does mean "true," but I cannot imagine any occasion (outside a certain specialized use among psychologists) when "true" is not very greatly to be preferred.

In my early days, I tried to imitate these adjectival examples of writing. My style was most ornate in the days before I had published anything. Some of the fat had been steamed out by the time I was publishing, and my writing has grown progressively leaner with the years. I am not sorry.

During 1931, I reached the stage where my pleasure in science fiction had bubbled over and could not be confined. I began to retell the stories I had read. I did this, I remember, in distinct imitation of my storytelling friend of three years earlier. Now it was *I* who had the audience.

Of course, the stories weren't my own, but I made no pretense that they were. I carefully explained that I had read them in science fiction magazines. My classmates couldn't afford to buy the magazines any more than I could and were glad to listen.

As for myself, I discovered, for the first time in my life, that I loved to have an audience and that I could speak before a group, even when some of them were strangers to me, without embarrassment. (It was a useful piece of knowledge, for twenty years later I was to become a professional after-dinner speaker at what turned out to be, eventually, very respectable fees. The childhood experience and training helped, I am sure.)

I well remember sitting at the curb in front of the junior high school with anywhere from two to ten youngsters listening attentively while I repeated what I had read, with such personal embellishments as I could manage.

And the specific story that I most vividly recall telling was "The World of the Red Sun," by Clifford D. Simak, which appeared in the December 1931 issue of *Wonder Stories*.

THE WORLD OF THE RED SUN

by Clifford D. Simak

"READY, Bill?" asked Harl Swanson. Bill Kressman nodded.

"Then kiss 1935 good-bye!" cried the giant Swede, and swung over the lever.

The machine quivered violently, then hung motionless in pitch blackness. In the snap of a finger the bright sunlight was blotted out and a total darkness, a darkness painted with the devil's brush, rushed in upon the two men.

Electric lights glowed above the instrument boards, but their illumination was feeble against the utter blackness which crowded in upon the quartz windows of the machine.

The sudden change astounded Bill. He had been prepared for something, for some sort of change, but nothing like this. He half started out of his seat, then settled back.

Harl observed him and grinned.

"Scared," he jested.

"Hell, no," said Bill.

"You're traveling in time, my lad," said Harl. "You aren't in space any more. You are in a time stream. Space is curved about you. Can't travel in time when you're still in space, for space binds time to a measured pace, only so fast, no faster. Curve space about you, though, and you can travel in time. And when you're out of space there's absolutely no light, therefore, utter darkness. Likewise no gravity, nor any of the universal phenomena."

Bill nodded. They had worked it all out before, many, many times. Double wall construction of a strength to withstand the vacuum into which the flier would be plunged at the move of the lever which would snatch it out of space into the time stream. An insulation to guard against the abso-

Copyright 1931 by Gernsback Publications, Inc.

lute zero that would rule where there could be no heat. Gravity grids at their feet so that they would still be able to orient themselves when flung into that space where there was no gravity. An elaborate heating system to keep the motors warm, to prevent the freezing of gasoline, oil and water. Powerful atmosphere generators to supply air to the passengers and the motors.

It had represented years of work, ten years of it, and a wealth that mounted into seven figures. Time after time they had blundered, again and again they had failed. The discoveries they had made would have rocked the world, would have revolutionized industry, but they had breathed no word of it. They had thought of only one thing, time travel.

To travel into the future, to delve into the past, to conquer time, to this the two young scientists had dedicated all their labors, and at last success lay beneath their hands.

It was in 1933 they had at last achieved their goal. The intervening months were spent in experiments and the building of the combination flier-time machine.

Miniature fliers were launched, with the miniature time machines set automatically. They had buzzed about the laboratory, to suddenly disappear. Perhaps at this very instant they were whirling madly through unguessed ages.

They managed to construct a small time machine, set to travel a month into the future. In a month's time, almost to the second, it had materialized on the laboratory floor where it had dropped at the end of its flight through time. That settled it! The feasibility of time travel was proved beyond all doubt.

Now Harl Swanson and Bill Kressman were out in the time stream. There had been a gasp of amazement from the crowd, on the street, which had seen the giant tri-motored plane suddenly disappear into thin air.

Harl crouched over the instrument board. His straining ears could distinguish the wheezy mutterings of the three motors as, despite the elaborate precautions taken to safeguard them, the inexorable fingers of absolute zero clutched at their throbbing metal.

This was a dangerous way, but the only safe way. Had they remained on the surface to plunge into the time stream they might have halted to find themselves and their machine buried by shifting earth; they might have found a great building over them, they might have found a canal covering them. Here in the air they were safe from all that might occur beneath them in the passing centuries through which they sped at an almost unbelievable pace. They were being fairly hurled through time.

Furthermore, the great machine would serve as a means of travel in that future day when they would roll out of the time stream back into space again. Perhaps it might serve as a means of escape, for there was no foreknowledge to tell them what they might expect a few thousand years in the future.

The motors wheezed more and more. They were operating on a closed throttle. At full speed they might dash the propellers to bits.

However, they must be warmed up. Otherwise they would simply die. It would be stark tragedy to roll out into space with three dead engines. It would mean a crash which neither of them could hope to survive.

"Give her the gun, Bill," said Harl in a tense voice.

Bill pushed the accelerator slowly. The motors protested, sputtered, and then burst into a roar. Here, in the machine, because of the artificial air, sound could be heard. Out in the time stream there could be no sound.

Harl listened anxiously, hoping fiercely that the propellers would stand.

Bill cut the acceleration and the motors, once more barely turning over, ran more smoothly.

Harl glanced at his wrist watch. Despite the fact they were in time, where actual time could not be measured by clocks, the little watch still ticked off the time-space seconds and minutes.

They had been out eight minutes. Seven minutes more and they must roll out of time into space.

Fifteen minutes was all that the tortured motors could stand of this intense cold and vacuum.

He glanced at the time dial. It read 2816. They had traveled 2816 years into the future. They should be well over 5000 when the fifteen minutes were at an end.

Bill touched his arm.

"You're sure we're still over Denver?"

Harl chuckled.

"If we aren't, we may find ourselves billions of miles out in space. It's a chance we have to take. According to all our experiments we should be in exactly the same position we were when we snapped into the time stream. We are occupying a hole in space. It should remain the same."

Their lungs began to ache. Either the atmosphere generators were failing or the air leakage out into the vacuum was greater than they had expected. Undeniably the air was becoming thinner. The motors still ran steadily, however. It must be a leakage from the cabin of the ship.

"How long?" bellowed Bill.

Harl glanced at his watch.

"Twelve minutes," he reported.

The time dial read 4224.

"Three minutes," replied Bill, "I guess we can stand it. The motors are running all right. It's getting colder, though, and the air's pretty thin."

"Leakage," said Harl gruffly.

The minutes dragged.

Bill tried to think. Here they hung, hypothetically, over the city of Denver. Less than a quarter of an hour ago, they were in the year 1935, now they were passing over years at a lightning-like speed—a speed of over 350 years in each space-minute. They must now be in about the year 6450.

He glanced at his hands. They were blue. It was intensely cold in the cabin. Their heat was leaking—leaking swiftly. It was hard to breath. The air was rare—too rare for safety. Suppose they became unconscious. Then they would freeze—would drive endlessly through time. Frozen corpses, riding through the aeons. The earth beneath them would dissolve in space. New worlds might form, new galaxies be born as they whirled on in the time stream. The time needle would reach the pin, bend back upon itself and slip past the pin, to slam against the side of the dial, where it would still struggle to record the flight of the years.

He chafed his hands and glanced at the time dial. It read 5516.

"A quarter of a minute," snapped Harl, his teeth chattering, his right hand on the lever, his wrist watch held in front of him.

Bill placed his hands on the wheel.

"All right!" shouted Harl.

He jerked the lever.

They hung in the sky.

Harl uttered a cry of astonishment.

It was twilight. Beneath them were the ruins of a vast city. To the east lapped a sea, stretching to a murky horizon. The sea coast was a desert of heaped sand.

The motors, warming to their task, bellowed a mighty challenge.

"Where are we?" cried Harl.

Bill shook his head.

"It's not Denver," said Harl.

"Doesn't look much like it," agreed Bill, his teeth still chattering.

He circled, warming the motors.

There was no sign of humanity below them.

The motors blasted a throaty defiance to the desert sands and under

Bill's hand, the machine came down in a long swoop, headed for a level stretch of sand near one of the largest of the white stone ruins.

It hit the ground, bounced high in a cloud of sand, struck and bounced again, then rolled to a stop.

Bill cut the motors.

"We're here," he said.

Harl stretched his legs wearily.

Bill glanced at the time dial. It read 5626.

"This is the year 7561," he said slowly, thoughtfully.

"Got your gun?" asked Harl.

Bill's hand went to his side, felt the reassuring touch of the .45 in its holster.

"I have it," he said.

"All right, let's get out."

Harl opened the door and they stepped out. The sand glittered under their boots.

Harl turned the key in the door lock and locked the ring to his belt.

"Wouldn't do to lose the keys," he said.

A chill wind was blowing over the desert, moaning among the ruins, carrying with it a freight of fine, hard granules. Even in their heavy clothing, the time explorers shivered.

Harl grasped Bill by the arm, pointing to the east.

There hung a huge dull red ball.

Bill's jaw fell.

"The sun," he said.

"Yes, the sun," said Harl.

They stared at one another in the half-light.

"Then this isn't the year 7561," stammered Bill.

"No, more likely the year 750,000, perhaps even more than that."

"The time dial was wrong then."

"It was wrong. Badly wrong. We were traveling through time a thousand times faster than we thought."

They were silent, studying the landscape about them. They saw only ruins which towered hundreds of feet above the sands. They were ruins of noble proportions, many of them still bearing the hint of a marvelous architecture of which the twentieth century would have been incapable. The stone was pure white, gleaming beautifully in the twilight which the feeble rays of the great brick-red sun could not expel.

"The time dial," said Bill, thoughtfully, "was registering thousands of years instead of years."

Harl nodded cheerlessly.

"Maybe," he said. "For all we know it may have been registering tens of thousands of years."

A creature, somewhat like a dog, dull gray in color, with tail hanging low, was silhouetted for a moment on a sand dune and then disappeared.

"These are the ruins of Denver," said Harl. "That sea we saw must cover the whole of eastern North America. Probably only the Rocky Mountains remain unsubmerged and they are a desert. Yes, we must have covered at least 750,000 years, perhaps seven million."

"What about the human race? Do you think there are any people left?" asked Bill.

"Possibly. Man is a hardy animal. It takes a lot to kill him and he could adapt himself to almost any kind of environment. This change, you must remember, came slowly."

Bill turned about and his cry rang in Harl's ear. Harl whirled.

Running toward them, leaping over the sands, came a motley horde of men. They were dressed in furs and they carried no weapons, but they charged down upon the two as if to attack.

Harl yanked his .45 from its holster. His great hand closed around the weapon and his finger found the trigger. It gave him a sense of power, this burly six-shooter.

The men, their furs flying behind them, were only a hundred yards away. Now they yelled, blood-curdling, vicious whoops which left no doubt that they were enemies.

No weapons. Harl grinned. They'd give 'em hell and plenty of it. There were about fifty in the mob. Big odds, but not too great.

"We might as well let them have it," he said to Bill. The two guns roared. There was disorder in the running ranks, but the mob still forged ahead, leaving two of its members prone on the ground. Again the .45's barked, spurting a stream of fire.

Men staggered, screaming, to collapse. The rest hurdled them, raced on. It seemed nothing could stop them. They were less than fifty feet away.

The guns were empty. Swiftly the two plucked cartridges from their belts and reloaded.

Before they could fire the mob was on top of them. Bill thrust his gun into the face of a running foeman and fired. He had to sidestep quickly to prevent the fellow tumbling on top of him. A knotted fist connected with his head and he slipped to his knees. From that position he drilled two more of the milling enemies before they piled on top of him.

Through the turmoil he heard the roar of Harl's gun.

He felt the grip of many hands, felt bodies pressing close about him. He fought blindly and desperately.

He fought with hands, with feet, with suddenly bared teeth. He felt bodies wilt under his blows, felt blood upon his hands. The sand, kicked up by many feet, got into his nostrils and eyes, half strangling, half blinding him.

Only a few feet away Harl fought, fought in the same manner as his companion. With their weapons knocked from their hands they resorted to the tactics of their ancient forebears.

It seemed minutes that they battled with their attackers, but it could not have been more than seconds before the sheer weight of numbers sub-dued them, wound thongs tightly about their hands and feet and left them, trussed like two fowls ready for the grid.

"Hurt, Bill?" called Harl.

"No," replied Bill. "Just mussed up a bit."

"Me, too," said Harl.

They lay on their backs and stared up at the sky. Their captors moved away and massed about the plane.

A loud banging came to the ears of the two. Evidently the others were trying to force an entrance into the machine.

"Let them bang," said Harl. "They can't break anything."

"Except a propeller," replied Bill.

After more banging, the men returned and untying the bonds on the feet of the captives, hoisted them up.

For the first time they had an opportunity to study their captors. They were tall men, well proportioned, clean of limb, with the stamp of well-being about them. Aside from their figures, however, they held a distinctly barbarous appearance. Their hair was roughly trimmed, as were their beards. They walked with a slouch and their feet shuffled in the sand with the gait of one who holds a purposeless existence. They were dressed in well-tanned furs, none too clean. They bore no arms and their eyes were the eyes of furtive beings, shifty, restless, as are the eyes of hunted beasts, always on the lookout for danger.

"March," said one of them, a large fellow with a protruding front tooth. The single word was English, with the pronunciation slightly different than it would have been in the twentieth century, but good, pure English.

They marched, flanked on either side by their captors. The march led back over the same route as the future-men had come. They passed the dead, but no attention was paid them, their comrades passing the sprawled figures with merely a glance. Life apparently was cheap in this place.

CHAPTER II

Orders of Golan-Kirt

They passed between monstrous ruins. The men talked among themselves, but, although the tongue was English, it was so intermixed with unfamiliar words and spoken with such an accent that the two could understand very little of it.

They reached what appeared to be a street. It led between rows of ruins and now other humans appeared, among them women and children. All stared at the captives and jabbered excitedly.

"Where are you taking us?" Bill asked a man who walked by his side.

The man ran his fingers through his beard and spat in the sand.

"To the arena," he said slowly that the twentieth century man might understand the words.

"What for?" Bill also spoke slowly and concisely.

"The games," said the man, shortly, as if displeased at being questioned.

"What are the games?" asked Harl.

"You'll find out soon enough. They are held at high sun today," growled the other. The reply brought a burst of brutal laughter from the rest.

"They will find out when they face the minions of Golan-Kirt," chortled a voice.

"The minions of Golan-Kirt!" exclaimed Harl.

"Hold your tongue," snarled the man with the protruding tooth, "or we will tear it from your mouth."

The two time-travelers asked no more questions.

They plodded on. Although the sand beneath their feet was packed, it was heavy going and their legs ached. Fortunately the future-men did not hustle their pace, seeming to be content to take their time.

A good-sized crowd of children had gathered and accompanied the procession, staring at the twentieth century men, shrieking shrill gibberish at them. A few of them, crowding too close or yelling too loudly, gained the displeasure of the guards and were slapped to one side.

For fifteen minutes they toiled up a sandy slope. Now they gained the top and in a depression below them they saw the arena. It was a great building, open to the air, which had apparently escaped the general destruction visited upon the rest of the city. Here and there repairs had been made, evident by the decidedly inferior type of workmanship.

The building was circular in shape, and about a half-mile in diameter. It was built of a pure white stone, like the rest of the ruined city.

The two twentieth century men gasped at its size.

They had little time, however, to gaze upon the building, for their captors urged them on. They walked slowly down the slope and, directed by the future-men, made their way through one of the great arching gateways and into the arena proper.

On all sides rose tier upon tier of seats, designed to hold thousands of spectators. On the opposite side of the arena was a series of steel cages, set under the seats.

The future-men urged them forward.

"They're going to lock us up, evidently," said Bill.

He of the protruding tooth laughed, as if enjoying a huge joke.

"It will not be for long," he said.

As they approached the cages, they saw that a number of them were occupied. Men clung to the bars, peering out at the group crossing the sandy arena. Others sat listlessly, regarding their approach with little or no interest. Many of them, the twentieth century men noticed, bore the marks of prolonged incarceration.

They halted before one of the cells. One of the future-men stepped to the door of the cage and unlocked it with a large key. As the door grated back on rusty hinges, the others seized the two, unbound their hands and roughly hurled them inside the prison. The door clanged to with a hollow, ringing sound and the key grated in the lock.

They struggled up out of the dirt and refuse which covered the floor of the cell and squatted on their heels to watch the future-men make their way across the arena and through the archway by which they had come.

"I guess we're in for it," said Bill.

Harl produced a pack of cigarettes.

"Light up," he said gruffly.

They lit up. Smoke from tobacco grown in 1935 floated out of their cell over the ruins of the city of Denver, upon which shone a dying sun.

They smoked their cigarettes, crushed them in the sand. Harl rose and began a minute examination of their prison. Bill joined him. They went over it inch by inch, but it was impregnable. Except for the iron gate, it

was constructed of heavy masonry. An examination of the iron gate gave
no hope. Again they squatted on their heels.

Harl glanced at his wrist watch.

"Six hours since we landed," he said, "and from the appearance of the
shadows, it's still morning. The sun was well up in the sky, too, when we
arrived."

"The days are longer than those back in 1935," explained Bill. "The
earth turns slower. The days here may be twenty-four hours or longer."

"Listen," hissed Harl.

To their ears came the sound of voices. They listened intently. Mingled
with the voices was the harsh grating of steel. The voices seemed to come
from their right. They grew in volume.

"If we only had our guns," moaned Harl.

The clamor of voices was close and seemed to be almost beside them.

"It's the other prisoners," gasped Bill. "They must be feeding them or
something."

His surmise was correct.

Before their cell appeared an old man. He was stooped and a long
white beard hung over his skinny chest. His long hair curled majestically
over his shoulders. In one hand he carried a jug of about a gallon
capacity and a huge loaf of bread.

But it was neither the bread nor the jug which caught the attention of
Harl and Bill. In his loincloth, beside a massive ring of keys, were
thrust their two .45's.

He set down the jug and the loaf and fumbled with the keys. Selecting
one he unlocked and slid back a panel near the bottom of the great door.
Carefully he set the jug and the loaf inside the cell.

The two men inside exchanged a glance. The same thought had occurred to each. When the old man came near the door, it would be a
simple matter to grasp him. With the guns there was a chance of blazing
a way to the ship.

The oldster, however, was pulling the weapons from his loincloth.

Their breath held in wonder, the time-travelers saw him lay them beside
the jug and the loaf.

"The command of Golan-Kirt," he muttered in explanation. "He has
arrived to witness the games. He commanded that the weapons be returned. They will make the games more interesting."

"More interesting," chuckled Harl, rocking slowly on the balls of his
feet.

These future-men, who seemed to possess absolutely no weapons, apparently did not appreciate the deadliness of the .45's.

"Golan-Kirt?" questioned Bill, speaking softly.

The old man seemed to see them for the first time.

"Yes," he said. "Know you not of Golan-Kirt? He-Who-Came-Out-of-the-Cosmos?"

"No," said Bill.

"Then truly can I believe what has come to my ears of you?" said the old man.

"What have you heard?"

"That you came out of time," replied the oldster, "in a great machine."

"That is true," said Harl. "We came out of the twentieth century."

The old man slowly shook his head.

"I know naught of the twentieth century."

"How could you?" asked Harl. "It must have ended close to a million years ago."

The other shook his head again.

"Years?" he asked. "What are years?"

Harl drew in his breath sharply.

"A year," he explained, "is a measurement of time."

"Time cannot be measured," replied the old man dogmatically.

"Back in the twentieth century we measured it," said Harl.

"Any man who thinks he can measure time is a fool," the future-man was uncompromising.

Harl held out his hand, palm down, and pointed to his wrist watch.

"That measures time," he asserted.

The old man scarcely glanced at it.

"That," he said, "is a foolish mechanism and has nothing to do with time."

Bill laid a warning hand on his friend's arm.

"A year," he explained slowly, "is our term for one revolution of the earth about the sun."

"So that is what it means," said the old man. "Why didn't you say so at first? The movement of the earth, however, has no association with time. Time is purely relative."

"We came from a time when the world was much different," said Bill. "Can you give us any idea of the number of revolutions the earth has made since then?"

"How can I?" asked the old man, "when we speak in terms that neither understands? I can only tell you that since Golan-Kirt came out of the Cosmos the earth has circled the sun over five million times."

Five million times! Five million years! Five million years since some event had happened, an event which may not have occurred for many other millions of years after the twentieth century. At least five million years in the future; there was no telling how much more!

Their instrument had been wrong. How wrong they could not remotely have guessed until this moment!

The twentieth century. It had a remote sound, an unreal significance. In this age, with the sun a brick red ball and the city of Denver a mass of ruins, the twentieth century was a forgotten second in the great march of time, it was as remote as the age when man emerged from the beast.

"Has the sun always been as it is?" asked Harl.

The old man shook his head.

"Our wise ones tell us that one time the sun was so hot it hurt one's eyes. They also tell us it is cooling, that in the future it will give no light or heat at all."

The oldster shrugged his shoulders.

"Of course, before that happens, all men will be dead."

The old man pulled the little panel shut and locked it. He turned to go.

"Wait," cried Harl.

The old one faced them.

"What do you want?" he asked, mumbling half-angrily in his beard.

"Sit down, friend," said Harl. "We would like to talk further."

The other hesitated, half wheeling to go, then turned back.

"We came from a time when the sun hurt one's eyes. We have seen Denver as a great and proud city. We have seen this land when the grass grew upon it and rain fell and there were broad plains where the sea now lies," said Harl.

The oldster sank to the sand in front of their cage. His eyes were lighted with a wild enthusiasm and his two skinny hands clutched the iron bars.

"You have looked upon the world when it was young," he cried. "You have seen green grass and felt rain. It seldom rains here."

"We have seen all you mention," Harl assured him. "But we would ask why we have been treated as foes. We came as friends, hoping to meet friends, but ready for war."

"Aye, ready for war," said the old man in trembling tones, his eyes on the guns. "Those are noble weapons. They tell me you strewed the sands with the dead ere you were taken."

"But why were we not treated as friends?" insisted Harl.

"There are no friends here," cackled the old man. "Not since Golan-Kirt came. All are at one another's throats."

"Who is this Golan-Kirt?"

"Golan-Kirt came out of the Cosmos to rule over the world," said the old man, as if intoning a chant. "He is neither Man nor Beast. There is no good in him. He hates and hates. He is pure Evil. For after all, there is no friendliness or goodness in the universe. We have no proof that the Cosmos is benevolent. Long ago our ancestors believed in love. This was a fallacy. Evil is greater than good."

"Tell me," asked Bill, moving closer to the bars, "have you ever seen Golan-Kirt?"

"Aye, I have."

"Tell us of him," urged Bill.

"I cannot," there was stark terror in the old man's eyes. "I cannot!"

He huddled closer to the cage and his voice dropped to an uncanny whisper.

"Men out of time, I will tell you something. He is hated, because he teaches hate. We obey him because we must. He holds our minds in the hollow of his hand. He rules by suggestion only. He is not immortal. He fears death—he is afraid—there is a way, if only one with the courage might be found—."

The old man's face blanched and a look of horror crept into his eyes. His muscles tensed and his clawlike hands clutched madly at the bars. He slumped against the gate and gasped for breath.

Faintly his whisper came, low and halting.

"Golan-Kirt—your weapons—believe nothing—close your mind to all suggestion—."

He stopped, gasping for breath.

"I have fought—" he continued, haltingly, with an effort. "I have won—. I have told you—. He has—killed me—he will not kill you—now that you—know—."

The old man was on the verge of death. Wide-eyed, the two saw him ward it off, gain a precious second.

"Your weapons—will kill him—he's easy to kill—by one who does not—believe in him—he is a—."

The whisper pinched out and the old man slid slowly to the sands in front of the cage.

The two stared at the crumpled form of humanity.

"Killed by suggestion," gasped Harl.

Bill nodded.

"He was a brave man," he said.

Harl regarded the corpse intently. His eyes lighted on the key ring and kneeling, he reached out and drew the body of the future-man close. His fingers closed on the ring and ripped it from the loincloth.

"We're going home," he said.

"And on the way out we'll bump off the big shot," added Bill.

He lifted the guns from the floor and clicked fresh cartridges into the chambers. Harl rattled the keys. He tried several before he found the correct one. The lock screeched and the gate swung open protestingly.

With quick steps they passed out of the cell. For a moment they halted in silent tribute before the body of the old man. With helmets doffed the twentieth century men stood beside the shriveled form of a man who was a hero, a man who had flung his hatred in the face of some terrible entity that taught hate to the people of the world. Scanty as was the information which he had given, it set the two on their guard, gave them an inkling of what to expect.

As they turned about they involuntarily started. Filing into the amphitheater, rapidly filling the seats, were crowds of future-men. A subdued roar, the voice of the assembling people, came to their ears.

The populace was assembling for the games.

"This may complicate matters," said Bill.

"I don't think so," replied Harl. "It's Golan-Kirt we must deal with. We would have had to in any case. These men do not count. As I understand it he exercises an absolute control over them. The removal of that control may change the habits and psychology of the future-men."

"The only thing we can do is fight Golan-Kirt and then act accordingly," said Bill.

"The man who captured us spoke of his minions," Harl said thoughtfully.

"He may be able to produce hallucinations," Bill hazarded. "He may be able to make one believe something exists when it really doesn't. In that case, the people would naturally believe them to be creatures which came at his beck and call."

"But the old man knew," objected Harl. "He knew that it was all mere suggestion. If all the people knew this the rule of Golan-Kirt would end abruptly. They would no longer believe in his omnipotence. Without this belief, suggestion, by which he rules, would be impossible."

"The old man," asserted Bill, "gained his knowledge in some mysterious manner and paid for its divulgence with his life. Still the old fellow didn't know all of it. He believed this entity came out of the Cosmos."

Harl shook his head, thoughtfully.

"It may have come out of the Cosmos. Remember, we are at least five million years in the future. I expect to find some great intelligence. It is physical, for the old man claimed to have seen it, and that should make our job easier."

"The old man said he was not immortal," commented Bill. "Therefore, he is vulnerable and our guns may do the work. Another thing—we are not to believe a single thing we feel, hear, or see. He seems to rule wholly by suggestion. He will try to kill us by suggestion, just as he killed the old fellow."

Harl nodded.

"It's a matter of will power," he said. "A matter of brain and bluff. Apparently the will power of these people has degenerated and Golan-Kirt finds it easy to control their minds. They are born, live, and die under his influence. It has almost become hereditary to accept his power. We have the advantage of coming out of an age when men were obliged to use their brains. Perhaps the human mind degenerated because, as science increased the ease of life, there was little need to use it. Some fine minds may still remain, but apparently they are few. We are doubters, schemers, bluffers. Golan-Kirt will find us tougher than these future-men."

CHAPTER III

The Struggle of the Ages

Bill produced cigarettes and the two lighted up. Slowly they walked across the vast arena, guns hanging in their right hands. People were filing into the place and the tiers were filling.

A roar came out of the tiers of seats before them. They recognized it. It was the cry of the gathering crowd, the cry for blood, the expression of a desire to see battle.

Harl grinned.

"Regular football crowd," he commented.

More and more poured into the arena, but it was apparent that the inhabitants of the ruined city could fill only a very small section of the thousands upon thousands of seats.

The two seemed lost in the mighty space. Above them, almost at the zenith, hung the vast red sun. They seemed to move in a twilight-filled desert rimmed in by enormous white cliffs.

"Denver must have been a large city at the time this place was built," commented Bill. "Think of the number of people it would hold. Wonder what it was used for?"

"Probably we'll never know," said Harl.

They had gained the approximate center of the arena.

Harl halted.

"Do you know," he said, "I've been thinking. It seems to me we must have a fairly good chance against Golan-Kirt. For the last fifteen minutes every thought of ours has been in open defiance of him, but he has not attempted our annihilation. Although it is possible he may only be biding his time. I am beginning to believe he can't read our minds as he could the mind of the old man. He killed him the moment he uttered a word of treason."

Bill nodded.

As if in answer to what Harl had said, a great weight seemed to press in upon them. Bill felt a deadly illness creeping over him. His knees sagged and his brain whirled. Spots danced before his eyes and a horrible pain gripped his stomach.

He took a step forward and stumbled. A hand clutched his shoulder and fiercely shook him. The shake momentarily cleared his brain. Through the clearing mist which seemed to hang before his eyes, he saw the face of his friend, a face white and lined.

The lips in the face moved.

"Buck up, old man. There's nothing wrong with you. You're feeling fine."

Something seemed to snap inside his head. This was suggestion—the suggestion of Golan-Kirt. He had to fight it. That was it—fight it.

He planted his feet firmly in the sand, straightened his shoulders with an effort, and smiled.

"Hell, no," he said, "there's nothing wrong with me. I'm feeling fine."

Harl slapped him on the back.

"That's the spirit," he roared. "It almost floored me for a minute. We've got to fight it, boy. We've got to fight it."

Bill laughed, harshly. His head was clear now and he could feel the strength flowing back into his body. They had won the first round!

"But where is this Golan-Kirt?" he burst out.

"Invisible," snarled Harl, "but I have a theory that he can't put in his best licks in such a state. We'll force him to show himself and then we'll give him the works."

The frenzied roar of the crowd came to their ears. Those on the bleachers had seen and appreciated the little drama out in the middle of the arena. They were crying for more.

Suddenly a spiteful rattle broke out behind the two.

They started. That sound was familiar. It was the rat-a-tat of a machine gun. With no ceremony they fell flat, pressing their bodies close against the ground, seeking to burrow into the sand.

Little puffs of sand spurted up all about them. Bill felt a searing pain in his arm. One of the bullets had found him. This was the end. There was no obstruction to shield them in this vast level expanse from the gun that chuckled and chattered at their rear. Another searing pain caught him in the leg. Another hit.

Then he laughed—a wild laugh. There was no machine gun, no bullets. It was all suggestion. A trick to make them believe they were being killed—a trick, which, if carried far enough, would kill them.

He struggled to his knees, hauling Harl up beside him. His leg and arm still pained, but he paid them no attention. There was nothing wrong with them, he told himself fiercely, absolutely nothing wrong.

"It's suggestion again," he shouted at Harl. "There isn't any machine gun."

Harl nodded. They regained their feet and turned. There, only a couple of hundred yards away, a khaki-clad figure crouched behind a gun that chattered wickedly, a red flame licking the muzzle.

"That isn't a machine gun," said Bill, speaking slowly.

"Of course, it's not a machine gun," Harl spoke as if by rote.

They walked slowly toward the flaming gun. Although bullets apparently whistled all about them, none struck them. The pain in Bill's arm and leg no longer existed.

Suddenly the gun disappeared, and with it the khaki-clad figure. One moment they were there, the next they were not.

"I thought it would do just that," said Bill.

"The old boy is still going strong, though," replied Harl. "Here is some more of his suggestion."

Harl pointed to one of the arching gateways. Through it marched file upon file of soldiers, clad in khaki, metal helmets on their heads, guns across their shoulders. An officer uttered a sharp command and the troops began to deploy over the field.

A shrill blast of a bugle drew the attention of the two time-travelers from the soldiers and through another gateway they beheld the advance of what appeared to be a cohort of Roman legionnaires. Shields flashed dully in the sun and the rattle of arms could be distinctly heard.

"Do you know what I believe?" asked Harl.

"What is it?"

"Golan-Kirt cannot suggest anything new to us. The machine guns and the soldiers and legionnaires are all things of which we have former knowledge."

"How is it," asked Bill, "that we see these things when we know they do not exist?"

"I do not know," replied Harl, "there are a lot of funny things about this business that I can't understand."

"Anyhow, he is giving the crowd a good show," observed Bill.

The bleachers were in an uproar. To the ears of the two came the shrill screaming of women, the loud roars of the men. The populace was thoroughly enjoying itself.

A lion, large and ferocious, growling fiercely, leaped past the two men. A thunder of hoof-beats announced the arrival of more of the brain creatures.

"It's about time for us to do something," said Harl.

He lifted his .45 high in the air and fired. A hush fell.

"Golan-Kirt, attention!" roared Harl, in a voice that could be heard in every part of the arena. "We challenge you to personal combat. We have no fear of your creatures. They cannot harm us. You are the one we wish to fight."

An awed silence fell over the crowd. It was the first time their god had ever been openly challenged. They waited for the two lone figures out in, the arena to be stricken in a heap.

They were not stricken, however.

Again Harl's voice rang out.

"Come out of hiding, you fat-bellied toad!" he thundered. "Come and fight if you have the guts, you dirty, yellow coward!"

The crowd may not have gathered the exact meaning of the words, but the full insult of them was plain. A threatening murmur rolled out from the bleachers, and there was a sudden surging of the crowd. Men leaped over the low wall in front of the seats and raced across the arena.

Then a sonorous voice, deep and strong, rolled out.

"Stop," it said. "I, Golan-Kirt, will deal with these men."

Harl noticed that the soldiers and the lion had disappeared. The arena was empty except for him and his comrade and the score of future-men who had halted in their tracks at the voice which had come out of nothingness.

They waited, tensed. Harl wriggled his feet into a firmer position. He slipped a cartridge in the gun to take the place of the one which had been fired. Bill mopped his brow with the sleeve of his coat.

"It's going to be brains now," Harl told his friend.

Bill grinned.

"Two mediocre intelligences against a great one," he joked.

"Look, Bill!" shouted Harl.

Directly in front and slightly above the level of their heads a field of light had formed, a small ball of brightness in the murky atmosphere. Slowly it grew. Vibrations set in.

The two watched, fascinated. The vibrations quickened until the whole field was quivering. As the vibrations increased the light faded and a monstrosity began to take form. Only vaguely could it be seen at first. Then it became clearer and clearer, began to take definite form.

Hanging in the air, suspended without visible means of support, was a gigantic brain, approximately two feet in diameter. A naked brain, with the convolutions exposed. It was a ghastly thing.

The horror of it was heightened by the two tiny, pig-like, lidless, close-set eyes and a curving beak which hung directly below the frontal portion of the brain, resting in what was apparently an atrophied face.

The two were aghast, but with a tremendous effort they kept close hold on their self-control.

"Greetings, Golan-Kirt," drawled Harl, sarcasm putting an edge to the words.

As he spoke, his arm swung up and under the pressure of his finger, the hammer of the gun slowly moved backward. But before the muzzle could be brought in line with the great brain, the arm stopped and Harl stood like a frozen man, held rigid by the frightful power which poured forth from Golan-Kirt.

Bill's arm flashed up and his .45 broke the silence with a sullen roar. However, even as he fired, his arm was flung aside as if by a mighty blow and the speeding bullet missed the huge brain by the mere fraction of an inch.

"Presumptuous fools," roared a voice, which, however, seemed not a voice, for there was no sound, merely the sense of hearing. The two, standing rigidly, as if at attention, realized that it was telepathy: that the brain before them was sending out powerful emanations.

"Presumptuous fools, you would fight me, Golan-Kirt? I, who have a hundred-fold the mental power of your combined brains? I, who hold the knowledge of all time?"

"We would fight you," snarled Harl. "We are going to fight you. We know you for what you are. You are not out of the Cosmos. You are a laboratory specimen. Unknown ages ago you were developed under artificial conditions. You are not immortal. You fear our weapons. A bullet in that dirty brain of yours will finish you."

"Who are you to judge," came the thought-wave, "you, with your tiny, twentieth century brain? You have come unbidden into my time, you have defied me. I shall destroy you. I, who came out of the Cosmos aeons ago to rule over the portion of the Universe I chose as my own, do not fear you or your ridiculous weapons."

"Yet you foiled us when we would have used our weapons on you. If I could reach you I would not need my weapon. I could tear you apart, destroy you with the strength of my two hands."

"Say on," rumbled the thought-waves. "Say what you believe me to be, and when you are done I shall obliterate you. You shall be dust floating in the air, ashes on the sands."

There was an unveiled tone of mockery in the brain emanations.

Harl raised his voice, almost shouting. It was a deliberate act, done in hopes the future-men would hear, that they might realize not too late the true nature of the tyrant Golan-Kirt. They did hear and their mouths gaped as they listened.

"You once were a man," Harl roared, "a great scientist. You studied the brain, specialized in it. At last you discovered a great secret, which gave you the power of developing the brain to an unheard-of degree. Sure of your technique, and realizing the power you might enjoy, you transformed yourself into a brain creature. You are a fraud and an impostor. You have mis-ruled these people for millions of years. You are not out of the Cosmos,—you are a man, or what once was a man. You are an atrocity, an abomination—"

The thought emanations which flowed from out the brain trembled, as if with rage.

"You lie. I am out of the Cosmos. I am immortal. I shall kill you—kill you."

Suddenly Bill laughed, a resounding guffaw. It was an escape from the terrible tension, but as he laughed a ludicrous angle presented itself —the twentieth century travelers millions of years ahead of their time.

wrangling with a cheat pawning himself off as a god on a people who would not be born until long after he was dead.

He felt the horrible power of Golan-Kirt centering upon him. Perspiration streamed down his face and his body trembled. He felt his strength leaving him.

He stopped laughing. As he did so, he seemed to be struck, as if by a blow. He staggered. Then sudden realization flashed through him. Laughter! Laughter, that was it. Laughter and ridicule! That would turn the trick.

"Laugh, you fool, laugh," he screamed at Harl.

Uncomprehendingly, Harl obeyed.

The two rocked with laughter. They whooped and roared.

Hardly knowing what he did, almost involuntarily, Bill screeched horrible things at the great brain, reviled it, taunted it, called it almost unspeakable names.

Harl began to understand. It was all a great game that Bill was playing. A supreme egoism such as was lodged in the brain pitted against them could not bear ridicule, would lose its grip before a storm of jeers. For uncounted centuries, through some miraculous power, it had lived and in all that time it had been accorded only the highest honor. Derision was something with which it was unacquainted, a terrible weapon suddenly loosed upon it.

Harl joined with Bill and hurled gibes at Golan-Kirt. It was a high carnival of mockery. They were not conscious of their words. Their brains responded to the emergency and their tongues formed sentences of unguessed taunts.

Between sentences they laughed, howling with satanic glee.

Through all their laughter they felt the power of the brain. They felt its anger mount at their taunting. Their bodies were racked with pain, they wanted to fall on the sands and writhe in agony, but they continued to laugh, to shout taunts.

It seemed an eternity that they fought with Golan-Kirt, all the time shrieking with laughter, while they suffered fine-edged torture from the tops of their heads to the soles of their feet. Still they dare not stop their laughter, dare not cease their hideous derision, poking fun at the huge intelligence which opposed them. That was their one weapon. Without it the engulfing waves of suggestion which poured with relentless fury upon them would have snapped asunder every nerve in their bodies.

They sensed the raging of the great brain. It was literally crazed with anger. They were "getting its goat!" They were ridiculing the very life out of it.

Unconsciously they allowed the pitch of their laughter to lower. From sheer exhaustion they lapsed into silence.

Suddenly they felt the terrible force of the brain renewed, as it drew upon some mysterious reserve strength. It struck them like a blow, doubling them over, clouding their eyes, dulling their minds, racking every nerve and joint.

Hot irons seemed to sear them, hundreds of needles seemed thrust in their flesh, sharp knives seemed to slash their bodies. They reeled blindly, gropingly, mouthing curses, crying out in pain.

Through the red haze of torture came a whisper, a soft, enchanting whisper, a whisper beckoning to them, showing them a way of escape.

"Turn your weapons on yourselves. End all of this torture. Death is painless."

The whisper fluttered through their brains. That was the way out! Why endure this seemingly endless torture? Death was painless. The muzzle against one's head, a pressure on the trigger, oblivion.

Bill placed his gun against his temple. His finger contracted against the trigger. He laughed. This was a joke. A rare joke. Robbing Golan-Kirt by his own hand.

Another voice burst through his laughter. It was Harl.

"You fool! It's Golan-Kirt! It's Golan-Kirt, you fool!"

He saw his friend staggering toward him, saw his face pinched with pain, saw the moving of the livid lips as they shouted the warning.

Bill's hand dropped to his side. Even as he continued that insane laughter, he felt chagrin steal over him. The hideous brain had played its trump card and had failed, but it had almost finished him. Had it not been for Harl he would have been stretched on the sand, a suicide, his head blown to bits.

Then suddenly they felt the power of the brain slipping, felt its strength falter and ebb. They had beaten it!

They sensed the gigantic struggle going on in that great brain, the struggle to regain the grip it had lost.

For years on end it had lived without struggle, without question that it was the ruler of the earth. They sensed the futile anger and the devastating fear which revolved in the convolutions of Golan-Kirt.

But he was beaten, beaten at last by men from out of a forgotten age.

He had met defeat at the hands of ridicule, something he had never known, a thing he had not suspected.

His strength ebbed steadily. The twentieth century men felt his dread power lift from them, sensed the despair which surged through him.

They stopped their laughter, their sides sore, their throats hoarse. Then they heard. The arena resounded with laughter. The crowd was laughing. The horrible uproar beat like a tumult upon them. The future-men were roaring, bent over, stamping their feet, throwing back their heads, screaming to the murky skies. They were laughing at Golan-Kirt, screaming insults at him, hooting him. It was the end of his rule.

For generations the future-men had hated him with the very hate he had taught them. They had hated and feared. Now they feared no longer and hate rode unchained.

From a god he had fallen to the estate of a ridiculous fraud. He was a thing of pity, an uncloaked clown, simply a naked, defenseless brain that had bluffed its way through centuries of kingship.

Through bleared eyes the twentieth century men saw the great brain, writhing now under the scorn of its erstwhile subjects, being laughed powerless. No longer did it hold control over these creatures of a dying world. Its close-set eyes glowed fiercely, its beak clicked angrily. It was tired, too tired to regain its rule. It was the end of Golan-Kirt!

The revolvers of the time-travelers came up almost simultaneously. This time the sights lined on the brain. There was no power to ward off the danger.

The guns roared rapidly, spitting hateful fire. At the impact of the bullets the brain turned over in the air, blood spurted from it, great gashes appeared in it. With a thump it struck the ground, quivered and lay still.

The time-travelers, their eyes closing from sheer weariness, their knees suddenly weak, slumped to the sand, the .45's still smoking.

Over the arena floated the full-toned roar of the future-men.

"Hail to the Deliverers! Golan-Kirt is dead! His rule is ended! Hail to the saviors of the race!"

Epilogue

"It is impossible to reverse time. You cannot travel back to your own age. I have no idea of what will occur if you attempt it, but I do know it is impossible. We of this age knew travel into the future was possible, but we lacked the technique to build a machine to try it. Under the rule of Golan-Kirt there was no material progress, only a steady degeneration. We know that it is impossible to reverse time. We, as a people, beg you not to attempt it."

Old Agnar Nohl, his white beard streaming in the wind, his hair flying, spoke seriously. There was a troubled frown on his face.

"We love you," he went on, "you freed us of the tyranny of the brain which ruled over us for uncounted time. We need you. Stay with us, help us rebuild this land, help us construct machines, give us some of the marvelous knowledge which we, as a race, have lost. We can give you much in return, for we have not forgotten all the science we knew before the coming of Golan-Kirt."

Harl shook his head.

"We must at least try to go back," he said.

The two twentieth century men stood beside the plane. Before them was a solid mass of humanity, a silent humanity in the shadow of the silent ruins of the city of Denver, the future-men who had come to bid the time-travelers a regretful farewell.

A chill wind howled over the desert, carrying its freight of sand. The furs of the future-men fluttered in the gale as it played a solemn dirge between the ruined walls of humbled buildings.

"If there was a chance of your success, we would speed you on your way," said old Agnar, "but we are reluctant to let you go to what may be your death. We are selfish enough to wish to hold you for ourselves, but we love you enough to let you go. You taught us hate was wrong, you removed the hate that ruled us. We wish only the best for you.

"It is impossible to go back in time. Why not remain? We need you badly. Our land grows less and less food every year. We must discover how to make synthetic food or we shall starve. This is only one of our problems. There are many others. You cannot go back. Stay and help us!"

Again Harl shook his head.

"No, we must try it. We may fail, but we must try it at least. If we succeed we shall return and bring with us books of knowledge and tools to work with."

Agnar combed his beard with skinny fingers.

"You'll fail," he said.

"But if we don't we will return," said Bill.

"Yes, if you don't," replied the old man.

"We are going now," said Bill. "We thank you for your thoughtfulness. We must at least try. We are sorry to leave you. Please believe that."

"I do believe it," cried the old man and he seized their hands in a farewell clasp.

Harl opened the door of the plane and Bill clambered in.

At the door Harl stood with upraised hand.

"Good-bye," he said. "Some day we will return."

The crowd burst into a roar of farewell. Harl climbed into the plane and closed the door.

The motors bellowed, droning out the shouting of the future-men and the great machine charged down the sand. With a rush it took the air. Three times Bill circled the ruined city in a last mute good-bye to the men who watched silently and sorrowfully below.

Then Harl threw the lever. Again the utter darkness, the feeling of hanging in nothingness.

The motors, barely turning, muttered at the change. A minute passed, two minutes.

"Who says we can't travel back in time!" Harl shouted triumphantly. He pointed to the needle. It was slowly creeping back across the face of the dial.

"Maybe the old man was wrong after—"

Bill never finished the sentence.

"Roll her out," he screamed at Harl, "roll her out. One of our engines is going dead!"

Harl snatched at the lever, jerked frantically at it. The faulty motor choked and coughed, sputtered, then broke into a steady drone.

The two men in the cabin regarded one another with blanched faces. They knew they had escaped a possible crash—and death—by bare seconds.

Again they hung in the air. Again they saw the brick-red sun, the desert, and the sea. Below them loomed the ruins of Denver.

"We couldn't have gone far back in time," said Harl. "It looks the same as ever."

They circled the ruins.

"We had better land out in the desert to fix up the engine," suggested Harl. "Remember we have traveled back in time and Golan-Kirt still rules over the land. We don't want to have to kill him a second time. We might not be able to do it."

The plane was flying low and he nosed it up. Again the faulty engine sputtered and missed.

"She's going dead this time for certain," yelled Bill. "We'll have to chance it, Harl. We have to land and chance getting away again."

Harl nodded grimly.

Before them lay the broad expanse of the arena. It was either that or crash.

As Bill nosed the plane down the missing motor sputtered for the last time, went dead.

They flashed over the white walls of the amphitheater and down into the arena. The plane struck the sand, raced across it, slowed to a stop.

Harl opened the door.

"Our only chance is to fix it up in a hurry and get out of here," he shouted at Bill. "We don't want to meet that damn brain again."

He stopped short.

"Bill," he spoke scarcely above a whisper, "am I seeing things?"

Before him, set on the sands of the arena, only a few yards from the plane, was a statue of heroic size, a statue of himself and Bill.

Even from where he stood he could read the inscription, carved in the white stone base of the statue in characters which closely resembled written English.

Slowly, haltingly, he read it aloud, stumbling over an occasional queer character.

"Two men, Harl Swanson, and Bill Kressman, came out of time to kill Golan-Kirt and to free the race."

Below it he saw other characters.

"They may return."

"Bill," he sobbed, "we haven't traveled back in time. We have traveled further into the future. Look at that stone—eroded, ready to crumble to pieces. That statue has stood there for thousands of years!"

Bill slumped back into his seat, his face ashen, his eyes staring.

"The old man was right," he screamed. "He was right. We'll never see the twentieth century again."

He leaned over toward the time machine.

His face twitched.

"Those instruments," he shrieked, "those damned instruments! They were wrong. They lied, they lied!"

With his bare fists he beat at them, smashing them, unaware that the glass cut deep gashes and his hands were smeared with blood.

Silence weighed down over the plain. There was absolutely no sound.

Bill broke the silence.

"The future-men," he cried, "where are the future-men?"

He answered his own question.

"They are all dead," he screamed, "all dead. They are starved—starved because they couldn't manufacture synthetic food. We are alone! Alone at the end of the world!"

Harl stood in the door of the plane.

Over the rim of the amphitheater the huge red sun hung in a sky devoid of clouds. A slight wind stirred the sand at the base of the crumbling statue.

■ ■ ■ ■ ■

Cliff Simak is a particularly prominent figure in the science fiction world. "The World of the Red Sun" was his first published story, and it was simply and straightforwardly told. It had a sad ending, too, and I remember that impressed me at the time. I could not help but recognize the force of a dramatic and ironic ending. ("The Man Who Evolved" had possessed one, too.)

Simak was unusual among the early authors in that he survived the Coming of Campbell. Most early authors did not. (It was rather like the coming of talking pictures, which proved the ruin of so many actors who had learned their job in the world of the silents.)

Meek, for instance, hardly wrote anything after 1932, and Miller wrote infrequently. Jones and Hamilton continued to write frequently but hardly ever appeared in Campbell's *Astounding,* which was all that counted through the 1940s.

Simak was quite different. He published four more stories in 1932 and then nothing more until the Campbell era began, in 1938. He then began to write prolifically for the various magazines, including *Astounding,* and was soon numbered among the recognized members of Campbell's "stable" —that is, those authors whom he had discovered or developed (or both).

Indeed, Simak went on to grow even larger in stature as the field expanded in the 1950s and 1960s, when Campbell no longer held the monopoly. Simak was Guest of Honor at the World Science Fiction Convention held in Boston in 1971, and just the other day I received the hardback edition of his most recent novel, *Cemetery World.*

In the gap between 1932 and 1938, I had forgotten Clifford Simak, though not "The World of the Red Sun." I rediscovered him when he wrote "Rule 18," which appeared in the July 1938 issue of *Astounding*

Science Fiction. What followed from that and how we grew to be close friends I mentioned in *The Early Asimov*.

It was not till a number of years after I had become friends with Cliff that I discovered, quite by accident, that it was he who had written the story I had once told with such pleasure and success to my junior high school classmates. What a happy discovery that was!

Simak was the first to teach me, by example, of the value of an un-adorned style. I explained that in *The Early Asimov*, and I want to mention that here, too.

In the fall of 1931 (inspired, perhaps, by my success in interesting my friends in the science fiction tales I retold), I began to try my hand at making up stories of my own.

I didn't write science fiction, however. I had a most exalted notion of the intense skills and vast scientific knowledge required of authors in the field, and I dared not aspire to such things. Instead, I began to write a tale of ordinary planetbound adventure called "The Greenville Chums at College."

I worked with a pencil and a five-cent notebook and eventually wrote eight chapters before fading out. I remember trying to tell the story of the Greenville Chums to one of those friends who had listened steadily to my retelling of science fiction. With a certain precocious caution, I had chosen the one who seemed most consistently enthusiastic. After I had told him what I had written that day, he asked eagerly if he could borrow the book when I was done.

I had either neglected to make it clear to him, or he had failed to understand, that I was *writing* the book. He thought it was another already printed story I was retelling. The implied compliment staggered me, and from that day on, I secretly took myself seriously as a writer.

BRIAN ALDISS
SPACE OPERA

The menace of galactic warfare; of science and genetics
run amok . . . Jewelled princesses, desperate guests,
doomed world's, exotic aliens and the deadly snicker of
sword blades. These are the rich themes which Brian Aldiss
has brought together in a tribute to red-blooded science
fiction of the golden age.

The authors include many of s.f's founding fathers such as
Asimov, Van Vogt, and Bradbury, as well as the lesser
known gems rescued from the obscurity of long forgotten
pulp magazines.

This unusual and entertaining anthology — the first in a
new series — will appeal to all lovers of 'hard core'
science fiction, but most particularly to the new generation
of readers who have rediscovered the stirring tales of
Edgar Rice Burroughs and E. E. 'Doc' Smith.

Enterprise Stardust

PERILOUS DAWN . . .

Major Perry Rhodan, commander of the spaceship STARDUST, found more than anyone had expected might exist on the moon — for he became the first man to make contact with another sentient race!

The Arkonides had come from a distant star, and they possessed a knowledge of science and philosophy that dwarfed mankind's knowledge.

But these enormously powerful alien beings refused to cooperate with the people of Earth . . . unless Perry Rhodan could pass the most difficult test any human being had ever faced . . .

ENTERPRISE STARDUST is the first novel in the Perry Rhodan series which sold more than 70 million copies in Europe and America.